PRAISE FOR ELLIOTT SUMERS

"Like 'The Man in the High Castle' this counterfactual story offers a unique twist to the Nazi thriller. The author brings a deep knowledge of West Point and the Hudson Valley to this World War II adventure, giving the reader a true sense of being there as the action unfolds. And there is a surprise reveal about Franklin Roosevelt that will shock even savvy readers."

PAUL M. SPARROW FORMER DIRECTOR
FRANKLIN D. ROOSEVELT PRESIDENTIAL
LIBRARY AND MUSEUM.

"A whale of a tale, well-told, with an impressive handling of the facts that makes the whole story move along smartly."

THOMAS E. RICKS, PULITZER PRIZE
WINNER, NY TIMES BEST-SELLING
AUTHOR OF FIASCO AND THE GENERALS

"*Operation Storm King* was a pleasure to read. I found it authentic, thoroughly immersive, and compelling to the last page.

As someone who has been associated with the military my entire life, I was especially impressed by the author's ability to seamlessly combine historical detail with story-telling flair. Indeed I often found myself forgetting that this is a work of fiction...or is it?

I commend it to anyone who enjoys consequential history—with a twist."

BENJAMIN PATTON, AUTHOR OF
GROWING UP PATTON

"*Operation Storm King* is a fast-paced alternate history military thriller that will keep readers furiously turning the pages. Based on a Nazi plot to kidnap President Roosevelt, this World War Two thriller with modern over-tones, is a fascinating must-read for military thriller and World War Two history buffs."

ANDREW KAPLAN, NEW YORK TIMES
BESTSELLING AUTHOR OF *BLUE
MADAGASCAR*

Operation Storm King

ELLIOTT SUMERS

Operation Storm King is a work of fiction incorporating historical settings, events and individuals. The technology and weaponry of World War II are accurate. All of the contemporary characters and all of the dialog is completely fictional.

ISBN (eBook): 979-8-9877301-0-2
ISBN (Paperback): 979-8-9877301-1-9
ISBN (Hardcover): 979-8-9877301-2-6
ISBN (Large Print): 979-8-9877301-3-3
ISBN (Jacketed Hardcover): 979-8-9877301-4-0
Library of Congress Number: 2023902038

Title Production by The BookWhisperer.ink

I am forever grateful to my wife Anne who has supported and championed my efforts. This book is dedicated to her and our undying love.

PROLOGUE

E ven as a young boy, President Franklin D. Roosevelt had loved maps. At the start of World War II, FDR converted the women's cloakroom in the White House basement into a command center modeled after Winston Churchill's War Rooms in London. Enormous maps of the European and Pacific Theaters covered the walls. Efficient military aides with top-secret clearance briskly posted updates, moving markers for troops and ships across the globe, noting weather conditions and obstacles, success and setbacks. With secure links to the nation's far-flung military, Roosevelt closely followed the progress of the war from this room on an hourly basis.

In January 1945, there was little action on the European front. This morning, it was quiet, with only a handful of staff answering phones. It was a good place for FDR to meet with his trusted chief of staff, Admiral William Leahy. Leahy was bald, with dark bushy eyebrows and a perpetual scowl. In his sixties, he was very fit, and still had the ramrod posture of a Naval Academy graduate.

FDR always enjoyed his briefings from Leahy, especially when the news was good. Roosevelt was wise enough not to meddle in the management of his armies, but he kept a close eye on the fighting. "Well, Admiral, it looks like General Patton has finally gotten control of things down in the Ardennes."

"It seems the Nazis have shot their bolt, Mr. President. We've rounded up the last of the infiltrators they sent in wearing American uniforms. That certainly caused a lot of confusion. Eisenhower thought they might assassinate him."

"No trick is too dirty for those Nazi bastards, Admiral."

"I don't think there's much fight left in the Germans. As soon as we can get the supplies up, we will go on the offensive."

"That's just what you said, right before they punched Hodges' First Army in the nose!"

"This time it's for sure, Mr. President. They have barely any armor, and the Luftwaffe can't fly without aviation fuel. It's time to plan for victory and peace. We need to talk about your schedule—that trip next month to Yalta is going to be grueling, Mr. President. It's seven thousand miles each way! Have you considered sending Mr. Truman?"

Roosevelt tipped his head back and laughed.

"Leahy! You jest. Send Harry to negotiate with Stalin? He'd get eaten alive! It has to be me. And you must accompany me. I need your advice. Oh, and please let's have my daughter Anna come along on the trip."

Leahy raised an eyebrow. "In addition to Eleanor?"

"God, no. I'd rather be kidnapped by the Germans than spend twenty-four hours a day with…that woman."

"Very well, Mr. President, I'll make the arrangements. I think we should keep the schedule light for when you return."

Leahy opened the large, leather-bound presidential calendar.

"I'm going to keep you in Washington for at least a month after you return. The only thing we can't miss is your visit to

West Point at the end of March. It's the cadet's Hundredth Night Ball—only three months to graduation. Since you can't make it to graduation this year, it seems only right."

"Tough for me up there, Admiral. It's not set for people like me." FDR laid his hands on his post-polio withered legs. There were few accommodations for the wheelchair-bound Roosevelt at West Point. The president and his staff had worked tirelessly to keep his disability hidden from the American public. He must not be seen or photographed in a wheelchair or being carried. Walking even a few steps to a podium was difficult, with heavy iron braces strapped to his legs, and required balancing on the arm of a son or bodyguard. He hated events where he might be exposed.

"I'm afraid it's already been announced to the press. We'll keep the visit to West Point short. An inspiring short speech, shake hands, salute, and go. It's only thirty miles to Hyde Park. You've earned a quiet evening up at Top Cottage."

FDR threw his head back again and roared. "You know me too well! Top Cottage! I love my cottage! But not alone, I expect?"

Leahy smiled. "Never alone."

FDR leaned forward, conspiratorially. "Can you make sure Eleanor has responsibilities somewhere else?"

"How's Alabama? She wants to revisit those Tuskegee Airmen. She's been pushing for it."

"Created a lot of headlines the first time! That sounds very far from New York. Excellent. And…companionship? You'll arrange it with Lucy? Discreetly, of course?"

Franklin Delano Roosevelt enjoyed the company of intelligent and beautiful women. Over the course of his marriage to Eleanor, he maintained enduring relationships with several women. Lucy Mercer Rutherford was the most profound and enduring. They had met back in 1920, when the beautiful and cultured, if impoverished, Lucy had been hired by Eleanor as her personal secretary. When Eleanor learned of their love affair, it had all but ended their marriage. Franklin and Lucy agreed to break off their affair, but it continued, on and off, for the next twenty-five years, even after Lucy married the fabulously wealthy Winthrop Rutherford. Rutherford died in 1944, and Franklin and Lucy began to see each other more frequently.

"Yes, Mr. President, we can pick Lucy up near her estate in New Jersey on the way up to West Point."

"Splendid. A speech for our brave boys at West Point before they go off to win this war, and then a private evening at Top Cottage with Lucy. I can't think of a better way to spend the day."

ONE

Generalmajor der Polizei and SS-Brigadeführer Walter Schellenberg had slept only two hours last night. Twin-engine Mosquito bombers of the RAF had hit Berlin at least a dozen times in the last two months—and they had come again last night. Schellenberg, and all of Berlin, were startled awake by the sirens. The raid was nothing as destructive as the raids of the previous winter, but that was no consolation. A few hundred dead from the bombing hardly matters, thought Schellenberg. The important thing was that the men like him, doing the important work of the Reich, needed a decent night's sleep.

Schellenberg had sheltered in the underground SS command bunker. With excellent ventilation, a chemical toilet, and a private sleeping area, it was luxurious compared to most bomb shelters in the city, but the rattle of antiaircraft fire and the thump of bombs made sleep impossible, even for the most powerful men in Germany.

And that was who he was. One of the most powerful men in Germany. Sleepless. Angry. Egomaniacal. Handsome, educated, and articulate, he favored smartly cut Hugo Boss uniforms and highly polished riding boots. A peaked officer's cap, with a death's-head logo, was usually perched on his head at a jaunty angle. Beneath his sophisticated exterior was a complete disinterest in the suffering of others. Schellenberg focused his considerable organizational and intellectual abilities on the interests of the genocidal Nazi regime. Schellenberg was plenipotentiary for Reichsführer Heinrich Himmler in charge of foreign intelligence, yet his conscience was clear: he was sure that history would see him, as he saw himself, as an intellectual, a statesman, far above the murderous thugs in the Gestapo.

Schellenberg's adjutant, Sturmbannführer Berger, limped into the office. He wheeled a cart with Schellenberg's breakfast: two large croissants, fifty grams of butter, a tub of real strawberry jam, and a double espresso. There was hunger in Germany that winter, but not at Prinz-Albrecht-Strasse. Berger clumsily steered the cart around stacks of papers that accumulated in great piles on the floor of the wood-paneled office.

Schellenberg grunted but didn't look up. He waved in the direction of the door. Schellenberg was physically revolted at the sight of his adjutant dragging himself around the office. Berger had lost the front half of his feet to frostbite in 1942, fighting with the SS Totenkopf in the Demyansk Pocket. Berger's sacrifice mattered not a whit to the Brigadeführer. This is the nerve center of the Reich for God's sake, thought Schellenberg. I need to be surrounded by strength, not weakness and deformity.

Schellenberg stirred his espresso and held up the demitasse to savor the aroma. His hand trembled and some of the precious coffee spilled out onto the polished floor.

"*Scheiss*," he screamed, and flung the china cup into the fireplace. That fucking cripple Berger must have overfilled the cup. He needed to get rid of that monstrosity once and for all. Schellenberg stared down at his trembling right hand. It was definitely getting worse. Should I go to the doctor? he wondered. That's ridiculous; it's just the sleeplessness. He'd double up on the Pervitin again today. He pulled a small aluminum tube with a red-and-white label out of his desk drawer. Bracing it against the desk, he opened it one handed. He spilled out several of the three-milligram methamphetamine tablets. He had started with the standard single tablet, but lately it seemed to lose its magic. He had taken three yesterday, He grabbed four and swallowed them together.

Schellenberg summoned Berger for another espresso. The adjutant was careful to avoid eye contact but noticed the china shards in the fireplace. He returned quickly with the coffee, and by then Schellenberg could feel the Pervitin restore his energy and bring his mind into focus. Some of his dysphoria cleared, and he stopped noticing the tremor in his hand. By God, there was work to be done! The Führer and the Reich needed him!

In recent years, he had generated detailed plans for the abduction or assassination of Tito, Churchill, and Stalin. To his frustration, none of these came to fruition. He was distracted by a creeping fear for his future. Perhaps it was time to settle scores and disappear?

Schellenberg fought a cold-blooded war with policies and directives, but his fantasy life was homicidal and graphic. He kept a handwritten "death list" of the traitors and rivals he should eliminate. The "Office Fortress" desk he had constructed concealed two pistols trained at the armchair in front of him. He could fire these with a button at his knees. The mere presence of the weapons was thrilling. He cleaned and polished them most days with a mildly erotic pleasure.

Schellenberg had a fondness for kidnapping. As a young SS Sturmbannführer, he lured MI6 Agents Captain Sigismund Best and Major Richard Henry Stevens to neutral Holland. They believed they were meeting a faction of anti-Hitler Germans. Schellenberg, posing as a disaffected German Army officer, held them at gunpoint and spirited them into Germany. They were brutally interrogated by the Gestapo, and the British spy network in Germany was smashed. Schellenberg grinned as he remembered the broken look on their faces as they were dragged off to Dachau. The Führer was delighted and insisted on personally decorating Schellenberg with the *Ritterkreuz*, the Knight's Cross. Could he work that magic again, he wondered?

It was time to buckle down. Schellenberg scowled as he paged through the reports and maps that detailed the current strategic situation. Germany's position was desperate. The December 1944 Ardennes Offensive, dubbed "Wacht am Rhein," had failed. The assault created a large bulge in the Allied line, but had failed to break through to Antwerp. On the Eastern Front, Soviet armies pushed into Poland. A crippling fuel shortage threatened to ground the Luftwaffe.

The Führer's promises notwithstanding, the much-touted Wonder Weapons like the V-1 rockets, Me 262 fighter jets, and futuristic electric submarines, had never been delivered, ineffective, or too few to have an impact on the fighting.

Germany was being bled white in the East and smothered by Anglo-American armies in the West. Something had to be done.

Schellenberg fervently believed that the Reich could be saved by an alliance with the Americans. Washington had to be convinced that America and Germany must work together to defeat the Bolshevik threat. Several weeks ago, Schellenberg had sent out feelers to the American government through the Swedish diplomat, Count Folke Bernadotte. There had been no reply. It was maddening.

The Brigadeführer alternately drummed his fingers on the table and toyed with the trigger of the pistol in his desk. He kicked a file resting on the floor. A request for clemency from Canaris fell open. How absurd! Schellenberg rolled his chair over Canaris's file. Admiral Wilhelm Canaris, his old friend, the former Chief of the Abwehr, was a traitor to the Reich! They'd shared afternoons galloping on horseback in the Grunewald, even as Canaris was plotting to kill the Führer. That swine! That bastard! Canaris was arrested with the other July 1944 plotters, who placed a bomb concealed in a briefcase under the conference table at the Wolf's Lair. After a quick trial, Canaris was found guilty of treason, and sentenced to death. Now he languished in a Gestapo cell, in the basement, no doubt praying for a speedy death.

Schellenberg snorted in disgust. Clemency! I should summon him to a meeting, right here in the office and shoot him, he thought. No, it would create such a mess in the office, and probably ruin the chair. Maybe a firing squad would be better. No, too honorable. They should hang him with piano wire, like the other traitors. Schellenberg made a mental note to call Himmler and push for that.

What, he wondered, could he do to bring the Americans to the table? The Americans would need Germany on their side to save Europe from Communism. It was obvious. Why couldn't they see it? The damned Swedish count just wasn't getting the job done. He needed some leverage or at least a direct channel to get through to the Americans and make clear to them the threat Stalin posed.

He thumbed through recent, rather thin, intelligence reports from the United States, searching for a clue. The reports were from public sources like newspapers and magazines, collected by cooperating neutral embassy personnel. They were nearly useless.

Schellenberg paged through an article from the *St. Louis Post*, really just a public boast of record American aircraft production. What garbage. Who needed to read that? Any idiot living in Germany could look up most days and see a vast armada of American B-17 bombers and P-51 escort fighters darkening the sky.

A report from the *Poughkeepsie Journal* reported an upcoming ceremony for the U.S. Military Academy on April 4th, when the president would address the cadets at West Point. He scanned the headlines. Random crap. Filler. Women refurbishing children's coats. How to grow winter potatoes for a victory garden. Mrs. Roosevelt's tips for economizing in running the house-hold…More drivel, he thought.

An astonishing thought struck him. In a dark corner of his twisted mind, the first elements of an audacious plan came together. But could it be done? It would require the right team. And unproven technology. And good fortune.

He jumped back to the *Poughkeepsie Journal*. He reread it care-fully and then summoned his adjutant. Berger stared at the floor as Schellenberg spoke. "I need the most detailed navigational charts we have of New York and the Hudson River. Make sure they extend as far north as Poughkeepsie. I also want all of the documentation we have available on the U.S. Military Academy at West Point."

"*Jawohl*, Herr Brigadeführer."

"And I will need to see Grossadmiral Dönitz. Inform him that I want to meet with him personally. This week."

"This week, sir? But—"

"By Friday, at the latest. It is of the utmost importance. He must drop everything. I need to see Type XXI *Unterseeboot*, the *Electroboot*, the one he is always boasting about. I will meet him in Hamburg, at the shipyard."

"*Jawohl*, Herr Brigadeführer." The aide snapped his notebook shut.

"One more thing. Contact the central personnel office. I must have the records of all Wehrmacht, Luftwaffe, and Kriegsmarine personnel who are fluent English speakers. I need an officer with an American accent. Have them pay particular attention to anyone with prior service in the U.S. Army."

The adjutant was puzzled, but knew better than to question Brigadeführer Schellenberg. Berger struggled out of the room, and Schellenberg shook his head in revulsion.

Later that night, Schellenberg sat at his desk, drinking cognac and studying the files provided by the SS personnel office. Sleep was out of the question. It was discouraging work. Most of the

English speakers were deserters of questionable reliability, some with criminal records. There was a small pile remaining; many native English speakers had been lost in the recent fiasco in the Ardennes.

At last, near the bottom of the pile, Schellenberg came across the file of Hauptmann Karl Krause from the Fallschirmjäger, the Luftwaffe parachute infantry. He had fought at Fort Eben-Emael and had been part of the team that rescued Mussolini at the Campo Imperatore. With rising excitement, Schellenberg noted Krause's childhood in America and then, with some incredulity, his time at West Point.

He'd found his man.

Schellenberg summoned his adjutant and handed him the file on Krause.

"Send Krieger for this man—immediately."

Schellenberg fondled the trigger of his pistol.

It was well past midnight when the name for his secret project came to him.

As he studied the topographic maps of the Hudson River, he saw the towering cliffs lining the river. It must look something like the Rhine, he mused.

Running his finger over the peaks near West Point, he made note of the names Dunderberg, Bear Mountain, and High Tor. Just to the north of West Point, his finger rested on a rocky peak dominating the river valley: Storm King Mountain.

Yes, that would do nicely! he thought. *Unternehmen Sturm König!* Operation Storm King was a longshot, but the future of the Third Reich rested on its success.

Germany had only a few chips left on the table. It was time to put them all on one number.

TWO

Blohm & Voss Shipyard was grim, noisy, and cold. A whipping wind raised white caps on the dark gray water of the bay. A flight of screaming seagulls swooped in the leaden sky. A dozen low concrete factory buildings, draped with camouflage netting and surrounded by 88-mm anti-aircraft guns, were clustered around the quayside. Enormous cranes poked skyward and hoisted tubular prefabricated sections of U-boat hulls into position.

Despite heavy bombing and extensive damage to key facilities, Hitler insisted on continued intense production of the top-secret Type XXI U-boats. Scores of slave laborers, many of them women, dressed in ragged pajamas and crude wooden clogs, swarmed over the nearly completed U-555. They were painfully thin, almost skeletal in appearance. Some had grotesquely swollen legs, others were covered with open sores draining pus. The prisoners filed down the welds on the sleek hydrodynamic hull and installed interior fittings. A handful of SS guards clad in warm great coats and wielding wooden truncheons goaded them on. The starving prisoners kept their sunken eyes on the ground and worked with whatever energy they could muster. A moment's eye contact with a guard could be fatal.

The toil went on from dawn to dusk, seven days a week. The prisoners slept three to a bunk behind the electrified barbwire fences of a subunit of Neuengamme concentration camp, directly adjacent to the shipyard. Over the past eight months, more than one hundred workers had died in the Nazi's drive to build this superweapon. Some fell from rickety scaffolding, others were crushed or burned. Many were beaten to death by their SS guards for inattention or suspected sabotage.

Grossadmiral Karl Dönitz was not accustomed to waiting for others. Immaculately attired in double-breasted naval uniform and great coat, he stood on a viewing platform above the ship-yard, and impatiently checked his gold watch. Tall and imperi-ous, a successful U-boat commander in World War I, he was Befehlshaber der Unterseeboote (BdU), Chief of the Submarine Force, and the architect of the German "Wolf Pack" tactics that had nearly won the war for the Nazis in 1942.

Four emaciated women staggered carrying a heavy subma-rine part, then the group stumbled, fell, and dropped the heavy metal piece. It fell with a sickening thud, crushing one woman's foot. She howled like an animal and collapsed to the ground, writhing, a heap of rag-draped bones. A guard kicked and stomped the prostrate figure until she stopped moving.

Grossadmiral Dönitz stamped his feet in outrage—but not about the beating. He barely noticed the brutality. What did he care about the suffering of a few Jews or traitors? As long as they worked! As long as the submarines were built! Goddamn it, he thought, they probably bent the part. They'll have to re-inspect before installation. Could no one do their job here? Why was he waiting for this functionary? Brushing a few wet flakes of snow from his coat, he glanced at his watch again. What a waste of his time! And why? An urgent summons from some SS bully boy.

At that moment, Brigadeführer Walter Schellenberg came bounding up the stairs to the viewing platform. He wore jodhpurs, highly polished leather riding boots, and a floor-length SS leather trench coat.

Schellenberg smiled broadly. "Sorry to be late! Thank you for meeting me on such short notice, Grossadmiral!"

Dönitz frowned. "Our Führer has given you great authority, Brigadeführer. We all serve the Reich with the last ounce of energy and resolve. Do try to be punctual. I'm quite busy. So, then. What do you need from me?"

Schellenberg pointed out toward U-555 with a riding crop. "Incredible design here! Looks like a something out of a science-fiction book, Herr Grossadmiral. More like a rocket ship than a submarine!"

Dönitz was flattered. He knew his U-555 was a work of unappreciated genius. It would change naval warfare! But many in the High Command resisted his innovations, emphasizing instead production of what they already knew. "*Ja*. It's an entirely new design, quite revolutionary. The hull is streamlined to reduce drag. We've eliminated the deck gun. It can go farther, faster, longer underwater than any submarine." As he spoke, a scuffle broke out in the shipyard and both men looked over to the submarine. There was a thickening thud as a guard slammed a prisoner across the face with his truncheon. "If I could only make these workers pay attention! Stupid and lazy! The Führer has authorized construction of more than one thousand of these U-boats, but I can assure you, Brigadeführer, I only need one hundred of them to bring the Americans to their knees!"

"Such a pleasing thought! Please pardon my ignorance, Admiral. The streamlining is very impressive, but explain to a non-sailor like me, what difference does it make? What makes you think you can win the war with this U-boat? My sources tell me that the *Ubootwaffe* is being defeated by aircraft. How will the hull design solve that problem?"

The SS man's condescension outraged Dönitz. What right

had this arrogant prick to interfere with the business of the Kriegsmarine? He forced himself to be polite. Since the July 1944 von Stauffenberg bomb plot, the apex of the Third Reich had become an extremely dangerous place. Hundreds of senior officers were arrested, subjected to show trials, and strangled with piano wire. Dönitz was staunchly committed to the Führer. Even so, it was dangerous to cross a man as powerful and ambitious as Walter Schellenberg. Whatever game Schellenberg was playing, Dönitz would have to go along.

"You are quite perceptive, Brigadeführer. We've lost many U-boats to aircraft because we had to operate predominately on the surface. Our old Type VII boats can only run for a few hours submerged, and at very slow speeds. Even if we did escape the aircraft, it meant diving, and crawling along blindly. The Type XXI will change all of that." Dönitz became increasingly animated. Maybe this functionary could help him, he thought. Send extra funding. Some decent workers. Dutch men. Finnish men. American prisoners. Not these weak, incompetent women. "We call it the *Electroboot*. The entire design is optimized for underwater propulsion. The battery capacity is three times our old Type VIIC. The latest twin 55 W, double electric motors put out 4900 hp. With the new motors and the streamlining, it will be faster below water than on the surface! We will be invisible from the air and at twenty knots, run circles around the escorts, let alone the merchant ships!" Dönitz smiled. "It will be like the happy days of 1942 again!"

"Still...even these boats will eventually have to surface to recharge the batteries," noted Schellenberg.

"*Ja*, good point, but not quite so. Look there—next to the periscope—do you see that pipe with the bulbous top? It's the snorkel, an extendable breathing apparatus. When we need to recharge the battery, we can stay just below the surface and use the snorkel! We can run the diesels while we are submerged. In three to five hours, we can completely recharge the batteries, without coming to the surface!"

"*Ach so.*" Schellenberg nodded. "Incredible! Does the snorkel have a radar signature?"

"You should have been an engineer, Herr Schellenberg. You're sharp. A very good question! Those damn B-24 Liberators with high-resolution radar are our bane. But we are one step ahead! We have coated our snorkel with rubber. *Schornsteinfeger*. It is genius! It dampens the radar return. In this boat, we are invisible!" Dönitz clapped his hands together. Surely he would get more funding.

"*Der Deutsche Technologie* is first rate!" said Schellenberg.

"Well, actually." Dönitz paused. "It was the Dutch who invented the snorkel."

"*Ja*, and we smashed the Dutch in 1940. Ha! So now it is German technology! Tell me, Grossadmiral, how far can this *Electroboot* sail without refueling?"

"The Type XXI has a range of 15,700 km, Brigadeführer. What are you planning? Taking a load of gold and running away with Reichsführer Himmler to Argentina?"

Schellenberg's face darkened. Dönitz had just cut far too close to the truth. "Idiotic comments about treason or surrender are not amusing to us in the SD, Grossadmiral. But in anticipation of your cooperation, I will ignore that."

Dönitz felt his intestines roil. Had he forgotten this man's power? Schellenberg could destroy him.

Schellenberg continued. "So. How far can it travel underwater without using the snorkel?"

"Twenty-seven nautical miles."

"Ah, so this is halfway…"

Dönitz couldn't help himself. "Halfway from where to where?"

"Never mind that, Herr Grossadmiral. I've heard enough. Tell me, which of your commanders has the most experience operating off the American coast? I remember quite a lot of celebration of Kapitänleutnant Hardegan after Operation Drumbeat."

"*Ja*, Hardegan had great success back in 1942 with U-123. He sank eighteen ships off the U.S. East Coast that year, some within sight of New York. I'm afraid he's out to pasture now. Kapitänleutnant Reichman was Hardegan's XO, and now he has his own boat, the U-576. He knows the American coast as well as any of our men," answered Dönitz.

"That settles it. This *Electroboot* will meet my needs. The SD will take possession of this vessel, and I need you to round up your best crew. Kapitänleutnant Reichman should report immediately to me."

Dönitz stiffened. "Don't be ridiculous, Schellenberg! I need this boat to win the war. It belongs to the Kriegsmarine."

"I'm afraid, Herr Grossadmiral, this boat now belongs to the SD. We need Kapitänleutnant Reichman by March 15."

"The Führer has promised me one hundred of these boats by year end. We have only a few of this type! What possible use does the SD propose? Surely we can provide a Type VIIC boat that will meet your needs."

"You will get your one hundred Type XXI boats in due time. Until then, the Kriegsmarine will have to make do."

"It's impossible! This boat won't be ready until mid-April, and Reichman just left with U-572 in the North Atlantic," said Dönitz.

"Nothing is impossible in our Reich, Grossadmiral! Recall Kapitänleutnant Reichman immediately! Inform my office as soon as he is in port. I will have my man Krieger bring him to Berlin."

"But under what—"

"And accelerate the construction. Do you need more workers from Neuengamme or Auschwitz?"

"Yes, and—"

"Then take them. Do it. Use my name," barked Schellenberg. "Take as many as you need. Pick the healthiest. Have no regard for their rest. And what about night work? Why not! I don't see any lights here, Grossadmiral!"

"What? Lights? But—"

"Do it! Set up lights! Why is there no night work? Crews should be working twenty-four hours a day." Schellenberg looked at Dönitz. "Dönitz. Listen. The fate of our Reich depends on your success."

Dönitz clicked his heels and stormed down the stairs and back to his waiting staff car.

Schellenberg lit a cigarette, leaned against the railing, and stared for a long while at the anthill of slaves working on the submarine. Perhaps Dönitz was right, he thought. Someday, it might be necessary to slip away for Buenos Aires or Montevideo with a load of gold. At the right moment, he might bring it up with Himmler.

Not right now, though. For now, he was working only for total triumph, complete victory.

Winners don't need escape plans.

THREE

Professor Tom Goldstein steered his battered Subaru Outback into a slow-moving line of cars at the security checkpoint at Thayer Gate, the main entrance to West Point, the U.S. Military Academy. A belligerent concrete eagle stared down at Goldstein from its perch atop the guard tower.

Set on a rocky bluff overlooking the Hudson River, the fortress-like buildings at West Point are home to four thousand cadets, training to become the future leaders of the U.S. Army. A cadre of Army officers and civilian faculty turn them in four years from clueless high-school students into confident, some would say arrogant Second Lieutenants.

That morning, the entire faculty seemed to be ahead of Goldstein in the slow-moving line.

A pimply faced military policeman in black body armor halted Goldstein at the checkpoint. The MP studied Goldstein's Department of Defense ID card and driver's license as though they were printed in Cyrillic, and then looked contemptuously into the messy back seat.

Goldstein stared straight ahead. There was no point in engaging the MPs. Yesterday, he had watched two young contractors thrown to the ground and handcuffed next to their van. Had they talked back? Carried in contraband? Who knew?

Goldstein had smoked weed again last night and the day got off to a slow start. Thank God they didn't drug test the civilian faculty, he thought. Earlier that morning, groggy, gazing into the bathroom mirror, he had been shocked into alertness by a cluster of gray hairs in his thick brown beard. He'd had the beard and unruly long hair since college, and it set him apart from the perfectly groomed cadets and military faculty at West Point. My God, he thought, I'm thirty-two years old! My high-school friends are bankers or doctors. They have families and careers! They own actual houses! What happened to me? Where did I go wrong? I was the smartest guy in the room all through school! I've got to do something different.

Goldstein was going to be late for class—again—if he didn't hustle. Being late was unacceptable in the Army. That morning, the kid at Dunkin' Donuts had forgotten to use oat milk in his latte and had to remake it. Goldstein told himself that he preferred the Dunkin' latte to the one at the Starbucks on post, but the reality was he drove the extra five minutes into town to save a buck. He drummed his fingers on the steering wheel and waited impatiently for the MP to return his card. For God's sake, he thought, what is taking so long?

The MP returned, handed back the IDs, and twirled his hand, gesturing for Goldstein to turn around. "Your car inspection. Out of date. You can't come on base."

Jesus Christ! What kind of Mickey Mouse bullshit was this! Everyone knew that inspections were just a scam to help the repair shops, thought Goldstein. He seethed, but managed not to pound on the wheel.

"I'm Dr. Goldstein, a history professor. I have important business on base," he rasped.

"I know you are, sir. And history is very important here at West Point. You are welcome to come on base, Dr. Goldstein. But your car is not." He pointed dismissively at the Outback. "Regulations. Pull over to the left, make a U-turn, and head off post, sir." The MP seemed ready to reach—for what? A radio? A Taser? A gun? Goldstein hesitated. "Now, sir. Turn around. Others are waiting." He gestured at the line of cars. No one dared honk.

Goldstein considered an outlandish lie about a medical emergency, then thought better of it. He decided to beg. "I have a class to teach in twenty minutes. I promise I'll get it inspected right after the class." He hated his own pleading tone of voice. He wanted to strangle this martinet. He was furious with himself, the MP, everything.

A second guard walked over, hand on holster.

"Trouble here?"

Goldstein groaned but made the U-turn, drove a few hundred yards back into the town of Highland Falls, and parked at a meter. He ransacked the center console, and even crawled around on the floor looking for quarters, but could find only one. Another parking ticket. Christ.

He grabbed his bag from out of the trunk, muttered "fucking Gestapo," and slammed the trunk closed. With a twinge of regret, he looked at the bumper where a blue-and-gold "Go Army, Beat Navy" bumper sticker had been inexactly placed over a Harvard College sticker.

Goldstein slung his tweed sport coat over his shoulder and rolled up the sleeves of his worn Oxford cloth shirt. He was a mile and a half to Thayer Hall. Goldstein slung his bag over his shoulder and set off at a jog. He still had the thin frame and the long stride from his days as a high-school cross-country star. He moved at a brisk pace.

As he passed back through Thayer Gate, the MP on duty

shouted, "Good luck, sir," and "Beat Navy." Goldstein waited until the guard's back was turned and gave him the finger. He ran past the tidy brick colonial homes of Colonels Row, past the "Slow Construction" signs for the new computer-science building, and past Mahan Hall.

Groups of uniformed cadets on their way to class stopped and stared. Running on campus was forbidden except in Army-issue physical-training gear. Let them stare, he thought. It felt good to run, even with his bag bumping him. The rules didn't apply to him.

As he approached the hulking mass of gray granite that was Thayer Hall, Goldstein felt a twinge of anxiety. Faculty at the U.S. Military Academy were judged more by punctuality and adherence to policy than by academic accomplishment. He picked up the pace, shouldered between two cadets, and raced down two flights of stairs toward his classroom, sweating and breathing hard.

The cadets in Goldstein's U.S.-history class were waiting. A few were clustered around Mai Zhao, a Firstie, or senior cadet, who was their natural-born leader. Zhao was the top student in every class she took. She did the optional supplemental reading, and her papers were works of scholarship. Given a choice of two topics to write a term paper on, she would often produce two papers, both brilliant. But Zhao was the exception; most of the cadets did mediocre work in history. They were smart kids, but they preferred their math and engineering classes. Goldstein emphasized reading original texts, writing original works, and critical thinking. It didn't come easily for them. Four of the twenty cadets in his section were in danger of failing, including two football players.

For most cadets, just getting through a day at West Point was a struggle. Aside from class, there was drill practice, military training, team practice, and mandatory physical-fitness sessions. They stayed up late doing problem sets; polishing their shoes, belt buckles, and buttons; and preparing for room inspection.

There weren't enough hours in the day to be soldiers, athletes, and students. They were chronically sleep deprived.

For the football players, schoolwork was a Herculean task. There was no "rocks for jocks" at West Point. The athletes studied the same curriculum as the other cadets. This included Calculus, Engineering, Physics, and Goldstein's U.S.-history class. The football team was often on the road for training or games. Some of the players made a good-faith effort to do the work, but most scraped by and relied on a wink and a nod from the faculty. Unlike most professors, Goldstein refused to compromise his standards.

The previous term, Tyrone Davidson, the fastest tailback in the Army backfield, copied a portion of a Wikipedia entry into a term paper. Goldstein had been irate. Tyrone's plagiarism was blatant; he hadn't even retyped it, just total cut and paste in a different font. Goldstein thought he was being taunted, and promptly failed Davidson, making him ineligible for the Army versus Air Force game. When Jim Priestly, the head football coach, called to appeal to Goldstein's patriotism, Goldstein was dismissive. Surely, thought Goldstein, Priestly would understand the need for honesty and discipline. Coach Priestly, the highest-paid employee in the entire Army, and on a first-name basis with the Chairman of the Joint Chiefs, then expressed his displeasure by threatening to throw Goldstein off the roof of Michie Football Stadium. Major Carlos Sanchez, the history department chair, intervened. Goldstein swallowed his pride and backed down, allowing Davidson to resubmit the paper.

If Goldstein resented the special status of the football players, he was fond of the cadets as a whole. Many had an earnest interest in U.S. history, and all were diligent and respectful. Goldstein admired their patriotism and selfless desire to work for the good of the country.

Only a few aggravated him, a few who were idiotic, bellicose, and irrationally nationalistic. Goldstein would make sport of them in class. He felt guilty, but he rationalized that it was worthwhile to

get them to question the validity of their beliefs in American excep-
tionalism. He wanted them to think critically, not to parrot the
doctrine thrust upon them by Fox News. He made up nicknames
for the most obnoxious cadets, like Fredo and Dr. Strangelove. Out
of earshot, those cadets called him Xi Xing Goldstein.

Goldstein had learned that making fun of right-wing cadets
had risks. Major Sanchez had summoned him to his office and
suggested that Goldstein take a more "supportive" attitude with
the cadets. Sanchez was an Air Defense Artillery specialist who
had made a midcareer switch to teaching. He had almost no
scholarly credentials but was a skilled bureaucratic infighter and
had a death grip on the history department.

"For God's sake, Tom. We need to graduate these men and
women. The Army didn't bring them to West Point to have you
fail them out."

"I'm frankly stunned by the academic standards here,
Carlos." He still wasn't used to referring to his department head
as major. "At Harvard—"

"Mr. Goldstein," barked Major Sanchez, cutting him off. "Call
me Major Sanchez! I've told you before, I'm tired, and everyone's tired, of hearing you talk about Harvard. Must I remind
you again that no one has tenure here? Davis Miller, the kid you
humiliated last week, is the son of Colonel Miller from the
Ranger Regiment. Does that mean anything to you? Colonel
Miller served in Iraq with the commandant. You can connect the
dots."

Goldstein backed off. He told himself: don't get fired. He
tried to make his face look neutral as Major Sanchez lectured on.
He heard snippets like: "this isn't Harvard" and "ease up on
your Ivy standards" and "align yourself with our mission."
Teaching at West Point wasn't a dream job, but it paid his rent
and impressed his parents' friends. There were few other
options. Too many history PhDs out there. At least he wasn't the
guy working at Dunkin' Donuts.

His job search had been a nightmare. Had he really not understood what the job market was? No. He'd applied to twenty-five colleges and universities for faculty positions. He got two Zoom interviews but no job offers. There were too many newly minted PhDs chasing too few academic jobs; musical chairs with not enough chairs at all. His PhD thesis on medieval naval warfare, his passion, was out of fashion. Goldstein's mentor suggested he do a post-doctoral fellowship and shift his academic focus to institutional racism or sexism in the military. Goldstein knew that a fellowship meant more years of poorly paid work, with no guarantee of a tenured faculty position down the road. Most importantly, he wanted to study war, not social justice.

Out of desperation, Goldstein applied for teaching positions at preparatory schools. He was offered a position at Harbor View, the elite private school in New York, where he'd graduated. He could teach A.P. History and coach the squash team. The job was appealing; the students were smart, and wanted to excel, and he would teach only three classes a day. The pay and benefits were decent, similar to many private colleges. And there was a lucrative side gig: he could tutor to supplement his income.

But could he face himself in the mirror? Was that all it was? A high-school teacher, scrabbling for tutoring cash. He didn't want to give up his dream of academia and scholarship, but what options did he have?

In the end, what dissuaded him was his firsthand knowledge of how the wealthy parents and students at Harbor View saw the faculty. The students bragged to their friends about the Harvard PhDs who taught at their school, but mocked them behind their backs for their failure to get college positions. The parents would hire him to tutor in their Park Avenue apartments, but use him as an example to their children that you could *never* make a decent living as an academic. They might fly him on a private plane out to Aspen over Christmas break to tutor, but they made it clear he was hired help, not a peer.

One day, when all seemed lost, a friend of his father, an old graduate of West Point, suggested he apply for a faculty spot at the U.S. Military Academy. It was only an hour from New York City, and although there was no tenure, it seemed a better option than a poorly paid fellowship or a job teaching snobby high schoolers.

At thirty-two, he was living in his parents' cramped apartment. His father looked at him balefully every evening.

Goldstein's Harvard PhD impressed the West Point faculty, and they offered him a position. His colleagues back in Cambridge were a bit puzzled. None of them had ever been to West Point or even knew the difference between the Army and the Marine Corps. No serious scholars or journal editors came from the U.S. Military Academy, but his mentor was relieved, and his parents were proud. Goldstein told himself that West Point was an elite academic institution, one that would value and support his scholarship. He was offered an inexpensive apartment on base. How could he go wrong?

Goldstein entered Room 400 of Thayer Hall. The young men and women immediately rose to attention in unison for roll call. They were fit and lean, with perfect posture. There were no baseball hats or knit caps. The cadets' white hats with black brims hung on a rack at the entrance to the room. The men's hair was cut high and tight to Army regulation, and the female cadets had their hair in tight buns or neat braids. Beards, visible tattoos, and nose rings, so common in the Ivy League, were forbidden.

Cadet Zhao looked at Goldstein and then at the clock. "At 0900—now 0910—one hundred percent of the class is present and accounted for, sir. Cadets, you may be seated." She was calm, stoic, and disciplined. Goldstein knew that female cadets were a special breed, some from Army families, some athletes, and others running away from something awful at home. Some female cadets were resented, others were lusted after, but Zhao stood out from the crowd. Her expression was somehow both serene and fierce, and Goldstein felt her magnetism.

Goldstein had prepared an exercise for the cadets about the Battle of Fort Montgomery. He thought it was particularly relevant, as it was fought almost within sight of the classroom. In 1776, the British stormed up the Hudson River from New York City with an armada of ships and two thousand Hessian troops. They planned to seize the entire length of the river from New York to Canada, and cut the rebellious colonies in half. The Americans made their stand just south of West Point. They built Forts Montgomery and Clinton on bluffs overlooking a narrow point of the river. The Americans dug trenches and dragged cannons into place, aiming at the river. They brought in a small fleet of warships to face the British Navy.

The Americans had a secret weapon, or so they thought. They dug iron from local mines and hastily forged a giant iron chain to block the British fleet. They floated it on logs and deployed it across the river. The British had other plans. Guided by a loyalist farmer, they marched swiftly through the wilderness and attacked both forts from their incomplete, and poorly defended, landward sides.

The forts were easily captured, and the British sank most of the American fleet. Two hundred and seventy-five American soldiers were packed off to prison ships in New York Harbor, where most died of disease and malnutrition. Although the standard West Point textbooks characterized the Battle of Fort Montgomery as a vital delaying action, Goldstein disagreed. He marveled at the Americans' bravery and resolve, but they had been soundly defeated. Goldstein used the battle to demonstrate to the cadets the price of poor leadership.

Goldstein needed a cadet to discuss the battle in front of the class. The U.S. Military Academy used the "Thayer Method" in most classes. The cadets were expected to come prepared, first mastering extensive materials independently, then defending their thinking in front of the class.

Goldstein asked for volunteers. As usual, Cadet Zhao had her hand raised high.

Goldstein called instead called on a broad-shouldered cadet with bright-red hair, cut to regulation. The young man had grown up on a wild rice farm in California. He spoke with the slow cadence of many from the American West. Goldstein had initially been impatient with Westerners. He judged them slow-witted, but at West Point he had learned measured speech could be the mark of clear thinking.

"Well, sir, I can't say this disposition of forces is very logical. We failed to anticipate a downriver flanking maneuver. Beyond that, sir, the Americans were very deficient in scouting and reconnaissance."

Goldstein was pleased and proud; the red-headed farm boy had done well.

Goldstein selected a defense man from the lacrosse team to continue the discussion. He was unprepared and inarticulate. The other cadets became disengaged. Goldstein himself started to lose focus. This is what it must be like to teach high school, he thought. Have I wasted all those years getting a PhD? I should really try to write a book. Major Sanchez didn't encourage research; none of the faculty did.

Goldstein had done hundreds of dives on the wrecks of sixteenth century Venetian warships. He had gathered an incredible about of data. He just needed to buckle down and start writing it up.

Goldstein's mind wandered to scuba diving. He'd taken six dive trips in the northeast this year, including the famed *Andrea Doria*, the Italian flagged cruise ship that sank in almost two hundred feet of water off Nantucket. For Goldstein, wreck diving was an obsession, like a tortured love affair, exhilarating and terrifying.

Technical wreck diving requires courage, perfect technique, and absolute attention to detail. The interiors of wrecks are a fascinating but potentially lethal web of broken pipes, large fragments of rusted jagged steel, and billows of wiring. Piles of sediment become blinding clouds with the slightest agitation. Wrecks are cramped, disorienting, and, for the ill-prepared or reckless, death traps.

Goldstein visualized the path he swam through the main dining room of the *Andrea Doria*. He was deep in the wreck, hoping to score some china to add to his collection. He remembered his panic when something snagged him, the terror of being stuck, thrashing trying to free himself, his uncoordinated movements raising clouds of sediment.

"Sir! Excuse me, Dr. Goldstein," said Cadet Zhao, waving at him. "SIR! Class is over. You have to dismiss us." The class was staring at him.

Goldstein's mind snapped out of the wreck and back into the classroom. The class hour was over, but the cadets needed his approval to leave. He was making them late—and the punishments were severe. As he dismissed them, they anxiously crowded the door and headed swiftly off to the Fieldhouse for football practice, Arvin Gym for boxing, or the pool for combat dive training.

As Goldstein gathered his belongings and prepared for the long walk back to his car, Cadet Zhao ambushed him. He couldn't read her expression. Was she angry?

"Professor. I need a minute with you."

"I'm just leaving—"

"Now."

"I know, I know, I'm sorry, I wasn't paying attention," he started. Was she going to report him? "And I was late —again—"

"I don't care about that. Look. I can tell you hate it here. Me too." Zhao lowered her voice. "Neither of us belong here. We both need a way to get out, get to a normal college where people don't wear uniforms and have their rooms inspected."

"What? You what? I don't..." Was she allowed to even say these things? Goldstein wondered.

"This place is more like a high school than a college, and the goddamn Army is just a prison. Am I right?"

Goldstein gulped. This? From the outstanding Cadet Zhao? "Uh, well, I'm not sure—"

"Look. Walk me over to the library. I have an idea. It just came to me."

"But…" Goldstein wondered what had come over her. Was she in trouble?

"I need your help." Zhao smiled. "I'm going to change your life. And you're going to change mine."

FOUR

After four months at West Point, Plebe Cadet Karl Krause had been angry, then depressed, and now despondent. Beast Barracks, the summer introduction to cadet life, had been six weeks of nonstop hazing and abuse. Compared to what would come later, it had been almost a holiday.

All through the hot and humid New York summer, the upper classmen screamed at, humiliated, and pummeled the plebes, the freshman cadets. With their shaven heads and ill-fitting uniforms, the new cadets in Beast resembled prisoners in a work camp. The upperclassmen detected the smallest mistakes—a missing button, a poorly made bed, a poorly ironed uniform—and meted out pushups and tirades of abuse. They preyed on the weak and broke the arrogant. Rebellion or resistance was crushed. Question authority? The upperclassmen would force you to clean the latrines with toothbrushes. For serious violations, or sometimes just for the joy of it, the upperclassmen beat them with fists and belts.

The plebes were sleep deprived and always hungry. There was never enough food at meals, and never enough time to eat it. Plebes had only twenty minutes to eat, and before they could start, the upperclassmen would quiz them on West Point military minutiae. Questions on the history, traditions, and song lyrics of the Army went on for an eternity. How many names on Battle Monument at Trophy Point? Who was Dennis Michie and where and when was he killed? Which Greek god is the statue in front of West Point Library? Get the question wrong, and the plebe would have to do fifty pushups. Krause lost fifteen pounds in four months, even as he grew two inches.

Most of the upperclassmen were average young men who enjoyed their power and dished out the abuse they themselves had received. A few were true sadists. As bad as it was, Krause hadn't been shaken by the abuses of Beast Barracks; his father, Otto, had been a far harsher taskmaster on the farm in Kansas.

Krause had grown up in Bremen, Kansas, about one hundred miles northwest of Kansas City. The community had been founded by *Volksdeutsche*, German immigrants who maintained their culture, language, and identities. Karl's father Otto, a decorated veteran, brought his family to Kansas in 1919, fleeing the chaos of post-World War I Germany.

Life on the Krause farm was harsh. There was no electricity. The children were expected to work hard, hauling water and working in the fields. The Krause family never assimilated; they spoke German at home. Krause's mother didn't speak any English. Krause learned his first English words at age six, when he went to school. He was a good-natured and outgoing child. He was befriended by the local librarian, who picked out books for him to read. When he finished middle school she gave him a complete set of William Shakespeare's works. He dreamed of a career on stage, but had not dared to share this fantasy with his father. Otto Krause had no patience for bookworms or actors. Otto felt that real men worked with their hands, or bore arms.

On Sundays, the family attended the Lutheran church. After services, Otto took Krause to the *Turn Verein*, a German social, cultural, and gymnastics club. Otto drank pilsner lager from the local German brewery, and socialized with his fellow expatriates. Over the years, Otto's conversations took on an increasingly dark tone, as the men discussed the worsening worldwide depression. Their conversations focused on the Jews and Bolsheviks, and they read aloud articles from the violently anti-Semitic Nazi newspapers, the *Völkischer Beobachter* and Julius Streicher's *Der Stürmer*.

Krause wasn't interested in the political discussions. His biggest hope was to somehow escape Kansas, the farm, and his domineering father. He was a gifted athlete and excelled on the rings, high bar, and pommel horse. Krause built a high bar and rings in the barn back on the farm to practice. In his senior year of high school, his team won the state championship. He was offered a scholarship to the University of Michigan, but there was no money offered for lodging or travel. Krause had also received an offer from West Point. He had never planned to be a soldier, but his father insisted that it was a noble profession, and Karl, the ever-dutiful son, enrolled. Anything was better than life on the farm. He had been sure of that.

Once Beast Barracks ended and classes began, conditions for the plebe cadets improved, if only a little. Plebes were forbidden to speak in public, unless directly addressed by an upperclassman or faculty members. They were forced to march on campus with their hands clasped into fists. They could be stopped for uniform checks or quizzed on arcane knowledge. If found lacking, they were "corrected" by upperclassmen with more pushups and kicks in the ribs. Between schoolwork, military training, and keeping their rooms prepared for white-glove inspections, the cadets never got more than five hours of sleep. Mealtimes remained a torment, with abuse heaped upon the plebes, who were forced to eat in silence while seated rigidly at attention and bring food to their mouths in two straight lines.

Despite a heavy academic load and the stresses of plebe year, Krause did well at West Point. He got passing grades, was in top physical condition, and stayed out of trouble. Before he went to sleep, Krause would often read from his treasured collection of Shakespeare.

His problems began shortly after helping his roommate, Mark, with his German homework. Mark was near tears. He couldn't grasp the convoluted sentence structure, and Krause was quick to help. For that small act of kindness, his life became hell.

The day after he helped Mark with his German, Krause found his way up the six flights of stairs to his French class in Washington Hall blocked by three upperclassmen. They were led by a towering Firstie, a senior cadet named Jorgenson. He was powerfully built with a thick neck, ash-blond hair, full lips, and pale blue eyes.

"Private Krause! I understand you speak German," barked Jorgenson. He spat out the words in a crude German accent.

"Yes, sir."

"Tell me, Cadet, how is that?"

"Sir, my father was born in Germany, sir."

"Did your father fight for the Kaiser? Goddamn Kraut! My father was shot by some fucking Hun! Probably your father or one of his friends!" bellowed Jorgenson. He shoved Krause in the chest, making him back down a few steps.

Krause's father had indeed fought in the war, and had been wounded while fighting in 1918. "No, sir," answered Krause. He looked down. He hated to lie. He was proud of his father's service. Proud of his German heritage. He looked at Jorgenson; he thought he could take Jorgenson in a fight, but he couldn't fight all three. Besides, if he punched a Firstie, he would be dismissed from West Point.

"No, sir, what?" shouted Jorgenson, pushing Krause again.

"No, sir, my father did not shoot your father. Sir."

"Shut up!" shouted Jorgenson, slapping Krause across the face, knocking off his cadet cap.

"Hey! Jorgie! Calm down!" protested one of Jorgenson's friends. "Don't take it too far."

Krause reeled, recovered his balance and hat, and staggered back to attention.

"Recite Worth's Battalion Orders!"

"Yes, sir," panted Krause, continuing, "Worth's Battalion Orders are 'An Officer on Duty Knows No One...To Be Partial is to Dishonor Both Himself and—'"

"Wrong!" bellowed Jorgenson, cutting Krause off. "Front leaning rest! Move! You miserable Kraut scum!"

Droplets of spit struck Krause in the face. He quickly dropped to the floor in pushup position and waited for the order he knew was coming. His heart sank. Jorgenson slammed the wall with his fist. "Pushups! Now! Keep going until I give the order to stop!"

"Yes, sir." He was going to do pushups for this madman until he collapsed or threw up.

Jorgenson stood over Krause and put his black, low-quarter shoe on Krause's back. "Push faster, harder, you fucking Kraut! This is for all the doughboys you people killed in France."

Krause was fit, and he did one pushup after another. Jorgenson put more weight on his foot. Straining, Krause continued his pushups. After another dozen pushups, Krause collapsed.

Jorgenson stepped off, then turned and kicked Krause twice in the ribs with his shoe. There was an audible crack. "We're watching you, Krause! We don't want any Krauts in the Corps!"

The upperclassmen stormed off, leaving Krause to recover his cap, stagger to his feet, and set off for class wincing.

The next morning, the real misery started. Krause said good morning to Mark, his roommate, who looked away and said nothing. Krause didn't think much of it; his roommate had never been one for idle chatter. Then in the bathroom, two cadets spotted him and quickly left without speaking or making eye contact. When Krause returned to his room after dinner, he offered to help his roommate Mark with his German homework. Mark shook his head.

It slowly dawned on Krause that he had been ostracized. No one would speak to him. Jorgenson had activated "The Vigilance Committee," an unofficial but very real network of influential cadets. They decreed that Krause was to be "silenced." No cadet would speak to him or even nod to acknowledge his existence.

Krause had always been proud of his family. His father was a stern but honest and upright man, who worked relentlessly to better the lot of his family. Now for the first time, Krause felt shame and anger. His father had fought on the wrong side of the war, but his enemies had been the British and French, not the Americans. Besides, that was before Krause was even born! It was all just so unfair.

As the weeks went by, Krause became increasingly desperate. He sought solace in his books, but found scant comfort. He fantasized about quitting, but couldn't imagine how he could face his family and friends. After all, they had thrown a town parade in his honor when he went off to West Point! The first in Bremen, Kansas to attend West Point! He could never go home again if he dropped out.

He had no friends. He was so lonely. He couldn't tell his family back home. They thought he was fine. He kept his letters brief and cheerful. He couldn't explain the shame that he felt about his father or the horror of the silencing.

Just when it seemed things couldn't get any worse, the plebes faced a room inspection. They stayed up the entire night before the inspection polishing shoes, blowing dust off the inside of light fixtures, and ironing every shirt that hung in proscribed order and angle in their closets. When his time for inspection came, three upperclassmen, two with white gloves and the sadistic Jorgenson, holding a clipboard, entered his room.

Krause and his roommate stood rigidly at attention as the upperclassmen opened drawers, inspected the bedding, and checked for lint in the corners of the room. One of the inspectors casually knocked Krause's volume of Shakespeare onto the floor.

"Cadet Kaiser," bellowed one of the inspectors. "Do you not know the rules? This room is a shithole! There are books all over the floor, and your belt buckle looks like it's never been shined!" He pointed at a black tarry smear on the inseam of a pair of gray dress pants. "This is atrocious! Cadet Kaiser, you don't mind if we call you that?"

Sabotage! Krause knew that his buckle had been highly polished, and the black smear on the pants must have been placed by one of the inspectors, but he could say nothing.

"No excuse, sir," said Krause. What else could he say? "Yes, sir," "no, sir," and "no excuse, sir" were his only options.

Jorgenson, the sadist, slammed him in the face with the clipboard and screamed, "You have failed room inspection, you fucking Kraut! Miserably, I might add. You and your roommates will forfeit all privileges until you correct these errors! And we are sentencing you to eight hours of marching as punishment."

Krause's roommates stared at him, their eyes full of hatred.

Krause despaired. Marching hours were used to punish a broad range of violations including alcohol use, missed assignments, and dress-code or room-inspection failure. On Sundays, after mandatory chapel services, cadets had eight precious hours of free time to walk to Highland Falls and eat in a diner, or study, or sleep, or write letters home.

Now Krause would spend those precious free hours marching back and forth in the main courtyard, publicly punished, for all the other cadets to see.

The following day after chapel, Krause changed into his full dress uniform and reported to the central area, a dreary cobblestone courtyard ringed with stone buildings. Eight other depressed cadets joined him. They stood at attention for an inspection of their uniforms and rifles. One cadet was dismissed because he had a loose button on his great coat. He returned to the barracks with tears streaming down his face. Four additional hours were added to his punishment; he had to wait until the following Sunday to begin marching.

On command, the cadets shouldered their rifles and marched from one end of the central area to another. It took about a minute to make the round trip circuit. They marched and marched, doing sixty circuits an hour. They were not allowed to speak to each other. Hour after hour passed, until finally at noon, they were given an hour off.

Even as they sat on a bench, resting their feet, the other cadets refused to acknowledge Krause. He had never been so miserable in his life.

Jorgenson then appeared, and Krause leaped to attention. "Enjoying your hours, you Kraut faggot? I hope so, because let me assure you, these aren't the only ones you have coming. You can plan on marching hours every Sunday! Do something smart, you fucking piece of shit: quit, go home to your Frau Krause, and tell her you don't belong in the United States Army!"

"Yes, sir," answered Krause. Jorgenson lost interest and stormed off. Before long, the cadets were back, marching back and forth.

Later that evening, as Krause sat in the washroom and washed his bloodied and blistered feet, he cried tears of frustration and rage.

There was no way out. He began to consider taking his own life. He had unspeakable murderous thoughts. He prayed for a miracle.

To his astonishment, the next day, salvation came from where he least expected it.

FIVE

Zhao and Goldstein left the classroom in Thayer Hall and crossed the street toward the new West Point Library.

"So don't keep me in suspense, Cadet Zhao; how are you going to change our lives?"

"The chain, sir. It's our way out."

"I don't understand, Zhao."

"The chain—it's a metaphor, but it's also the answer."

"Zhao, you aren't making any sense."

"It's a bit of a story, sir. Should we sit down?" Zhao and Goldstein sat on a bench beneath a statue of Douglas MacArthur. "You see, sir, we both feel chained to the Army..."

Zhao sighed and explained her dilemma. On Affirmation Day, the first day of her third year at West Point, Zhao had carefully braided her hair, donned her India White dress uniform with gold buttons and U.S. insignia on her collar, and joined the other members of her class in the Thayer Hall auditorium. They swore a solemn oath to the Army, one that obligated them to five years of service after graduation. At the time, it had seemed like a noble and grand adventure.

Today, it felt miserable. How did she get here in the first place?

Unlike most West Point cadets, Zhao was prior service; she had started as a private. The day after her eighteenth birthday, she had driven down to the recruiting center on Woodward Avenue in Detroit and thrown in her lot with the U.S. Army. Some enlisted soldiers had come from a background of troubled families and academic failure. Not Zhao. She was the treasured daughter of highly devoted parents. "The Tiger Baby of a Tiger Mom," her dad called her.

Zhao's mother was furious.

"We moved eight thousand miles for you, ungrateful daughter," she screamed. "Your father and I sacrificed everything for you. I was the Department Chief in the Party Hospital in Shenzhen! Your father was a civil engineer for the city! In China, people paid top dollar for good medical care! We had a car and a driver! No one got a building permit in Shenzhen without your father's permission. We barely had to work, and we were rich."

"Mother."

She wouldn't let Zhao get a word in.

"No! No! You listen to me now! You not allowed to talk! We came here when you were four so you could have every advantage, so you could learn English perfectly. Now Father and I work every day from dawn to dusk." The angrier she got, the worse her English grammar got. She switched to Mandarin, which she did when she was really outraged. Which was often.

Zhao lowered her head. She handled this as she always handled confrontations with her mother.

She would appear docile, but then go on and do exactly whatever she intended to do. "I thank you every day for that, Mom. I know how hard coming to the U.S. has been for you," Zhao replied sweetly in Mandarin.

Zhao had swimming lessons at age four. Violin at six. By

middle school she competed with the high-school math Olympic team. Her parents sent her to Oaktree, a prestigious private high school, where she was state champion in the 400 Individual Medley swim. On weekends, she went to Chinese school, which gave more homework than her regular school. Zhao had complied with every expectation, but felt completely suffocated and controlled.

One day, she was served an Army recruiting video ad on her Instagram. She saw soldiers, some women, scale tall wooden obstacles and rappel from helicopters. She clicked on the like button and was served more and more videos, each more exciting than the next. She watched soldiers paddle boats and leap out of helicopters. Zhao was hooked. These were her people.

Her mother shoved her into a chair. "You were supposed to go to Harvard," she screamed, "and then Goldman Sachs! Now, you join the Army without even asking us! Why are you dishonoring the family and playing soldier? How can I tell my sister in Vancouver that you threw everything we gave you away and now you are in the Army?" She became short of breath from the screaming and aggravation. "I told my sister you were choosing between Harvard and MIT. She will think you must have trouble with the police."

"Mother, I think a good officer should start as a regular soldier, learn to care about ordinary people…Didn't you tell me that back in China—"

Zhao's mother cut her off and continued her tirade. "Don't talk back to me! We came here for you! In the United States, your father and I are nobodies! I couldn't afford to spend ten years retraining to be a doctor, so I'm a nurse! Your father learned to program and now commutes every day by bus to a bank in Detroit! His boss is awful. We worked weekends to send you to Oaktree. Twenty-eight thousand dollars a year! Scholarships for minority people but not for Chinese. For our daughter Mai, we pay full price. FULL PRICE!"

"You can always tell them I'm a drug addict," Zhao spat in a perfect flat Midwestern-English accent. When she fought with her parents, she would switch to English. If she spoke quickly, they struggled to follow her, and it put them off balance.

"You are ruining your life!" her mother raged. "You have ruined our lives!"

Deng, Zhao's father, sat silently through the confrontation. He had always been closer to Mai than her mother. He was by nature relaxed, and sought reconciliation. "I'm sorry your mother is so upset, Mai. We love you, and your mother shows it in her own way. You are eighteen now, an independent American citizen, and we are very proud of you. I hope you will remember us when we are older. There is nothing more for us to say."

"Oh, Dad," answered Zhao in Mandarin. "You know I love you and Mom, and I am very grateful for everything you have sacrificed for me. I won't disappoint you, and I will be there to look after you as life goes on." She paused. "And Dad, hey, tell Mom I'm not an addict."

The day after high-school graduation, Zhao's father drove her to the Greyhound bus station in Detroit. Twelve hours later, she was at boot camp at Fort Benning, Georgia. Three months after that, she was the honor graduate in basic combat training, and breezed through advanced infantry training.

Her father came down to Georgia for her graduation.

"How is Mother?" asked Zhao

"It's hard for her. She still doesn't understand."

"Tell her I love her and will make her proud."

They hugged for a long time. So much unsaid.

Zhao then posted to Fort Campbell to join the 101st Airborne. When she made corporal, her father flew out to Kentucky for the promotion ceremony.

"Your mother had to work, Mai, but she sent these," said her father, presenting her with her mother's special pork dumplings.

A year later, she was one of very few enlisted women

selected for the notoriously difficult Army Ranger School. The Ranger program was designed to train leaders in realistic small-unit combat settings, under maximum tolerable physical, mental, and emotional stress. For sixty-one days, Zhao conducted missions twenty hours a day in rough terrain varying from swamps to rugged mountains, and in all weather conditions. She carried loads up to ninety pounds of supplies and ammunition. She slept three hours a night, lost twenty pounds, and developed stress fractures in both feet, but passed with distinction.

Her mother and father came together to Victory Pond at Fort Benning to pin the Ranger tab on her uniform. Her mother was still puzzled by Zhao's choices, but proud and respectful. Zhao was relieved to be back on good terms with her family.

After the ceremony, a powerfully built Black woman major with a Ranger and a Sapper tab on her uniform took Zhao aside.

"Very impressive, Corporal Zhao. The Army is lucky to have you."

"Thank you, ma'am."

"You've done great things as a soldier, Zhao, but I think the Army needs your talents at a higher level. If women are going to make systemic change in this Army, we need to be in the room where decisions are made. There aren't any corporals in those rooms. Have you considered West Point?"

"The U.S. Military Academy? But don't I need to know a senator? Or something?"

"I can speak to the commandant at West Point. I served with him in Afghanistan. With that Ranger tab on your shoulder, it will be an easy sell. I know you will crush it at West Point."

Zhao had indeed crushed it at West Point. With one year to graduation, she had been at the top of the class, respected by cadets and officers, and looking forward to service as an officer in the U.S. Army, but then it had all gone wrong.

So terribly wrong.

She thought back to the oath of commitment she made last

year and cursed her bad judgement. She owed the Army five years of her life.

They might as well wrap an iron chain around my waist and throw me in the river, she thought.

"You see, Dr. Goldstein. The chain, sir, it's going to make us famous!"

Goldstein looked confused. "What chain?" he asked.

"The 1776 iron chain you told us about in class. The one the Americans put across the Hudson to block the British ships."

"Oh, that. It's gone. It sank, or they melted it down, Cadet. How is the chain going to save us?" answered Goldstein, turning away.

Zhao wasn't discouraged. She came closer and smiled.

"We should scuba dive down and check. You told the class how much you love to dive. We might even find those ships that the British sank," she added earnestly.

"Excuse me, Cadet. Did you suggest we make a dive—out there?" Goldstein pointed to the Hudson River beyond. "In those murky tidal waters? This isn't Aruba!"

"Yes, sir. I think there could still be pieces of the chain out there. Sir, they fought that battle right there. You said that no one has tried looking for the ships the British sank or the chain since 1804."

"Do you have dive experience, Cadet Zhao?"

"Yes, sir. I went to the Combat Dive School on Key West last summer, sir. I'm Cadet in Charge of Cadet Scuba Club."

"If I remember correctly, the cadet scuba club is an excuse for a spring-break trip to the Bahamas. But combat dive—that does sound impressive." He nodded. "But you know it's deep out there, freezing cold, with rapid tidal currents, and terrible visibility. More importantly, why do you care if we find a few links from an old metal chain?"

"I want to win a Rhodes Scholarship, sir. I need to raise my profile, to make a splash as it were, sir. Everyone knows that the media loves West Point, and the media loves shipwrecks and mysteries."

... − −−− ·−−·

GOLDSTEIN STARTED to dismiss the idea. It was silly, he thought. The ships that sank were small and insignificant, and besides, ship worms would have reduced them to dust a hundred years ago. The chain would have rusted away, too.

"It's perfect for *National Geographic* or *Inside Edition*, sir!" Zhao continued.

"*National Geographic*?" Goldstein repeated quietly.

Goldstein's mind raced. Maybe this girl was on to something. Cute Asian West Point Girl and Harvard PhD find Revolutionary-War relics in the deep waters of the Hudson River at West Point. She's right. *National Geographic* would eat this up. He started to think. If things broke his way, he could quit teaching and move into TV! Maybe he would host his own show! *Ancient Mysteries of the Deep* with Dr. Tom Goldstein.

He looked over to the cadet. Her uniform tag listed only her last name, and he struggled to remember her first name.

"Zhao, how much diving have you done?"

"Fifty dives, sir."

"Have you been deep?"

"I've been to one hundred and twenty feet."

Goldstein frowned. The river was almost two-hundred-feet deep opposite West Point.

"Were all your dives in Key West?"

"Except for the ones here in the pool," said Zhao. "Seriously, I've never been in water as deep and dark as the Hudson, and I've never been on wreck, but I'm dry-suit certified, and I even learned how to blow underwater obstacles at Combat Dive School."

Goldstein struggled to keep a straight face. "Let's leave blowing shit up to the combat divers, Zhao."

"I could get Captain Haskins to help. He's the officer in charge of the scuba club. He has a Boston Whaler. He'd be interested; it's cool. Historic, and right here at West Point...and besides, I think he's a little soft on me." Zhao looked down. She didn't like to show vulnerability, but she had to make this happen. "I need that Rhodes Scholarship, sir. I'm top of my class and on the scuba team and all, but my advisor says, it's really hard to win without doing something special. I know that seems selfish, sir. But the Rhodes committee doesn't understand the military. I think they are actually put off by it. I don't blame them, actually. I've had it up to here with all the saluting and military braggadocio. Two years at Oxford, that's what I really want. That will give me time to figure out my life. I think if we find this chain, or even get people fired up about it, they'll punch my ticket, sir."

"Let's not get ahead of ourselves, Cadet. Are you free this Saturday?"

"Sure. At 1500 hours. After the football game, sir."

"Football game? Who cares about football?"

"No one, sir, but every cadet must attend every football game, and stand and cheer the entire game, or we get punishment hours."

Goldstein shook his head, only at West Point, he thought. "Probably no pre-gaming or beer pong afterwards?"

"Ahhh, no, sir," Zhao almost choked. "No." Being caught drinking alcohol could result in dismissal. Definitely not joking material.

"No wonder you want to get out of this place. Okay, reach out to Captain Haskins. I'll arrange with the dive shop to get us eight tanks. We can go with regular air, no need for Trimix. I've got a magnetometer. If that chain is down there, it shouldn't be hard to find."

"Thank you, sir. I'll meet you at the dock at 1500 on Saturday. You won't be disappointed with this cadet, sir."

"Take it easy, Zhao." He laughed. "Let's try to make this fun."

"West Point is where fun went to die, sir. I'll have my fun in Oxford." Zhao turned and headed off briskly to practice for her combatives class. She'd been knocked around enough, she decided; it was time for her to throw some punches.

Goldstein headed back along Thayer Road to his uninspected car with a spring in his step. *Ancient Mysteries of the Deep*, he thought. That had a nice ring to it.

SIX

Cadet Krause's ribs still ached with every breath from the beating he had received, but the mental anguish was worse. The "silencing"—complete ostracism—undid him. He was a complete outcast. It was an impossible situation for him. Social isolation and rejection were much harder than the physical torment. He was called Cadet Kaiser by the upperclassmen, and they rained physical and mental abuse on him at every opportunity. His father was a hard man, and Krause had grown up with a steady diet of harsh physical punishment, but his mother and sister loved him, and he'd had a wide community of friends. He had never felt so alone.

Sitting alone in his dreary room, rereading the letters his mother mailed him in German, made him feel even more alone and ashamed. He could never tell her about this.

Few cadets could tolerate "the silence." Most dropped out. Only one, a few years before, survived four entire years of complete ostracism: Benjamin O. Davis, Jr., the fourth African

American graduate of West Point, and the first since 1889, had been shunned. During his time at West Point, no cadet would room with him, eat with him, or speak to him outside of class. Somehow, Davis had persevered, and graduated thirty-fifth in his class of two hundred and seventy-six.

Davis had anticipated he would not be welcome at West Point. He had an iron will. Krause was completely blindsided. He had grown up proud of his German heritage. Back in Kansas, German heritage was nothing unusual. Now, he was confronted with the ugly anti-German feeling still widespread in the U.S. after World War I.

Inflamed by Jorgenson, the huge Firstie, the other cadets continued to shun Krause. Even his roommates wouldn't make eye contact. As the weeks wore on, Krause's ribs healed and he kept his head down. He went to Protestant church services at the Cadet Chapel on Sundays, and he tried to take some solace from the prayers. He didn't believe in God, but chapel was one of the only places on campus he felt like a human being.

One day near the end of the term, he found an envelope in his room, addressed to him in a fluid calligraphy, from the wife of Lt. Colonel Wilson, the BTO, or Brigade Tactical Officer, inviting him to dinner at their home the following Saturday. After the commandant and superintendent, the BTO was the highest-ranking officer at West Point; he supervised all military training for the cadets. Colonel Wilson was a World War I Veteran with a fierce military bearing, and he had unbending standards for discipline and conduct.

Krause was shocked. Cadets generally tried to avoid direct contact with the BTO, and now he was invited to dinner at his house. Why? Krause showed the invite to his squad leader, who passed it along to the First-Class cadet commanding their company. He, too, was puzzled. Plebes were occasionally invited to the home of "sponsor families," West Point staff or faculty, for a dish of ice cream, but a formal dinner invitation for a plebe to the home of an officer, let alone the BTO, was unheard of. The

Firstie grumbled, but had no choice but to allow Krause to go. Krause penned an affirmative response on his best West Point stationery.

The following Saturday, as Krause returned to his room to dress for dinner, he found Jorgenson sitting at his desk with his feet up, trimming his nails with a knife.

Krause sprang to attention.

"I guess you aren't joining us in the mess hall for dinner tonight, Krause. Not very sociable."

"No, Cadet Sergeant."

"Why not?"

"I've been asked to dinner at Lt. Colonel Wilson's house."

"I don't know what kind of fucking Jew-loving Kraut bullshit this is, Kaiser, but let me warn you. Company problems stay in the company. Be sure you keep your mouth shut with the BTO."

"Yes, Cadet Sergeant."

Jorgenson turned and left, slamming the door behind him.

A few minutes later, Krause, still shaking, walked out of the cadet central area, turned right past Grant Hall, and set out for Colonel Wilson's home on Thayer Road. Krause's dress uniform hung loosely. He'd lost a lot of weight. There was a brilliant sunset over the Hudson, and the maple trees in the Hudson Highlands had turned red and orange, but Krause barely noticed. Arriving at the two-story brick home, he nervously rang the bell.

Cheer up, he thought, Colonel Wilson wouldn't be inviting him to dinner to make him do pushups. Mrs. Wilson answered the door. She was a stout, middle-aged woman, hair in a bun, with a kindly smile. Krause removed his cover and awkwardly handed her a small wooden dog he had carved from a piece of scrap wood.

"I'm sorry, ma'am, I know it's not much. My mamma told me you should always bring something when you go calling and well, ma'am, plebes aren't allowed in the company store," stammered Krause.

"Oh, it's lovely, Cadet! Karl, is it? You are very talented! Thank you!"

"Yes, ma'am." He felt his throat catch. This woman was so kind! "Thank you, ma'am, Karl is my first name. I don't think anyone's used it in months. My papa is a really good wood carver. He taught me a little."

"Well, thank you, Karl. Please come in!" said Mrs. Wilson ushering Krause into a spacious sitting room with woolen rugs and overstuffed couches. Krause was overwhelmed by the delicious aroma of home-cooked food. He was ravenous! As they entered the room, Mrs. Wilson gestured to a couch. After months spent in the hard and cold confines of the barracks, Krause found the carpeting and upholstered chair incredibly luxurious.

Colonel Wilson came down the stairs and into the room. To Krause's surprise, Colonel Wilson had exchanged his exquisitely turned-out uniform and boots for khaki pants and a cardigan sweater. Civilian clothing notwithstanding, his posture was ramrod straight, and his bearing unmistakably military.

Krause jumped off the couch and snapped to attention. Wilson smiled warmly.

"Please, Cadet Krause, sit down. Be comfortable. The whole purpose of a visit with a sponsor family is a chance to relax and feel like you are back home."

"Yes, sir, thank you, sir," answered Krause uneasily.

"I'm having a whiskey and soda, Krause, can I make you one?"

"No, sir, thank you, sir," answered Krause. How much did Colonel Wilson know? he wondered. Was this a trap? He was wary.

"Don't worry about those regulations, son. They don't apply when you're a guest in an officer's home," said Wilson, stepping over to a side table, where he mixed Krause a drink.

Mrs. Wilson excused herself to check on dinner.

"So. The lady has left the room. Tell me straight. I hear plebe year has been pretty tough for you, eh?" said Colonel Wilson.

"Not too tough, sir," lied Krause. "I get by." He was afraid to bring up the silencing.

"Certainly wasn't fun when I was a plebe! The Firsties were a rough bunch."

"Yes, sir," answered Krause weakly. If he only knew! Krause wanted to tell him. But how?

Mrs. Wilson returned with some crackers and cheese.

Colonel Wilson raised his glass. "To the Corps!" he said.

Mrs. Wilson and Krause echoed him.

"And let's hope that goddamned man in the White House doesn't wreck the country," said Colonel Wilson, taking a swig of whiskey. "I can't even say his name!"

Krause didn't ask why Colonel Wilson thought President Roosevelt, "the man in the White House," was wrecking the country. Wilson seemed to hate Roosevelt passionately.

Krause took a big sip of his drink and nearly spit it out. He'd never tasted whiskey before, and it burned his mouth and throat. He felt his face flush.

As Colonel Wilson droned on about the dangers of Bolshevism, and Mrs. Wilson poked the fire and added kindling, Krause listened politely and ate as many crackers as he could without appearing greedy.

Krause wasn't sure what to think about President Roosevelt. Growing up, Krause had worshipped FDR. He eagerly anticipated FDR's fireside chats, when the president explained banking and the things they were doing in Washington to fight the Depression and get every citizen employed. But last summer, his father, and some of the other Kansas farmers, felt abandoned by FDR. Otto Krause didn't share much, but Karl understood that his father blamed FDR for the trouble with the bank. They watched newsreels of millions of trees being planted by the Civilian Conservation Corps. But in their part of Kansas, the soil continued to blow away. Loans were due. Crops were failing. His father spent more and more time at the community center, *Turn Verein*, reading the *Völkischer Beobachter*, the weekly publication of the Nazi Party, and the vulgar and virulently anti-Semitic *Der Stürmer*.

"You know what I'm saying, Krause. Bolsheviks in our government! Giving handouts to folks who just don't want to work!"

Krause recognized Wilson wasn't looking for a political discussion. He wanted a good listener, and Krause could do that. Easily. Nod, smile, and sip this delicious whiskey. The warmth of the crackling fire, the delicious smells coming from the kitchen, the whiskey—he'd agree to any political point, just to stay relaxed in this comfortable deep chair.

Krause was startled when a willowy young woman strolled into the room. He jumped to his feet, barely avoiding knocking over his drink.

"At ease, Cadet. This is my daughter Margaret."

Krause stood, unsure what to do. He stood there dumbly, his head spinning from the whiskey, the warmth and comfort of the room, and the beautiful young woman in front of him.

"Hi, soldier, call me Peggy! Not Margaret, Daddy, that's so—formal!" said the young woman. She held her hand out to Krause. Was he supposed to shake it or kiss it? He held it awkwardly. "You can give me my hand back, soldier, whenever."

Peggy laughed. And Krause laughed too.

She was gorgeous. He was in love. No one had even spoken to him in months, and now this vision was standing in front of him. He wanted to grab her hand—and so much more!—even with her father standing right there. Peggy Wilson was sixteen, with wavy blonde hair and deep-blue eyes, an easy smile and charming laugh. Krause sensed her energy and mischievous nature.

He'd seen her around West Point. Everyone had. Peggy, the BTO's daughter, an indifferent student and dedicated trouble-maker, beautiful, athletic, disobedient, and passionate about horseback riding. She kept her big white mare, Star, in the West

Point stables and was often caught by the MPs breaking rules—jumping cannons on Trophy Point or cantering past the marching cadets. When caught, Peggy apologized energetically, brought cookies to MPs, charmed everyone, and promised never to break rules again. "Star and I will be good, sir!"

Until the next time.

Peggy featured in the dreams of many of the cadets. Lt. Colonel and Mrs. Wilson kept a close eye on her, knowing full well the temptations an Army base bursting with young men held for their daughter. Colonel Wilson loved his high-spirited daughter, but hoped she'd settle down. Mrs. Wilson kept most of Peggy's adventures from her husband, and hoped one of the cadets—maybe this one?—would marry Peggy before her antics torpedoed her husband's military career. Or a baby showed up.

Krause tried to speak, but his tongue felt dry and stuck to the roof of his mouth. Finally, he croaked, "I'm Cadet Krause. A pleasure to meet you, ma'am—I mean miss, I mean Miss Peggy—may I call you that?"

Peggy smiled at Krause, looked directly in his eyes, and tilted her head very slightly. "My pleasure, Cadet Krause," she said, and giggled slightly. Turning to the colonel, she continued, "Mother asked me to tell you that dinner is served." She took Krause's elbow, snuggled a bit closer than actually needed to get through the doorway, and steered him to the dining room.

"Do you like Wiener schnitzel, son?" said the colonel, sitting down at the table. "I hope so! Mrs. Wilson has taught our cook Betty how to make all her recipes."

"Wiener schnitzel! That would be amazing, sir."

They were seated at a heavy rectangular table with a lace tablecloth. The Colonel and his wife sat at opposite ends of the long table. Krause and Peggy sat across from each other near the middle. The cook brought heaping bowls of schnitzel, Spätzle, and green beans, slathered in butter. The food was delicious. For the first time in months, Krause was able to enjoy his food. He didn't have to worry about being rushed or abused.

Looking up after a few minutes, Krause was startled when he realized that he had completely cleaned his plate. Colonel Wilson, and Mrs. Wilson, and Peggy, were all looking at him. They had barely gotten started on their meal. He was mortified.

"Ma'am, I've forgotten my manners. This is a most wonderful dinner. It reminds me of home." He felt like he was going to cry.

Colonel Wilson exchanged a glance with his wife. Mrs. Wilson flushed with pride. "It makes me so happy to see a young man enjoy his food! Please. Have another helping. Betty! Get in here!" she said.

The meal was delicious, but the dinner conversation was stilted. Krause still didn't understand why he was being favored with this invitation. And looking at Peggy across the table was so distracting! Was she smiling at him? Would his napkin cover his erection? What if he had to stand up?

Colonel Wilson droned on; now he was holding forth about the multitude of new technologies available to the Army. "Our German friends are very wise, Krause. They've taken the opportunity to learn and practice their craft in Spain. They use aircraft, tanks, and infantry together. Have you read the book *Achtung Panzer*, by Heinz Guderian? He's way ahead of his time. Guderian understands the potential of massed armored forces."

Krause struggled to focus, fighting the whiskey, the warmth, the food, this damned girl so alluring and so close.

"Uh, yes, yes, sir. What is the potential of massed armored —what?"

Krause was startled by something brushing against his leg. A cat? he wondered. The second time it happened, he caught Peggy's smile. Her stockinged foot was stroking his calf. He was dying. This girl!

Krause struggled to focus his attention on the colonel's lecture. What was he even talking about? Fortunately, Betty burst through the swinging doors with a chocolate cake covered with whipped cream and decorated with maraschino cherries.

"Ah! This is Mrs. Wilson's specialty!" said the colonel.

"Mrs. Wilson. It's beautiful. This is my favorite—my mother makes a cake like this, but only for very special occasions."

"Really? Well, this is a very special occasion. You are our new friend! It's a Black Forest gateau, although I bet your mother calls it *Schwartzwälder Kirschtorte*," said Mrs. Wilson, adding as she smiled, "*Der Kuchen ist lecker, nicht wahr?*"

"*Ja, er ist wunderbar!*" burst out Krause, and the room fell silent. Krause stared down at his plate. My God, he thought, now I've done it. I've spoken in German!

"*Schon gut, Karl, ich bin auch deutsch aufgewachsen,*" Mrs. Wilson said gently. And then again in English, "It's all good, Karl, I too grew up German. We are both German—and also American."

She smiled.

Karl was flabbergasted.

Colonel Wilson came to his rescue. "You see Karl, my wife was raised in a German-speaking family, just like you. Her maiden name was Kaltenthaler. Doesn't make her any less pretty or any less American," said Wilson reaching out and putting a fond hand on his wife's shoulder. "And Karl, my wife and her family are as patriotic as anyone." He paused. "Of course, I'm Scotch Irish. My family's been here for generations—fought proudly for the South in Virginia!—but that doesn't make my family any better than hers."

"Americans with German blood should be proud, not afraid," said Mrs. Wilson. "It's not as though we are Jews." Nodding toward the kitchen, she lowered her voice and said, "Or *Schwarze.*"

"Mom!" Peggy objected. "They're just people, too..."

Krause squirmed. There were no Black or Jewish people in Kansas, or at West Point, for that matter. He bore no malice to either.

Colonel Wilson broke the awkward silence. "So, Karl, let me explain why you are here today. I know about your silencing. I won't stand for it in my Brigade. You'll see that bastard Jorgenson marching penalty hours all day Sunday and the following Sunday, too. He'll put the word out—anyone harassing cadets of German heritage, or shunning them, is on the top of my shit list, and that's the last place they want to be."

Karl felt like he was floating. It was magical. All his problems solved. A powerful ally. His enemy vanquished. Could it be true?

Colonel Wilson continued. "We'd like to make you part of the family, Krause. We'll have you over regularly for family dinners. My wife would love to speak German with you. And she'd love to play some German music for you. Wagner. Mozart. German culture stuff, you get it."

"That sounds just swell," said Krause, who cared little for music, but was digesting one of the best meals of his life, and thinking wild thoughts about Peggy.

He gulped another slice of the Black Forest gateau—my God, it was good—and listened to the colonel hold forth about the importance of combined arms in the next war. He looked at Peggy as much as he could without staring. She smiled back. She was interested! He wanted to spend more time with this alluring girl. He could tolerate Wagner and the BTO's lectures. Easily.

"Peggy and I can wash the dishes, Mrs. Wilson," Krause offered.

Mrs. Wilson waved dismissively and said, "Oh, no, Betty will do that, Cadet. Officers' wives don't do dishes."

Peggy, who had been silent most of the meal, spoke up. "Papa, Cadet Krause is so handsome and well mannered. Don't you think so? Maybe he can escort me to his military ball this year! I'd love to go! I'm old enough now, I know!" She smiled at Krause. He melted.

Wilson looked at Krause with a steely eye. "Cadet Krause. Pay attention to me here. My daughter is sixteen. She is a good girl, from a good family, but she has a little wild streak. If you even think of touching her, I'll throw you back to the Firsties and let them eat you alive."

Mrs. Wilson handed Krause his cover. "Don't be silly, Margaret. You're not old enough to be escorted to a military ball, and anyway, cadets don't have a ball until Yearling Winter Weekend. It's getting late. Don't you have some high-school homework to do, young lady?"

Peggy laughed and stood up. "Good night, Cadet Krause. My Papa, the colonel, has dismissed me, and I am obedient...at least today." She laughed and Mrs. Wilson flinched. "And so I must go. Please come back sometime?"

Krause shook hands with Colonel Wilson. "Sir, I do hope to return and learn more about military strategy." He turned to Mrs. Wilson. "*Und ich freue mich darauf, deutsch zu sprechen und deutsche Lieder zu singen*—speaking German and singing German songs with you." Then he looked directly at Peggy, holding, not shaking, her hand. "And sir, I'd be honored to escort your charming daughter to anything—when and if you give us permission, of course."

Peggy walked Krause to the porch, still holding his hand. With her parents out of her line of sight, she gave him a smile and a wink. "Who needs permission?" she whispered.

Over the next few months, Krause's world was transformed. Cadet Jorgenson was charged with abusing the Honor Code and Conduct Unbecoming an Officer. He was convicted, stripped of his rank and privileges, and sentenced to two hundred and fifty punishment marching hours. He spent every free moment left at West Point in dress uniform, marching back and forth in the central area. Jorgenson would be allowed to graduate, but was posted to the hot and snake-infested Fort Polk in Louisiana.

Krause's silencing ended immediately, but his classmates never warmed to him. He heard the occasional hiss of Kraut or Hun in the shower, and felt unwelcome even on his gymnastics team. Although he received high marks for his military and physical skills, and his academic performance excelled, he deeply resented West Point, the silencing, the anti-German bias, the Army.

Krause loved visiting the Wilsons' home. Mrs. Wilson instructed Betty to prepare German favorites: Bratwurst or schnitzel and potato salad. After dinner, the family would gather around the piano and sing *Lieder*.

Peggy Wilson was thrilling. She was everything he could want. Exciting, beautiful, charming, and she fell in love with him. And he with her.

Krause and Peggy were never left alone, or at least, that's what the Wilsons reassured themselves. After all, on Sundays, wasn't that young cadet gallant when they attended Lutheran church services as a family! Colonel and Mrs. Wilson smiled when they observed Krause and Peggy discreetly holding hands during the church services. As far as her parents knew, they were only alone while walking together to and from the chapel.

Colonel and Mrs. Wilson were very strict about rules, absolutely forbidding dating, but Peggy was inventive in finding ways to see him alone. "Meet me at the stables. I'll tell them I'm riding!" Her conspiratorial chuckle gave him an instant erection. They could never meet in his barracks room; women weren't allowed anywhere in the cadet area, and definitely not in his room. Other cadets met their girls outdoors in the park, on "Flirty Walk." Not his Peggy.

She became the model of the obedient daughter. Her mother was relieved. Peggy did her homework. She did her housework. She had a strict curfew, which she scrupulously obeyed. Always home by 8 p.m! She went to the stables as often as ever, but somehow Star was ridden less and less.

One warm afternoon, in the horse's stall, Krause laid down some horse blankets over the straw, and turned to kiss her. What a wonderful woman, he thought. He said out loud, *"Ich bin ein glücklicher Mann."*

Peggy laughed. "What does that mean?"

"I'm a lucky man," he said, smiling.

As she unbuttoned her blouse, she laughed again. "And getting luckier by the moment, soldier."

Later, while they were lying in the straw, spent, she said, "You know, someone should tell her. My mother thinks you can only have sex after dark!" She laughed, long and hard.

At Christmas 1937, the upper-class cadets were granted leave to go home to their families, but the plebes stayed on at West Point. It snowed Christmas morning and the trees were rimed with snow. Krause and Peggy walked across the Plain; the sun glinted off the snow-covered trees. They stood at Trophy Point and looked out over the ice-covered river and snowy mountains. It was breathtakingly beautiful.

Krause went down on one knee in the snow. He'd prepared a speech. Couldn't remember a word.

"Peggy—would you...?" and presented her with a ring, a simple silver band with their initials. There was an identical ring for Krause to wear.

Peggy choked back a sob of joy. "Yes!" She offered her lips for a deep and lasting kiss unreservedly for him. They'd only known each other a few months, but this was pure passionate love. That morning they pledged to spend the rest of their lives together. But Peggy was only seventeen, still a high-school junior; they'd have to keep the secret from her parents, and his.

He couldn't marry until graduation, and would need her parents' consent. They would wait, and keep their engagement secret for now. Both solemnly swore to wear their matching rings on silver chains around their necks.

They walked arm in arm back to the Wilsons' home, stopping to make snow angels. Under Mrs. Wilson's watchful eye, Betty made a traditional German Christmas dinner of roast goose, sausage apple stuffing, and potato dumplings.

For Karl Krause, a farm boy from Kansas, the world was filled with marvel that Christmas day. A beautiful woman had pledged him her eternal love, he had a powerful future father-in-law, and a promising career ahead of him in the Army.

How could he imagine that it would unravel so spectacularly?

As Krause returned to the barracks, the cadet on duty handed him a telegram.

"It's for you, Krause, from Kansas. It's marked urgent."

SEVEN

The telegram that summoned him home was cryptic and alarming: "Family Emergency STOP Come Home Immediately STOP."
What was going on? A series of awful scenarios occurred to him. Had there been an accident? A fire? Would they have told him in a telegram if his mother or sister were ill? Or dead? Farms were dangerous places. The neighbors' boy had lost an arm in a threshing machine, and a little girl two farms over had suffocated in a silo. What if his father had cancer, or his sister had polio?

West Point sent him home that afternoon. There was no time to say goodbye to Peggy.

Krause barely slept on the two-day journey from West Point. Normally ferociously hungry at all times, he'd barely touched the bag of soggy diner-car sandwiches.

His gnawing concern about the emergency telegram was coupled with a deep homesickness, an ache to be with his family, roam with his dog, feel like himself again in the comfort of his home. He had been away from home eight months; it seemed far longer. The cigar smoking and enforced Christmas camaraderie amongst the plebes didn't make up for the loss of a family Christmas. Even the passionate romance with Peggy couldn't completely compensate for the absence of family. He would tell them about Peggy, at the right time; his parents would be very upset at the whirlwind romance.

Krause especially missed his sister Hildi, and their dog Schatzie. Schatzie was just a regular old farm dog, nothing special, but he loved her, and fed her scraps from the table. She was good company, following him around the farm all day as he did his chores, and always slept at the foot of his bed.

Krause thought back to the time last fall when he met a visitor's dog at West Point who reminded him of Schatzie. It had hurt him so much he nearly cried.

Krause was filled with anxiety as his train pulled into Kansas City. He had only left West Point two days ago, and he missed Peggy terribly. He was falling apart. He needed to sleep. He needed to eat. He needed to know that everyone was okay. God, he hoped everyone was okay, even Schatzie.

As he waited for his father to meet him outside the station, Krause stood out amongst the rumpled farmers and beaten-down women; he was nineteen, tall, muscular, with West Point ramrod-straight posture. The civilian population was unused to the sight of men in uniform. Women smiled at him, and young boys stared in admiration. The dress uniform and high collar were uncomfortable, but they had their advantages. The conductor between Chicago and Kansas City was a World War I veteran and, seeing the West Point uniform, insisted on moving Krause up to First Class.

He was taken aback by the noise and hustle and bustle of the train station. His only experience away from the farm and West Point was the few hours he had passed in the Chicago train station. Newsboys hawked papers with headlines about the "Rape of Nanking," porters pushed carts piled high with luggage, their breath condensing in the cold air. Traveling salesmen with valises raced for their trains. A few undernourished beggars cadged handouts; one even pulled a half-eaten sandwich out of the trash.

Krause's family finally arrived. Krause's father Otto was a thin, weather-beaten, muscular man in his early forties, with a carefully groomed handlebar mustache. His face was deeply lined from years working in the fields. The struggle of trying to provide for his family was etched in his brow. He wore his only set of Sunday church clothes—a worn black jacket, high-collared shirt, and well-worn boots. To Krause's surprise, his ten-year-old sister Hildi and his mother Eva were also riding on the family wagon. His mother and sister almost never left the farm. There was simply too much work for them to leave: laundry, cooking, cleaning, and caring for the livestock.

His mother Eva wore a handmade, worn-out dress, a heavy men's wool coat, and worn leather shoes. Her graying hair was pulled into a tight bun. She looked old, and tired, and frightened.

When Eva saw Krause, her deeply lined face lit up with love.

Hildi waved gaily. "Karl! Karl! Karl! Here we are!"

Otto nodded stiffly at Krause. Thank God, Krause thought, at least they are all here. So what was this "family emergency"? Why was he here? Everyone seemed well.

His father would explain when he was ready. And not before. Pushing him would get no answers. Otto gestured to Krause to throw his suitcase in the back of the wagon.

His parents looked defeated, the family wagon decrepit, and their belongings bedraggled. Even the old workhorse pulling the wagon looked dusty and tired. But what was all this stuff in the back of the wagon? Why the high pile of boxes, parcels tied with twine, and the family's battered valises? Those suitcases that had gathered dust in their farmhouse attic for a decade! Had they assembled their entire worldly belongings? But why?

Krause clambered up and the father and son awkwardly

shook hands. Otto was a hard man of few words and steely determination. He had come home to postwar Germany from the trenches in 1918 to witness bread riots, hyperinflation, and heavily armed fascist Stahlhelm men fighting it out in the streets with communist mobs. In 1919, Otto emigrated with his pregnant wife Eva, escaping the chaos and misery of Germany for hard work and hopes for a fair chance in America. Eva had cousins in the German community in Bremen, Kansas so they settled there. Karl was born soon after they landed in the United States, and Hildi eight years later.

Neither Otto nor Eva spoke English when they arrived in Kansas. Otto managed in agricultural English, and understood most people if they spoke slowly and were discussing cattle feed, tractor repair, or wheat prices. Otto's heavy accent made him difficult to understand, and to Americans, he always sounded angry. Krause's mother spoke only a few words of English, and always tentatively, so they spoke German at home. If they spoke at all. Most meals were passed in silence.

No one spoke as the family wagon moved slowly away from the train station.

Krause was frustrated. Were they really not going to talk? What was going on? Why were they heading away from the farm? Finally, Krause could wait no longer. He broke the silence.

"Why do you have all of those boxes and the suitcases, Papa?" Krause asked. "What's the emergency you wrote about in the telegram?"

"*Nicht hier*! Not here. *Ich werde es später erklären.* I will explain. Later. When we get to the hotel," Otto replied.

"Hotel? Where? Why aren't we going back to the farm? Papa? I don't understand," said Krause.

His father stared straight ahead. He ended every discussion the same way. "*Ich habe gesprochen!* I have spoken! Later, Karl."

Krause knew better than to challenge his father.

Krause's sister Hildi couldn't resist speaking. "I missed you so much, Karl! It's so sad and lonely without you! Tell us about West Point Military School?"

"Oh, Hildi, it's good to see you, too. West Point, what can I say? We work hard there, Hildi. It's a lot of work to become a soldier."

"Papa says the German Wehrmacht is much better than the American Army. He said they're better than the French, too. Our papa was in the Wehrmacht, did you know that? One day we are going to teach those nasty French a lesson, Papa says!"

"*Sei still, Kind!*" snapped Eva, silencing Hildi with a stern look. "*Nicht hier!*"

Krause changed the subject. "Well, at West Point they don't feed us like Mamma does." His stomach rumbled and he thought of his mother's cooking. Karl hoped she'd made schnitzel and Spätzle for dinner back at the farm tonight. "I can't wait for some of Mamma's food, and to see Schatzie. I wish you'd brought her! You would be proud of me, Papa. The schoolwork is hard, but the rest of it, it's not a problem. The discipline, the marching, and the uniforms, it's easy compared to farm life."

Krause thought of the West Point cadets from Florida and Virginia and Alabama complaining of the New York winter cold. They should try feeding cattle in midwinter Kansas, in below zero temperatures, or looking for baby lambs in the snow in the spring.

But Otto Krause didn't answer. Mother and Father sat unspeaking and staring forward as the old farm horse plodded on. The family rode on in silence. Otto brought the wagon to a halt in front of a run-down hotel and dismounted, hitching the wagon to a post.

"We will stay here tonight, Karl. Help me with the bags."

"Why aren't we going to the farm—Papa? I want to see Schatzie! I don't understand what we are doing here."

Otto stood up straight and spoke sternly to Karl.

"*Unser Hof ist verloren!* There is no more farm, Karl! Understand? There was no rain! The crops failed! No harvest, none worth selling. Then the bank—those bastards…"

Krause was reeling. "No more farm? I don't understand. The bank said they'd help! President Roosevelt said he would take care of us! The farmers!"

"FDR!" Otto spat. "FDR is nothing but a lying Jew, Karl. *Wir haben nichts, nichts!* We have nothing! Do you know what is this 'foreclosure'? We paid what we could. They threw us out. All the farmers! Everyone! Out of our own farms! They couldn't wait a few months for their money. All we have left is in this wagon. These rags, and tools, and our dignity as German *Volk*."

Krause felt dizzy and nauseated. How could this be? he wondered. There had been nothing about these problems in the letters he got from home. All those months at West Point, he had wanted nothing more than to come home to the farm and see his family.

"And Schatzie? What about Schatzie, Papa?"

"We…we left Schatzie at the neighbors' farm," said Otto. Karl's mother looked away.

"Why, Papa? Why didn't you write and tell me? Where are we going? Why did you give Schatzie away?"

Tears welled in Krause's eyes. Both Eva and Hildi started to cry.

Otto slapped Krause across the face. "For God's sake, Karl! Get a hold of yourself! You are supposed to be a soldier! *Sei keine Frau!* Don't be a woman!" Otto glared at his son. Then his tone softened. "How could we say this—*diese Katastrophe*—in a letter? Help me take the bags up to the room. I will explain more, in private."

Otto and Krause manhandled their bags up four flights of stairs and stacked them in a shabby and cramped hotel room. Otto theatrically checked the tiny closet and then firmly closed the hotel room. He turned to address the family.

"There is nothing here in America for us. FDR makes nothing but empty promises. The Jews at the bank have stolen our farm.

Foreclosure! It's theft! *Gestohlen!* Our future is in Deutschland, Karl."

Krause struggled to understand. The farm was gone. Schatzie was gone. His parents were moving to Germany? But why? What about Hildi? She was as American as he was!

His father thundered on. "Times are changing! Germany is rising! Here: read this," he said, thrusting a copy of *Der Stürmer* at Krause. A cartoon caricature of a leering Jew embracing FDR with one arm, and fondling a German maiden with the other, jumped out at him. "The Führer Adolf Hitler has called the *Volksdeutsche* back to the *Vaterland,* and we must answer his call! We are returning home! To Deutschland! Vater, Mutter, Hildi! All of us to help the Führer, to build the destiny of the Volk!"

"But, Father, no! All of us? Me too?"

Otto looked sternly at Krause. "All of us, Karl, but especially you. You have the most to give. You must come."

Krause was stunned. It was too much. He'd never been to Germany. Krause had paid little attention to politics and events in Europe. Now his family was moving to a country on the other side of the world, and insisting he join them.

He thought of President Roosevelt, the Commander in Chief, the only president he had ever known. Krause had believed FDR, trusted FDR, and thought of him as a friend, or kind uncle.

FDR had promised it would all work. Put your money back in the banks, he said. We are in this together, he said. We'll save the banks, he said, and the banks will save your farm. We heard it all on the radio, right in our kitchen.

Now it turned out to be a lie.

Now they have no money. No farm. No home. Krause felt as though he didn't fit in anywhere.

Otto edged closer and put his arm around Karl's shoulder. "Don't worry, Karl. *Mach dir keine Sorgen, Kind.* I know it seems strange. We are Germans inside. You will belong there! You will have friends, good friends. You will love it there. It's beautiful, it's clean and orderly." Otto pointed to the caricature in *Der*

Stürmer. "In our Deutschland, there are no Jews or Negro men to steal from us, or defile our women with their gorilla blood."

"But Papa," said Krause, "my training at West Point—my fellow cadets—I can't just leave them…"

"Forget them, Karl! Soon you will join the Wehrmacht and understand true *Kameradschaft*, like I did during the war. It will be all right—*es wird alles gut!* Deutschland is our *Heimat*, Karl, and our destiny is with the Führer."

Krause thought about Peggy and the future they planned together. Could he bring her back to Germany with his family? She spoke no German, and how he could convince her parents? He quietly stammered, "Papa. I must tell you. I-I met a girl." Krause whispered to himself, "I've asked her to marry me…"

Otto didn't hear Krause, or pretended not to. He thrust his right arm stiffly outward at eye level with his palm down. Eva and Hildi quickly followed suit and in unison the three shouted, *"Heil Hitler!"*

Otto looked at Krause. "You too now, Karl. We all must show our loyalty."

Krause wavered, images of beautiful, loving Peggy and vicious-bastard Jorgenson alternating kaleidoscopically in his mind. He had no choice: his future would have to be in Germany. Krause told himself he would write to her and explain, and keep their love alive. After he was established, and had money, he could send her a ticket, and they could build a life together in Germany.

Finally, under the stern stares of his family, he raised his hand.

He found his voice. *"Heil Hitler!"* He was a West Point cadet no longer.

He still loved Peggy, but he would fight for the Third Reich.

EIGHT

UNITED STATES MILITARY ACADEMY

WEST POINT

PRESENT DAY

As Goldstein came down the steep hill from campus toward the dock, he looked across the Hudson at the small town of Cold Spring. The town was nestled at the base of the rocky Breakneck Ridge, and several steeples created a small skyline. As Goldstein looked on, a Metro North commuter train, bound for New York City, pulled into the station, and a small cruise ship carrying leaf-peeping tourists from New York City motored up the river toward Beacon.

Goldstein steered his newly inspected Outback past the old West Point train station, turned north up the river, and parked by the Army Crew House. Eight lanky members of the men's team cheerfully balanced a fiberglass shell on their shoulders and headed toward the river. Goldstein was reminded of his days in Cambridge, and admired their easy camaraderie with a sense of longing.

He popped the trunk and shouldered his bulky dive gear. He walked toward the south dock, where a twenty-two-foot Boston

Whaler was tied up. He was startled to see a woman with long dark hair and a clinging one-piece swimsuit sitting on the dock, leafing through a book.

"Hello, Dr. Goldstein, sir," said the woman, giving him a friendly wave.

Goldstein was confused. He didn't know many people at West Point and certainly no one who looked like they belonged in a swimsuit ad.

"I'm sorry," he stuttered.

"Hello, sir! Don't recognize me?"

Suddenly Goldstein understood. Out of her loose uniform and black-framed Army glasses, and with her hair cascading over her muscular shoulders, Zhao was transformed. She had long powerful legs, sculpted triceps, and a leonine grace. He looked at her a moment too long, and then at his feet. He struggled for words.

Zhao pulled on a West Point fleece jacket and tucked her hair in her cap. She raised an eyebrow and waited.

"Ah yes, Cadet Zhao. Sorry, I'm a little preoccupied. Wind just picked up, huh?"

••• ▬ ▬▬▬ •▬▬•

ZHAO HAD SEEN this all before. Since she was fourteen, most men, and some women, would stare at her body. She felt their desires and understood the power, but didn't want to be defined by her looks. Taking advantage of her beauty was not her style. She had outperformed almost everyone, man or woman, wherever she served. As much as she had suffered at Ranger School, she loved the complete abnegation of typical femininity. Head shaved, unwashed, and largely sleepless, she passed, indeed excelled, because of a relentless desire to succeed. Surrounded by men at West Point, she generally chose to disguise herself behind the loose-fitting uniform and heavy glasses. As far as this adventure went, she hoped Dr. Goldstein would turn out to be a good partner, not just another creep.

"Come on, let's start bringing the tanks over to the dock," said Goldstein.

Goldstein and Zhao made four trips carrying tanks, buoyancy compensators, regulators, and assorted hammers, lights, and chalkboards to the dock.

"Tell me, Zhao, I've met more than a few cadets. Nobody really likes being here, but most Firsties are excited to get out into the Army. A Rhodes Scholarship would be amazing, but what's got you so down on the Army?"

"That's rather a long story. I'm trying to look forward, not back."

"I don't mean to pry," said Goldstein, "but there is no sign of your Captain Haskins. We've got nothing but time."

Zhao leaned back against the pile of tanks and stretched out in the sun. She closed her eyes. How to explain? What did she want her professor to know?

Zhao looked away and was silent.

She thought back through her time at West Point. It had all started so easily. Zhao had cruised through Beast Barracks, six weeks of hard military training and indoctrination. She was unfazed by heat, physical pounding, and verbal harassment. It's like Ranger School, only much easier, she had thought. She seemed built of ripcord and steel, and used to long, punishing ruck marches. Her Ranger tab and ribbons from prior service and, equally important, her fierce demeanor, served to ward off any upperclassman who might have been tempted to single out a female cadet for abuse.

As a plebe, she aced her classes and got top marks in physical fitness and military conduct. She was rewarded with a prized summer slot at the Army Airborne School. Her mother came down to Fort Benning to watch her make a night parachute jump. She proudly pinned the Jump Wings on Zhao's uniform, and her father wore a miniature set of Jump Wings as a tie tack.

When she went home for Christmas, Zhao and her mother had a video chat with her aunt in Vancouver. "Yes, sister, West Point is more prestigious than Harvard! Three American presidents are graduates! And yes, it's very big on Wall Street. Mai can go right to Goldman Sachs when she leaves the Army!"

"Is the U.S. Army corrupt like the People's Army back home?" asked her aunt in Mandarin.

"Mai says no, but I'm sure she's just too little a fish to understand yet. But don't worry about her, Mai is someone who will look after herself!" her mother said, quickly adding, "And her family."

Two years later, Zhao was a Firstie—a First-Class Cadet. She had added a gold star and gold wreath to her uniform for outstanding academic and all-round performance. She studied Arabic and civil engineering. She loved to pummel other cadets in combatives class, jumped off a ten-meter diving board without hesitation, and rappelled from a helicopter. She even seemed to enjoy holding her breath for minutes at the notoriously difficult Army Special Forces Combat Dive School in Key West, Florida.

Cadet Zhao sighed. "What I really love about West Point is the people," Zhao told Goldstein. "Most of them, anyway. My classmates. The upperclassmen. I tried to be a good leader and mentor, too." The past summer, Zhao had been selected as the Cadet in Charge of Beast Barracks, the summer training for the incoming plebes. "I was at my best running Beast. We were hard on those kids, but not unreasonable. Everything that we did had a purpose." Zhao had led by example and carried the West Point culture of discipline, teamwork, and camaraderie. By the end of the summer, the new cadets she supervised had been transformed from civilians to soldiers. They were fit and disciplined, with neat uniforms and positive attitudes, and they worshipped Zhao, who cared deeply for them.

"I'm jealous," said Goldstein. "I wish I could bond with my students, or the other faculty, like that. Sometimes I feel very alone here. But you still haven't told me about what happened for you to lose your love for the Army."

Zhao looked at her watch. Last summer had been wonderful; the best months of her life. "I don't want to talk about it. Enough of memory lane," she said. "I think you intimidate some people, Professor. If you lightened up a bit, I think you might like some of the other faculty, like Captain Haskins. He's really into history."

Goldstein changed the subject. "Okay then, let's go over the gear. And text Haskins, would you?"

Goldstein could check his gear blindfolded, but they weren't taking any chances. They dove with neoprene dry suits, hoods, and 5-mm gloves, all absolutely essential in the cold river water. They would each take two tanks, mounted on a back plate and wing. In addition, they each would dive with a small deco tank filled with an oxygen-rich mixture to breath at their final decompression stage. They carried dive computers which tracked their oxygen consumption and depth, and calculated when they needed to surface. They each took a spare, in case their primary computer failed.

Satisfied that everything was in order, they went over the dive plan.

"We're going down to one hundred and seventy feet. It's not quite deep enough for us to use Trimix, but we will almost certainly get nitrogen narcosis. It creeps up on you, you don't realize anything is wrong, but it affects your judgement. Divers with narcosis make stupid mistakes, sometimes fatal ones," said Goldstein.

"Yes, I know." Zhao nodded.

"It should take ten minutes to descend, and we will have enough air for twenty minutes at the bottom. We'll need about an hour to ascend, including a couple of stops to decompress."

As Goldstein finished up, a muscular young man with high-and-tight hair and Ray-Bans joined them on the dock. "Sorry I'm late," said Haskins. "I got stuck in the gym helping some guys from the CrossFit team." Haskins spent most afternoons in the weight room, and had an astonishingly large and detailed tattoo of Caesar Augustus on his bulging tricep.

"Thank you so much for helping us, Captain," said Zhao. I'm sure you know Professor Goldstein from the history department."

The two men exchanged nods. They had crossed paths, but seemingly had little in common.

••• — ——— •——•

REJECTED by West Point out of high school, Haskins had settled for ROTC at Rutgers. Eight years later, he had Captains' bars, a Ranger tab, and a Silver Star, and had done two tours in Afghanistan. Haskins came to USMA, the institution that had rejected him, as junior faculty. He had no formal teaching experience, but loved history, and was widely admired by the cadets because of his combat experience.

Cadet Zhao was Haskins's kind of cadet. She was prior service, completely squared away, and completely committed to the Army. There were two other girls in the scuba club, but both were soft. Those girls had joined the scuba club with the hopes of getting to dive in the Caribbean over winter break. They planned to serve their commitment to the Army in a non-combat branch like logistics and leave as quickly as possible. Haskins resented it. He could not understand why the West Point took girls like that—but hadn't found a place for him.

Getting the gear and eight dive tanks onto the boat was awkward. Haskins looked on as Goldstein smashed the tip of his left fourth finger with one of the tanks. Goldstein's finger throbbed, but he tried to ignore it, hoping Zhao and Haskins wouldn't notice.

Zhao handled the equipment gracefully, and with Haskins's help, they got the gear stowed and were quickly ready to go. As they were ready to push off, Haskins's phone vibrated and he looked down at the number.

He jumped up and leaped back onto the dock.

"Whoa! That's the BTO. I need to take this call."

He walked off, deep in conversation.

••• — ——— •—•

"Wow, that certainly got his attention. The VTO?" asked Goldstein.

"Not the VTO. It's the BTO. The Brigade Tactical Officer. He's like the assistant principal when you were back in high school, the disciplinarian. Actually, he's more like the assistant warden. He can make your life miserable—cancel your passes, assign you to extra work details. You definitely want to stay on the right side of the BTO."

Goldstein looked up at the campus on the edge of the cliff. The mass of Thayer Hall loomed over them like a medieval fortress.

"God, this place really looks like a prison, doesn't it?"

Zhao ignored him and pulled a chemistry text out of her camouflage backpack. She put it aside and pulled out a copy of Doris Kearns Goodwin's *No Ordinary Time* and started to read.

Goldstein tapped on the book.

"What class are you reading that for?"

"No class. I'm just really into the Roosevelts. Especially Eleanor, she was amazing. She really cared about ordinary people. And she was effective! Child labor laws. Civil rights. Franklin trusted her judgement and relied on her. They were true partners."

"In government, if not in marriage," added Goldstein. He was intrigued. Very few cadets read for pleasure; if they had any free time, which they rarely did, they usually watched videos, or napped.

This girl is something else, he thought. She's thoughtful.

She's so graceful—she moves like a panther, and she doesn't buy into the Army bullshit.

He wondered if she was straight.

They smiled at each other.

"I loved that book. It was really sad they fell out of love," he said.

"I'm not sure he ever loved her," said Zhao, "not in the romantic way. She was President Teddy Roosevelt's niece. I think he wanted to be close to power."

"Well. You know, they did have six children."

"Yeah. True. But all the while he was cheating on her with her best friend, Lucy."

His eyes lingered a little too long on her lips and eyes and she broke eye contact.

Zhao pointed up to a row of the red-brick, Georgian-style homes above the river.

"Is your house up there, sir?"

"Hardly," said Goldstein. "That's Colonels Row. Those are for department chairs."

Goldstein lived up in one of the new ticky-tacky base developments by Stony Lonesome Gate. He'd been there for eighteen months and barely unpacked. Thirty boxes of books filled the spare bedroom. The master bedroom shared a thin plasterboard wall with the adjoining unit. He couldn't decide which bothered him more, the din of the children screaming, the loud country music, or the incessant noise from their television. His neighbor, evidently a senior NCO in the fitness department, had a neck like a tree trunk, and spent most of his time working on the trucks in the driveway or pumping iron in the gym which filled his garage.

"It won't take long for them to make you chairman. What with your PhD from Harvard and all."

Goldstein flushed, despite himself. He was pleased that she was impressed by his academic pedigree. "I'm afraid I'm a long way from chairman, Cadet. I'm not sure Major Sanchez wants to renew my contract."

"When we find this chain, and we're on the cover of *National Geographic*, you're going to be a hot commodity. Major Sanchez will be begging you to stay at West Point."

Goldstein still wondered what Zhao was all about.

What had really gone wrong for her at West Point?

He wondered if she would go out with him. Cool it—great way to lose your job, he reminded himself.

"We should go up to Hyde Park one day, Cadet," said Goldstein. "It's only an hour from here. There's a great museum about Roosevelt's life and his presidency. We could go to Top Cottage where FDR went to be alone and Val-Kill, Eleanor's place."

"Are you asking me on a date?" Zhao flashed a smile. "Fraternization is an Honor Code violation, you know."

"Class trip, I mean. With the class, and you know…the other cadets, your history class," Goldstein added awkwardly.

"I'd love that. I'd love to see Val-Kill."

At that moment, Haskins returned to the boat and Zhao dropped the book back into her bag.

They cast off the lines and Haskins steered the Whaler south on the Hudson. There was only a very light chop on the river. There were no other small craft; it was too cold for the usual jet skis and speedboats. Off in the distance, the afternoon sun glinted brightly off a fire-engine-red oil tanker carrying ten thousand barrels of heating oil from Brooklyn up to the depot in Newburgh.

Fifteen minutes later, they were out in the Hudson just off Fort Montgomery and across from Anthony's Nose, the rocky bluff that marks the southern edge of the Hudson Highlands. The soaring towers and steel cables of the Bear Mountain Bridge loomed overhead. They were directly over the site of the 1776 Fort Montgomery chain.

Haskins cut the motor and they dropped anchor. It seemed to

take forever to reach the bottom, but finally held at one hundred and seventy feet. Beneath them was "World's End," an underwater gorge and the deepest part of the Hudson River.

"Okay, you two battle buddies, let's get going!" said Haskins. "No time to waste! It's slack tide now, and you won't want to be in the water when the current starts running."

The Hudson is a tidal estuary, and currents are particularly treacherous between Peekskill and Poughkeepsie where the river is narrow.

Zhao and Goldstein wriggled clumsily into their heavy dry suits. Attached to each of their suits were a hammer, dive lights, crowbar, and dive knife. They mounted GoPro cameras on their hoods. Zhao carried a slate and marker. Goldstein had the magnetometer, and Zhao took along her iPhone in a Kraken waterproof case.

"Okay, one more time. I'm Diver Number One. Follow my lead. We should have enough air for twenty minutes at the bottom, if we stay relaxed. We are doing this dive together. Stay close."

She rolled her eyes but nodded yes.

Goldstein continued. "When it's time to go up, stay along the line to ascend. We will take an hour to surface. We'll take a ten-minute stop at forty feet and a twenty-minute stop at thirty feet. At the decompression stops, we'll switch to the deco tanks. Follow me!"

Goldstein put the regulator in his mouth, bled air from the dry suit, and started down the anchor line. The world darkened quickly. Soon his vision was limited to the beam of his lamp and the myriad reflections from the silt particles in the water. His regulator hissed and bubbles ascended to the surface. Zhao followed close behind. Intermittently, he did jaw thrusts to open his Eustachian tubes and equalize the pressure in his ears. As he approached the bottom, he maintained neutral buoyancy by adding air to his buoyancy compensator.

Five minutes later, they made a final adjustment to their

buoyancy compensators and floated effortlessly just above the river floor. The bottom was muddy and the visibility poor. Last night's rainstorm had carried a load of sediment into the river. There were a few scattered ill-defined bumps on the bottom covered with silt. Zhao and Goldstein swam a rectangular search pattern with their magnetometer, but recorded no activity. After a few minutes, frustrated, Goldstein kicked off the surface of a lump with his flipper, briefly exposing the rock below and releasing a storm of silt in the water.

Damn, he thought. Getting frustrated isn't going to help. Cool it.

With ten minutes of bottom time left, Goldstein got a faint signal on his magnetometer. Intrigued, he probed the bottom with a crowbar, but found only a rusted garbage can.

When their dive computers indicated only a five-minute buffer of air, Zhao and Goldstein headed up the anchor line toward the surface. At forty feet, they paused for ten minutes and switched to their deco tanks. The oxygen-rich mixture helped drive the dissolved nitrogen out of their bodies. The two divers stared into the blackness, each in their own dysphoric world.

Another dead end, Goldstein thought. What a waste of a day. I need to really get to work revising my thesis. Maybe I can get a book publication out of it. I'll apply for some grants. If I'm funded, maybe Yale will take another look at me.

••• ▬ ▬▬▬ •▬▬•

ZHAO WAS CRESTFALLEN. She knew swimming around on a mud bottom in near-zero visibility wasn't exactly the stuff of *National Geographic*. How could she get the attention of the Rhodes Committee? She had to come up with something! Otherwise, she'd be stuck going off for six months at Fort Benning, Georgia, for the Infantry Basic Officer Leader Course.

Stranded. Benning was awful. The honky-tonk town was filled with pawn shops, fast food, dollar stores, and tattoo parlors. The bars played country-and-western music and were packed with drunken, testosterone-soaked soldiers, sporting high-and-tight haircuts, flirting with high-school dropouts with fake ID and too much makeup. Zhao would have preferred a posting on the moon.

If the thought of Fort Benning depressed Zhao, the thought of five years at Army bases like Fort Polk in Louisiana filled her with dread. Polk was hot and humid, and the housing was filled with mold. Alligators and poisonous snakes were everywhere. They called it Fort Puke. No bookstores, no museums or boutiques or even coffee shops, no hiking, sailing, or camping.

Zhao briefly considered going AWOL and heading to Canada. She wondered if the Army would be able to extradite her.

Coming to the surface, they struggled to reenter the boat, until Haskins finally stuffed a wad of chew in his mouth and helped haul them over the gunwales like sacks of potatoes.

They sat in silence.

Finally, Haskins said, "From these sad faces, looks like the professor and the Ranger girl haven't found very much."

"How insightful of you," replied Goldstein. "You missed your calling, Haskins. You should have branched into military intelligence."

"Hold the sarcasm, soldier. Without my boat, you two couldn't have even tried this little science project. Besides, last I checked, you Harvard boys don't have a monopoly on diligence. You and your battle buddy—Zhao here—you owe me one. Have some respect for a guy from Rutgers. One day he may save your bacon. Besides, I have another idea for you guys."

Goldstein and Zhao looked unimpressed. But why try to stop him? He was going to tell them, whether they encouraged him or not.

Haskins continued. "I was on the phone with an old friend of mine from college, Peter Kim, last week. I told him about your plan to find the chain. He was super excited—he's really into Revolutionary-War history. Kim is super smart. He started out at McKinsey and now works for one of the government agencies in D.C. Can't tell me which one. Probably the CIA. Anyway, he talked my ear off about the other chain."

"What other chain?" asked Zhao, brightening a bit.

"The Great Chain. They built it in 1778, and it ran from West Point up to Constitution Island. Each link was three-feet long and weighed one hundred and fourteen pounds. They used logs to float it like the other one. It was forged in—"

"I know all about that chain," Goldstein interrupted. "There are some links up next to the cannons at Trophy Point. There's nothing interesting about that chain, either."

"Not unless we find some other pieces. The thing was always breaking. All you need to do is find one link for a front-page story. We have about ninety minutes before the tide gets strong— that should be enough time for you let you do another deep dive. Let's head up there and pop you in the water. It's right across from West Point."

Goldstein brooded.

Zhao looked at him. "Can we?"

He nodded agreement. "Sure thing. We're not winning you a Rhodes Scholarship sitting here in this boat."

Haskins turned the boat upriver, and they drew near the town of Cold Spring on the east bank of the river opposite West Point. Most of the houses were simple; a few larger mansions could be seen near the top of the hill. Despite the million-dollar views of the Hudson, Cold Spring had always been a working-class manufacturing town.

Going into professor mode, Goldstein explained, "During the Civil War, there was a huge foundry over there. They built thousands of artillery pieces and millions of shells. Something like a thousand people worked there. The nice houses up on the hill were for the managers. The workers lived in hovels down near the swamp."

Zhao pointed across the river. "What happened to it?"

"After the Civil War, someone found cheaper iron ore up in Michigan and drove these guys out of business," answered Goldstein. "When the foundry closed, Marathon Battery opened a factory over there. They spilled an incredible amount of heavy metals onto the river floor. Incredibly dangerous stuff. It was a Superfund site. One of the most polluted spots in the country."

"That's nasty! Is it safe to dive here?" asked Zhao.

"They say it is. They spent twenty years dredging that crap out of the river. Cost a fortune."

"Who paid for that?" asked Zhao

"Take a guess, Zhao."

"I bet the government paid."

"Exactly. The American people paid. The company declared bankruptcy, and we the taxpayers were left holding the bag."

Zhao wondered if the river water was really safe. She didn't trust the government. They could be lying about that. My God, thought Zhao. Maybe my parents were right about this country after all.

It occurred to her that the Superfund site might be a way to be famous. An exposé about the pollution would certainly attract the press and the interest of the Rhodes committee—of course it might get her into trouble for insubordination. Nobody likes a muckraker. Especially the U.S. Army.

Captain Haskins brought the boat to a halt between Trophy Point and Constitution Island. Satisfied with the position, he shut the engine. "This is the spot. And hey! Look at that! The depth finder is showing an anomaly."

Goldstein peered suspiciously over his shoulder. "That's no small anomaly. Probably too big to be our missing links."

"Maybe a shipwreck," offered Zhao.

"Could be," said Goldstein. "After World War II, there were almost two hundred surplus ships anchored just south of here on the Hudson. They called it the Hudson River Reserve Fleet, but people around here called it the Mothball Navy. Of course, they started falling apart. Became navigational hazards. Pulled out in the seventies for scrap."

"Wow, that's cool!" said Zhao. "Maybe it is a shipwreck, then. Maybe one of them broke loose and sank."

"Well, you two aren't going to find any secrets sitting here in the boat," said Haskins. He released the anchor, which wound down into the murky water.

Five minutes later, they slipped below the surface and descended along the anchor line. Goldstein initially had difficulty equalizing pressure in his ears, and he waved Zhao down ahead of him. She slipped out of sight; the only sign of her presence was the bubbles from her scuba unit, rising up past him. As he moved slowly down the line, he was immersed in total darkness. The beam of his flashlight illuminated only dark and silty water.

Reaching the bottom, Goldstein nearly landed on top of Zhao, who was motionless, pointing at a giant shape, like a whale, shrouded in the darkness. The two played their headlamps over the huge ovoid structure.

What was this? An underwater ridge? A sunken city? A sunken Liberty ship? They couldn't see the beginning or end of it.

My God, thought Zhao, this must be nitrogen narcosis. It was all an illusion or a hallucination. Up close, it seemed to be a giant slime-covered wall, but overall it had a tubular outline.

Goldstein reached out and brushed away the slime. It was smooth, and tiny welds were visible. This was no hallucination.

It was huge. It was man-made.

And it would change their lives forever.

NINE

After two years of relentless training, Karl Krause was reborn as a German warrior. His feet had blistered on long marches. The blisters burst and then bled, soaking his socks. Now his feet were calloused and his heart hardened. Krause was sustained with *Kameradschaft*, a powerful bond with his fellows, forged in shared suffering. His unit included other *Volksdeutsche* who had joined the Reich when their homelands were absorbed. Krause felt no different than the ethnic Germans of Bohemia or Poland who fought by his side. At West Point, he had been silenced and ostracized. Today, his glider mates were his brothers, and he would live or die fighting alongside them.

Krause wanted victory and honor, but he also wanted to live. He didn't miss America or West Point, but he hoped victory would come quickly. He had learned to believe in the master race, but he was a soldier, not a politician, he told himself. When it was over, he wanted a real family—four kids, at least. He fingered the ring around his neck and wondered what Peggy had done with hers. He wished he had said good-bye, but how could he have explained? In Germany, his father forbade him to write her. Krause knew his father was right—a letter sent to America was sure to attract the attention of the SD or Gestapo.

Now, as Germany went to war with France and Belgium, the fate of the invasion rested on the shoulders of Karl Krause and his new comrades. Their mission was to tear open a gap in the Belgian line, and allow the German Panzer divisions to pour in behind them. Squeezed into a thin-skinned glider, Obergefreiter Krause and the eight men in his squad squatted on a bench that sagged beneath the weight of their combat loads. They were burdened with submachine guns, Bangalore torpedoes, gas masks, and wire cutters. Krause squinted through a plastic window. Where was Eben-Emael?

There! It looked tiny! From five thousand feet, the most impregnable fortress in Europe looked like a postage stamp.

The guns of Eben-Emael covered some of the vital terrain in Europe. For the German invasion of France to succeed, the Panzers would need to cross the Albert Canal. The canal bridges were lightly defended, but Fort Eben-Emael's 120-mm guns were trained on the bridges. The fort's thick walls were surrounded by multiple rows of barbwire, minefields, and antitank obstacles. The massive guns on the roof were set in ferroconcrete bunkers and shielded by steel cupolas akin to battleship turrets. Five miles of tunnels shielded the one thousand two hundred defenders as they moved between command posts, ammunition storage, and fighting positions.

Eben-Emael was vital, and seemingly unassailable.

Krause shivered in the unheated glider. His breath condensed in the cold air. Conversation was out of the question. He went over the attack plan in his head. He knew it backwards and forwards. He had spent hours spent studying aerial reconnais-sance photos and carried out endless practice assaults on scale models of the target. Krause was determined. He wouldn't let his men down.

It was Adolf Hitler himself who recognized Fort Eben-Emael's Achilles heel, and conceptualized the assault. The fort's thick walls and powerful armament made it difficult to attack from the ground, and the heavily armored gun positions were invulnerable to bombing. Hitler recognized that the fort's flat roof was its vulnerability. Eben-Emael's large guns would be nearly useless against infantry fighting on the roof, but how could they get there?

The roof was too small for a parachute landing. Instead, for the first time in history, Hitler ordered combat infantry delivered to the battlefield by glider. In the years between the wars, Germany had secretly developed the DFS-230 glider, capable of carrying nine heavily equipped soldiers. Bringing a heavily loaded glider down for a short field landing proved hard for ordinary pilots. For this mission, the Germans recruited a team of world-champion sport-glider pilots. They were an undisciplined and difficult bunch. Krause prayed that they could pull this off. At least the pilots had been locked in the barracks last night—otherwise those fool pilots would have been out at the bar.

••• ▬ ▬▬▬ •▬▬•

A MILE ABOVE THE FORT, the pilot released the tow rope. As they separated from the Junkers, silence descended on Krause and his glider mates. The DFS-230 dropped sharply, carrying them silently toward their destiny.

The fort came into view. There were sporadic flashes of anti-aircraft fire that rose up like strings of burning pearls. They were seconds from victory, or disaster. On landing, Krause and young Unteroffizier Schmidt would assemble the top-secret Hohlladung charge. The Hohlladung's 50-kg, shaped hollow charge generated a highly focused blast wave, capable of smashing the thick ferroconcrete and steel barriers shielding Eben-Emael's guns. Schmidt was a farm boy from Silesia. He wasn't particularly bright, but he was dogged and strong as an ox. He worshipped Krause and was proud to be selected as his teammate. Schmidt was prepared to die for him. Krause wasn't going to let that happen. Not today.

Clutching their weapons, the nine silent men in the glider braced for impact on the fortress roof. The DFS-230 landed hard and, with the screech of metal on concrete, braked to a stop. A burst of machine-gun fire tore through the glider's skin, miraculously missing the soldiers.

"*Raus! Raus! Raus!*" screamed Krause. Was anyone hit? Not yet. "Don't drop your weapons! Stay together!"

The squad quickly followed Krause out of the aircraft. Their pilot had managed to avoid multiple coils of concertina wire snaked across the fortress roof. Other gliders were less fortunate. One aircraft had landed directly in the obstacle. Krause saw soldiers caught in the razor wire. It tore through their uniforms and into their flesh. They screamed and fought desperately to free themselves.

Mentally referencing the models he had studied, Krause oriented himself. With a quick hand signal, he directed his team toward their primary target, Casemate 18. Thankfully, there was no significant fire directed at them from the emplacement.

Unteroffizier Schmidt fell to his knees at the base of the casemate. He quickly fitted the 50-kg Hohlladung together, and Krause armed the weapon. They ducked around the corner of the casemate. There was a brilliant flash and a deafening explosion. Dense gray smoke billowed from a gaping hole at the base of the casemate. They choked on the acrid smell of cordite.

Schmidt, trembling, unclipped stick grenades and prepared to toss them into the breach, but Krause waved him off. "No one is firing, Unteroffizier. I think they are finished. Let me go ahead and see if anyone is alive inside."

Krause donned a gas mask and crawled through the breach of the wrecked casemate. A few minutes later, he emerged, dragging two stunned Belgian defenders. One Belgian was bleeding heavily from a jagged wound in his neck, and the other had an open chest wound, which hissed and foamed with each breath. Strips of burned flesh fell from their faces. He laid the wounded men down next to the shattered bunker. Krause offered them water from his canteen. Poor kids, he thought. They'd soon be dead. They must have mothers and wives.

There were more explosions and intermittent bursts of small-arms fire from other attack teams. Krause signaled his men to follow. He passed an open ventilation vent and dropped a 2-kg explosive charge, which exploded down in the lower level. They ran through the smoke toward Casemate 15, their secondary objective. There was a distant roar of a heavy machine gun. There was a deafening blast, and then silence. Smoke and screams were everywhere.

Within hours, the fight was over. The fort's stunned defenders, isolated in the hot and smoke-filled interior, were no match for the commandos. By early afternoon, they surrendered. The bridges across the Albert Canal were open, and Panzers roared toward France.

Krause and his men celebrated that night with fine Belgian ale. They swapped stories of confusion, and heroism, and raised a glass to the six men they'd lost. There were many choruses of *Das Lied der Fallschirmjäger, Wir Fahren gegen Engelland* and many toasts to the Führer and Fatherland.

"We'd follow you anywhere, Krause!" a very drunk Unteroffizier Schmidt shouted.

"*Zum Sieg!*" Krause raised his glass. "To Victory!" No one could stop them.

"*Sieg Heil! Sieg Heil! Sieg Heil!*"

The mess hall roared. Krause felt at home and with his people.

As he dropped off in a drunken sleep that night, Krause

gently rubbed the band he wore on a chain around his neck. Germany will win this war quickly, he thought. There would be no need for America to be involved. Things will work out for the best.

One day Peggy would join him here in Europe.

Anything seemed possible.

TEN

Floating at the bottom of the Hudson River, Goldstein ran his gloved hand along the slime-covered rectangular metal wall. Flakes of rust broke off and glimmered in his headlamp. The depth finder was right; there was an anomaly here, it was man-made, and it was enormous. This was no piece of Revolutionary-War chain. This was something much bigger, much more important.

Okay, keep your shit together, Goldstein told himself. Breathe slowly. Think calmly. Goldstein fought to control his respiratory rate as he peered into the darkness. Don't pant. Stop panting! Visibility was awful. He could barely make out the wreck. Maybe it was one of the Liberty ships, broken loose, but it was hard to imagine that it wasn't salvaged. More likely, it was a barge, or some sort of steam tender. In the nineteenth century, there was an enormous amount of river traffic on the Hudson. Ships laden with oysters, ice, and iron stoves plied the river. There must have been uncharted wrecks. This had to be one.

There was rust and surface incrustation that spoke to decades of submersion, but in places Goldstein could discern a smooth, subtly curving surface. He could barely perceive the welds. Goldstein's mind raced. This wasn't nineteenth-century metalwork. He was sure of it. He snapped photos, then swam along the hulking mass.

They should have enough air for another twenty-five minutes at the bottom. He felt his heart racing, and paused again. Zhao tapped Goldstein on the shoulder and startled him. They checked their dive computers. Goldstein had only fourteen minutes left. Christ! He was breathing too hard! Zhao held up ten fingers. Damn! They had to make the most of their time. Goldstein started swimming. Zhao followed.

Their first job was to estimate the size of the wreck, do a general survey, and classify the vessel. Goldstein signaled to Zhao to start filming, and they began to swim slowly around the perimeter.

Even with the murky darkness pressing upon them, he could appreciate a general cigar-like shape. Was this some sort of enormous storage tank? he wondered. Maybe from the Space Shuttle? Goldstein thought fleetingly of an alien craft before discarding the thought as ridiculous. He wondered how much of this could be narcosis. Goldstein's pulse began to hammer. Maybe they should go up, right now, before something bad happened?

They reached one end of the wreck, where an oversized propeller extended out on a shaft. A second shaft was bare. The second screw lay mangled nearby on the river bottom. This was clearly the stern of a sea vessel, not a spaceship. Goldstein regained control. He felt a euphoria like that of an archeologist finding a lost city overgrown with jungle. A calmness descended on him. The whole world seemed to slow down.

Finally, the answer became absolutely clear to him. A superstructure took shape through the gloom. There was only one explanation for the cylindrical contour and bridge—this had to be a submarine! The idea seemed insane. How could there be a submarine, right here in the Hudson?

Whose was it? How did it get there? Why did no one know? Was it American? Goldstein thought of the *Thresher*, an American submarine lost in 1963 with all hands. The official naval report had never been released to the public. Maybe there was a training accident covered up years ago? Maybe some sort of crazy Naval Academy prank related to the Army–Navy game that went off the rails? Or Russian! Maybe it was Russian, he thought. The streamlined hull reminded Goldstein of the 1960's Soviet Whiskey-class submarines. Zhao and Goldstein swam to the superstructure and up toward the bridge. Goldstein hoped to find markings to confirm his hunch. There was a rusted, slime-encrusted mass that Goldstein thought he recognized as a twin 20-mm antiaircraft gun.

There were no markings around the conning tower. No plaque or numbering. There was nothing to betray the origin of the wreck. Fifty feet ahead, they both stopped short. There was a large gash in the flank of the sub. They swam over carefully, avoiding a tangled cloud of wires billowing out from the hull. A web of bent metal and broken pipes partially screened the opening. The hull plates bordering the aperture were crumpled and angled into the ship. There must have been a powerful explosion to tear a hole like that into a submarine. The deformity of the plates suggested that the explosion had been on the outside of the submarine. Had it been depth charged?

Clearly the best place to look for an answer was to swim through that gash. It was tight, but if they were careful, it was probably doable. Inside there would be artifacts that would solve the mystery. Findings that should change history, make them famous, maybe even rich—if they didn't die trying.

Goldstein was exultant. This was big. Bigger than anything since the *Titanic*. They would be scientific rock stars!

The opening into the sub looked very tight. Goldstein shuddered.

He flashed back to his last dive on the *Andrea Doria*. He had been one hundred and fifty feet into the wreck, and down two decks. Goldstein's dive buddy had gone ahead to check out the next room, when a strap on Goldstein's buoyancy compensator had snagged on a claw of twisted metal. Goldstein had struggled for what seemed like an eternity, and he was nearly over-whelmed by frustration and then blind panic. After what seemed forever, but was only five or six minutes, his buddy returned. Goldstein's frantic breathing had exhausted most of his spare oxygen. A single swipe with his partner's knife freed him, but Goldstein had sworn he would never again do a deep-wreck penetration dive. What choice did he have now?

Zhao efficiently made video and took still shots of the opening from multiple angles. She looked at her computer again and held up two fingers. It was time to ascend. Goldstein knew there was no arguing with a dive computer. Well, you can argue, but you won't win. You'll die.

At seventy-five feet, they had to pause for thirty minutes to decompress.

During the pause, Goldstein gestured to Zhao, putting his index finger over his lips. He pointed down at the wreck, made a quacking gesture, and wagged his index finger. He then pointed to himself, up to the boat, and back and forth, still making the quacking gesture.

Of course, thought Zhao, of course, you think I'm a moron. You think I'll blabber to Haskins. No, I won't say anything when we get to the top. Of course, I'll let you do the talking, you mansplaining asshole.

She nodded and waved. Thumbs up, you idiot.

It was late in the afternoon when they hauled themselves back onto the boat.

"So? Any luck?" asked Captain Haskins, looking closely at their faces.

"Nothing definite," said Goldstein, "But worth a trip back for sure."

"How about that anomaly on the depth finder?"

"Must be some sort of artifact. We didn't see anything to explain it."

Haskins looked at them suspiciously. "What's going on? Am I part of this team? Are you guys hiding something?"

Goldstein looked quickly at Zhao. "Of course not, Captain. If your CIA friend hadn't suggested diving up here, we would be out of ideas."

"Okay, whatever. And just saying, my friend Peter hates it when you say he works for the CIA," said Haskins. "Want to make another try? I can probably get the boat next weekend. Maybe a little further upriver?"

"This spot feels lucky to me, Captain, if that's all right," Goldstein said. It was important to placate this guy. They needed him. "We can use the depth-finding anomaly to localize the spot. Let's try right here next week."

They rode back to the West Point dock in silence, cleaning their gear and stowing it away. Back on land, they hauled their tanks over to Goldstein's Subaru and stored them in the back.

"Next Saturday after the football game?" Goldstein asked Haskins.

"Sure, that works for me."

"Go Army!"

Haskins waved to Zhao, and drove carefully up the steep road to campus, away from the dock. When he was out of sight, Goldstein and Zhao let out huge whoops and hugged excitedly.

"Holy shit! I mean holy cow!" exclaimed Zhao. "What the hell! We found a freaking submarine! We're making history here —today. *National Geographic* will beg us for the story."

"Zhao. Slow down. We have to move very carefully here. I want to go down again and get some more proof before we tell anyone," cautioned Goldstein.

"Proof? You have the video! What more do we need?"

"I'm not sure what this is. We don't know if it's American or Russian. My best guess is that it's a Russian, Whiskey-class from the Cold War. Who knows, maybe we captured one and stashed it here."

"I wouldn't put anything past the government. You're right about being cautious. This could turn out to be a national-security or public-relations nightmare," said Zhao.

"I'm going to do some research. I'll meet you tomorrow after my last class at four."

"Sir, if you mean 1600 hours, I can't, I have formation. I can meet you at 1800 hours, that's 6 p.m. for a Harvard man. Let's have dinner at Grant Hall. You can buy me a submarine sandwich."

Goldstein nodded his assent.

"Sir. That's a joke."

Goldstein looked distracted. "Sure. I get it. A submarine sandwich."

ELEVEN

Three years had passed since Hauptmann Karl Krause first fought for Hitler's Germany. Now Krause, Unteroffizier Schmidt, and seven grim-faced infantrymen were again tightly packed in a frigid DFS-230 glider. High above the Apennines, they were poised to dive onto their target. The troopers wore camouflage smocks and carried *Maschinenpistole* 40 submachine guns. Braces of M24 *Stielhandgranate*, stick grenades, hung from their combat webbing. The euphoria of Eben-Emael and the rapid victory over France in May 1940 was long gone. The loss of the Sixth Army at Stalingrad hung over the Wehrmacht like a pale. Final victory for the Reich was no longer in sight and at best seemed uncertain. The men kept their heads down and waited.

Krause fingered the ring he wore on a chain around his neck. It had been five years since he'd left West Point. He had had no contact with Peggy. To Krause the ring stood for the possibility, however small, of a future together. He clung to that possibility.

One day at time, he told himself. Pay attention, look after the men, the future will have to take care of itself.

Earlier in the month, Adolf Hitler's close friend, Benito Mussolini, had been toppled in a coup. The new Italian government had arrested Il Duce and held him prisoner at the Gran Sasso Massif, a mountain-top ski resort in the Italian Alps. The new Italian government sued for peace with the Allies.

The Führer was outraged.

Hitler wanted Mussolini returned to power. Immediately!

It was again up to Krause and his men to execute the Führer's plan.

Krause led ninety Fallschirmjäger paratroopers to rescue the captive fascist dictator. At Hitler's command, they were accompanied by Obersturmbannführer Otto Skorzeny, the ruthless head of SS Special Forces. Skorzeny was not officially in command, but he was a wildcard, always more likely to take charge than take direction.

A thousand meters below they could barely make out their target. The hotel was perched on a cliff hundreds of meters above the valley floor. The gliders were equipped with a parachute break and designed for short field landings, but Krause wasn't sure there was enough room to land. There was no going back without Il Duce. On Krause's signal, the pilot released the tow wire, and the roar of the tow-plane engines faded away. Swooping silently toward the mountain top, the gliders passed terrifyingly close to jagged mountain ridges.

"*Achtung!* Brace for landing!" yelled the pilot.

The glider bounced hard across the field directly in front of the hotel, and the tail skid dug into the earth. The port wing struck a rock and with a tearing sound broke away. With a lurch, the glider screeched to a halt, within meters of the cliff. The troopers tumbled off their bench into a tangled heap and struggled to get upright.

"*Aus! Aus!* Out! Out! To Il Duce!" shouted Krause.

The heavily loaded infantrymen struggled to their feet and

poured out of the escape hatch, clutching their machine pistols. The shattered glider was only twenty meters from the hotel.

Even as they ran ahead, the other gliders from the assault force were swooping in. One glider was caught by a gust, stalled, and pitched over the edge of the cliff. It shattered on the rocks two hundred and fifty meters below. No one emerged from the wreckage.

Krause and his men raced into the hotel lobby unopposed. A dozen shocked sentries quickly surrendered. Sporadic firing continued from the upper floors of the hotel. With the help of an interpreter, Krause began to question the Italians. A middle-aged captain of the Carabinieri insisted that Mussolini had been taken away the day before. At that moment, two hulking SS officers burst into the lobby.

"I am Skorzeny," declared the giant of a man with a long dueling scar on his cheek. "I am now in command here."

"Hauptmann Krause of the Luftwaffe," responded Krause. He pointed at the Italian captain. "This man is telling us that Il Duce was evacuated yesterday."

"How convenient," said Skorzeny. "Sturmbannführer Krieger, take over the interrogation. We have no time for this foolishness."

Krause got a quick look at Krieger's face. He was struck by the complete lack of emotion and Krieger's thick lips and sinister, piercing blue eyes. Krause flashed back to the sadist Jorgenson who tortured him at West Point.

Krieger walked over to a captured Italian private, wounded in the leg. The prisoner sensed the menace in Krieger. He whimpered and cowered. Krieger drew his Luger, put it to the prisoner's temple and fired, splattering blood and brain tissue onto the pavement. The Italian captain gibbered and cried.

Krieger trained his gun on the captain. "You're next, Captain! Where is Il Duce?"

Krause screamed, *"Um Gottes Willen!* For God's sake!"

"I'll shoot every one of these Italian bastards if I need to! And you, too!" screamed Krieger. He turned to the translator. "Tell this traitorous pig he has ten seconds to tell us where Mussolini is, or we'll shoot him next."

The Italian began to babble, pointing to a staircase behind them.

The interpreter translated. "Up the stairs, to the third floor, turn right, it's the last room on the right, Sturmbannführer."

Krieger smiled. "*Grazie.*"

Then he shot the Italian captain between the eyes, and holstered his Luger.

Krause turned around and vomited. He had been proud to be a German soldier, but this was cold-blooded murder. Were these his comrades in arms?

Krieger and Skorzeny took four SS troopers and dashed up the stairway.

There was a brief burst from an automatic weapon and shortly after, Skorzeny and Krieger came down the stairs with a rumpled but triumphant Mussolini at their side. Il Duce looked haggard, and stubble covered his usually immaculately shaven head. He was draped in a long overcoat and wore a soft hat with a broad brim. His clothing was worn and ill-fitting, but he retained a jaunty and dominating air.

"I knew my friend Adolf Hitler would not leave me!" the Duce announced in fluent but accented German to the assembled soldiers. "*Danke schön.*"

"The Führer never forgets his friends, Il Duce," answered Skorzeny. "Or his enemies!"

"Where is my family?"

"We have everything in order, Duce. We've sent another detachment to Rocca delle Caminate. I'm sure they are free. Now we must be off to Wolf's Lair. The Führer is anxious to meet with you."

With his prize in hand, it was time to escape. The plan had been to seize the nearby Italian airfield at Aquila de Abruzzi, descend the mountain by cable car, and meet the aircraft there, but Skorzeny had other ideas.

··· – ––– ·––·

THE LUFTWAFFE PLANNERS said the plateau near the hotel might be long enough to land a Fieseler Storch, but was too short for takeoff. Skorzeny decided to prove them wrong. He ordered the radio operator to summon the aircraft.

The captured Carabinieri were put to work at gunpoint, moving rocks to create an improvised landing strip. The sloping, irregular, and rocky field appeared impossibly short. They would chance it.

A few minutes later, Hauptmann Heinrich Gerlach of the Luftwaffe, and General Student's personal pilot, brought the Storch in for a rough landing. With the engine still running, Skorzeny and Mussolini hurried over to the Storch. Skorzeny bundled Mussolini into the rear seat and started to get in himself.

"*Nein*. No. Get out. I can't take you," said Gerlach. "It's barely possible with two people on board."

"I am personally in charge of Il Duce and have command over this operation—directly from the Führer!" screamed Skorzeny, piling into the back.

"Be reasonable. There's no way we can get off this mountain with three people aboard. The strip is too short, and the air is too thin," said Hauptmann Gerlach. "We'll all die. Get out, now."

Skorzeny pulled out the Luger and said, "I've already had two unhelpful men shot today. You have two choices, Hauptmann. Be a hero for the Fatherland, and fly us out of here—"

"Or?" said Gerlach grimly, looking at Skorzeny. He already knew the answer.

"Or I'll shoot you, toss your useless carcass off this cliff, and fly the damned aircraft myself!"

Gerlach threw his pack out the window and signaled Skorzeny to do the same, tightened his seatbelt, and firewalled the throttle.

The engine ran at a deafening roar and the plane tugged against the blocks.

Gerlach signaled the troopers restraining the aircraft, and it surged forward.

The Storch lifted briefly, bounced back down, and plunged over the edge of the cliff. Krause and the other soldiers held their breath. The light plane plummeted toward the rocks below as Gerlach pulled back on the stick with all his might.

With only meters to spare, the Storch got lift, climbed out of the ravine, and rose into view. Waggling its wings, it flew off down the valley and on to Vienna.

The SS Commandos and Fallschirmjäger cheered loudly.

Krieger turned to Krause and said, "That Skorzeny is a superman! Dr. Goebbels calls him the most dangerous man in Europe. Thank God he's on our side!"

Krause shook his head warily. "As usual, Dr. Goebbels is right. Skorzeny's dangerous, no doubt—but, you know—"

"But what! He's a hero!" objected Krieger. "Watch what you say, Krause. You sound weak. Victory is for the strong"

Krause saw no emotion in Krieger's cold blue eyes.

Krieger was right, victory would go to the strong, thought Krause. That just might not be Germany.

TWELVE

K apitänleutnant Reinhard Reichman stood on the bridge of U-154 and peered impatiently into the inky darkness through his Leitz targeting binoculars. He'd pulled his scarf over his face, but it was little protection against the bitter east wind. The deck crew hunched over lumpy shapes in full winter gear: heavy sea boots with black overtrousers, large waterproof black coats, balaclavas, and sou'wester waterproof hats. He couldn't tell one from another.

No one spoke.

The lookouts scanned the horizon.

Reichman's XO, Karlson, peered at his stopwatch.

The light of a waning crescent moon outlined a large tanker, drifting low in the water, barely moving. A convoy dropout, he thought. Maybe engine failure. No doubt their crew was working frantically inside the crippled ship.

Everyone knows what happens to stragglers on a convoy.

Karlson counted down the seconds. *"Sechs, fünf, vier, drei, zwei, eins."* Several more seconds went by. They waited silently. The only sound was the howling February wind.

"Scheiss!" muttered Reichman under his breath. They were within eight hundred meters! How could they have missed?

Moments later, the sky was illuminated by a blinding flash, followed by a deafening roar. The tanker exploded into a gigantic fireball. Burning tanker fragments flew hundreds of feet in the air and splashed into the ocean. The smell and smoke of burning fuel made breathing painful.

Christ, she must have been carrying aviation gas, thought Reichman.

A massive secondary explosion knocked Karlson and Reichman off their feet. Karlson smashed against the voice tube, his face taking most of the force. Blood streamed from his nostrils. His right eyeball was driven backwards in the socket, and the force fractured his orbital floor.

Reichman staggered to his feet and looked over at Karlson. His right eye was swollen shut and the lid blood red. Karlson vomited, and collapsed in a heap on the deck.

The burning aviation gas coated the ocean, and the inferno illuminated the sky and U-154.

The lookout pointed wildly to port.

An American destroyer! Heading directly for them at high speed.

The crippled ship had not been unprotected.

In the early years of the war, stragglers from Allied convoys were left to fend for themselves. There were not enough escorts to protect the rest of the convoy, but by February 1945, American naval yards had produced hundreds of escort vessels. Now the fleet could spare a destroyer escort to shepherd a single ship that fell behind. The Edison DE-439 had U-154 in its sights, and was charging in for the kill.

Through his binoculars, Reichman glimpsed the DE three

thousand yards on the port beam, knifing through the water, its prow lifting a huge bow wake. "Alarm! Dive the boat!" he ordered in a quavering voice. He lunged for the hatch.

To his astonishment, the lookouts didn't move to the hatch, or react to his command. What was wrong with them? It was inexplicable! Flames from the immolating tanker lit the U-boat like a searchlight. Reichman felt panic rising. They were completely exposed, almost naked on the bridge. He glanced back at the American destroyer, which was closing fast. His heart fluttered and he felt his breathing catch.

"Dive the fucking boat!" he screamed. The crew didn't respond.

Reichman saw a splash from the DE's deck gun, far off, soundless, but still menacing. Why soundless?

We're deaf, he suddenly realized. All of us. Everyone on the bridge was deafened by the tanker's explosion. He shoved the stunned and bleeding Karlson first, then slammed his men on the shoulders, pushed them down and in, and jumped below after them, slamming the hatch.

Reichman took the boat down to one hundred and fifty meters and crept along at two knots on the electric motor. They had no hope of outrunning the DE on battery power. The best they could hope for was to creep away. "Silent running!" he signaled.

By some miracle, the DE never acquired them on sonar. They managed to slink away.

Their tanker was fourteen thousand tons. That would put Reichman at two hundred thousand career tons, enough to earn the *Ritterkreuz*.

Reichman thought of a café back in Potsdam. With a Knight's Cross at his throat, he'd be irresistible. He thought of some girls known to be particularly patriotic with Knight's Cross winners.

It was 4 a.m. Soon the sun would be up, and the crew faced a long day waiting submerged for sunset. Reichman visited Karlson, who was completely blind in his right eye. Karlson joked weakly about a war-wound badge. The medic gave him a morphine ampule and he fell into a deep slumber.

Reichman updated his log, then circulated through the ship, congratulated each crew member, and thanked them for their efforts. He started aft, in propulsion, then worked his way through engineering, the kitchen, the control room, and finally the forward torpedo room. Four MK 2500 torpedoes were loaded into the forward tubes. These two-ton black beasts, each with four hundred kilograms of high explosive in the warheads, could easily break a ship's back. Two more torpedoes lay in cradles. Empty cradles had been converted to sleeping berths for the men. On a U-boat, the only thing more valuable on a U-boat than space was oxygen.

"Congratulations, Herr Kaleun!" whispered the sweat-soaked torpedo handlers.

As Reichman went on his tour, power from the ships eight thousand kilograms of lead acid batteries pushed the ship ahead slowly, and fans circulated the fetid air in the ship. Having toured the entire boat, an exhausted Reichman went to his cubby, drew the curtain, and fell deeply asleep.

At 1800 hours, Reichman awoke, came to the control room, and slowly brought the boat to periscope depth. Comfortable that there were no lurking escorts or hovering aircraft, he ordered the ballast tanks blown and brought U-154 to the surface.

Baffles opened and blowers exchanged the foul air of the boat for cold clean air from the surface. The diesel intakes were opened and the four V18 Heinkel engines throbbed to life. Energy flowed into the batteries, and the lights on the ship came on fully.

It was like Lazarus coming back from the dead, thought Reichman.

Scrambling up the metal rungs of the conning tower to the

bridge, the Kapitänleutnant was met by his XO, Karlson, his face bruised, wearing a large black bandage over his right eye.

"Deck report, Lieutenant?"

"Burning debris in the water, Herr Kaleun," pointing on the port bow, "and one boat with British seamen."

"And your eye?"

"I see perfectly well with the other eye, Herr Kaleun."

"Pull down that bandage."

The eye was hideously swollen. Reichman felt nauseated just looking at it.

Reichman reached for a pair of Leitz binoculars and trained them on the small open boat. A dozen oil-coated men lay sprawled in the boat. A few worked oars ineffectually. As they neared, Reichman could read the words "Queen of the Nile" stenciled on the bow.

"It's our tanker from last night. I guess the DE didn't hang around to pick up survivors."

The U-boat pulled up near the lifeboat. Reichman turned to the XO. "Tell them their best shot is to aim for the Irish Coast. It's one thousand two hundred kilometers due east."

In that open boat, in February, even Ernest Shackleton wouldn't stand a chance, thought Reichman. They are dead men. He looked at their weary and terrified faces. They looked injured, and very young, in their late teens, like his youngest sailors. But U-boats do not take prisoners. He wished they could.

Taking survivors on board was not just impractical. It would interfere with the mission and might be seen as treasonous.

Reichman couldn't afford even a whiff of political scandal. Talented U-boat captains were valuable tools of the Third Reich and weren't easily replaced, but Reichman knew what had befallen his brother. Expressing unpopular opinions, questioning authority, not appearing patriotic enough. Only complete fervor and commitment was acceptable. His brother had fallen from a very great height and been crushed. Reichman was a careful man.

"Karlson, put out a raft with a compass, fresh water, and additional provisions."

"Herr Kaleun? Herr Dr. Goebbels and the Führer have ordered *totaler Krieg!*" Total war!

"We're sailors, Karlson, for God's sake, not murderers."

Reichman returned to the officers' mess, hoping XO Karlson wouldn't report the aid they gave to the survivors. He hoped the crew of the *Queen of the Nile* could miraculously make it to Ireland. He wanted people to know the captain of the U-154 was an honorable and decent sailor, not a sadistic monster like Richter, who was known to machine-gun survivors for sport.

Reichman settled down in the mess with a plate of pig knuckles, and thought wistfully of a plate of greens. The last of their fresh provisions were exhausted the week before.

His meal was interrupted by the signalman with a message.

"It's from the BdU, Herr Kaleun."

The BdU, or Befehlshaber der Unterseeboote, the U-boat High Command, was presided over by Grossadmiral Dönitz.

"Have they detected another convoy?"

"No mention of a convoy. We're ordered to return to base—"

"Now?"

"Immediately, Herr Kaleun."

"That can't be! We still have most of our fish! That message must be for another U-boat. Are you having problems with the Enigma?"

"The four-wheel system is a little cumbersome, Herr Kaleun, but this is definitely directed to our boat."

Reichman felt his throat dry up and his palms sweat. He fought down the anxiety. "Set a course for Bremen, XO," he said calmly.

The signalman read the anxiety on Reichman's face. As he left the compartment, he turned back and said, "I'm sure we are being recalled so the Führer can personally award you that *Ritterkreuz*! They probably want to get some heroic pictures of you for *Signal* magazine. We can send copies to our *Mütter*! Maybe we can get our pictures in, too! Your faithful crew!"

The signalman's words barely registered with Reichman. "Of course," he added, without conviction. An urgent recall to Germany in the middle of a cruise? This was unheard of! What trouble was he in now? Could it be the Gestapo? He put on a brave face.

"Let's get back to Bremen, before they drink all the decent beer left in Germany."

••• ▬ ▬▬▬ •▬▬•

FOR THE NEXT SIX DAYS, Reichman and the U-154 circumnavigated Great Britain, then cruised on the surface of the North Sea.

Three hundred kilometers off the coast, a forward portside lookout screamed, "*Achtung! Ankommende Flugzuege!*" Incoming aircraft!

"Prepare to dive the boat!" ordered Reichman. He studied the intruder through his Zeiss binoculars and recognized the silhouette of a twin-engine Ju 88. "No! Cancel dive! She's ours!"

Seconds later, the long-range Ju 88 flew low over the U-154 and waggled her wings. Now they had air cover, thought Reichman. They would make it!

Word was sent below. They were saved.

A few men quietly studied pictures of loved ones and fervently thanked God. Most of the crew became boisterous. "My God, Herr Kaleun has brought us home with victory!" shouted the signalman. There was singing in the engineering department and discussions of where they would get their first drink and who would be the first to get laid.

Fifty kilometers from shore, Reichman radioed word of their impending arrival, and the crew made the final arrangements to enter the harbor. They decorated the conning tower with pennants and flags, each carefully chosen to reflect their successful cruise. Finally, with land in sight, they crowded the bridge and deck. Although their cruise had been truncated, they were proudly sporting long beards and ample mustaches, a sign of a long cruise and proof of submariner toughness.

The celebratory mood was dampened by the realization that the war continued and they were unlikely to survive it. Inside the Weser estuary, they steered for the enormous steel-reinforced concrete pens which sheltered the *Ubootwaffe*. The massive structures were built in 1941 by the Todt organization. At the Führer's orders, they were constructed with roofs of five-meter thick ferroconcrete.

The Allies had dropped thirty thousand bombs in twelve different missions on these giant buildings, but not one aerial bomb ever penetrated a U-boat pen. The rest of the port took a beating, though, and many apartments and shops lining the harbor were reduced to smoking rubble.

The U-boat passed slowly through the cave-like entrance and entered the vast, dark, and dank world of the U-boat pen. U-155 and U-501 were at dock, being provisioned for cruising. The sounds of the loading crew echoed through the concrete space. Sparks from arc welding flew over U-501. Shadows danced on the roof and wall.

Reichman, First Watch Karlson, and the second-watch officers stood on the bridge. They were a rough-looking crew, Karlson especially with his battered face and a jury-rigged patch over his injured eye. Reichman had made a modest effort to trim his beard and straighten his uniform. He fingered the U-boat war badge, the *Kriegsabzeichen*, on his breast pocket.

Their urgent recall suggested that something had gone terribly wrong, but Reichman still wasn't sure what. He had thought on departure that he would die or win the *Ritterkreuz* and the *Kriegsabzeichen mit Diamant*. Now his fate seemed uncertain.

"XO, give the crew two days' leave. Make sure the men use those condoms. Don't let them stray too far. As soon as I hear from High Command, we sail. For now, we need to get refueled and rearmed. And please, get a medic to look at your eye. You've done good work. We need you."

As Reichman walked off the gangway, he was quietly intercepted by an old comrade, Korvettenkapitän Erich Topp. The two walked together along the quay.

"Nice work, Reichman! Forty thousand gross tons!"

"Credit to Hershmann and U-404, they made the initial intercept and vectored us in."

"I need to speak with you—alone."

"Tell me, Erich, what is happening? Why were we recalled? We still have half our fish!"

"Yes, well, I'm sorry, Reichman. Bad news. A man from the SD, waiting for you. I wanted to warn you."

Reichman's skin crawled. "The SD! For Christ's sake, I risk my life on patrol! What else do I need to do to demonstrate my loyalty to the Fatherland?"

"No one here has said anything about your loyalty, Reichman, but no one questions the Sicherheitsdienst. You know, Admiral Dönitz protects us, as he can. Still, my friend." Topp lowered his voice and looked around. "You are too outspoken for your own good."

Reichman flinched. Topp was right. But it made him furious. Was he not allowed to think? Have opinions? Must it always be unctuous submission?

"Remember, I'm your friend…"

"If I've spoken out, it's only because they are tearing the guts out of the *Ubootwaffe*! For God's sake, Erich! You know it, and I know it! We've lost four U-boats in the last two weeks—Hertzer, Grossman, Schiedle, and Tedesco."

"Now five boats. A Sunderland caught Scheister and U-444 on the surface two days ago."

Reichman clenched his fists.

"We can't keep on like this, Erich. Someone needs to speak

up. When are they going to give us the Type XXI Dönitz always promises?"

"There's a new problem. The snorkel," said Topp. "Last month, in the Baltic, the official report says, 'crew dies in heroic battle.'"

"And what really happened?"

"Those sailors definitely died. But not a heroic U-boat battle," said Topp. "The truth? We suffocated an entire crew in a XXI last month in the Baltic when a valve got stuck. A faulty valve killed them! Carbon-monoxide poisoning. Don't quote me, I never told you, of course."

"Poor design? Bad maintenance?"

"Or rushed production? The wrong valve? Jewish sabotage? Incompetence? The XXI isn't working. Whatever it is."

"But we need it now!" Reichman pressed on. "It's a suicide mission in these old subs—you know it yourself."

Topp held out his hand. "Stop right there. Questioning the war effort is treason. In any aspect. I can't continue this conversation. This SD man is impatient. He brought orders from Brigadeführer Schellenberg. He is taking you straight back to Berlin. He wouldn't tell me anything more. Wouldn't even accept a schnapps while he waited! We both know what they did to your brother. With your family history—you need to be careful—"

Reichman cut him off. "I had nothing to do with the July plot. You know that. I was at sea when it happened! I've sworn an oath to the Führer."

Topp pressed on, "They strangled him with piano wire, Reinhard. It went on forever! They made a movie of it, for God's sake. I've told you what I can. There is nothing I can do for you directly, but, here." Topp handed Reichman a Walther P38. "As your friend. It's your choice, Reinhard. If you're mixed up in something, it would be better to make a stop now in the bathroom and take care of matters yourself."

Reichman stared at his old friend. He was deeply offended.

Shaking his head, he shouldered past the Korvettenkapitän. He bounded up the steps to the headquarters, leaving Topp behind.

At the top of the steps, Reichman wheeled and looked down at his friend. *"Heil Hitler!"*

"Heil Hitler!" answered Topp, and muttered, "God protect you, Reinhard, my impetuous old friend."

THIRTEEN

Hauptmann Karl Krause and Oberfeldwebel Dietrich Schmidt marched warily at the head of a column of Volkssturm. Since their triumphant rescue of Mussolini in 1943, they had been fighting on the Eastern Front. Their elite airborne unit was no more. Now they led a motley group of pubescent boys, old men, and wounded veterans, scraped from the bottom of the manpower barrel for the last-ditch defense of the Reich. Since late morning, they had heard the rumble of artillery fire, which had gotten progressively louder. The sky was gray and it threatened to snow.

The Volkssturm shivered in their mismatched clothes: Hitler Youth uniforms, battle dress, and work clothing. The adolescents were excited to finally be real soldiers, away from home, not children anymore—they laughed and joked as if they were on a scouting trip, not about to go into combat in a few hours. The youngest boys, some no more than fourteen, stooped under their knapsacks, marched eagerly at the front of the column. The battle-injured veterans were the most reluctant, lacking a hand or an eye or limping; they knew what awaited them.

Krause and Schmidt passed the time on the march swapping stories of farm life and abusive fathers. They had each heard the other's stories many times, but it was soothing nonetheless. They bonded over their appreciation of healthy cattle and well-maintained wheat fields. Schmidt always loudly assessed each farm, and farm wife, sharing his loud and vulgar opinions with the other men, and claiming the best as his own, "Ach, boys! This farm is mine! Mark it down! I could live there! And farm it much better. And she looks very strong, this one! And look! Still has some teeth!"

Over the years, they had marched with many comrades. All those men they'd laughed with were now dead: frozen, shot or starved.

They passed through carefully tended fields and small villages of neat houses. War had just come to Germany. The old women and children stood watching as the Volkssturm marched by, some waving handkerchiefs, and others passing wrapped bread to the soldiers. Each man was armed with a Panzerfaust, a crude but potentially devastatingly effective antitank rocket. A well-aimed Panzerfaust could disable the largest Soviet tank, but had an effective range of only one hundred meters, meaning that a soldier firing it was often blown to pieces before he could fire.

Schmidt was unusually mournful and dark. "We're dead men, Krause. This rabble won't last three minutes under fire. They'll piss themselves or have heart attacks. Does the High Command think we can slow the Russians down?"

"We're not in Russia anymore, Schmidt! This is German soil we are defending. The boys are brave and the Panzerfaust is a good weapon. I wish we'd had it when we were in Kharkov. With decent cover, and a little luck, this crew will knock out a dozen T-34s."

"You may be right, but the next dozen, or the dozen after that, will grind them into bloody mush with their treads."

Krause moved closer to Schmidt and spoke in a confidential tone. "Choose your words carefully, Schmidt. It's not that I think you're wrong, but these little Hitler Youth boys haven't lost their hearing like us! A few words from them to the military police and you could find yourself dangling from a lamppost with a sign reading 'defeatist' hung around your neck."

Krause knew that Schmidt was right. What point was there in leading a few old men and boys to the slaughter? He had come to believe that all war was insane, but still he fought on. Fighting to the death was madness, but his duty, the oath he had sworn to the Führer, and his devotion to his men left him no choice. Better to die in combat than hanging from a tree.

"Enough of that kind of talk. Let's keep working on your English. You'll need it after the war," said Krause.

"If you can find us a way to be captured by the Americans," added Schmidt.

"Sound trumpets! Let our bloody colors wave! And either victory, or else a grave!" said Krause.

"I like that," said Dietrich. "Did the Führer say that?"

"Not exactly."

"Dr. Goebbels?"

"Shakespeare. Henry VI, Part 3."

Schmidt smiled genially.

Krause and Schmidt continued their conversation in English, Schmidt struggling mightily with English f's and w's.

"Keep practicing, Schmidt. I am a vulgar fellow—"

"I am a wulgar vellow—"

"Well, maybe just smile at the Americans, and keep your hands up."

"I know! Hello wovely wady!"

"Okay. Stick with that. Your English is atrocious. Despite all my lessons!"

"Tell me, Hauptmann, do you still think about that girl—"

"Peggy, yes, I think about her all the time." Krause fingered the ring he wore on the chain. "You never forget your first girl."

What a woman Peggy was, he thought. In another life, they might have very happily married. He remembered her allure, her warm laugh and inviting smile, her soft body pressed close to him.

Krause and Schmidt were startled to attention by the roar of an engine and the grinding sound of a heavy-tracked vehicle.

"*Raus! Raus!*" shouted Schmidt. "Everybody off the road! Firing positions, wait for my order." The column of Volkssturm took cover behind the berm and small trees. "Wait for my orders to fire!"

The terrifying sounds intensified. It seemed to be coming from behind them. Suddenly, a camouflaged half-tracked vehicle burst into view, belching smoke. The Volkssturm cowered behind the berm.

A skinny teenaged boy in a patched tweed coat and short-brimmed cap got up on one knee and tracked the vehicle with the crude sight on his Panzerfaust. He depressed the firing lever of the weapon, and the rocket propellant ignited, sending the warhead jetting off toward the half-track. The vehicle swerved abruptly, and the charge exploded yards away, harmlessly cratering the road.

The Sd.Kfz. 251 half-track skidded to a halt in front of them. It was painted a green-brown camouflage pattern. A large black iron cross was clearly visible on its side.

"Halt! Cease fire! I never gave an order to fire! Idiots! It's one of ours!" screamed Krause.

The enormous armored vehicle was deafeningly loud. In the front seat of the Hanomag towered a Sturmbannführer of the SS, wearing the SS M42 camouflage battle smock with a Knight's Cross at his neck.

The SS man vaulted from the vehicle and strode over to the Volkssturm soldiers.

"Who fired that rocket?" he bellowed, pulling his pistol from his holster.

The old men looked at their feet and the boys cowered. The

boy with the patched tweed coat and hat stood to attention and looked directly ahead.

"M-m-me, Herr Sturmbannführer."

"What's your name, boy?"

"Willie, Herr Sturmbannführer."

The SS officer slapped the boy across the face with his pistol, knocking off his cap and bloodying his nose. The boy staggered and fell to the ground. The SS man stood over him screaming, "*Schweinehund!* You could have killed me!"

The SS man raised his Walther P38 and pointed it at Willie's head. The boy's pants darkened as he wet himself.

Krause ran over to intervene. He grabbed the SS man by the shoulder and spun him around. At that moment, to his dismay, he recognized the thick lips and pale blue eyes of Sturmbann-führer Krieger, who had shot the defenseless Italian Carabinieri with Mussolini.

Krieger shook free. "What kind of unit is this? What the hell, this snot-nose kid almost blew me to pieces!"

"You're right, Sturmbannführer, he's a child. He's fresh from the schoolroom. At least he showed a fighting spirit. If anyone should be blamed, it's me for failing to control my troops."

The SS man turned back to the boy and holstered the Walther.

"You are lucky to have such a forgiving officer, boy. If he wasn't here, I would splatter your fucking brains on the ground. I hope your aim improves. There won't be any second chances with Ivan."

Krause touched the boy's shoulder. He reached into his pockets and took a piece of candy to give to the boy, whose hand trembled so violently he could barely hold it. "Go on back to your mates, Willie. And remember next time, wait for your offi-cer's order to fire."

The boy offered a shaky Nazi salute and joined the other Volkssturm.

Krieger walked back to Krause.

"Ah, Krause, always such a gentle soul. I remember how you trembled when I put the fear of God into those Carabinieri guarding Mussolini."

"That man was a prisoner. You shot him in cold blood. What you did was the work of a murderer, not a soldier."

"Liquidating traitors isn't murder, Krause. They're vermin, like the Jews, and need to be exterminated. We are fighting a war of annihilation. The soldiers of the Reich must be pitiless. There's no room for weaklings. Frankly, I couldn't believe it when they told me to bring you back to Berlin."

"On whose orders am I to leave my men?"

"Dr. Walter Schellenberg of the SD."

"What does the SD want from me?"

"Dr. Schellenberg is organizing something he calls *Unternehmen Sturm König*, and for some reason they need to involve a washed-up Fallschirmjäger like you."

Krause had never heard of Dr. Schellenberg, but knew the SD arrested and obliterated the enemies of the Reich.

Krause hesitated. "What's this really all about?"

"Perhaps in the Fallschirmjäger you are taught to question orders, Krause. In the SS, we do what we are told. Dr. Schellenberg has a job for us to do. Get in the Hanomag. We're going to Berlin. I'm not asking again." He snorted with derision. "Or perhaps you would rather be facing a battalion of T-34s with your little friend Willie and that pathetic lot of children."

Krause started to climb aboard the half-track, but paused and huddled with Schmidt. "Try to keep the boys safe, Oberfeldwebel, and practice your English!"

"*Jawohl*, Herr Hauptmann," answered Schmidt, and switching to fractured English, "Hello! I spreche Englisch! Hello, lovely lady! Thank you, Krause."

Schmidt waved his rag-tag unit of Volkssturm forward, and started down the road toward the sound of the artillery. Krause looked at Schmidt marching away with the children and the old men, and knew he'd not live out the day.

Schmidt was a good man, a vulgar fellow, kind-hearted, and would have been happy on any farm with any chubby wife.

Maybe in his next life.

Krause climbed into the back of the half-track. The driver gunned the engine and headed back toward Berlin. The Reich had a plan for him and it involved Krieger.

God help me now, Krause thought.

FOURTEEN

Goldstein sat in Grant Hall, waiting for Zhao. Grant was the mediocre alternative to eating at the cadet mess in Washington Hall. Grant was cool, dark, and very busy. Goldstein didn't notice the hubbub. The submarine they had stumbled upon yesterday was all he could think about.

Grant was one of the few places at West Point where cadets and staff could gather informally. It was a stately space, with a lofty coffered ceiling and arched leaded windows. The walls were hung with oil portraits of generals, including Dwight David Eisenhower and John "Blackjack" Pershing. The food at Grant Hall was, if anything, worse than the mess hall. The Army knew how to build grand buildings, but they subbed out the food service to the lowest bidder. The cadets ate the cardboard pizza and precooked hamburgers without complaint. Anything was better than the mandatory meals with their company in Washington Hall. The food there was free, but there was no escape from the relentless, testosterone-fueled cadet culture. Two nights a week, cadets were allowed to skip dinner at the company table. Since most cadets were chronically broke and not terribly choosy, it was either go to Grant Hall, order from American Burrito, or get greasy Chinese food from Dong Fong.

Cadets in Army combat uniforms sat together at long tables eating junk food and working on problem sets, gossiping and bitching about life at West Point. Goldstein, in a tweed blazer with leather arm patches, felt conspicuous as the lone civilian. He sat alone below a portrait of a steely eyed General Douglas MacArthur.

His foot would not stop tapping. He knew the discovery would completely change his life. He would become well known and his scholarship widely quoted. Goldstein spent several hours the night before discreetly reaching out to colleagues and searching the internet for clues about missing submarines. What, he wondered, would Major Sanchez and the superintendent do when they found out about the submarine? Would he get credit for a historic find, or criticized for diving without authorization? Would they make him bring in other investigators?

When he finally went to bed around 3 a.m., he had a nightmare about the *Andrea Doria*. He awoke lathered in sweat and breathing hard. Goldstein felt increasingly out of place and scrutinized at West Point, and more than a little paranoid. He was terrified to penetrate the wreck, but even more scared of having someone else get credit for their discovery.

They would have to go back to the wreck to solve the mystery. If the news broke prematurely, they might lose control of the discovery before they could tell the world. Every military historian and ambitious marine archeologist would jump in to steal the credit. Even worse, the Army might shut them down completely and declare it a matter of national security. They might bury the story forever.

... – ––– .–––.

ZHAO APPEARED RIGHT ON TIME, composed and confident, her uniform crisp and her hair tucked neatly into a bun. She had finished her schoolwork early, then did hours of research on lost submarines. Despite a general contempt for "PowerPoint Warriors," she had spent extra time on the presentation that she had on her laptop.

Zhao spotted him alone at the booth. "Prof? You okay?" Zhao stood over Goldstein holding a plastic tray piled high with wilted salad, two milkshakes, and a pile of chicken nuggets.

Goldstein jumped from his reverie. "I'm sorry, Zhao, I'm so distracted. I barely slept last night."

"No kidding. Welcome to my world! At least you don't have a mechanical-engineering exam in an hour. Did you remember to eat? This is for you. I brought you dinner!"

"Oh, hey, thanks." He pulled out his wallet. "Let me repay you."

Zhao laughed. "One, no one uses money anywhere. It's all Venmo, all the time. Two, I used my cadet discount, on seriously subsidized food, so this is on me. Don't thank me. Thank the American taxpayer. Now, eat! Your nuggets are getting cold." Zhao sat down next to him and pushed the chicken nuggets in his direction. "They get seriously disgusting when they get cold. Here, have some ranch dressing. So. I gotta run in forty minutes, let's get to work." Zhao pulled out her laptop and pulled up her PowerPoint, starting with her dive video. "You can think while you eat. Here, look at this."

Goldstein froze the image of the wreck and pointed at the curve of the hull. "This streamlining means it's definitely post-war, and we can pretty much rule out it being one of ours."

"But no, I disagree—" Zhao started.

Goldstein stepped on her words, declaring, "You really think we lost a nuclear power sub? Then we covered it up?"

Zhao hated to be interrupted. "That's not what I meant, it's just—"

Goldstein cut her off again. "We only lost three submarines

after the war: *Thresher, Stickleback,* and *Scorpion,* and they've all been accounted for. No. Our find—this sub has to be a Russian, probably a Whiskey-class. Those Russian sub commanders were wild men. They ran one aground just outside Karlskrona, a big Swedish base. The Russian built and launched over two hundred. I'm sure there are some that aren't accounted for. You can only imagine what the Russian's record-keeping is like. They exported them to Albania and Bulgaria, for God's sake. The Chinese built twenty-one under license…"

Zhao's frustration at not being heard mounted. As Goldstein lectured to her about the certainty their find could only be Russian, she finally managed to get a word in edgewise.

"What I meant, Dr. Goldstein, is that I disagreed when you said it had to be postwar."

"But the streamlining, Zhao."

"Sir, I think it could be German U-boat. It looks just like a Type XXI."

Goldstein swallowed hard. Damn, Zhao might be right. "Good thought. It could be a German U-boat. After all, the Russians had modeled their Whiskey-class on the Nazi Type XXI U-boats. I still think it's Russian. But Zhao, what would the Germans be doing in the Hudson River? We really can't prove anything until we penetrate the wreck. We have to get in there, and soon," Goldstein said, gesturing at the gash in the submarine on the video screen.

Goldstein thought about being trapped inside the *Andrea Doria.* He felt queasy.

Zhao continued through her PowerPoint. "I checked with a friend at the Naval Academy. There is only a single report of a Whiskey-class boat, the S-80, which went missing in the mid-fifties, but the Russians found that one sunk in the Barents Sea in the mid-sixties."

"That doesn't mean much," said Goldstein. "The Russians wouldn't necessarily announce to the world that they've lost a sub. You can't believe anything they say."

"But what is a Russian sub doing here? In the Hudson River?"

Goldstein began to speak more quickly. "Maybe we hijacked it! Did you read *The Hunt for Red October*? Maybe the captain arranged to defect. After we took all the tech off the sub, we ditched it here and everyone pretended it was lost at sea."

"I'm glad your contribution to this mystery extends to reading some Tom Clancy novel," scoffed Zhao.

"My apologies. Your idea is much better. It's a Nazi submarine carrying hidden gold, or Hitler's DNA," snapped Goldstein.

"Don't mock me!" Zhao said loudly. Several cadets at the nearest tables turned their heads and stared. Raising your voice in public was not done at West Point. Zhao continued in a more modulated tone. "I'm sorry, Professor. None of this makes any sense right now."

"You're right. We'll have the answer on the next dive."

Zhao impaled a piece of her salad. "Where do we stand with the law on this? Who has legal ownership of the sub? Could we be accused of trespassing?"

"We should be fine," said Goldstein. "The sub is covered under the Abandoned Shipwreck Act of 1987. The Federal Government has transferred authority over embedded wrecks on state land to the states. New York may have a claim on the vessel, but the Federal Government has no jurisdiction if it's not a U.S. naval vessel."

"How about the Russians or Germans?" she asked.

"The Russians or the Germans might make a legal claim if it's their boat, but I don't see why that should stop us from exploring."

"I'm a bit worried about how Major Sanchez and the superintendent will respond," said Zhao.

"Don't worry about the man, Zhao. This is our shot, we need to take it!" Goldstein struggled to appear nonchalant. He pushed back his memories of being trapped on the *Andrea Doria*. This was the opportunity of a lifetime. His future rested on swimming into that iron coffin. For once in his life, he wouldn't worry about what other people thought of him. "Screw the Army— they'll just have to wait to find out what was on the bottom of that river until we are ready to tell them. Better to beg for forgiveness than ask for permission."

"Hooah! Sir! I'll confirm with Captain Haskins. We'll go next Saturday."

"After the football game," added Goldstein.

"That's right, it's still West Point." Zhao smiled. "You should come to the game. I'm jumping that day."

"I'm really not much of a football fan, Zhao"

"Just come, Professor, it will be fun, I promise. And don't be late!"

FIFTEEN

Reichman left Topp behind and entered the fleet office, which was dominated by a huge map of the North Atlantic, overlaid with a grid. The positions of the U-boats were shown with markers. The walls were simple, unadorned, poured concrete, a far cry from the old BdU headquarters in Lorient, France, which had been decorated with antiques and hung with tapestries.

Sturmbannführer Krieger, clad in a floor-length black leather raincoat, rose and gave the *Hitlergruss*. Reichman returned the salute with more vigor that usual, doing his best to appear enthusiastic. Reichman had his guard up. He briefly locked eyes with the pale-eyed brute.

"Kapitänleutnant Reichman, I have orders from Dr. Walter Schellenberg of the SD to accompany you to Berlin. Immediately."

"Dr. Schellenberg of the SD? What…what crime am I charged with?" asked Reichman. His heart was racing, and he struggled to speak evenly or breathe normally. The Sicherheitsdienst, or SD, was the most terrifying element of the SS. It detected and rooted out the enemies of the Nazi Party, real or perceived. So this is it, he realized. The inevitable catastrophe. It was happening. He felt Topp's P38 in his pocket. He'd missed the opportunity to die easily. He wondered if should try to shoot this monster and then take his own life.

"There are no charges. I am bringing you to the Reich Chancellery."

"The Reich Chancellery? I don't understand," said Reichman. "If I am not under arrest, what are you doing here? Why am I being summoned?"

"Don't ask so many questions. This is a matter of great urgency, Kapitänleutnant," said Krieger. "Grossadmiral Dönitz has put your name forward. There are plans for a special mission. The Führer wants to meet you personally. You seem rather jumpy, Kapitänleutnant. Guilty conscience?"

"Not at all. No one is more committed to Germany than I am."

"And the Führer?"

"Yes, of course."

"*Genau.* Precisely. They are waiting for us in Berlin, Herr Kapitänleutnant."

Reichman was jubilant. Not under arrest? A special mission? What was this about? Reichman could feel his heart thudding in his chest. Summoned by the Führer himself! Unbelievable! Finally, a chance to explain exactly what the U-boat force was struggling with! Surely once the Führer understood he would make things right!

They climbed into a black Horch with SS pennants and roared into the dusk, led by a motorcycle escort. Krieger sniffed and ostentatiously opened the window. Reichman had not bathed in four weeks. U-boat life. Nothing to be done.

The four-hundred-kilometer trip from Bremen to Berlin should have taken five hours, but they were intermittently forced to the side of the road by convoys of troops and armored vehicles. Allied airpower had made road travel dangerous in daylight, so roads were congested at night. With dimmed and hooded headlights, the visibility was poor. Reichman slept uneasily through most of the trip. He had a nightmare, reliving the sinking of the *Queen of the Nile*, and the close call with the escort.

He awoke in a cold sweat just outside of Berlin.

"We would have preferred to give you a few hours to clean up before the meeting, Herr Kapitänleutnant," Krieger remarked, "but my orders are to bring you directly to the Reich Chancellery. In whatever condition."

Arriving at the Reich Chancellery, their papers were closely scrutinized by the SS guard with an MP 44. They were waved through the checkpoint and came to a stop in a cobblestone courtyard.

"I have not been authorized to attend the meeting," said Krieger. "Apparently this is for Navy men only," he sniffed. "No matter, I'm sure the Führer will decorate me personally after the mission." Krieger waited with the car.

Several SS guards with machine pistols escorted Reichman to an entryway, and they descended 4 stories underground in the elevator. His papers were inspected again by an unsmiling SS trooper, and he stepped through a massive steel door into a narrow concrete-lined hallway with industrial lighting. Despite the whirl of the air handlers, the atmosphere was humid and heavy. The SS guard led him through a series of corridors until they entered a small conference room with a felt-covered table and half a dozen chairs.

Reichman was stunned. Adolf Hitler, his Führer, was reduced to leading Germany from this small warren of underground rooms!

Reichman was greeted by Grossadmiral Dönitz in his starched blue uniform and Knight's Cross. "Have a seat, Reinhard," said Dönitz, gesturing at the chairs and offering

Reichman a glass of schnapps. "The Führer will be pleased with your good work on this cruise, Reinhard—forty thousand tons. Excellent."

"I had half my fish left, Herr Grossadmiral. Why did you call me back? What, for God's sake, are we doing here? Is this our chance to tell the Führer that sailing out in Type VII is just suicide?"

Both men knew that the battle for the Atlantic was lost. Dönitz pointed at the light fixture and then his ear, raising an eyebrow, signaling caution.

"Relax, Reinhard. The Führer is well aware of the sacrifice our U-boat crews have made for the Fatherland. As to your presence here, the Führer has authorized an extremely important mission. He's requested a captain with experience operating off the East Coast of the United States. There was no one in the Kriegsmarine with more experience operating in Atlantic coastal waters off the United States than you, my friend." Dönitz smiled and raised his schnapps. "Reichman! None of us will forget your triumphs of 1942! When you sank ships off of New Jersey and Long Island! The Americans panicked! And now...Now you must go back to America! Back to New York!"

Reichman slammed the table with his fist. "New York? Are you joking? This isn't 1942, Grossadmiral! With the American aircraft and new radar, we wouldn't get within five hundred miles of the Atlantic seaboard!"

Dönitz lit another cigarette, offering one to Reichman. "Very likely true, Reinhard, with the old Type VII boat. That's why we will be giving you one of the new Type XXI with the snorkel. You will make the entire crossing submerged. Come up to periscope depth only intermittently to recharge with the snorkel. And there will be no need to rendezvous with a Milch Cow. You'll return to Bremen with half of your fuel still left."

"Take the fight to New York, Grossadmiral? Why go all that way? With a Type XXI, we can hunt the Ami's anywhere. And New York? There must be defenses..."

"This is all Schellenberg's plan. He has the Führer's ear. They have insisted on taking this Type XXI and demanded our best captain. That is you. The Führer insists on meeting you and judging your fitness to command the boat. At times like this, Kapitänleutnant Reichman, we do well to bend with the wind."

At that moment, the door swung open, and an SS attendant in crisp uniform and polished boots entered and announced, "Achtung! Der Führer, Adolf Hitler!"

Dönitz and Reichman leaped to their feet as Hitler entered. They gave the *Hitlergruss* and shouted, *"Heil Hitler!"*

Hitler tossed off a causal return salute. He wore a simple tunic with his Iron Cross. "Good day, Herr Grossadmiral. So this is the intrepid Captain Reichman?"

"Jawohl, mein Führer," answered Dönitz. "Kapitänleutnant Reichman has sunk more ships off the Atlantic seaboard than any of our active U-boat commanders."

Hitler's hair was limp, and his arm trembled, but he turned to Reichman and fixed him in a fierce glare. "We are at a historic moment, Kapitänleutnant Reichman, a providential moment. Our Germany suffered a few reverses, it's true, but these are times which separate the weak and the brave. The Fatherland's finest warriors have always fought hardest in times of peril. The SD tells me that you have expressed concerns about the U-boat war."

Reichman felt himself drawn into Hitler's eyes, like a rabbit staring helplessly at a cobra. "Mein Führer, I-I-we," he stammered. "The *Ubootwaffe,* we will fight to our last breath for Germany, we only need weapons we can win with. I know—"

Hitler cut him off. "Weapons, great weapons, are here, Captain. Our Type XXI boat is undetectable—we have hundreds planned! We will sweep the seas clear of the Americans. And jet bombers, ballistic missiles, too! By year end, the Anglo-Americans will make peace and join us against the Bolsheviks!" Hitler paused. "But for now, now we need a bold strike, a shocking blow to knock the Allies off balance. This will buy us time—a few months to produce those great weapons. I am the ultimate judge of warriors, Captain. I can see in your eyes you are just the man we need. You, Kapitänleutnant, are the man to strike that blow!"

Hitler stood uncomfortably close to Reichman, and put a shaking hand on his shoulder. His breath was fetid. "My dear Reichman, we are surrounded by cowards, traitors, backstabbers. I see through them all. These men would give up and turn our Germany over to that scoundrel Roosevelt and his Jewish cabal. You are different! I can see your determination, your patriotism, your willingness to give your last breath for the Fatherland. This is what Germany needs right now. You are the man to take the superweapon on this voyage. As a sign of my faith and your contributions to the Fatherland, I am promoting you to Korvettenkapitän!"

Reichman felt hypnotized. Nothing made sense. How can a single U-boat, even one with a snorkel, stop the Allies, or even slow them for a day? What possible reason was there to go to New York?

Hitler sat down heavily. "Dr. Schellenberg's plan will shake the American's resolve. It will bring them into the fight with the Russians on our side! Go home, Reichman, get something to eat. Get some rest. Report to Dr. Schellenberg at Prinz-Albrecht-Strasse tomorrow. That's all. You are dismissed."

Trapped in Hitler's piercing glare, Reichman's questions became irrelevant. He felt his shoulders square. He had no control of his speech. "*Jawohl*, mein Führer! You command and I will follow."

SIXTEEN

Obersturmbannführer Otto Skorzeny and Brigadeführer Walter Schellenberg drank espresso and chatted amiably in Schellenberg's wood-paneled Prinz-Albrecht-Strasse office. Six floors below, prisoners writhed and screamed under Gestapo torture, but the two men were oblivious. They sat in comfortable leather armchairs and gossiped about the recent political machinations in the Nazi hierarchy.

"Propaganda Minister Goebbels seems to have regained some of the Führer's respect," said Schellenberg.

"*Ja,* that little dwarf is everywhere in Berlin! Ever since he whipped them up with the *'Totaler Krieg'* speech in the Sportpalast last year, the people adore him," said Skorzeny.

"He's a hideous little club-footed monster," said Schellenberg, "and his conduct with that Czech movie actress—he's shameless. Himmler tells me to watch out for Bormann. He's dangerous, and he has the Führer's ear."

"Ach, if only I had the Führer's ear," said Skorzeny. "Since that cock-up in the Ardennes, I have not been welcomed at the Führer Hauptquartier. If only we could have gotten through to the Meuse River bridges."

"It's true, Obersturmbannführer, you failed to achieve your objectives, but your men in American uniforms certainly wreaked havoc."

Schellenberg put down his coffee and leaned forward. "You've inspired me, my dear Skorzeny. I have a project in mind, a most interesting project, one that will change the entire course of the war. I have in mind to use your man Krieger. I need someone bold, ideologically sound, and unafraid to act."

"Krieger is my best man, Brigadeführer. The man is absolutely ruthless. He served with Einsatzgruppe C in the Ukraine. He puts his personal total at thirty thousand."

"Jews?"

"Of course. Enemies of the Reich, all of them."

"Excellent. What I have in mind is much smaller in scale, but equally vital to the war effort. We will also need some assistance with equipment—"

A knock on the door interrupted the conversation.

Three men stood at the door.

Sturmbannführer Krieger wore his crisp field-gray Waffen-SS dress uniform. His SS honor dagger, with a tassel and sword knot, hung on his right hip. He gave a crisp *Hitlergruss* and clicked his heels. Krieger was followed by Krause in his soiled Fallschirmjäger camouflage jacket and dusty boots. Reichman, now showered and wearing freshly pressed naval dress, with his new rank of Korvettenkapitän, came last.

Reichman and Krause exchanged uncomfortable looks, and gave the *Hitlergruss* as well. It was terrifying just to be in the neighborhood of Prinz-Albrecht-Strasse. They asked themselves the same questions: What kind of wild plan was afoot? And why were they involved?

Schellenberg directed the group to a conference table. Reichman smelled the aroma of real coffee and sniffed the air.

"Can I offer you gentlemen an espresso?" asked Schellenberg.

"Real coffee?" asked Reichman. "Why not? I haven't had a real coffee in years. I've been drinking that ersatz acorn shit since 1942!"

"There are a few minor benefits for those most loyal to the Führer," said Schellenberg, smiling.

"I guess the loyalty of the fighting man must be its own reward," said Krause.

"The Fallschirmjäger hardly has a monopoly on combat experience or loyalty, Hauptmann Krause," responded Krieger icily.

Krieger and Krause glared at each other.

Reichman broke the silence. "It would be a pleasure to fight alongside you both." He tore open a pack of Turkish cigarettes and offered one to each man.

Krause refused. "No, *danke*. As you know, our Führer teaches us that smoking is unhealthy."

Krieger laughed coarsely, flashed a smile of jagged teeth, and lit a cigarette. He took a deep drag and exhaled. "War is unhealthy, Krause, yet it's the only vocation for true men."

"I completely agree, Sturmbannführer," interjected Schellenberg. Then turning to Krause, he asked, "Well, Herr Hauptmann, enough talk about smoking and health. How are our brave soldiers faring in East Prussia?"

Krause thought it was time to be honest. "My men—well, as you know, many are just boys, or very old men—are doing their best, Herr Brigadeführer. We are badly outnumbered. We have no air support, and little artillery. We have been facing hundreds of Russian tanks with nothing more than the Panzerfaust."

"*Harte Zeiten, harte Pflichten, harte Hertzen.* Hard times call for hard hearts, Herr Hauptmann. Sacrifices will be necessary to stabilize the front for a couple of months while the Führer finalizes his Wonder Weapons." Krieger crossed his arms.

"Of course, Herr Sturmbannführer. Ultimate victory will be ours," murmured Krause.

Schellenberg rang his adjutant, who limped into the room with more espresso and small chocolates. Krieger was oblivious. But Krause smiled and offered the disabled man a nod of recognition, which the adjutant reciprocated gratefully.

"Gentlemen, thank you for making yourselves available at such short notice," said Schellenberg. "As you know, the past months have been a challenge for the Reich. Reichsführer Himmler and I believe Germany's best hope lies with bringing the Americans and British on to our side in the struggle with Bolshevism. To that end, we plan to invite FDR to Berlin to discuss this natural alliance."

"Quite so," agreed Skorzeny. "If only he was not so horribly misguided by his Jewish cabal, FDR would understand. Soon enough we will be fighting side by side with them against the Russians."

"FDR? Invited to Berlin?" repeated Krause. What was Schellenberg talking about?

"Perhaps I should clarify what I mean by invitation. We intend to kidnap FDR and bring him to Berlin," explained Schellenberg. "And that is where you men come in."

Reichman and Krause looked at Schellenberg in astonishment.

Krieger's face was impassive, his pale eyes unblinking.

"Brilliant!" shouted Skorzeny, slamming his hand on the desk. "We will do it!"

Schellenberg held out his hand. "Not so fast. As you know, Herr Obersturmbannführer, the devil is in the details." Schellenberg then switched to English and spoke directly to Krause. "Hauptmann Krause, we understand you are a native English speaker."

Krause was surprised to be addressed in English, but responded, "Yes, sir, I am. I grew up in Kansas."

"Excellent. I understand you graduated from the U.S. Military Academy at West Point?"

"No, Herr Brigadeführer, I spent only eight months there before our family answered the Führer's call to return to the Fatherland."

"Ah yes, I see." He turned to the group. "This man, Krause, is at the center of our plan."

Skorzeny leaped to his feet. "*Das ist fantastisch.* I too English speaking. I too go with Krause! Tomorrow!"

"Please sit down, Herr Obersturmbannführer. No. Not you. Sit down. You are simply too famous," said Schellenberg, diplomatically omitting any mention of Skorzeny's fractured English. "Sturmbannführer Krieger will go in your place. His face is unknown, and, as you know, he does what is necessary without remorse."

Skorzeny remained standing. "But surely..." Skorzeny protested. "My mission—"

Schellenberg cut him off. "Sit down, Obersturmbannführer!" he said harshly, switching back to German. "It is not your mission! I am working with the complete authority of the Führer. We must put the interests of the Fatherland ahead of our vanity. The fate of the German Reich depends on our success."

Skorzeny sat down unhappily and nodded his head.

Krause rubbed his hands nervously together. Where was this all going?

Krieger withdrew his SS dagger from its sheath and meticulously polished the razor-sharp blade with a soft cloth. The words *Meine Ehre heisst Treue*, "My Honor is Loyalty," were acid etched in the blade.

Krieger had spent much of the ride back from East Prussia with Krause polishing the dagger. He had proudly reminded Krause that "Reichsführer Himmler issued a decree. All SS men are authorized to use their dagger to defend their honor." Krause imagined that Krieger often felt insults to his honor.

Schellenberg cleared his throat, unrolled a nautical chart of

New York Harbor and map of the lower Hudson River valley, and began. "Gentleman, I give you *Unternehmen Sturm König.*" He paused and looked directly at Krause. "Operation Storm King, for those of us more comfortable in English."

Krause looked at the men's faces studying the maps of New York Harbor and the Hudson River. They were shocked. He looked at Reichman, who silently shook his head. He didn't speak but his face revealed his thoughts: this is complete insanity.

Schellenberg continued, undeterred. "This is a bold stroke, but we have history within our grasp. Providence has provided us the opportunity and tools to win the war. Here, look." He pointed to the map. "President Roosevelt will visit the U.S. Military Academy at West Point on the afternoon and evening of April 4 to deliver a speech to the cadets. Our plan? Seize Roosevelt during that visit and bring him back to Germany." Schellenberg looked pointedly at Krause, who stiffened. "With that devil Roosevelt in our hands, we will convince the Americans to align against Bolshevism. At the very least, it will buy us time, enough time, we believe, for the Führer's new Wonder Weapons to turn the tide!"

Krause knew he had to speak. "May I have permission to, er…speak freely?"

Schellenberg frowned. "Of course."

"West Point isn't just a college, it's an active military post. There are always hundreds, if not thousands, of uniformed personnel on base. Guards will be surrounding the president at all times!"

Schellenberg scowled. "We have done the research. At West Point, he stays at the military hotel, the Thayer. In very secure locations such as West Point, the president has only a small personal-security team, a few men at most."

"How large a force are we sending on this mission, Brigade-führer, and how are we supposed to gain access to the base?" asked Krause.

"Just you and Krieger here."

"By ourselves!"

"Precisely," said Schellenberg. "You will be dressed as American officers. I have tasked Obersturmbannführer Skorzeny to provide you and Krieger with captured uniforms. The Amis will be their usual lax and unprofessional selves. They believe the war is almost over. Krause and Krieger will be gone before they know what hit them. For you, Krause, this is sort of a homecoming. It should be a sweet revenge."

Revenge and homecoming, thought Krause. Which one? Or both? A chance to strike directly back at the bastards at West Point—or see Peggy? Was there any chance of a life together with her? Could he bring her back with him to Germany? Maybe this was an opportunity to switch sides again and escape with Peggy into the wide-open American West?

Schellenberg continued. "Hauptmann Krause, we will count on you to do the talking. I think we will give you a promotion!" He laughed. "Does Major in the U.S. Army suit you? We will make Sturmbannführer Krieger your adjutant! That way, no one will pay him much attention. Reichman's men will row you from the U-boat down to the dock area here around 1900 hours." Schellenberg pointed at the map of West Point and the Hudson River. "It's less than a kilometer to the Thayer Hotel. You should have no trouble making it back to the dock with Roosevelt your prisoner no later than 0100 hrs. That will give you five hours to get downriver and out of the harbor before sunrise. Presumably, the Americans will discover FDR missing soon after daylight, if not before."

"Brilliant!" said Skorzeny, nodding enthusiastically.

"I believe that after a few days here in Prinz-Albrecht-Strasse, Mr. Roosevelt will agree that an alliance with Germany is in America's best interest," continued Schellenberg.

Reichman, who had been listening uncomfortably, finally burst out, "But this is preposterous! You can't possibly expect me

to take my U-boat through New York Harbor and fifty kilometers upriver!"

"Yes, we do. You've done it before. Grand Admiral Dönitz
assured me that during *Unternehmen Paukenschlag,* you operated
with impunity in New York Harbor," said Schellenberg.

"Clearly you misunderstood! It's true, back then, we worked
very close to shore. Hardegan and I enjoyed seeing the lights of
Coney Island! All of that was risky enough in 1942 before the
Americans had the Liberator aircraft and radar. We can barely
cross the Atlantic now, let alone operate inside a heavily guarded
harbor.

"We are providing you with a Type XXI U-boat! You can use
the snorkel and stay submerged the entire way across the
Atlantic. Or so your Admiral Dönitz told me."

Reichman took a deep breath. "*Ja,* with a Type XXI boat it
should be easy to reach the East Coast. I could land the raiding
party on the beach in Long Island, like we did in 1942. They
could go by land to West Point. It's just not feasible to enter the
harbor, let alone go fifty kilometers upriver."

"That is unacceptable. This is an abduction, not an assassination. Once we abduct FDR, any movement by road or rail will be
impossible. Krause and Krieger must go in and out by submarine," said Schellenberg, "and only in one night."

"The New York Harbor entrance has antisubmarine nets and
mines," Reichman protested.

"Our sources in Staten Island tell us that the harbor defenses
are quite lax. The submarine nets are set in the open position.
Besides, you will have your snorkel!"

"Snorkel!" said Reichman, raising his voice. "We can't navigate submerged in confined waters with the periscope and
snorkel. We'll have to be on the surface. It's impossible!" He
slammed his open hand on the harbor map with fingers splayed
apart, covering the New York Harbor.

"Coward! Remember that Günther Prien took U-47 into

Scapa Flow! And sank the *Royal Oak*! He was using a Type VII!" shouted Skorzeny.

"And now Prien is dead! Along with the rest of my comrades!" yelled Reichman.

Krieger lunged toward the table and, in a flash, slammed his SS dagger into the map. The blade passed between Reichman's thumb and forefinger and impaled deeply into the mahogany conference table.

The room became silent. He slowly removed the dagger from the table.

Krieger spoke in an icy and composed tone. "Let me remind you, Korvettenkapitän, you are going to West Point under the orders of our Führer Adolf Hitler. To me, you are just a bus driver. Figure a way to get us to Roosevelt, or the next time you see this dagger, I'll be slitting your throat with it."

SEVENTEEN

Zhao had seemed very interested in having Goldstein come to the football game. He wasn't sure why, but since they couldn't dive until the game was over, Goldstein decided to go. Attendance at home games was mandatory for all cadets. This was not a suggestion—Zhao had told Goldstein that her roommate had been caught sleeping in her room one Saturday morning and given forty hours of punishment marching.

In his months at West Point, Goldstein had never attended a game. He was not much of a college-football fan and spent most weekend days diving. What the hell, he thought, he had to wait for Zhao anyway. She had said something about jumping at the game, whatever that meant.

Goldstein walked from his office up the hill to Michie Stadium. It was a *gorgeous* fall day; he enjoyed passing Lusk Reservoir amongst a crowd of high-spirited cadets. Cadets recognized him and waved. One yelled, "Hey Professor! Great day for a game." The red-headed cadet from his history class called him over, and they exchanged high fives and cries of "Beat Bucknell!" For once, Goldstein felt like he belonged.

Outside Michie Stadium, there was a swarm of Army fans, some old graduates, others young officers and families, wearing Army fan gear, tailgating, and tossing footballs. The men were fit, with great posture and neatly cut hair; the wives were trim and attractive. Even the Army children were polite and well behaved. After their picnics, they collected their trash and neatly disposed of it. There was little or no drinking. He was part of the Army family, thought Goldstein. He bought an Army baseball cap and blended into the crowd.

He entered the stadium just as the 2nd Regiment paraded onto the field in neat columns, led by their officers. When the Army band played the National Anthem, the Corps of Cadets and fans sang lustily, projecting a sense of dedication and commitment. Reluctantly at first, and then enthusiastically, Goldstein sang along with the crowd. This is a great country, isn't it? he thought. After the anthem, the 2nd Regiment cadets piled into the stands and joined the rest of the Corps. The rowdy mass of young men and women, wearing camouflage uniforms, waved flags, stomped, and cheered until they were hoarse.

When the cheering subsided, the stadium speaker blared, "Ladies and gentlemen, please turn your attention to the Army Black Knights Parachute Team!" A helicopter appeared high overhead. With the cry "The jumpers are out!" four black dots appeared in the sky next to the helicopter. The skydivers popped their yellow and black chutes and the crowd roared. Goldstein watched in admiration as the jumpers soared over the stadium. The first three jumpers landed around the forty yard, each receiving an appreciative roar. Goldstein stood and cheered along with the crowd. He had never felt as proud to be an American and a part of West Point.

The last jumper flew between the stadium lights, trailing an American flag, and nailed the landing, right at midfield. The crowd went wild. Looking up to the Jumbotron, Goldstein watched as the last jumper handed the game ball to the official, pulled off her helmet, and shook out her long black hair—wait, it's a girl? he thought—and she flashed a dazzling smile.

My God! It was Zhao! So that's what she meant about jumping into the game! She was on the parachute team. And their best jumper, the one honored to bring the flag! What a woman! What other secrets was she keeping from him? he wondered.

Goldstein was surprised how much he enjoyed the game. He stood and cheered with the crowd. He'd always resented Army football. But not today! The Black Knights jumped to a huge lead before halftime.

As always, the cadets stood for the entire game and cheered loudly with their company mates. Many cadets resented the compromises the USMA made to field a winning team; most resented their mandatory attendance at the games. But right now, the cadets were happy in the moment, reveling in a few hours of unrestrained fun and celebration.

At halftime, Goldstein used his binoculars to study the cadets, and he found himself searching for Zhao in the sea of camouflage. He was embarrassed and jealous to see her laughing and smiling with several handsome young cadets. Zhao accompanied the plebes in her company down onto the field each time Army scored a touchdown. They did pushups, one for each point in the score. Even after Army's sixth touchdown, and forty-two more pushups (on top of the one hundred and five she had already done), she looked happy and energetic.

Midway through the fourth quarter, an Army tailback took a pitch and made a spectacular run for a touchdown, driving the crowd into waves of deafening cheers. Returning to the bench, the athlete removed his helmet and was congratulated by his teammates. His handsome face was projected on the stadium Jumbotron and Goldstein's blood ran cold. It was Tyrone Davidson: that kid from his history class—the one he'd caught cheating last year.

So that was it, Goldstein realized. Winning at football was so important to these people—even himself for a few minutes—that they were willing to compromise the very bedrock values of Duty, Honor, and Country that West Point and the Army was built on.

Tyrone Davidson. Football tailback. Hero of the hour.

Flagrant cheater.

No one seemed to care, except him.

Goldstein walked out of the stadium, uncertain what to think of West Point. He headed down to the dock to meet Zhao and Captain Haskins, more conflicted than ever.

"Holy cow, Zhao! That was amazing! How come you didn't tell me you were on the parachute team?"

"I thought you'd enjoy a surprise, Professor." Zhao nodded toward Haskins. "This dive will probably be nothing special, so I thought I would brighten your Saturday."

"My Saturday was amazing," said Goldstein. "That is until I recognized that Davidson kid—the one who cheated in my class. I guess the generals love him now."

"I know exactly how you feel about football, Professor, and most of the cadets agree with you. West Point has made a deal with the devil. Somehow the brass thinks it's okay to compromise our standards—not just academic, but moral too, all for the sake of beating Navy."

Goldstein and Zhao carefully rechecked their gear. The plan today: penetrate the wreck. Goldstein brought specialized gear: wire cutters to clear the way in, sample bags outfitted with inflatable balloons to raise artifacts to the surface, strobe lights, and polyethylene guiding line to help them find their way out.

Haskins watched them closely, but said nothing. His face betrayed no emotions behind his aviator sunglasses. Goldstein sensed Haskins's suspicion, but Haskins would ask questions only when he thought he'd get answers.

Setting out onto the river, they easily found the anomaly on the depth finder and dropped anchor. Zhao and Goldstein did one last check on their gear, reviewed their dive plan, and splashed over the side. They descended quickly and found the anchor had snagged on the sub itself, just aft of the opening and associated wreckage. They briefly searched a debris field adjacent to the gaping hole in the sub.

Goldstein entered the sub first. The opening was extremely tight. He trimmed a few wires and squeezed in. He moved very deliberately, careful not to be snagged by wires or pieces of jagged metal. He meticulously maintained neutral buoyancy to avoid contacting and disturbing the silt that coated every surface.

Playing his torch across the wreckage, Goldstein found a pipe at the entrance and clipped a reel of polyethylene line to it. It would unspool as he went deeper into the wreck. Goldstein also activated a strobe light, which he secured at the entrance. Should they become disoriented, both the strobe lights and polyethylene line would guide them back to the entrance, and survival.

Goldstein moved cautiously deeper into the wreck. Zhao followed close behind. She had an athletic grace but only limited wreck experience, and she occasionally touched the floor or walls of the wreck with a flipper, raising billows of silt. Goldstein tried to stay relaxed and ignore her missteps.

They found themselves in a large room with pieces of mangled equipment. Whatever had blown up inside the sub had largely destroyed the fitting. Goldstein swam over to the remains of the periscope. The base was partially intact, and a small metal plate was visible.

Gently brushing away the silt with his glove, Goldstein read the inscription: "Blohm & Voss, Hamburg." As he stared at the plate, Goldstein felt a shiver down his spine. Blohm und Voss: the storied German manufacturers of submarines and ships—most famously the *Bismarck*.

There could be no doubt now. This was no Russian Whiskey-class submarine—this was a Nazi U-boat!—from World War II. Hands shaking, Goldstein used a screwdriver to pry the plate free.

Goldstein had known in his heart that Zhao was right about the wreck, but he was baffled by its existence. What was a Nazi U-boat doing in New York, in the Hudson River, opposite West Point?

Zhao and Goldstein locked eyes.

Goldstein scribbled "OK! Type XXI" on the white board.

Zhao gave him a thumbs up, drew a small swastika on the board, and wrote "Told you!"

They spent the next few minutes exploring the compartment, searching for artifacts. They were careful not to disturb the large gray lumps on the floor that might be human remains. Goldstein found several pieces of encrusted metal, one of which appeared to be a knife. Zhao grabbed a heavily encrusted ceramic plate and put it into the sample bag.

Before they knew it, they were short on air. Despite the silt that Zhao had stirred up, the visibility was adequate. They returned carefully along the line they had laid, retrieved the strobe light, and carefully swam back through the opening. As they waited to decompress at fifty feet, Goldstein pointed up at the boat and made the shushing sign. He wrote on the white board "Let's talk in private."

After the long decompression, they hauled themselves up on the dive boat where Captain Haskins waited. They put on long faces and did their best to hide their exultation.

Goldstein explained they had found some debris but nothing of interest. Haskins seemed disappointed that they hadn't found the chain, but didn't question them in any detail.

··· ▬ ▬▬▬ ·▬▬·

ZHAO AND GOLDSTEIN walked up from the dock to Library Corner, looking for somewhere to sit and be alone. They walked along the edge of the Plain, the main parade grounds, Zhao careful to stay on the paths. Cadets walking on the grass could receive punishment hours. They found an empty bench beneath a bronze statue of a helmeted general with pistols at his waist and binoculars around his neck. Goldstein imagined that he was protecting them, looking out for trouble. Before they could speak, a major stopped to look at the statue. Zhao jumped to her feet and gave a snappy salute. Finally, he wandered off. At last out of the earshot of others, they couldn't contain themselves. Goldstein and Zhao exchanged whoops of triumph and high fives.

"My God, Zhao! You were right, it's a U-boat—a Type XXI."

"We should go the commandant right now," said Zhao.

Goldstein held up both palms. "Not so fast. We need to control the message here. I'm not sure if the commandant is the first person we should tell. We might be better to submit a brief publication to *The Journal of Maritime Archeology*, as a place marker, then hold a press conference."

"Press conference? No, no. This is the Army. Everything needs to go through proper channels. You know how the Army would feel about a press conference, Professor."

"Okay, okay. It's the weekend, we don't have to do anything right away. The sub has been there forever. The more information we have the better. We need to present ourselves as professionals, not two random divers who stumbled on a wreck. Let's give it some thought. See if you can find anything about Type XXI U-boat missions and I'll make a few phone calls. We have to be able to come up with some idea of what this thing is doing here. Where's a good place to meet on Tuesday night?"

"I'll meet you at The Firstie Club, 2000 hours. The music is a bit loud, but we can have a booth to ourselves."

They stood to leave. "Who is that guy?" asked Goldstein, pointing at the statue behind them.

"George S. Patton, class of '09," answered Zhao reflexively. "It's part of the mandatory cadet knowledge. Apparently, he was a better general than student; they say he is facing away from the library because he never went inside."

"I feel like he's looking out for us, Zhao. Trust me, we're doing the right thing here."

Zhao shook her head. "I hope you are right, sir. We're playing with live ordnance."

Zhao headed back to her barracks and Goldstein to his office, both intent on unraveling the mystery that lurked in the dark river below them.

EIGHTEEN

The forty freighters and six escorts of Convoy HX 320 sailed out of New York bound for Liverpool. High winds and enormous rolling waves made life miserable for the deck crews of escort vessels and merchantmen alike. Ships were lifted to the top of each wave, and then plunged down into the trough, burying their prows in the churning ocean. To go overboard was certain death. Men clung to the railings, lashed to their posts with icicles hanging from their beards. Those men lucky enough to serve below decks fought a losing battle with seasickness, vomiting bile from their empty stomachs.

At 40 meters, the cold sea was still and the submarine moved ahead, unaffected by the storm. The Type XXI U-boat was the first vessel to be faster submerged than on the surface. Unlike the Type IXC long-range boat she replaced, the Type XXI boat had a streamlined contour. Enormous banks of batteries fed power to a pair of powerful electric motors.

The Funkmeister monitoring the hydrophones detected the

throbbing noise generated by the freighters' propellers beating against the ocean. "Herr Korvettenkapitän! We have a sound contact, multiple ships. Sounds like a convoy. Approximately five to ten kilometers, almost dead in front of us!"

"Maintain our depth and heading!" said Reichman

"But, Herr Kapitän, shall we at least bring the boat to periscope depth? If Providence has put these lambs in our way, shouldn't the lion strike them?" said the XO, Karlson.

"Very poetic, my dear Karlson. I'm afraid not this time. Our orders are very explicit: avoid all contact. We have bigger fish to fry than a few thousand tons of merchant shipping."

The convoy and U-555 passed less than a mile from each other and then continued on to their separate destinies.

Cruising at fourteen knots, the U-boat's passage from Bremen across the North Atlantic was uneventful. Since 1943, U-boats traveling west on the surface followed the route north of Iceland, through the Denmark Strait. The detour added two days to the voyage, but reduced the chance of contact with Allied surface vessels or aircraft. By 1944, the VLR Liberator bomber equipped with HSV III centimetric radar had made the North Atlantic passage a near death sentence for U-boat crewmen, but the Type XXI boat was a game changer. On this voyage, Reichman charted a direct course across the North Atlantic.

The Type XXI remained submerged during the voyage, operating with battery power. Periodically, the batteries would run down and, Reichman would bring the U-Boat close enough to the surface to extended the snorkel. The ten meter telescoping tube allowed the submerged U-Boat to run the diesel engine and recharge the batteries. Under a blanket of cold dark seawater, U-555 was invisible to radar when fully submerged and proceeded without risk of detection.

The snorkel was a huge improvement, but imperfect. While almost impossible to spot with the naked eye, the snorkel could be detected by the Allies' HSV III ultrashort wave radar. The Germans had countered the ultrashort wave radar with the

Naxos Radar Warning System. Naxos could detect search radar up to four kilometers away. In theory, this allowed the U-boat time to withdraw the snorkel before they were spotted visually by aircraft. Even undetected by radar, the snorkel was a threat. If it malfunctioned, the diesel fumes would flood the sub and rapidly asphyxiate the crew. The men were always alert and anxious when the snorkel was up.

Krause and Krieger shared a closet-like compartment, barely large enough for their bunks. They passed the days in the ward room, reading and getting on each other's nerves. Krieger read old copies of the *Völkischer Beobachter*. He freely quoted Goebbels and lectured Krause on the genetic superiority of the Aryan Race and the necessity of destroying the Jews.

Krause had no love for the Jews, nor hatred. He just didn't know any. He hadn't met any in Kansas or at West Point. Krieger, on the other hand, seethed with anger: it was directed at communists, Russian, Poles, Americans, traitors, weaklings, defeatists, and shirkers, but mostly at the Jews. Krause wondered how much of the murderous rage was related to the Pervitin capsules Krieger swallowed by the handful. Krieger couldn't live without Pervitin. The smallest provocation, and he would fly into a frenzy.

Krieger was a strangely self-educated intellectual. He'd been expelled from school after he'd beaten a vagrant to death, and joined the SS. He'd read some philosophy and was familiar with Shakespeare, although he had only read it in a clunky German translation. Krieger had a small collection of Shakespearean quotations which supported his twisted world view. He would frequently end a conversation with Krause with his favorite: "War gives the conquerors the right to impose any condition they please upon the vanquished." Krause recognized it as Julius Caesar. He was appalled by Krieger's world view. The more time Krause spent with Krieger, the less faith he had in National Socialism and the future of Hitler's Germany.

"Tell me, Herr Hauptmann, I am not completely convinced of

your commitment to the ultimate triumph of National Socialism. If I asked you, would you repeat the oath you swore to the Führer?" prodded Krieger.

"I have no need to convince you. You have no right to command me to repeat that oath, Sturmbannführer. I've sworn it. My commitment to Germany and my *Kameraden* is unshakable."

"A commitment to comrades in arms or the German nation is not the same as an absolute commitment to our Führer. I may have to report you to the Reichsführer-SS when we return"

"Listen, Sturmbannführer, there are two outcomes of this mission. If we succeed, we will change history and Dr. Goebbels will celebrate us as the greatest heroes in the history of German Arms. Somehow, I don't think your concerns about my loyalty to the Führer will impress anyone."

"And if we fail?"

"Neither of us is coming home, and it will hardly matter."

Several hours after passing the convoy, Reichman knew it was time to extend the snorkel and run the diesel engine. He had no choice. The air in the boat was foul, the batteries needed to be recharged, and using the snorkel was by far safer than running on the surface.

Chief Engineer Mueller, a squat man with black hair and beard, turning to gray, waited impatiently while Korvettenkapitän Reichman studied a chart in the control room. "It's time, Herr Korvettenkapitän. We are down to ten percent power."

Reichman nodded and barked to the executive officer, Karlson, "Periscope depth Number One."

"*Jawohl*, Herr Korvettenkapitän."

"Give me one-half ahead. Bow up ten degrees." The boat slowed and, with the slight angulation of the hydroplanes, U-555 glided upward, holding at fifteen meters below the surface.

"Wide angle scope up." Reichman pressed his forehead to the rubber eyepiece and spun three hundred and sixty degrees, scanning the empty gray sky. He always marveled at the optics. Of course, he reminded himself, it's a Zeiss. Satisfied with his search, Reichman called, "Deploy the snorkel!"

The crew waited eagerly for the cool air from outside to circulate into the dank control room.

"Radar man. Snorkel is deployed. Is Naxos functioning?" asked Reichman.

"*Jawohl*, Herr Korvettenkapitän. The Naxos system is operational."

Seconds ticked by and there was still no rush of cold air.

Chief Engineer Mueller manipulated the snorkel controls. After a few minutes of tense work, Mueller saluted Reichman. "Herr Korvettenkapitän, I regret to inform you, the snorkel is not operational. It is fully deployed, but the pressure is very high and the airflow minimal. I think the valve is jammed."

Before Reichman could answer, Krieger appeared in the control room. "Nonoperational?" He fumed.

Mueller started to speak, but Reichman cut him off. "Prepare to surface. All the crew to alert."

Krieger thundered, "This is sabotage! Treason! Who is responsible? Bring them to me!"

"No," Reichman answered, "you are wrong. This is what happens when you take a new boat out without a sea trial. We have no choice. We are out of battery power. If we run the diesels with the snorkel valve jammed, we will be dead in a matter of minutes. We need to surface and recharge the batteries. Once we are up there, we can troubleshoot."

Reichman put on oilskins, and the four lookouts jammed into the control room, ready to go on deck. Chief Engineer Mueller began to dress for the surface, but Reichman stopped him.

"Stay down here, Chief—you are getting a bit old for this. Send up your number two."

Mueller looked pointedly at Krieger. "With respect, sir, I owe it to my brothers here, and my honor."

"And the Führer," added Krieger.

"As I said," said Mueller, pulling on his foul-weather gear.

With the deck crew in readiness, Reichman ordered the boat to the surface. The lookouts scrambled up the ladder in the conning tower, spun open the hatch, and leaped into position. They scanned the four quadrants of the sky like men whose lives depended on it.

Mueller had the main vents opened, and the diesel engine roared to life. Cool air circulated in the boat. Power began to surge into the depleted batteries.

"Ahead full!" ordered Reichman.

Karlson started up the ladder, but Reichman pulled him back.

"It will be very tight up there, No. 2. I'll go up and keep an eye on Mueller while he checks out the snorkel."

Mueller and Reichman climbed up onto the bridge. As they got their footing, the boat pitched down off a wave, and they were lashed with freezing spray. Water swirled around their waists, then drained quickly away. When the boat steadied briefly, Mueller, his tool belt at his waist, unclipped his harness and climbed up on the superstructure to inspect the balky snorkel, carefully clipping to the new location.

Mueller, lashed by the ocean waves, gripped the snorkel and peered into the snorkel mouth. "A piece of *Schornsteinfeger*! Blocking the valve!" Mueller shouted. The *Schornsteinfeger*, or "Chimney Sweep," was an experimental composite applied to the snorkel to reduce the radar signature. Mueller stripped away the decaying composite, pulled the pieces from the snorkel, and swept the shredded pieces into the dark Atlantic.

At that moment, the loss of a portion of the radar-dampening *Schornsteinfeger* seemed like a small price to pay for a functioning snorkel. Much relieved, Reichman ordered the boat down to snorkel depth. The streamlined U-555 slipped completely beneath the waves and, with its diesel engines throbbing, continued on its stealthy journey toward unsuspecting New York.

NINETEEN

Korvettenkapitän Reichman, Sturmbannführer Krieger, and Hauptmann Krause stood in the control room of U-555. They were ten meters below the surface. They had traveled almost four thousand miles submerged, surfacing only once when the snorkel had malfunctioned. Reichman studied the shore lights through the periscope.

"Can you see the harbor, Herr Korvettenkapitän?" asked Krieger

"Not yet. We'll swing around this peninsula, turn north, and run parallel to Brooklyn, and follow the Ambrose Channel," answered Reichman.

"Are there shore lights?" asked Krause.

"*Ja*, very bright. Not much different than our mission here in 1942 with U-123."

After the terrible losses inflicted by U-boats on American coastal shipping in 1942 during *Unternehmen Paukenschlag*, the United States had responded by introducing a coastal blackout.

Now, after three years without U-boat activity, and no threat of aerial bombing, the city lights were back to normal.

"Those silly Americans are too busy enjoying their Jazz to defend their harbor," jeered Krieger.

"Complacent or not, I'm concerned about the antisubmarine barrier at the mouth of the inner harbor. If it is in place, we have absolutely no chance of entering the harbor," said Reichman.

"Our asset in Staten Island tells us that it is routinely left open, and only closed when an alarm is sounded," said Krieger. "Admiral Dönitz assured Brigadeführer Schellenberg that on a moonless night we can cruise on the surface, right through the front door."

"On the surface? That's insane!" said Krieger.

"We will run submerged on electric power with the periscope through the Ambrose Channel. That should allow us to escape detection by surface radar. When we are a few kilometers from the Narrows of Staten Island, we must surface."

"But why don't we stay underwater?" asked Krause thoughtfully.

Reichman laughed gruffly and shook his head. "I'm not a magician! We can't sail blindly underwater through a narrow harbor mouth. My view through the periscope at night isn't good enough to avoid obstacles. The moon doesn't rise until 2130. The window is narrow, but at seventeen knots, we should make it to West Point before moonrise. As we enter the Verrazano Narrows, we will have to make a high-speed run on the surface and hope we catch them napping!"

"Like Günther Prien, *Der Stier von Scapa Flow*! The bull of Scapa Flow!" exclaimed Krieger. In 1940, Kapitänleutnant Prien had guided U-47 through a forty-meter wide gap in the defenses at the Royal Navy's Anchorage at Scapa Flow. Once inside the harbor, he sank the battleship *Royal Oak*. Prien won the *Ritterkreuz* and became a tabloid sensation in Germany.

"*Genau*," said Krause, nodding. "I read his book, *Mein Weg nach Scapa Flow—My Way to Scapa Flow*."

"Prien was my friend, and a very brave man. Too brave," Reichman said. "But he paid for his audacity. With his life."

A silence fell over the group.

Reichman cleared his throat. "By my calculations, it's fifteen kilometers from here to the Narrows. At seventeen knots, we can be there in about twenty-five minutes. Now, gentlemen, our adventure begins. Let's hope we are right about those antisubmarine nets! XO Karlson!"

"*Jawohl*, Korvettenkapitän!"

"Sound the alarm! Dive the boat, and bring us to snorkel depth."

"*Jawohl.*"

"*Willkommen* in New York!"

••• – ––– •––•

LESS THAN THREE KILOMETERS AWAY, four young American seamen and a petty officer sat in a ferroconcrete bunker sealed with an airlock. They manned posts in the Harbor Defense Command Center in Fort Tilden, Rockaway Point, New York. It was the nerve center for the defenses covering the eastern approaches to New York Harbor. The blockhouse was unheated, and the men wore heavy coats, hats, and gloves.

The seamen were bored, trying to stay awake by playing endless rounds of gin with worn playing cards, wondering when the shift would end, and keeping a desultory eye on the outputs they were assigned to monitor.

Nothing interesting had ever happened on their guard shifts. And they expected nothing ever would. In theory, New York Harbor was protected by multiple sophisticated electronic systems designed to detect intruders. Admirals and government contractors displayed impressive maps of the overlapping networks. But each was plagued with technical difficulties, false alarms, and poor inter-service communication.

Underwater microphones detected the sound of propellers, even at great distances. But they provided neither range nor bearing on the contacts. The seamen ignored the frequent alarms, assuming they were false. They always were. The SCR-582 surface radar was capable of detecting ships at a range of forty-five miles, when it was working. But it was unreliable, and often broken.

The mainstay of harbor defense was the electronic loop detectors. Multiple cable loops crisscrossed the floor of the harbor approaches, extending from Fort Hancock on Sandy Hook in New Jersey to Fort Tilden on Rockaway Point in Brooklyn. The steel hulls of ships and submarines are mildly magnetic, and as they passed over the cable, their magnetic fields induced a detectable electrical flux in the cable. An unscheduled or unannounced ship was obvious; it would be immediately intercepted, illuminated with search lights, and challenged.

If an intruder was detected, an alarm went out. Powerful winches would pull massive steel nets across the Verrazano Narrows to block the harbor entrance.

Petty Officer Steven Jacobs worked on the *New York Times* crossword puzzle. The three sailors played gin and casually monitored the readout from the indicator loop, radar, and hydrophones. In civilian life, Jacobs taught math at a junior high in Coney Island. After Pearl Harbor, he enlisted in the Navy, hoping to avoid serving in the infantry. A high score on the service aptitude test had sent him into the signal branch.

Most of the other graduates of the Navy Signal School deployed to the Pacific on radar pickets ships. These pickets had proved to be favorite targets for Japanese Kamikaze aircraft. Several of Jacobs' classmates had already been killed. He was bored and cold, sitting in the windowless concrete bunker, but grateful for a posting where he wasn't risking his life.

At 1930 hours, as U-555 cruised up the Ambrose Channel toward the Narrows, the invisible electromagnet waves from the SCR-582 surface radar struck the U-boat's snorkel. Most of the beam was muffled by the *Schornsteinfeger*, the decaying radar-absorbing coating. But Mueller had stripped off some of the defective coating when it had jammed the snorkel. Now the bare metal of the snorkel reflected back radar waves.

The enlisted sailor monitoring the SCR-582 noticed a faint blip in the Ambrose Channel.

Heading toward the harbor.

"Sir, I have a signal on the radar in the channel!"

Petty Officer Jacobs, engrossed in his puzzle, barely looked up. "Lots of anomalies on the radar, Seaman. Keep an eye on it." Everyone knew the SCR-582 was a buggy system, endlessly mistaking floating debris for a ship.

"Hydrophones detecting propeller activity!" reported the second sailor.

"Meaning...exactly nothing. Probably a fishing boat out of Seabright," muttered Jacobs, stymied and annoyed by his stupid job and his impenetrable crossword. "Keep an eye on it."

Annoyed by the interruptions, and unable to solve 5 Down, he turned to the sailor monitoring the indicator loop. "So, any flux in the loop?" he asked. "Also, five letters, band leader?"

"No, sir!" responded the sailor. "And five letters? Benny! Benny Goodman!"

"Strong work, sailor."

But the men of Harbor Entrance Control did not know that earlier that evening, merchant ship *John Mahedy* had traversed the Ambrose Channel, sloppily dragging its uncoiled anchor line. The *Mahedy*'s anchor snagged the loop cable, dragged it a dozen yards, and then snapped it, tearing a two-thousand-yard gap in the electrical early-warning system for New York Harbor.

The *Mahedy*'s alcoholic captain, fearing yet another sanction would cost him his job, declined to report it.

"Must be a bug in the radar. No way the loop fails to pick it up." Petty Officer Jacobs debated calling an alarm. Jacobs remembered the last time he shut the sub gates for an anomaly, he had a rear admiral up his ass about delaying convoy traffic to

Europe. Jacobs typed up an entry about yet another false signal on the radar and hydrophones, and returned to his crossword. "Famous Jewish physicist...8 Across—this is impossible!"

... – ––– .––.

WHEN U-555 WAS a few kilometers from the Narrows, Reichman ordered it to the surface and up to flank speed. Reichman, Krause, and Krieger crowded the bridge of U-555 as it knifed through the still waters of the lower bay. It was dazzling. The lights of Coney Island Amusement Park! Most of Europe lay in ruins, and the Americans were riding roller coasters and merry-go-rounds!

The bay funneled inwards, and the sea in front shrank to a tight passage through the Narrows. The heights of Staten Island loomed up on their left, and they could see Fort Wadsworth and a few small ships anchored at the Narrows. An automobile with undimmed headlights raced along the Belt Parkway on the Brooklyn Shore.

When they had just one thousand meters' clearance on either side, it seemed they must be spotted, until, holding their breath, they sped through into the waters of the inner bay.

"We're through!" exulted Reichman.

"Grossadmiral Dönitz was right! These Americans are like children! They know nothing of war!" thundered Krieger. "Merry-go-rounds! Coaster-rollers!"

The skyscrapers of lower Manhattan twinkled ahead of them, reflected in the still waters. Now that they were through the harbor defenses, they just needed a small run of good fortune to run up the river without detection.

A ferry bound for Staten Island appeared well to their starboard. "Even if they see us, they will assume we are part of normal harbor traffic," said Reichman.

Looming out of the darkness on their left was a towering

statue, a single arm raised in triumph with a flame flickering in the torch it held aloft.

"*Die Freiheitstatue. Das ist fantastisch!*" murmured Reichman

Yes, it is, thought Krause, remembering an afternoon he had spent on the harbor as a West Point cadet many years before. Maybe it was a sign? Was there a way he could go back to his old life?

Krause kept silent, keeping his thoughts his own, as U-555 glided up the peaceful cliff-lined Hudson River.

TWENTY

Tuesday evening, Zhao left MacArthur Barracks, nodding at the cadet on duty as she passed his desk. It had been three days since they had made their last dive on the U-boat. It was hard to think of anything else. She had to convince Dr. Goldstein to bring their discovery to the commandant. Zhao set out for The Firstie Club, the beer hall on campus exclusively for seniors. She crossed the central cadet area, a barren and depressing courtyard that resembled the exercise yard of a high-security prison. A few miserable cadets in full dress uniform, with rifles on their shoulders, marched robotically back and forth across the cobble stones, serving out punishment hours. Zhao ducked through an archway onto the vast grass-covered Plain.

Zhao waved to a group of cadets in physical-fitness uniforms and reflective belts, leaving Arvin Gymnasium and headed out for a run. It was never too late or too cold to exercise at West Point. As she passed the Academic Dean's cottage, Zhao was joined by a boisterous group of cadets angling toward the Beat Navy pedestrian tunnel and headed for the Firstie for beer and relaxation.

They emerged from the dank tunnel, turned right down the hill, and then entered a low-slung building with an unmarked entrance. The Firstie, or First Class Club, was the only place at West Point where cadets could legally drink. Some cadets smuggled booze into their rooms; Zhao thought they were crazy. She liked getting a buzz on, but certainly wasn't going to risk one hundred hours of marching back and forth in dress uniform for a shot of illicit tequila.

Zhao displayed her military ID card to the cadet manning the entrance desk and went into the dark bar. The cadets shouted over a foot-stomping country-and-western anthem. It took a moment for her eyes to adjust. Groups of muscular, male cadets pounded back pitchers of beer and flirted with the townie girls serving burgers and fries. Every few graduations, a senior cadet, a future Army officer, married one of the barmaids; a girl could hope. And a guy could go for it.

Zhao spotted Goldstein in a corner booth and slid in across from him as a heavily made-up young waitress appeared. "You owe me a beer—or have you decided that Blohm und Voss, Hamburg built Whiskey-class subs for the Russians!" said Zhao.

Goldstein smiled at Zhao. "Soldier, scuba diver, skydiver, and humorist. You have so many talents, Zhao."

He turned to the waitress. "Two Sam Adams, please."

"And food? To eat?"

"Do you have truffle fries?"

The waitress gave him a quizzical look.

"Okay. Fries, please."

The waitress turned away to the bar.

Goldstein leaned over toward Zhao

"Okay, Zhao, you were right, it's a U-boat—Type XXI. I was wrong. You were right. Okay, the beer is on me, but we still need to keep a lid on this."

"Keep a lid on what? That I was right and you were wrong?"

"Never going to happen again."

"Seriously, we need to tell the commandant. Why keep it a secret? This is starting to feel like an honor-code violation. Remember the parts about not lying, cheating, or stealing. It's not our sub, and we can't just keep it secret. It's a good thing. We just made the greatest underwater find since they located the *Titanic*! We're famous, or will be a couple of hours from now."

"Take it easy, Zhao. I did some digging today. There is something very odd going on. I checked with a colleague at the Naval War College. He had never heard of a Type XXI U-boat lost in American waters, but here, look at this."

Goldstein opened his L.L.Bean briefcase and pulled out a ceramic plate. In the center, there was a black eagle with a swastika suspended in its claws. Along the bottom it was marked U-555.

He handed it to Zhao, who let out a low whistle and handed it back.

"Keep it. You found it. I just cleaned it. There will be plenty more when we go back inside."

Zhao burst out, "Back inside? Are you nuts? You were the one scared to penetrate the wreck! We have an answer—we even know what specific sub this is! Goldstein, listen. We have to go to the commandant and tell him what we found!"

A few cadets heard the words "Go to the commandant," and as one their heads swiveled to Zhao and Goldstein.

Goldstein stared daggers at Zhao.

The waitress returned with the beers and fries. She hesitated for a moment before leaving.

"Listen," said Goldstein, lowering his voice. "You said it yourself. This is the biggest find since the *Titanic*, and there is something extraordinary going on. I checked with the U-boat archives in Cuxhaven. The file for U-555 was removed from the archives in 1945. The record shows that it was turned over to the OSS."

"OSS—what's that?" asked Zhao.

"Office of Strategic Services—it's what they used to call the CIA."

"I think you watched *The Hunt for Red October* too many times."

Goldstein ignored her. "It's possible that we captured it at the end of the war, but didn't want the Russians—or the British, for that matter—to know. Remember in 1945, the Type XXI was the most advanced submarine in the world. Hell, even in 1960, it was pretty much state of the art."

Zhao looked skeptical. "But there were twenty other Type XXI subs made, and the British and the Russians both had access to one of those."

"True," he said. "My best guess is that U-555 was on a special mission. In 1945, we captured U-234 it on its way to Japan. It was carrying five hundred and forty kilos of uranium oxide. That's enough to make 3.5 kg of uranium-235—about a quarter of an atomic bomb! We kept that secret from the Russians until 1965! Whatever it is, the CIA thinks it's important enough to stop anyone from finding out. Look, I want to make one more dive before we go public. I'm pretty sure that once we break the story, the government is going to shut us down. Keep the plate, but don't show it to anyone. Let's ask Haskins to get us the boat for one more dive. This is bigger than naval history, Zhao—we're going to rewrite the history of World War II."

Zhao hesitated, then nodded agreement. She thoughtfully reached for a French fry.

"Third time's a charm," said Goldstein. "Trust me."

Those words would come back to haunt her.

TWENTY-ONE

Cathy Howell looked in the mirror and admired the cut of her new top. Silk was unobtainable in the stores, but her friend Carl had somehow found it on the black market, and had triumphantly presented it to her. Carl was sweet that way. He was good-looking too, but he was married. She wondered what he'd given his wife. Cathy knew she could do better than him, she always had.

Cathy had always had her choice in men. She still did, in a way. But there just weren't many men around. Three-quarters of workers at Remington Arms were women and the others were geriatric. Now, in 1945, with the U.S. Army vacuuming up manpower to patch the hole torn in the Army at the Battle of the Bulge, there were fewer uniformed men around as well.

She didn't feel like going to her sister Betty's birthday party at that snooty Sleepy Hollow Country Club. It would be the same crowd talking about golf and complaining about rations. There were never any new men at these parties. Still, the country club managed to always have liquor available, and if she didn't get out, she'd never meet anyone.

Looking in the mirror, she made an impulsive decision. She decided her glasses made her look schoolmarmish. She'd leave them home. It was only a few blocks away. Besides, she had learned, sometimes in life it was better for things to be a little blurry.

She left her bedroom and turned into Kevin's small room. His bed was neatly made and he sat intently at his desk, drawing a picture. Kevin was only seven, but he had inherited his father's brilliance and focus. He could sit for hours flipping through a picture book or playing with his models.

"What are you drawing, sweetkins?" Cathy asked. Kevin didn't react to the question and kept drawing. "Sweetkins. You have to look at my face. You have to answer me."

Cathy couldn't put a name on it, but it was clear to her that Kevin didn't interact with people the way most kids did. After his father left, he seemed to get worse. He never smiled and didn't like to be hugged. He was a bright boy and he could stay focused for hours with this books and models. He knew every aircraft in the American, British, Japanese, and German Airforce, and had notebooks crammed with clippings and drawings.

Recently, Kevin had shifted his obsession to ships. He read every book in the community library about naval vessels. "It's a U-boat. Mom, a German submarine."

"It's a very nice drawing. We need to go over to Sleepy Hollow now for Aunt Betty's party." She handed Kevin the first model she reached for, a tank of some sort. "And here! You can bring a model with you. But just one."

Without her glasses, she could barely make out his face, but she knew the blank look on it. It never varied. "It's a Sherman. The gun is a 75 mm. I'd rather bring my battleship," said Kevin, carefully restoring the tank to its proper position and selecting a ship. "And don't touch my models, Mom. You always set them down wrong."

"Good choice! Remember the last time we went to the country club, you talked to the man about tanks?" Kevin didn't connect well to people, but he could talk endlessly about planes, ships, and tanks.

"Mom. Two things. I will bring two. I will bring this one: Battleship Missouri. And I want to bring my binoculars."

She knew better than to argue. When he got angry, he was intractable. "Yes, Kevin. And we can stop and look out at the river traffic before we go into the party. It will be dark soon."

She sighed and took Kevin by the hand. They crossed the street and walked up the long tree-lined driveway to the country club, gorgeous in the golden light of the setting sun.

Originally built as a Vanderbilt family mansion, Sleepy Hollow had been converted to an elite private club just before World War I. Early members included the Astors and the Rocke-fellers. During the war years, the club had fallen on hard times, but the mansion was beautiful and commanded sweeping views of the river.

They paused on the terrace and looked out on the Hudson. Without her glasses, the landscape was a blur to Cathy. Scanning the Hudson with a pair of cheap binoculars, Kevin could see the brown cliffs of the Palisades that loomed over the west shore of the river. Looking north, he could see Anthony's Nose where the Bear Mountain Bridge spanned the Hudson and the Highlands began.

The setting sun glinted on the river and the wake from a tugboat and oil barge rippled. Kevin was disappointed that there were no Navy ships to see, and after a few minutes they went inside. The birthday party was a small affair, mostly family, a few children, and older friends. As Cathy had predicted, there were no young men to flirt with, and no dancing. Cathy consoled herself with a couple of gin and tonics.

By nine, the party was breaking up.

··· ─ ─── ·──·

Down on the river below Sleepy Hollow, U-555 raced up the Hudson, Reichman and Karlson on the bridge. To Reichman's dismay, they had miscalculated moonrise, and the full moon appeared on the horizon, casting an eerie glow on the river. After passing through a vast, open stretch of water, labeled "Tappan Zee" on the chart, the river had again narrowed to less than two kilometers, with tall cliffs on the west shore. It reminded Reichman very much of the Rhine, near Köln, but he had no time to focus on the natural beauty before him.

"*Scheiss!*" said Reichman. "This moonlight! Thank God there are no patrol vessels." He called down to the engine room and urged Chief Mueller to coax every possible horsepower out of the diesels.

"*Mein Gott*, I'm sorry! We're close to West Point, Herr Korvettenkapitän," said Karlson. "In just one hour, we'll be safely on the river bottom!"

··· ─ ─── ·──·

Up at the country club, Cathy went over to collect her son and head home. Kevin sat by himself, deeply engrossed in a drawing of an aircraft carrier. "That's very good, Kevin! Look how many guns it has."

"The guns are just for defense, Mom! To protect it from the Jap aircraft!" Kevin sounded exasperated and pointed at the drawing. "We use our torpedo bombers and dive bombers to attack the Japs!"

Cathy nodded and sighed. "That's right! Well, time for us to go home, Admiral. It's past your bedtime."

"Can we look at river on our way home, Mom?" asked Kevin.

"Of course." He was being so good on such a disappointing evening. Cathy took Kevin by the hand and headed out onto the mansion patio. A rising moon illuminated the landscape and glinted off the river. Kevin raised his binoculars to his eyes.

He screamed, "Mom—it's a submarine!"

Out in the Hudson, U-555's diesels throbbed, and her stream-lined hull knifed through the water at twenty knots.

Without her glasses, Cathy couldn't see anything. The river, the mountains, were all a blur.

"But Mom, look!" Kevin jumped up and down, pointing. He tracked the submarine with his binoculars as the moonlit shape glided up the river. "You have to see it! You must!"

"I'm sorry, Kevin, honey, I just don't." What was he seeing?

After a few moments, the submarine vanished northward, leaving only ripples in the water.

Cathy and Kevin walked down the club driveway and headed home, Kevin chattering nonstop the entire way. Cathy was fairly sure it was all Kevin's imagination, but the boy was persistent. When they got home, he made a drawing of the sub and flipped through all of his books on ships.

"It was a U-boat, Mom! I'm sure of it," he repeated, pacing back and forth in his room. "We need to call the Navy and have them send a destroyer to depth charge it!"

Cathy hadn't seen anything at all on the river, but she knew how Kevin's mind worked. The only way she got him into bed was by promising she would call the Navy in the morning. Long after Cathy fell asleep, Kevin lay awake in his bed clutching his battleship model and pretending to depth charge the U-boat.

... - --- .--.

As KEVIN TOSSED and turned in his bed, U-555 continued upriver. Nearing Charles Point, Reichman saw a huge industrial complex on the east shore. A strong, sweet smell hung in the air, and a sign declared it to be the Fleischman's Yeast factory. Heavily forested cliffs rose steeply on both sides of the river. The Hudson narrowed to five hundred meters, and the graceful Bear Mountain Bridge loomed overhead.

Stupid Amis, thought Reichman, why build an enormous bridge in the middle of a forest?

Krause pointed at the bridge. "This is where the Amis tried to block the river when they were fighting the revolution against the British. They called it Fort Montgomery and they strung a great chain across the river."

"Did it work?" asked Krieger.

"No, not really. They only managed to delay the British for a few hours," answered Krause, "but somehow they think of it as a victory. They keep a piece of the chain at a place they call Trophy Point at the Military Academy. It's surrounded by cannons they captured in their wars with Spain and Mexico."

"Maybe you can show us the chain while we are stealing FDR out from under their noses," spat Krieger. "These Americans are so full of themselves. Those trophies are from wars with third-rate armies. Just once they should fight us on even terms. We'd teach them a lesson!"

The hair stood up on Krause's neck, but he held his tongue.

A few kilometers upriver, the Hudson bent sharply to the left and, on the cliffs high above the west bank of the river, they could see the fortress outline of Thayer Hall. Soaring above it, in the distance, the Cadet Chapel appeared like a Gothic cathedral. They'd made it!

"All stop!" barked Reichman. "Funkmeister, radio Berlin. Inform them that we are on station at West Point. Karlson, check the depth beneath our keel."

"Sixty meters, Herr Korvettenkapitän!"

"Clear the decks! Dive the boat!"

U-555 slipped gently beneath the Hudson and settled quietly on the river bottom, to wait.

••• ▬ ▬▬▬ •▬▬•

KEVIN WAS up at dawn and badgered his mother to call the police about the submarine. Cathy knew he'd be relentless, so she walked with Kevin to borrow the neighbor's phone. She dialed the police precinct, and reported the sighting of a submarine in the river. Kevin hung on her every word. The policeman was sympathetic, but seemingly more amused than interested.

He promised to forward a report to the relevant authorities. It hardly seemed to matter.

TWENTY-TWO

Sturmbannführer Krieger and Hauptmann Krause made their preparations in the officers' quarters of U-555. U-boat men lived like pigs. The crew never bathed or shaved; there was no room aboard for showers, sinks, or mirrors. Krause did a meticulous job shaving. He squatted on a crate of condensed milk with a bowl of warm water, a hand mirror, and a viciously sharp hand razor he'd had since the 1940 assault on Eben-Emael. Skorzeny had warned him that during *Unternehmen Greif*, the false-flag operation at the Bulge, Germans who had been captured in American uniforms were easily identified—wrong haircut, facial hair—and shot. When Krause had been a plebe at West Point, he'd spent thirty long hours marching punishment for one missing epaulet. The success or failure of the mission, and for Krause and Krieger, their lives, might depend on their appearance. Krause had come too far to be shot for side-burns that were a fraction too long.

Krause's gaze lingered on his image in the mirror. The war

had aged him some, but also given him a confident mien. He knew he could do what was necessary to succeed. Taking lives didn't thrill him, but he learned to kill without remorse when the situation demanded.

He had done well with women since West Point. His experiences with Peggy had taught him how to satisfy a woman in bed. He was not particular about looks; he favored the intelligence and independence that reminded him of Peggy. He had never found a girl that measured up to her. She had been energetic and uninhibited; his German girls were obedient, but inhibited. Peggy dreamed of seeing the world, but his German girlfriends wanted to have babies and keep house.

Seven years and many girls later, he often thought of Peggy, wondering where she was, and with whom. Had she married? Probably. Gone to college? Unlikely. Was she in love? Always, with someone, I'm sure, he laughed to himself. Peggy had been passionate and volatile, a thinker and a reader, questioning life as it was. She had strong opinions she was eager to discuss with him. The immorality of killing. Her father's brutish love of war. He wished that he had paid more attention to her philosophical leanings; he'd thought mostly about sex. But after he abandoned her so abruptly for Germany, he missed her terribly. He realized he had loved her as a person.

Krieger shaved and dressed, and meticulously sharpened his SS dagger with a whetstone. It was already sharp as a surgical scalpel, but he worked away, nonetheless. The shard of carbon steel was an extension of his hand. He had killed men—with a pistol, a submachine gun, grenades, and even with his bare hands. He preferred killing with his SS dagger. Silent and efficient, and very personal. Krieger got particular pleasure from his proximity to the victim, the quick, shocked struggle and the complete collapse.

Krause and Krieger put on identical four-pocket, four-button, olive drab 51 U.S. Officers' jackets, and carefully knotted the olive drab ties. They slipped on Russet Brown Type I shoes and sported U.S. officers' caps with gold and black piping. Their uniforms with the blue and red U.S. 1st Armored Division insignias had been captured at the Kasserine Pass. Each man wore a white and yellow ribbon for service in North Africa.

To his vast annoyance, Krieger wore the single silver bar of a 1st Lieutenant—he was outranked by Krause, who was a major. There was little choice. Their mission depended on Krause's English and familiarity with American military conduct.

The men checked, then rechecked, the mechanism of their Colt 1911A .45 caliber pistols. "It's not as elegant as a Luger," said Krause.

"It's heavy as hell," Krieger said, "but the stopping power should be excellent."

"There is no silencer."

"That's why I brought these," Krieger said, pulling out two silenced CZ27 pistols. They strapped them into ankle holsters.

The first-watch officer came into the officers' quarters. "It's time. No moon yet, no surface activity."

Krieger and Krause stepped through the watertight door into the overcrowded control room. Two torpedomen had manhandled an inflatable raft forward. Krieger unbuttoned his blouse pocket and pulled out a packet of pills. He swallowed two and offered the others to Krause.

"None for me, Sturmbannführer. I've never liked Pervitin."

"Relax, Krause, this is much better! They call it D-IX. It still has the methamphetamine, but they've added oxycodone and cocaine! You feel like you can fly!"

"None for me thanks. I'm afraid it will interfere with my English."

"Suit yourself. More for me!" Krieger gulped the second pair of capsules. He turned to Reichman. "Listen carefully, Korvettenkapitän—"

"I know," said Reichman, cutting him off. "At midnight, we do a periscope search for your signal light, every half hour until 0600."

"We should be back at the dock with the package by 0100. I will flash twice, then once, then twice." Krieger chuckled. "Why don't you have the cook do up a special meal for us when we return? We can dine with FDR! Pig knuckles and cabbages—yes, a good Bavarian dish for that Jew."

Reichman grimaced and was silent. After eighteen days of close proximity with Krieger, the Korvettenkapitän could barely stand his arrogance and racism.

Reichman did one more periscope search of the surface and turned to the watch officer. "Surface the boat."

"*Jawohl*, Herr Korvettenkapitän."

U-555's sleek hull gently breached the Hudson, and the lookouts scrambled up the ladder to the bridge. The torpedomen dragged up an inflatable rubber raft and paddles. As the crewmen worked to inflate the raft, Krieger and Krause scanned the shoreline, but saw no guards or activity. The vast stone towers of the U.S. Military Academy rose high above them, only a few hundred meters away.

They double-checked their uniforms and gear, and slipped into the raft, signaling the torpedomen to start rowing quietly. Minutes later they landed on a rocky beach just below Thayer Hall.

The lights of Cold Spring twinkled in the distance behind them as the raft returned to the U-boat. Krieger and Krause stepped briskly off the exposed shore into a forested area. Krause recognized the spot immediately, and led Krieger past the dock and across the railroad tracks, and up a path toward Thayer Hall, a cavernous structure built for horseback-riding instruction. The campus seemed unusually deserted. They headed for the Thayer Hotel.

They didn't speak. Krieger seemed even more menacing than usual. It was just after 1930 hours. By this time, the presidential ceremonies with FDR would be over, the president safely in the hotel, and the cadets confined to the barracks. As he passed the familiar landmarks of his West Point cadet years, Krause felt his breath quicken and his heart pound in his chest.

His mind flooded with memories of the bullies who had tormented him, and the roommates and teammates who refused to speak to him. Those bastards! No one had stood up to the injustice! They call themselves the land of the free, but they are as close-minded and hateful as the Bolsheviks! He had never fought against American troops, and up until now wasn't sure how he would feel, but the memories of the months of abuse infused him with rage. He would show them courage and loyalty, and how real men fought and stood by their comrades!

As angry as he was, Krause wondered if they could pull it off. Did Schellenberg think they could just bluff themselves past the array of guards that no doubt surrounded FDR? Besides that, the war was almost over! Anyone could see that. What were they going to accomplish? Maybe they had a chance of killing FDR. Even if they succeeded it would only bring further ruin on Germany.

Krause looked over at Krieger. He projected menace. Krause knew there was only one way they would return to that submarine and that was with Roosevelt as their prisoner. If the mission failed, either Krieger or the Americans would kill him. The briefing they had received from Schellenberg had few details of FDR's visit to West Point, other than that he was to address the cadets on the occasion of their Hundredth Night celebration. Schellenberg was sure that FDR would spend the night, most likely at the Thayer Hotel.

The Thayer, where visiting dignitaries were usually quartered, was the only decent accommodation within fifteen miles of the base. A few enlisted men in uniform snapped sharp salutes as they approached. The six-story, neo-Gothic granite and brick building, with a crenellated façade, had an enormous sign:

Welcome to the USMA West Point. Beat Navy!
Commandant Brig. General Henry Wilson.

Krause swallowed hard. He clutched at the ring he wore on the chain around his neck. Brig. General Wilson, Commandant of West Point! Wilson was still here! He was a Brigadier General and the Commandant. And Peggy, thought Krause, could she still be here? He had run off to Germany without even saying goodbye. He was ashamed. She was really just a child back then, but Krause had never felt as strongly about any other woman.

Memories of the Wilson's home flooded back. Cozy afternoons sipping iced tea and eating ice cream, listening to Colonel Wilson drone on about World War I, while playing footsie with Peggy under the table. Singing *Lieder* with Mrs. Wilson. Wild afternoons in the straw at the stable. Seven years ago, but it seemed like yesterday.

Krieger poked Krause in the ribs, jarring him from his reverie. The hotel loomed above them.

Where was the security? The faux-Gothic lobby was empty. Regimental flags hung from the walls. "Welcome Mr. President" signs, and tables and chairs were piled at the perimeter, the aftermath of a formal event. They'd missed whatever had happened. Or perhaps it hadn't happened at all.

There wasn't any security at all, just a single fat balding clerk behind the reception desk, looking at the photos in an old copy of *Life Magazine*. Krause gestured to Krieger to take a seat and walked over to the reception.

"Good evening, Major, how can I help you?" asked the clerk. "The bar is still open! Meeting some ladies?"

"Good evening. Seems very quiet here tonight," said Krause. "I thought the president was staying here?"

"Oh, I shouldn't tell you but—well, what a royal screw-up!" answered the clerk. "They booked out most of the hotel for FDR, and then at the last minute they canceled everything! Do you and the lieutenant need a room? We have plenty!"

"No, not exactly—I was ordered up here to brief the president."

"Something top secret, I bet!" said the clerk with a wink. He looked around to make sure no one else was listening in the lobby. "Well, I can let you in on something that might help you out, Colonel. My manager, on the phone, he was so angry! Seems like FDR went off at the last minute to stay at his own house, up in Hyde Park. It's a big estate, not far—up near Poughkeepsie. So our hotel is empty! And can you believe the government is stiffing us on the bill!"

"Really," murmured Krause. "How unfair."

"Yes! Our manager is furious! He says FDR meets women up there." He snorted. "Can you blame him? Married to Eleanor, the battleaxe!"

"Be careful running your mouth," said Krause, pointing sternly. "You could get in a lot of trouble with that loose talk. Spies are everywhere."

The clerk stiffened and stood up straight, almost at attention. "You're quite right, sir. Are you sure I can't get you a room? Special military rates, of course. There are usually pretty girls up at our Zulu Time bar most nights."

"I'm afraid not," said Krause. "The lieutenant and I must be on our way. Do you know how we can get up to Hyde Park? I have urgent business with the president."

"The Officer in Charge on base can direct you." He picked up the phone. "I can ring him for you—"

"No, no, that's fine. We'll..." Krause realized he didn't have a plan. What could he say?

"Oh, just have your driver ask. Everyone in Hyde Park knows where the Roosevelts are. If he needs directions, the security check-point is just out and to the right, you'll see it. I can call them now—"

"No, no, no bother," Krause said quickly, "and thank you." Krause waved Krieger toward the door. They walked down the hotel driveway onto Buffalo Soldier Field and, walking in the darkness away from the security checkpoint, toward the darkness of the cadet stables.

Krause was flooded with relief! FDR was gone! There was no

need for a suicide mission! Could this be his chance? He had a uniform and superbly forged papers. The war would be over soon. There was no need to die! Krause wondered if he could give Krieger the slip. He knew the campus like the back of his hand. He could find Peggy, and they could run off together! Anything was possible in America! Wasn't it? They could take new identities and run off to California!

"Sturmbannführer, he's not here! FDR left early! The mission is blown," he whispered.

"*Scheiss!* Where did he go? Another hotel?"

"He's in Hyde Park. It's at least thirty miles or so, on the other side of the river, up past Poughkeepsie. We can't walk it. We don't have a boat. We don't have a car. Krieger, it's over. Back to the river. We have to get picked up."

Krieger grabbed him by the neck, knocking him to his knees. Krause felt the prick of Skorzeny's SS dagger under his jaw. His mind was flooded with a mixture of panic and rage. "The Führer has sent us for that Jew FDR! We are not crawling back to the sub on our knees! We must go to this Hyde Park place and snatch him there. You lived here, Krause! You must know where we can get a vehicle!"

"For God's sake, Wilhelm!" choked Krause. "Cadets don't have cars!"

"We can steal one—"

"No one has cars, only big shots like the commandant and superintendent!" Even as he choked out the words "commandant and superintendent" the answer came to him. "Sturmbannführer! Take the ice pick out of my neck! I have an idea."

Krieger released Krause, who dusted off his uniform as Krieger sheathed his dagger. "Let me make myself clear, Hauptmann. We are going to bring that Jew Roosevelt back to the Führer, or die trying. We've sworn an oath to Adolf Hitler, and I'll kill you or anyone else who gets in my way!"

Krause thought of Peggy, fear, guilt and longing flooding

together. Was she here? Would she agree to see him? Could he convince her to help him?

"*Jawohl*, Sturmbannführer! I had one friend here. I might be able to borrow—"

"Or steal."

"Or steal a car from her father. Follow me."

The two men started back down Thayer Road, cutting across the central cadet area, and headed for the commandant's house.

The mission was now infinitely more complicated.

Could they actually find FDR?

Was Peggy still here?

Was Providence finally on his side?

TWENTY-THREE

WEST POINT
PRESENT DAY

G oldstein was out of ideas. The U-boat archives at Cuxhaven in Germany had been scrubbed by the OSS right after the war. A call to his contact at the Naval Academy wasn't returned and he found nothing about U-555 on the internet. He toyed with the brass plate they found at the base of the periscope hoping to find something, anything to help explain the mystery. The only thing he could see with his naked eye was the Blohm & Voss logo. He got out a magnifying glass and saw only scratches.

Then it hit him—of course, how could he have forgotten! His old friend and casual hookup Angela Kunisberg had taken a job with B & V. German companies were obsessive record keepers. Angela had left her academic position to be the archivist at B & V. Maybe the OSS had forgotten to scrub those records. A visit to Hamburg could pay dividends—on many fronts. He opened up his laptop and launched Expedia and started looking at flights.

Major Sanchez, the department chair, barged into Goldstein's office, red-faced and out of breath. "Goldstein! The Secret Service is in my office! Waiting for you!" He paused. "What have you done now!" It wasn't a question. It was an accusation. Goldstein quickly closed his laptop.

"What? Why?" Goldstein was stunned. "In your office?"

"They won't tell me. Have you been on the internet? Goldstein. I told you. Department of Defense policy is very clear. All DOD personnel are forbidden to make political statements online, even—"

Goldstein cut him off. "Yes, yes, I know. Even on our personal accounts, if you can be identified as a DOD employee, which I am."

"So why did you?"

"I didn't! Well, I did, that one time months ago. Come on. That one time. Everyone—even you—knew the president was being a total ass. But no, not since then. And why would the Secret Service care about that?"

"Goldstein. Have you threatened the president?"

"Steve, Major...For God's sake, no. And I'm not engaged in counterfeiting, either. I have no idea what this is about. Maybe they have an interest in naval history?" Goldstein's heart hammered in his chest. This had to be about the sub. But why the Secret Service? he wondered.

"I sincerely doubt that. Come on, to my office. Now!"

Standing by the window in Sanchez's office was a young Black man with the build of a wrestler and a nose that had been broken one too many times. An older agent with gray streaks in his hair sat at Sanchez's desk, studying the papers. He had tortoiseshell glasses, which gave him a scholarly look.

"Hey, that's my desk!" Sanchez croaked. "Am I under investigation, too?"

The agent at the desk smiled genially. "Didn't open any drawers...just looked closely at the top of your papers. Secret Service habit."

"You might pay your golf fees, Mr. Chairman," said the Black agent. "I'm Agent Cadell, my nosy colleague here is Agent Fitzpatrick." Cadell glanced at Goldstein dismissively. "So. This the guy causing all the trouble? This...guy?"

"Let me state right now: The Department of History is fully cooperating with the Secret Service," declared Sanchez. "Complete assistance and full cooperation!"

"Hey, Prof.," Agent Cadell leaned over to Goldstein. "FYI. Your boss here, he just threw you under the bus."

"What can I do to help with your investigation?" Sanchez asked. He looked terrified.

"Very kind of you, Major," said Agent Cadell. "Get out. Leave."

"But this is my office!"

"Yes, it is. And we need your office. But not you."

"Excuse us, Major. It's a lovely day outside, maybe you want to go hit a few golf balls?" Fitzpatrick said. "Agent Cadell and I need to have a...have a few friendly words with Dr. Goldstein."

"He can't stay?" Goldstein croaked. He'd never wanted Sanchez's company more than he did now.

"With Dr. Goldstein. In private," said Cadell, opening the office door. He pushed the stunned Sanchez out, and firmly closed the door. Then locked it.

"Dr. Goldstein, we have a little problem," Agent Fitzpatrick began. "Please, sit down and—"

Goldstein interrupted and said quickly, "Look, guys, it was a mistake. I didn't understand the rules governing DOD employees and political posts. I thought I was protected by Free Speech. As soon as Major Sanchez brought it up, I took the posts down, all of them."

Agent Cadell broke in, "As my partner was saying, sit down and shut up."

Goldstein persisted. "If I'm under investigation, don't I need a lawyer?"

Agent Fitzpatrick smiled. He offered Goldstein a mint. "Relax, Dr. Goldstein. Back off for just a minute, Cadell. Let's all take a seat." The agents settled comfortably into their seats.

Goldstein squirmed. "Dr. Goldstein, Tom, right? So, Tom? Agent Cadell and I are here to clarify a small matter that has come to our attention. No need for you to be upset."

Agent Cadell broke in, "If you tell the truth."

Agent Fitzpatrick continued, "An...issue has come to our attention. We wanted to offer you some...shall we say, guidance."

"Guidance about what?"

"You have been in contact with the German U-boat archives in Cuxhaven, Germany, about a Type XXI Submarine."

"Yes, but it's not 'X, X, I.' We actually say 'type 21.' Those are Roman numerals," corrected Goldstein. Oh my God, had he just actually said that. Was he trying to piss these guys off?

Cadell's eyes narrowed. He clenched his fist. Goldstein wasn't sure if he was threatening him or just rubbing his knuckles.

"Of course, Type XXI, specifically U-555. We are concerned about those inquiries. Why are you interested in that class of U-boat?"

"Well, um, I'm a naval historian. I'm just writing an article about them. They are remarkable pieces of engineering, decades ahead of anything we were building. That hardly seems like something the Secret Service would be concerned about. How about you, Agent...Cadell, you a history buff?"

"Don't get cute, Dr. Goldstein. We didn't come up from Washington to play games. You could be in deep shit." Cadell stood up, moving toward Goldstein.

"Easy now, gentlemen," interjected Fitzpatrick, opening his palms in a friendly gesture.

"I don't understand what my research has to do with the Secret Service. Don't you guys protect the president?"

"Yes, that's right. We protect the president, but we also investigate a variety of other...concerns," Fitzpatrick said. "Let me be direct, Dr. Goldstein. Your inquiries into these Type XXI submarines involve you in a matter of national security. I'll make it simple. Desist making inquiries in these archives."

"Desist?"

"Keep to medieval naval warfare. Phoenicia. Egypt. Ostrogoths in the Adriatic."

"Yeah," added Cadell, "Ostrogoths. Shit no one cares about."

Goldstein shook his head. They had researched him. They knew all about him! Read his papers! "I don't understand, but why?" said Goldstein.

"We don't have to explain. Listen, Dr. Goldstein, we're trying to help you stay out of trouble." Fitzpatrick looked disappointed in him. "But I see we're not getting through to you. Major Sanchez tells us that you're not well liked here, you don't fit in, and there's no tenure here at West Point. Understand me? You might be fired. Your annual contract—it might just not be offered again. No reason. Doesn't have to be one." Goldstein looked down at his hands. They were trembling. "Tom. No need to make trouble. Surely you can find other topics to research," Fitzpatrick added gently.

"Yeah, like them Ostrogoths..." added Cadell. "Dusty history shit. Do that."

Agent Fitzpatrick rose to his feet. "Really, Dr. Goldstein, we'd like to see you succeed here at West Point. I'm sorry your research has taken you into areas that are sensitive. Let's just chalk this up to a learning experience. Go back to your students and your research, in some other area. In fact, I believe we have some contacts that might be willing to fund other lines of research." Fitzpatrick looked at his notes. "There's funding, for instance, in the invention of the torpedo by the Syrian Hasan al-Rammah in, ahhh, 1275. A rocket system with explosive gunpowder—"

Cadell interjected, "Now, that's cool! Torpedoes, Tom!"

Fitzpatrick looked firmly at Goldstein. "That medieval 1275 torpedo grant—it's all pre-approved. Please, for your own sake. No more questions about U-555." He handed Goldstein his card.

"Reach out to my office next week. They'll line something up for you."

"Yes, I see," said Goldstein, smiling weakly. "That should be no problem at all. I'm really more interested in Venetian and Genoan galleys from the 1600s."

Fitzpatrick was dismissive. "Okay, Prof. We gave you the message. You can leave now."

Goldstein stumbled out of the building.

He started to text Zhao, but his hands were trembling too badly to work the keyboard. He stood overlooking the Hudson River, trying to get his bearings, deep breathing and visualizing a deep-blue Caribbean ocean. What did these goons really want? he wondered. He knew he hadn't broken the law. They clearly didn't have anything real to go on; all they did was make some vague threats. His calls to the U-boat archive had stirred up a hornet's nest, but not really turned up anything useful. Clearly the Secret Service didn't know that they had been diving on the wreck.

He pulled out the brass plate and looked at the inscription: Blohm & Voss.

He wouldn't be bullied.

He was going solve the mystery of the Nazi submarine in the Hudson.

He was going to Hamburg.

TWENTY-FOUR

After her husband Dale was killed in action, Peggy Wilson had hit the bottle, hard. The year after his death was a gin-soaked blur of binge eating, depression, and isolation with her small son.

But now, things were looking up. She'd left Fort Benning and moved back in with her parents at West Point. Being back with her parents helped. She lost weight and could fit into her old clothes. Her son Devon had stopped asking for Dada. She was drinking less. Not completely stopped, but less. She reenrolled at Vassar and was working on a nursing degree.

Peggy and Dale met when she was a sophomore at Vassar and he was a Firstie, a fourth year cadet at West Point. A pretty girl on the West Point campus got lots of looks, but few cadets were brave enough to speak to a colonel's daughter. There had been that one cadet, Karl Krause, who captured her heart, then broken it, in high school, but he had disappeared from West Point without even saying goodbye.

Dale was brave, even reckless, in his pursuit of Peggy. He invited her to a military ball for their first date, and proposed on their third date. When Dale was summoned to her father's office —the colonel's office—in Nininger Hall, Dale feared he'd be expelled. The middle-aged officer and the young cadet bonded over their love of the Army. Wilson was a hard man, but he loved his daughter. Reassured of Dale's commitment to Peggy, Colonel Wilson welcomed Dale into the family.

The day after graduation, they were married in the Cadet Chapel. Despite barely knowing each other at the altar, their honeymoon on Cape Cod was blissful. They spent two weeks together basking in the sun and walking on the beach.

When they returned from the honeymoon, they moved down to Fort Benning, Georgia, where Dale trained for the infantry. Four months later, Dale shipped out for North Africa.

Peggy was six months pregnant when Dale was decapitated by an 88-mm shell in the Kasserine Pass. He was awarded the Silver Star posthumously. The citation described "uncommon gallantry." It was delivered with a folded American flag, a folded uniform jacket, and some cufflinks.

Peggy rapidly slipped into a deep depression. When her mother made a surprise visit to Fort Benning, she found Devon bawling in a dirty diaper and Peggy asleep with an empty gin bottle beside her. They had a terrible row, and her mother said she would take Devon back to West Point with or without her.

Colonel Wilson had been promoted to Brigadier General and appointed Commandant, and the Wilsons moved into the commandant's residence. The white-brick house had a broad veranda that overlooked the Plain where the cadets drilled. Peggy often sat there with Devon, watching him play with wooden soldiers.

Please God, she thought, anything but that.

She should be content. After all, she was safe in her parents' home. Devon asleep upstairs in his crib. Celia, the maid, banging around, closing down the kitchen. Her parents asleep already upstairs. It was safe. It was peaceful. But Peggy was restless. She never went out, never dated or went dancing. Her social life was limited to accompanying her father at tedious military events, chatting with generals' wives, and visiting congressmen's families. She missed fun. She missed having a man in her bed. It was so claustrophobic and boring. She was living in a nunnery with a toddler.

Today had been fun, though. The president visited and FDR chose her, Peggy Wilson, to ride in the back seat with him for the parade and inspection of the troops! That is, until that woman, Lucy, arrived. FDR was so engaging and jolly, with his jaunty hat and cigarette. "The war's won!" FDR had told her in the backseat of his car. "Look, there's a bar, relax, take a snort from the brandy snifter, and have a cigarette!" But of course, she couldn't; her parents were watching. She just giggled and enjoyed the attention. FDR was fun.

She tried to focus on her thick nursing textbook. She tried hard not to think about sneaking a little drink from her parent's closely watched bar. She knew her mother measured the liquid left in the liquor bottles.

But FDR declared today it was fine to celebrate! And he's the president! She owed herself a little drink. She poured a quarter cup of her dad's Jack Daniel's Old No. 7 Tennessee Whiskey into Devon's sippy cup and took a snort. It burned all the way down and filled her with a delicious warmth. She laid back on the soft living-room sofa and the textbook fell to the floor. She'd study tomorrow. She'd drink tonight. She closed her eyes and thought about dancing.

Celia, a middle-aged Black lady in a starched domestic outfit, stepped discreetly into the living room. Celia had been with Peggy since she came back from Benning with Devon.

"Excuse me, Mrs. Roberts, a Major Krause at the door asking for you."

"For me? Not Dad? I'm don't know any majors. Besides, it's much too late for visitors."

"Yes, for you. He says you will remember him as Karl. He studied at West Point and that you were friends when you were in high school." Celia smiled. "And he's quite handsome."

Major Krause? Karl Krause? Could he really be the plebe she knew all those years ago? She was thunderstruck! Suddenly, she felt very alive.

She felt herself flush with excitement, anticipation...and anger. "But you know, Mother and Daddy, they're not awake." She thought for a moment. "Celia, tell you what, watch Devon for me. I'll just speak with Karl on the porch."

"Yes, ma'am."

"And don't turn the porch light on. We don't want to wake the general!"

Peggy stopped to look at herself in the hall mirror. She was a few years older, but judging from the way the West Point cadets and officers looked at her, she knew she was very attractive. How many men had suggested they take a walk together?

But this was Karl! Returned! She'd never forget sneaking out to Flirty Walk with him. Flirty Walk was a nearby park area with dense forest and shadows and private areas; cadets, not allowed to have girls in their room, would bring dates to Flirty Walk and get as far as they could, second base, third, in all weather. It was the first time anyone had touched her...there.

She deftly applied some lipstick, smiled at the mirror, and opened the front door. Krause and Krieger waited, caps in hand.

"Peggy! It is you! It's Karl, Karl Krause! Gosh, it's good to see you!"

She flushed and her heart raced. "Karl! Major Krause! Oh my God! But, what are you doing here?" Karl looked better than ever—fit, strong, big, and very attractive. And the sharp major's uniform suited him perfectly.

"Peggy. You are so beautiful!" He laughed. "And yes, I'm a major! Promotions come quickly in wartime. But now you are Mrs. Roberts? You're married? Your husband home?" Karl looked around. He felt desperately exposed standing out on the porch. "My lieutenant and I—can we come inside?"

"What, come in now?"

"And just talk?"

She slapped him across the face. "Are you kidding? You and your creepy friend? You think my father—the general—lets me entertain soldiers in his home? Just talk? What else would we do! I'm a mother and a widow, Karl. You bastard."

He winced, but stood still. "I'm so sorry, Peggy. I didn't mean—"

"Not a letter? No call? No explanation? What are you even doing here? I was sixteen, Karl! We were engaged! You disappeared! You never—I never even heard from you again!" Peggy's breath was ragged, and she started to cry. "I've got a child, Karl. No, you can't come in. Of course you can't. Go away. Get out of here." Peggy regretted the whiskey. She felt the porch spin.

"I'm so sorry, Peggy," Krause repeated gently. There was a yearning and warmth in his eyes, and he reached out and touched her gently on the shoulder. "It's been so hard for everyone. There is so much suffering in this war, on both sides."

She looked at him quizzically. "On both sides?" She closed the screen door firmly, and stood behind it. "Leave now, Karl."

"I mean, not both sides—suffering both at the front and at home." Krause realized he was pushing her too hard. Peggy looked like a frightened deer. Krieger retreated silently into the deeper shadows, further away from the house. "Of course, you're right, we mustn't come in." He stepped back off the porch, down the three steps. Away from the house lights.

Peggy looked confused. "Karl...?" She opened the screen door, and took a few tentative steps onto the porch. "Karl? Oh, I'm sorry, don't go..."

His big hands reached out to her. She hesitated, stepped forward, lost her balance, and stumbled down the three steps, throwing herself into his arms. "Karl, I missed you so much. It's so lonely," said Peggy, choking back a sob. "I never thought you'd come back."

"Peggy, I've missed you so much. I need just a few minutes—just to talk." Krause held her closer. "I need to tell you something, a secret. We can walk along Flirty Walk. It's private there."

Peggy stepped back abruptly and let go of his hand. "No, Karl! Not Flirty Walk!"

He laughed. "You have nothing to worry about, Peggy, your honor is safe with me! My aide will chaperone." As though having Krieger around made anyone safer. Like having a loose tiger at your back. But Krieger kept a respectful distance, and didn't speak.

She tilted her head. Celia could watch Devon. Her parents were asleep. Krause looked so appealing. She had not touched a man in years. Karl's arms felt so strong holding her. A man's man. He was no longer a homesick farm boy.

And a secret! She loved intrigue.

"All right, Karl." Peggy buttoned her sweater. "Just a quick walk…"

··· ▬ ▬▬▬ ·▬·

KRAUSE REACHED OUT HIS HAND. Her hand in his was electric. He pulled her gently, closer, and they strolled down the dark street, speaking in low tones. They could hear the quiet evening sounds of the base, a distant truck starting, the wind in the trees.

Krause didn't see Krieger but knew he was close behind them. Stalking them in the dark. Watching precious minutes ticking by. He was flooded with a sense of affection and a desire to protect Peggy. Was there a way to give Krieger the slip?

Peggy squeezed his hand. So big. So comforting and familiar. "But Karl, what happened to us? One minute we were planning our lives together—and the next you were gone without a trace!

I wore the little ring you gave me for such a long time. I still have it, wrapped in a drawer."

Krause put his arm around her shoulder. He pulled out the ring he still wore around his neck. "I will get you a better ring, when you marry me."

"Karl, you mean this?"

"Oh, yes." Part of him sincerely meant this. Her warm, soft body pressed so close to his felt incredible. But part of him would tell her anything to get her to give them the car keys. He was completely winging this. "I had to withdraw. Abruptly."

"You never called me! West Point acted like it was a secret! Dad wouldn't tell me anything. Was there trouble? An Honor Board? Did you lie, cheat, or steal? Did you cover for a friend?" Peggy knew the strict West Point Honor Code: "A cadet will not lie, cheat, or steal, nor tolerate those who do."

"Oh, no," Karl lied. "Nothing like that. Peggy. My father passed suddenly, we lost the farm—we had nothing. I had to help my mom and sister. We were hungry, desperate…"

"There wasn't another girl at home, was there?"

"Oh, no, Peggy, nothing like that at all. It's always been only you—I thought only of you." Krause was thinking quickly. "I always planned to come back to marry you, but I was ashamed how poor I was. I couldn't feed myself, let alone a wife."

They stopped at the entrance of Flirty Walk, and she gave him a deep and passionate kiss which made his heart race. She tasted and smelled of smoky whiskey. She's drunk, he realized.

Krause thought quickly. How to persuade her? "I did come back, you know."

"To me? You did? When?"

"When I finally had rank, I was promoted, a good salary. I wanted to see you, to explain, to propose marriage—but by then you had married your officer. I was crushed."

She held him close and whispered, "If I'd only known! I would have married you! Poor, rich, I don't care, I would've waited, Karl, you know that." She kissed him again.

Karl murmured, "You were a married woman. I'm an honorable man. Your husband a hero." He kissed her again. How was he going to move this along? He needed the car! Now! "But when I saw today that your father is commandant, I just had to see him, to explain—and then I couldn't help myself when I saw you." He kissed her again. "I just had to see you, one last time—"

"But no! Where are you going now?" She pulled away from him.

"Peggy, no one knows. I'm heading out on a secret mission, I might die…"

Peggy looked at him with tears in her eyes. "But FDR just told us! The war is over! No Karl, you can't. I find you and just lose you again—a secret mission? You might die? No." She pulled away. "Let go of me. I'm drunk. This is all wrong, I'm going home."

Karl held her close. "But Peggy, I love you. I need your help. I'm begging—for our future."

"What can I do? I'm just a housewife." Peggy was intrigued.

"You don't realize. You are very important." Krause stopped, held her shoulders, and looked down at her. "May I tell you something in complete confidence?"

"Of course, Karl."

"You can't tell anyone, not your dad or anyone—"

"Karl. Put your hand on my heart. You can trust me."

"I've been advising the president—first it was just German translations, but there was so much more—"

"My Karl? You've been advising FDR?" Peggy gasped. "That's why you're here today! But I didn't see you, you weren't at the tea—"

"No teas for majors, we're too busy working."

"FDR is wonderful, but so complicated. He smokes and drinks and tells stories. He says we've won the war!" Krause almost choked. "And now we are going to teach Stalin some manners! Karl, I wish you'd seen me! I rode in the president's car. With FDR! I like him, but you know, he is a little bit of a phony. He brought this women to tea—it wasn't Eleanor. It wasn't a secretary. It's his girlfriend...I think everyone knows it, too. Oh, the whispering! Her name was Lucy—Lucy Mercer. She's beautiful. Poor Eleanor—and she's the one who really cares about ordinary people."

Lucy? Eleanor? Krause's mind raced. What in God's name was Peggy prattling on about? We need a car. We need to find FDR. Right now. Krause saw Krieger in the shadows, watching him. It was like being stalked by a leopard.

Peggy chattered on. "So this Lucy shows up to West Point, and instead of staying the evening at the Thayer, where he was supposed to stay, the president decides to take Lucy up to his new house, Top Cottage! Can you believe it? The brazenness of that woman!"

"What? I thought Hyde Park. My orders are to go and meet him up there. My top-secret orders."

"Oh, it's all in the same area—the estate, at Hyde Park, near Springwood. Top Cottage is just a small little house in the forest. Everyone's calling it FDR's love nest. My mother says Eleanor's not allowed there at all!"

"Really."

"Ever!"

"Look, Peggy, I have a favor to ask. Lieutenant Harris and I, we need to get up to Top Cottage. Tonight. Now. We need your help."

"So just go requisition a car and driver. That's what Mom does. When she's too drunk to drive."

"Peggy, you can't tell anyone. The circumstances are...irregular. Top secret. We must get to the president as quickly—and discreetly—as possible."

"Mom says motor pool is full of blabbermouths, it's true. So. What's this all about? Is it this Lucy Mercer thing?" she asked.

Krause nodded knowingly. "Smart girl. You're a clever one.

So. Let's have you tip toe back and get your dad's car? We three can all drive up together..."

"No, can't, no." Peggy shook her head. "He'll never let me take his car! Are you kidding? No!"

"Peggy. You have to. You must."

"I don't have to do anything!"

"Peggy, your dad won't know. We'll run up to Top Cottage, deliver the message, and be back well before dawn. FDR will be so proud of you!" He pulled Peggy close, kissed her neck, and pulled her body close to him. He lowered his voice and growled, "I need you, Peggy." He meant it, but with Krieger breathing down his neck, he had to get the car. There was no escaping Krieger, not now. Maybe after they got Roosevelt, he could run off with Peggy. Krieger would have to stay with his prize.

"Peggy, please."

Peggy gave him one long kiss and shivered, no doubt remembering long, passionate, incredible sessions in the back of her dad's car. "I'll meet you up by the Cadet Chapel in half an hour."

Krieger looked at Krause. "What the hell? We're taking her with us?"

Krause shrugged. "We need the car."

"That took too long. And now we have baggage."

"Fuck you, we have a car."

··· — ——— ·—·

PEGGY ARRIVED at Cadet Chapel before Krause and Krieger. She'd slugged a double shot while grabbing the keys. Waiting in the warm Packard staff car, she turned on the radio and slipped off her panties. She closed her eyes and waited.

Peggy was startled when Krause and the taciturn lieutenant —what was his name, anyway?—appeared out of the darkness.

She handed the keys to the lieutenant, who almost snatched them from her and got in the driver's seat.

Krause reached forward and pulled across the curtain separating the drivers and passengers. "Drive carefully, Lieutenant, it's two hours till we get to the Mid-Hudson Bridge. Mrs. Roberts and I have a lot of catching up to do. Please turn up the radio. She and I have to compare notes about the Roosevelts, so you will excuse us."

He embraced her, brushing her neck and cheek with his lips. Peggy pressed her back and buttocks into Krause's muscular frame, and moaned gently. Krause pulled her onto his lap, caressing her full breasts. Her lips were very full and moist. Krause's hands moved skillfully over her body.

After several minutes, she broke the embrace. "Are you telling me anything about the Roosevelts? Or the truth about where you've been?"

He smiled. "Oh, confidential. I can't tell you the details, but believe me, I thought of you every day. Especially this..." He unbuttoned her blouse, and put a probing hand between her legs.

"You're a liar," she said, feeling him swell through his Army uniform. "A big fat liar, but I don't care," she said, unzipping his pants.

Two hours later, Krieger crossed the Mid-Hudson Bridge in Poughkeepsie and brought the Packard to a stop. Krause shook Peggy gently. "Wake up, baby. Peggy, sweetheart, we need directions."

Peggy stirred, deeply asleep. She smiled and murmured, "Come back to bed, you strong man."

Krause spoke sternly, "Wake up, it's important!"

"Come snuggle baby, I'm still all warm." She rolled over, snuggled her jacket, and closed her eyes.

Krieger looked at Krause and narrowed his eyes. He didn't speak but he looked furious.

Krause shook Peggy hard. "Peggy! Listen! We're in Poughkeepsie now. Lieutenant Harris and I need to see FDR immediately. Where the hell is Top Cottage?"

Peggy finally woke up, straightened her skirt, and ran her hands through her hair. Her face took on a surly look. "Why are you so mean?"

"We need to go to FDR, now. It's important. There's a war on, remember?"

"Listen, I don't exactly know the way."

"For God's sake, Peggy, you told us you came up to Hyde Park all the time."

"Well, every time I've been here we go to Springwood—it's the big mansion house. It's much bigger than my dad's house back at West Point. My dad told me that FDR doesn't even own the big house. It actually belongs to his mom, Sara. Well, it did anyway, until she died last year. The superintendent's wife told me all about it last year. I was telling her about how mean my mother was, and she laughed and told me all about how horrible Eleanor's mother-in-law Sara was to her. Actually, my mother-in-law—"

Krause finally interrupted. "Please! Peggy! Lieutenant Harris can get nasty when he's upset."

"Then why don't you get a different adjutant? I'm awake now. I'm sure I can find Top Cottage. Go left. We'll head north on Route 9. We can always ask directions!"

Krause shook his head at Krieger, then directed him to get back on the road and head north.

Krause turned his head back to Peggy. "And then, where do we turn?"

"I'll point it out. Tell me something. When you were in Africa, did you meet Dale? Was he famous? Did his troops really love him?"

"What are you talking about, Peggy? I never met Dale. I've never been to Africa."

Peggy studied Krause's jacket pocket. Just above it was a white and yellow ribbon identical to the one she had at home on her dresser. It was for service in North Africa. It was the ribbon on Dale's jacket, the one they sent home with the flag.

Never been to Africa? That doesn't make any sense. Something's not right, she thought. Her head was clearing. The bourbon was burning off. She had to pee. This didn't seem the time to confront him, but sooner or later she would get him to explain. He seemed very grumpy now. Not nice like last night.

"Just keep going north up Route 9," Peggy said. "It's four or five miles along the river to Hyde Park. There's a checkpoint there, and they'll direct us." Peggy was worried. Something was very wrong. What was Krause really up to? Why the North Africa ribbon if he's never been to North Africa? Why didn't the creepy lieutenant speak?

In her mind Peggy, visualized the stone building with the white-frame portico up ahead. There were MPs there, from the 240th MP Battalion, stationed to guard FDR. They'd know what she should do.

••• — ——— •—••

CORPORAL PAT DUGAN rubbed his hands against the early spring chill. It had been warm earlier that afternoon, and he had chosen his summer weight for the overnight shift at the guardhouse. During the day when there was more traffic, the guards worked in pairs. If the weather was bad, they took turns sitting in the house, out of the wind. For the overnight watch down on the Route 9 checkpoint, the military police worked alone. Dugan passed the time listening to the radio.

He noticed a pair of appropriately dimmed headlights snaking up the road.

No one had told Dugan anything special when he took over from the Day Watch. Nothing much happened up here, and he liked it that way. Unanticipated late-night visitors were definitely not common up at Hyde Park. Dugan straightened his

Sam Browne belt and adjusted his peaked cap. He ran his hand over his holstered .45 caliber pistol. He found its heavy presence reassuring.

••• ▬ ▬▬▬ •▬▬•

THE PACKARD PULLED up to the road barrier and came to a halt. Krause addressed him through the open window.

"Excuse me, Corporal, we have urgent business with the president. Direct us to Top Cottage."

"I'm sorry, Major. I'm expecting no vehicles. Where's your written authorization from the base commander?"

"Open the gate, and we'll be on our way." Krause spoke in an imperious tone which rubbed Dugan the wrong way.

Krieger unsheathed his dagger.

Krause tried a final time. "This is a matter of highest priority, Corporal. We have urgent matters to discuss with FDR. Which way is Top Cottage?"

"I'm quite sure it is, Major." Dugan started back to the guard-house. "I'll just make a quick call."

Peggy opened the back door of the Packard and tried to scramble out.

"Officer!" she shouted. "These men are liars! He's wearing a medal he never earned!"

Dugan turned as Peggy screamed and frantically stumbled in his direction.

Too late, Dugan saw Krieger running directly at him. With a practiced grace, Krieger thrust his dagger into Dugan's solar plexus, the sharp steel penetrated Dugan's left lung, which immediately collapsed. The tip on the dagger tore through the Dugan's heart and a torrent of blood flood his left chest. The big man collapsed to the ground wordlessly.

Peggy fell to her knees, sobbing, and vomited. What was happening? Who were these men?

Krieger dragged Dugan's limp body into the stone guard-house and rolled him under a desk.

Krause held the sobbing Peggy. "I can explain, just calm down."

Krieger spat. "We have no time for niceties, Karl. Give me the girl."

Peggy wailed, and tried to bolt. Krause held his hand over her mouth and held her down.

"Give me a minute, Krieger. The girl can be useful to us," said Krause.

"You can't be serious! We have no time for this."

Krause gripped Peggy tightly and spoke earnestly. He really loved this girl. But she was making this impossible. "Peggy, my love, listen to me. Get a hold of yourself! Your life depends on it!"

Peggy stopped struggling, and Krause took his hands off her mouth.

Peggy closed her eyes, shook her head, and then tried to focus. "Who are you? You killed that guard!"

"You have two choices, darling—either calm down and listen, or Lieutenant Harris here will kill you, too."

"Oh my God, oh my God. No," she sobbed, collapsing on the dirt road.

"Peggy—darling—listen…"

Krieger shouted at Krause, *"Dafür ist keine Zeit."* There's no time for this!

The president was just minutes away. Someone could call the guardhouse at any time.

"Peggy, darling," Krause started. "I'm German, you're German…"

"No, my mother is, but you're American. I'm American! You're an American soldier with a uniform and medals!" she cried.

"But Peggy. I went back to Germany, back to our home. I fight for the Fatherland now, and we are winning!"

Peggy moaned. "Are you insane? You're a Nazi spy! Everyone knows the war will be over in weeks!"

"Now listen. Mr. Roosevelt is coming back to Germany with us for peace talks."

"Peace talks? How? You're kidnappers!"

"Either you help us, or Lieutenant Harris here—actually, his name is Sturmbannführer Krieger—will kill you."

The hair on the back of Peggy's neck stood up. Could she run? Scream? Sound an alarm? Warn someone?

Krause gripped her tightly. His speech was pressured, the words pouring out of his mouth. "You will come back to Germany with me! We will be famous—like Bonnie and Clyde. The people will worship you. I'll worship you. Mr. Roosevelt isn't all he claims to be. You know that. He cheats on his wife. He said he would save my family farm, but he didn't. He's a tool of the Jews! We won't hurt him. He will have peace talks with the Führer and Dr. Goebbels, and we can fight together against the Russians. Our real enemy is the Mongol Horde. They've always been the enemy, your father always said that!" He was spitting in her face.

Peggy twisted her face away. "You are insane! You are murderers! I don't want to be German! I want to go back to Devon!"

"We will take him with us! He will be German, too! And proud of it! Peggy, anything is possible. The Führer might send me back to America! One day, I will be the superintendent at West Point. Or I could be Ambassador or Gauleiter, governor of the whole U.S., with you at my side!"

Peggy screamed, "No! You're a monster!" She broke away from Krause's grip, and staggered down the road.

Krause bounded after her. "No, Peggy. Stop!"

··· ─ ─── ·──·

KRIEGER PULLED his silenced revolver from his ankle holster, and shot her in the back. He ran up to the fallen body and fired another shot into the base of her skull. Krieger dragged her body off the road into the dark forest.

Krause fell to his knees sobbing.

Something inside him died. Krause's dream of a life with Peggy, in the United States or Germany, were over. There was nothing left for him. Peggy was dead, Schmidt was dead, the Americans hated him, and he was fighting alongside monsters.

Krieger slapped Krause on the back of his head. "Finally! Thought you'd never shut up. Let's go. Get in the car, Major."

Krause had no choice now. He was a zombie, but he got in the car.

••• ▬ ▬▬▬ •▬▬•

AT FDR's TOP COTTAGE, the two guards heard the high-pitched noise in the wood. They thought it was a coyote, or a fawn being killed.

••• ▬ ▬▬▬ •▬▬•

TOP COTTAGE WAS AHEAD of them in the forest. Which fork? Which driveway to take? They'd have to guess. They'd been lucky so far. They took the right fork.

A mile up the road, there was another guard post, a neat fieldstone building with a peaked roof. Two guards this time. Maybe more? Krieger halted the car.

One guard leaned in. "Excuse us, sirs. This is a protected zone. Do you have authorization?"

"Yes, of course," answered Krieger, swiftly pulling his silenced pistol from his coat. Before either could react, he shot them both in the face. Krieger and Krause then dragged the bodies into the guardhouse. They cut the phone line and jumped back in the car.

Where was the Secret Service? The guards with machine guns? The razor-wire protections?

Krause looked around. A little hideaway cottage in the woods. It didn't look like a presidential retreat. A small veranda, no guards sitting outside. A few lights on downstairs and up. They could see through the window: FDR and a butler, both seated in the living room, drinking together.

Looked like only the two of them.

"Remember, I'll do the talking," said Krause.

He rang the doorbell at Top Cottage.

TWENTY-FIVE

G oldstein threaded his rented gray VW Passat through heavy traffic on the Hermann-Blohm-Strasse along the Hamburg Quay. The GPS guided him to a five-story brick building on the waterfront. The headquarters of Blohm und Voss was modest, fitting the Germanic ideals of understatement and practicality.

A chilly receptionist and a severe security guard glared at him while he waited in the lobby. A huge mock-up of a luxury mega-yacht dominated the lobby. *"Nicht anfassen!"* hissed the receptionist. Like he was going to touch it. He stood up, pointedly turning his back to the receptionist, and studied the beautifully framed architectural prints of warships and aircraft.

He was excited to see Angela Kunisberg, the Blohm und Voss historian and archivist, again.

He hoped she had information, and he hoped she'd share it. Also, he had high hopes for the evening. A few years before, at the naval history conference in Stockholm, they'd had a boozy hookup. He'd liked her a lot. And she liked him.

Angela greeted him in the lobby. She looked terrific, wearing a form-fitting cashmere sheath dress and high heels, more stylish than she'd been in her academic years. Her blonde hair was swept back in a professional chignon, but a few stray wisps were coming loose.

She flashed a warm smile, and they embraced more enthusiastically than typical for academic colleagues. Goldstein took Angela's hand and clasped it gently, then bent forward to kiss her softly on her cheek. The handshake and kiss lingered slightly.

"Such a pleasure to see you again, Herr Doktor Professor Goldstein. It isn't often we get American academics here at our modest place—especially famous scholars from Harvard," said Angela formally, but with a sly smile. He felt like her speech was an act for the receptionist and the security guard, who were watching them closely.

He replied equally formally, "You are overly generous, Frau Doktor Kunisberg. Of course, as you know, I'm no longer in Cambridge. I have a faculty appointment at the United States Military Academy, at West Point."

"Well, from Harvard to the U.S. Army. How you have moved up in the world! I'm so very pleased to see you again. I hope I can help you in your scientific research!" She looked at the security guard, indicating he should let them through. "You are already registered as an official visitor. Come, let's talk in my office."

The two historians rode the elevator to Angela's fifth-floor office. Large windows overlooked the Hamburg harbor—an enormous shipyard with cranes, ships, construction vehicles, activity everywhere. Angela took a seat behind the desk, and Goldstein pulled a chair up next to her. Bookcases lined the walls, and books and documents overflowed onto the floor. Four large red document folios sat on a modern chromium-steel desk.

"Angela. It's just so good to see you. You look amazing. This office is beautiful! That view! But what are you doing here? You were a professor at Heidelberg University! You had an academic career! Why would you leave Heidelberg to work at Blohm und Voss?"

"Oh, I miss the academic life. The prestige. The intellectual challenge. But you know, I'm raising two boys—they are teenagers now!" she laughed. "Amazing."

"I can't believe you're the mother of teenagers!" He wondered about the father. Where was he?

"Well, you can't eat prestige, or use it for school fees. You know, I'm raising them on my own—and I was so tired of being chronically short of cash. That twelve-year Opel—remember my car?—the engine light always coming on, smoke in the exhaust every time I accelerated! It lived at the repair shop. And our cramped apartment! The boys' sports equipment, always trip-ping over it, no place to put anything." She smiled. "Now, it is so much better! Double the salary, a full house for the boys and me. And later, I will show you! My pride and joy—the red BMW Roadster!"

"In some ways, I miss the university, but I certainly don't miss the politics."

"Oh, that I understand. Politics are a huge problem in every American university. Especially at our military academy."

"Not that kind of politics, Tom. When I was a child in East Germany, you had to be very careful. My parents warned me that you never knew who worked for the Stasi."

"The Stasi?"

"Yes, the security police. Informants were everywhere."

"That must have stopped when the wall came down."

"Not completely, some people maintained allegiances to the old order."

Goldstein didn't completely follow.

"And your work here? What are you doing?"

"The research opportunities, Tom! Blohm und Voss has been building ships since 1877. Imagine! Access to one hundred and fifty years of continuous and meticulous documentation! A historian's dream! They file every scrap of paper they generate!" She sighed. "I can write my scholarly articles. But, unfortunately, we—the archive—are technically in the public-relations department. They turn out a glossy quarterly publication for our clients and business partners and the media and to make the CEO happy, and I create content with a positive spin—you know, emphasizing B & V's—we like to call ourselves B & V, that's our new name, not emphasize the German, you know—B & V's role as a technology leader and an enlightened employer. We are focusing on our work refitting and building new ocean-going luxury yachts. Our customers are the mega rich. We sell to Arab sheiks and Silicon Valley billionaires, but mostly Russian oligarchs! The Russians have absolutely no taste. They want everything covered in gold! Plus, swimming pools and helicopter landing pads. The money is probably stolen, but we don't ask a lot of questions."

"B & V has never really asked a lot of questions. They never cared where the money came from. After all, you built the Bismarck and all those U-boats for the Nazis."

Angela looked at him sharply. "Are you here as a friend, Tom? And you are asking of me favors today?"

Goldstein knew he should drop it. But the truth! The truth was important. "But Angela—you cannot deny, Blohm und Voss used slave labor, prisoners of war—"

"Dr. Goldstein. I am paid not to talk about that," she said sharply. In fact, she was paid to absolutely ignore it. Not deny it, not change the record, but never bring it up, never include it in any of her articles or lectures. "Let me quote our CEO on this point: B & V is a forward-looking company. Our publications stress our efforts to better the lives of people everywhere, not wallow in the mistakes of our grandfathers."

The CEO, Hermann Muller, made it very clear that Angela was to ignore B & V's contribution to the Nazi war effort, and particularly around the use of slave labor from the Neuengamme concentration camp. She couldn't deny it, because it was true; to deny it would create a firestorm. Most major German corpora-tions, from BMW and Mercedes, to BASF and Siemens, acknowl-edged their participation in the Nazi war effort, but all sought to downplay it.

Angela wasn't entirely happy with that approach, but she loved the red BMW she drove around town.

Goldstein, realizing he was losing her, changed the topic. "It's so good to be here—and I am very appreciative of your help! I'd love to take you to dinner tonight, after this—if you are free…"

She softened. "Of course, I'd love that. But I don't think you came this far to just have dinner with me!" She turned to the pile of folders on her desk. "So, Tom. Let's get started! You mentioned in the text a new interest in Type XXI U-boats? This is a pivot for you, I think. In Stockholm, weren't you all about the Venetian Navy?"

"I'll be completely honest with you, Angela," lied Goldstein. "I've been approached by a group of divers who think they've found a Type XXI boat, somewhere off the East Coast of the U.S. I was obviously skeptical at first, and when I checked with the U-boat archives in Cuxhaven, I got nowhere. Cuxhaven claims are no existing records of U-555. The photo of the plate I shared with you clearly indicates it is a U-555 and it was built by B & V."

Angela tilted her head slightly toward Goldstein.

"Yes, I know, it's quite mysterious. When I got your text messages, I dug a little bit into the archives. Of course B & V doesn't encourage me to delve too deeply into certain things. Still, it is intriguing. The official record was no help. Do you know, there's absolutely no record of any U-555 in the main archives! Nothing in the official record."

Goldstein slumped. "Nothing? Angela! Surely you didn't have me travel all this way on false pretenses!"

"No, no, Tom. You're a historian! You know. The moment official records disappear—that's when it gets interesting. Everyone knows the U-555 was designed and built here. I did some digging into the papers from Neuengamme. Look—I found some correspondence from SS-Brigadeführer Walter Schellenberg to Admiral Dönitz regarding your mysterious U-555. It was copied to Standardenführer Max Pauly, the Lagerführer at the Neuengamme camp."

Goldstein interrupted. "Whoa! Angela! Who is Walter Schellenberg and what was in the correspondence?"

"Always so impatient, Tom! Please let me finish." She handed him a letter and a photo of a fit man in crisp SS uniform, death's head on his jaunty cap, smiling and squinting into the sun. "You don't know of him? I'm surprised. Well, you're a naval historian. Schellenberg was a Major General in the SS and head of the SD Foreign Intelligence Branch. Very high up. He reported directly to Heinrich Himmler. He was a ruthless man, endlessly hatching plots to advance the Reich. How's your German?"

"*Weiterführende Schule*—just high-school German."

"Some historian! You Americans! So parochial. Well, then—here, this letter. It's a bombshell. I'm surprised it wasn't destroyed. I found it in the requisition files." She unfolded the letter. "Look at this! Schellenberg demands a Type XXI for top-secret purposes. He insists it be delivered to him on time. No later than March 1, 1945. And he authorizes Standardenführer Pauly to divert as much labor—that's the slave labor from the concentration camp we don't talk about—as necessary to get that done."

"So it exists! But what was the secret mission? Does he say?"

"Ah, Tom." Angela sighed. "No. First, say thank you. In German!"

"*Danke Varrater*," he said, smiling. "Thank you, teacher." He took her hand and kissed it.

Angela laughed. "You sound like a high-school student! A charming one, and very forward! But I'm afraid that's all I have here, Tom. I do not know your Schellenberg's secret mission."

Goldstein held the photo and letter. It was something. Something very big. He couldn't wait to share it with Zhao. The trip to Hamburg had already paid off, and he'd only gotten started.

Angela held out a Post-it with a number and an address on it. "I do have one more thing for you. I made a few calls; a colleague from mine at Heidelberg is an expert on Walter Schellenberg. Schellenberg died in 1952, but he was very close with his niece. She's quite elderly, perhaps a bit demented, depends on the day, but she's agreed to meet with us."

"*Wunderbar!*"

Angela snorted. "Maybe. My colleague says she's just horrible, an unrepentant Nazi, but she has all sorts of letters and memorabilia. And memories. He's published quite a bit from her trove. I can translate, and keep you from misbehaving. Perhaps I will hit you with a ruler when you, how do you say, put my foot in your mouth?"

"My foot in my mouth. I know. I'm sorry. I'm a hothead. I'll be polite."

"You better be! So, she's in Schwerin. It's just a few hours' drive from here."

"Let's go!" said Goldstein rising.

"Not so fast, cowboy. She can't see us until tomorrow morning, but there's a lovely inn in Schwerin. I booked us a room." She smiled and lowered her voice. "In the meanwhile, I thought we should make a start right here."

She got to her feet, closed and locked the office door, and shook her long blonde locks free from the chignon. Sweeping the papers off her desk, she put her arms around Goldstein, and pulled his hips to hers.

"Research can wait," he agreed.

TWENTY-SIX

After his speech at West Point and teatime with the generals, FDR had waved goodbye to the adoring cadets. Chatting. Laughing. Heading for a romantic dinner and interlude at Top Cottage. FDR loved to drive out in the rolling farms and river vistas of Dutchess County countryside in his Blue Ford V-8, license plate FDR-1. It was specially fitted out with hand controls of his design. With the top down and Lucy at his side, screaming and laughing as he accelerated on the narrow country roads, he roared through the wooded countryside giving the Secret Service the slip. Security at Top Cottage was usually light, even during the war years. FDR's Security Chief Mike Reilly was uneasy, but FDR enjoyed himself more with fewer prying eyes.

FDR built Top Cottage as an escape—to escape from being president, to escape from his wife, and to escape from his mother. It was the only home that was truly his. Located on high ground above the family home of Springwood, and Eleanor's Val-Kill retreat, it had sweeping views of Dutchess County and the Hudson River below.

Roosevelt designed the building himself to accommodate his disability, which was kept secret from the public. There were nine rooms, including three bedrooms, all on one floor, with a large forty-foot living room. The doors were built wide enough to easily accommodate FDR's specially designed wheelchair, made out of a dining chair and bicycle wheels—light and flexible and looked like a regular chair. He also designed an extra-low, custom-built stove allowing him to scramble eggs for himself, and for overnight feminine guests. And there were frequent overnight feminine guests.

Top Cottage was a perfect spot for Roosevelt to avoid his mother Sara, who had dominated Springwood, the family home where she lorded over Eleanor and harangued FDR. Eleanor escaped to the rustic comfort of her cottage, Val-Kill, with intimate female friends, notably Lorena Hitchcock, a journalist. FDR would retreat to Top Cottage. During his presidency, he made over two hundred trips to Hyde Park. He traveled by private rail car, sometimes stopping at a private stop near Allomanchy, New Jersey, to pick up a special passenger, Lucy Mercer.

Although FDR publicly described Top Cottage as a retreat where he could study and write, he pursued other interests there. Women. FDR loved women, and they loved him back. He had multiple intimate female friends throughout his marriage, and always juggled several simultaneously. He was handsome, charming, and powerful, a potent combination. Far from Washington, and reasonably separate from his dominating mother and outspoken wife, he could enjoy a few cocktails and entertain.

Of all of his numerous liaisons, Lucy Mercer was the most enduring. The two had become lovers when the beautiful and accomplished Lucy was Eleanor's private secretary during

World War I. When Franklin, then Under Secretary of the Navy, returned from a European inspection trip ill and near death with pneumonia, Eleanor discovered Lucy's passionate letters while unpacking Franklin's luggage. Humiliated and despondent, Eleanor agreed to a divorce, but Franklin's mother intervened, threatening to disinherit Franklin. Forced to choose between his love affair and his political aspiration, he agreed to end the relationship.

FDR had promised Eleanor he'd never see Lucy again. But he did. Over the next twenty years, through FDR's paralysis, Lucy's marriage to the fabulously wealthy Winthrop Rutherford, and FDR's ascent to the presidency, they remained lovers. Lucy loved Franklin with a deep enduring love that had survived his paralysis, and twenty years of separation. Lucy called on FDR frequently at the White House under a pseudonym, visiting whenever Eleanor was away, as she often was.

Fashionable, animated, poised, bright, and lighthearted, Lucy was well read, a great listener, and she worshipped FDR. Eleanor was outmatched: physically ill-favored, socially awkward, unable to make small talk, and, when she saw FDR, lapsed into haranguing an overworked Franklin to advance her progressive causes. Eleanor had a huge heart and tremendous empathy for the oppressed and downtrodden of the world. She advocated for many groups whose suffering she personally embraced. All too often her pleas to help the downtrodden were ignored by FDR, who was exhausted by the challenges of fighting a Great Depression and a World War. After work, relaxing with a cocktail in hand, FDR much preferred the company of the more relaxed and worshipful Lucy.

FDR enjoyed cooking at his special low-set stove. Alonzo, his body man, a discreet, strong, patient man in his fifties, set everything up, then vanished into an upstairs room, available if needed, but giving FDR and Lucy time alone.

FDR prepared a light supper for himself and Lucy of steak, fried tomatoes, and creamed potatoes. FDR and Lucy ate on the same veranda where FDR had famously served the English King and Queen hot dogs in 1941.

After dinner, they relaxed in the comfortable living room. FDR talked of his plans for the United Nations and a framework for permanent world peace. Lucy had no official security clearance, but FDR often enjoyed lifting the veil of power to female admirers.

FDR had been unwell most of winter, but seemed to have rallied recently under the care of Dr. Bruenn, who was treating his hypertension and heart failure. Lucy smiled at him. "Yalta really set you back, Franklin. You look exhausted...I wish you could have sent Truman in your place."

The truth was, Franklin Roosevelt felt exhausted; he sensed that he had only weeks to live. Still his fighting spirit and sharp sense of humor never left him.

"Truman!" snorted FDR. "The man is a failed haberdasher. Really now, he'd let Winston snatch back the entire British Empire! And Stalin! Stalin would eat him for dinner."

"But Franklin. You can't do everything."

"No, Lucy, you're wrong!" He laughed. "I can't let him do anything! Even you know more than he does!"

It was true.

Truman was not FDR's choice for vice president. His running mate in 1932, Henry Wallace, chosen in 1940, was too progressive, and had alienated the southern states. Truman was the practical choice to balance the ticket in 1944, but FDR had little regard for the two-term Missouri senator. Truman was kept out of important affairs. Truman wasn't in the room where it happened. Truman didn't even know where the room was.

"He's too green. He isn't stupid, just parochial. Inexperienced in global affairs. We needed a strong hand in Yalta. I had to go."

"I would have loved to go with you, Franklin. I'd love to travel by your side."

"One day soon, Lucy. After the war, and the United Nations, when that's established." He was delighted with her, so happy to have her here with him in cozy Top Cottage. He waved his hand expansively, "Ah, my beautiful Lucy. We'll travel the world together! Let's plan our first cruise. What's your pleasure? The Baltic? Peloponnese Peninsula? Amalfi Coast? You choose!"

"I'd go anywhere with you. Or we can stay here, together, alone at Top Cottage. We'd be out of the limelight. You could be a scholar, like Winston, and write your memoirs."

"Ha! Did you hear what Winston said? 'I know history will be kind to me, for I intend to write it.'"

"He didn't!"

"Well, maybe not that succinctly. You know Winston uses twelve big words when three little ones will do! But I must deal with Winston. He's demanding we form a unified front against Stalin. My God! I wish he would stop talking about the Balkans."

"You'd think he was losing Scotland to the Russians!" Lucy laughed her musical laugh. FDR was enchanted. Beautiful, brilliant, and witty.

"Oh, just blustering about the British Empire and which colony he absolutely must keep. None! He'd sooner give up a testicle than see the Indians independent!"

"Franklin!" Lucy laughed. "Gracious! Are we in a barn?"

FDR grew serious as he held her hands. "Lucy. You must understand. It's so important what America does next. The people of the world must be free to rule themselves. We can guide them. No to the British Empire. No to communist-dominated Europe. Every nation must fully commit to the United Nations. That's the future for peace. That's the future for mankind, Lucy. If we don't get some form of international cooperation, there's no future for people on this planet."

"Franklin. I agree. But let's talk about the immediate future. Your immediate future. You know I can't stay the night—I must leave in a couple of hours." Lucy stood up, and kissed him long and slow. "Let's not think about Churchill. This is our time. Alone. Together. Let's use it wisely. Don't you want to...relax?"

"Oh, yes. Let's." He smiled at her, but added, growling, "But you do see, don't you, it's too important to leave to a greenhorn like Harry!"

"Of course it is. Forget Truman. Forget Harry! And get in here." She laughed again. "You're still giving a speech! And I might already have my stockings off!"

FDR maneuvered his wheelchair toward the bedroom.

Two hours later, Lucy stood next to Franklin at the door of Top Cottage. Her chauffeur waited, holding the door open to her Bentley touring car.

"Lucy, my love..." FDR started.

"Shhhhhhh. I'll be in touch when I can. Let me just take care of a few things, then we can really enjoy ourselves."

"I love you."

"I know you do." They embraced and kissed one last lingering time.

Lucy headed back to Rutherford Hall, her majestic, lonely Tudor mansion in New Jersey.

Alonzo, FDR's body man, closed the front door gently. "Ready for bed, sir?"

"Thanks for making yourself scarce, Alonzo."

"She's a nice lady. Good to hear you laugh a little, sir."

"I'll hope that's all you heard!" FDR laughed, and Alonzo blushed. "Bring me the drinks tray, Alonzo. I'll fix us both a nice cocktail." He poured two very dry gin Martinis, his favorite, and presented one to Alonzo. "Sit down with me, Alonzo, you look concerned. Is everything all right with you? Your family?"

"Well, Mr. President, I've never liked that man Stalin. And you know—"

"Just spit it out, Alonzo. I can handle the truth!" FDR chuckled.

"Frankly, every time you come back from one of those big trips, you're tired, Mr. President, and very cranky."

FDR tilted his head back, giving a loud open-mouthed roar of delight. "Ha! Well, you're not exactly so easy to please, either, Alonzo. Let's drink to cranky old men!" The two chatted on comfortably while sipping their drinks. With their glasses dry, Franklin offered another round.

"Oh, no, thank you, Mr. President, we should be getting you ready for bed. We're making an early start—"

The ring at the front door jolted them both. Normally, the guardhouse called ahead for visitors, and escorted them to Top Cottage. It gave them time if a young woman had to be quickly escorted out the back.

Alonzo opened the door, and was surprised to see two Army officers. "Major. Lieutenant. Good evening. You weren't announced—"

"We have an urgent matter to discuss with the president."

"This is most unusual. It's after eight! Is the president expecting you? Where's your guard?"

"This is an emergency. We must see him. Now."

"I don't understand. Why didn't someone call up? I have to call the guardhouse. No, no, you can't come in!" Krause and Krieger pushed their way past Alonzo, who lifted the phone and tapped the cradle a few times.

Alonzo put down the phone. "I don't understand, phone's not working—"

Overhearing the exchange, FDR wheeled himself over toward the door. "For goodness' sake, Alonzo, let them in," said FDR, waving exuberantly. "Let me get you a nightcap, Major! I'm sorry, I didn't catch your name?"

"It's Krause, Mr. President, Major Karl Krause. I work with General Donovan." Wild Bill Donovan was the founder and director of the OSS, the U.S. foreign-intelligence bureau. "This is my adjutant, Lieutenant Harris."

Krieger offered a salute.

Krause and Krieger were astonished to see FDR in a wheel-chair. There had been nothing in their briefings about that.

"Let me make you two gentlemen a cocktail," Roosevelt offered jauntily.

"Excuse me, Mr. President, I don't want be rude, but this really is a matter of grave importance."

"Surely it can wait for a cocktail?"

"I'm afraid not, sir." FDR sat up taller, put down the cocktail shaker, and appeared annoyed.

"All right then, Major. I've been commanding the war on five continents for four years, and we are just weeks from winning, so tell me what is so urgent?"

"Sir, your life is in danger. We got word from Springwood about an attack—before communication was cut off. All phone lines are down."

"Attack? At my Springwood? I'm incredulous! Alonzo, get security on the phone!"

"Oh my God, sir, they are right! I already tried! I can't get security on the phone! The line is dead, Mr. President."

"Where the hell is the Secret Service?"

"They may have been killed, sir. We think it's German Commandos, Mr. President. A last-ditch assassination attempt. We're bringing you back to West Point and safety, sir. The garrison is secure and has excellent radio communications."

FDR had survived an assassination attempt before his inauguration. The shooter had killed the Mayor of Chicago, sitting next to him. He assumed his practiced calm mien. "I see. This is all rather cloak and daggers. A nice ride down to West Point would be in order. General Donovan there? Wild Bill will have everything sorted out by the time we get to West Point."

"Sir, we must hurry. I hope it's a false alarm. We can take no chances. Let's get to the car."

Alonzo pushed FDR's chair out toward the waiting car, and helped transfer him into the back seat, slipped in to sit next to him. Krieger motioned to him to get out.

"But I always travel with the president!" Alonzo protested.

"No, Lieutenant Harris will assist us. Are you injured, Mr. President? The West Point Hospital is standing by." Krause motioned to Krieger. "Lieutenant Harris, walk him back to the house and give him those documents from General Donovan."

Krieger saluted. He was ecstatic. "Yes, Major."

"And hurry! I'll turn the car around—"

Alonzo hesitated at the door, turning back to FDR. "But, sir— I should stay with you!" he said, as the burly lieutenant took his arm and pushed him back to the house.

"Alonzo," said FDR. "Stay safe inside Top Cottage, turn off all the lights, lock the doors. When the phones come on, let them know where I've gone."

••• ▪ ▬▬▬ •▬•

KRIEGER PUSHED Alonzo through the door, shut it quickly, pulled Alonzo's right hand toward him sharply and kneed him in the face. As Alonzo staggered forward, Krieger spun the butler around and drew his SS dagger. With a single powerful motion, he slashed at the butler's neck with the razor-sharp blade. It tore through both carotid arteries and the larynx, and the butler sagged gurgling to the floor.

Krieger bounded back to the car, jumped into the driver's seat, and took off, with gravel flying, throwing the president back in his seat. They headed back down the dark Dutchess County roads toward the Hudson River.

"An attack on Springwood! I hope no one was hurt. The family and staff aren't there, but—it's horrendous. I mean, who is behind this? Intriguing. I wonder if it was that Skorzeny fellow that Hitler had rescue Mussolini. He seems to be their top man for these sort of covert operations. Skorzeny is said to be quite clever. You know, he was behind those false-flag attacks during the Battle of the Bulge. We could use more men like him on our side," said FDR.

Krause studied the shadow of FDR through the rearview

mirror and said, "Perhaps one day, he will work with you, Mr. President. We will have to fight those Russians soon enough."

"Ha! I certainly hope not. Stalin is a difficult man, but we have a solid agreement for a United Nations. We need world peace," said FDR. "What has happened? The lights of Newburgh are on. Well, I expect General Donovan will clarify when we get to West Point."

Silence quickly descended on the car. By the time they had crossed the Mid-Hudson Bridge, FDR was dozing.

"The man's legs don't work! He's a cripple!" Krieger whispered.

"Shhhhh. We have the car—we won't have to carry him far," whispered Krause. He couldn't believe they were still alive, with FDR in the back of their speeding car.

They were waved though the checkpoint at Thayer Gate, and headed across the garrison and down to the boat dock where they had originally landed.

At exactly 0200, Krause saw the blue signal light from the U-boat. He flashed back the pre-arranged response code. Minutes later, the assault raft that had dropped them the night before pulled up at the deserted dock.

They tried to move the sleeping FDR without disturbing him, wrapped in a blanket, but he woke agitated and confused. "What's going on? Is this West Point? Where is General Donovan?"

Krause pointed up at the castle-like outline of Thayer Hall on the bluff above them. "Mr. President, we are at West Point, as you can see. The Navy brought this submarine up from New York. General Donovan is here—in the sub—he will meet you aboard and brief you. After that, you can head directly back to the White House."

"I see."

"It seems as though they have things under control at Springwood. There were four Nazi commandos. They're all dead."

"Any of our boys?"

"Six, I'm afraid, Mr. President."

Roosevelt sighed. "Well, I'm sorry. Let's get aboard that submarine then, and get back to D.C. This war won't win itself!"

"Yes, Mr. President."

Krieger and Krause lifted FDR out of the car and carried him across the deck to the raft. With two crewmen from the U-boat, it was a tight fit, but they all scrabbled aboard and paddled out into the river toward the dark form of the U-555.

TWENTY-SEVEN

Angela Kunisberg sang along to the radio in her red BMW Roadster. Their previous night at the inn in Schwerin had been beyond passionate. Now as they headed toward their meeting with Trude Schellenberg, Brigade-führer Walter Schellenberg's niece, Goldstein was lost in his thoughts.

The sky was clearing, so they pulled off the autobahn to remove the rag top on the Roadster.

"So quiet this morning, Tom," said Angela.

"I'm just hoping it has some payoff. How do we even know this Nazi witch will see us?"

"I think you got your payoff last night! Ingrate!" said Angela, touching Goldstein's thigh. "Besides, my friend Johanna says Frau Schellenberg will see anyone who brings cigarettes. The old lady has good and bad days, but she likes cigarettes, and she loves to talk about the glory days of the Third Reich. When she can remember them. Cheer up, Tom! Maybe the old lady knows what Schellenberg planned to do with U-555. Maybe she'll tell us where Hitler's gold is buried, and we can run off together!"

Goldstein woke up that morning with a terrible headache, but now with the sun out and the wind in his face, he felt better. He felt guilty that he hadn't told Angela that he had actually already found the U-boat. She was really quite something. Running off with her wouldn't be the worst thing in the world. She was sassy and a total wild woman in bed.

Half an hour later, they left the autobahn at Stettin and pulled up to Trude Schellenberg's assisted-living facility. It was a neatly landscaped, low brick institutional building. A few ancient bundled-up residents were in wheelchairs smoking on the front patio, wrapped in blankets.

The receptionist turned them away. Frau Schellenberg was not receiving visitors. Not today.

"But please, tell Frau Schellenberg that we have a special package from her friend Johanna," said Angela.

The receptionist returned, shaking her head in wonder. "Frau Schellenberg will see you in the day room. *Sie ist eine sehr schwierige Frau.*"

Goldstein looked at Angela, trying to remember his German. "She's taciturn? Shy?"

"She's difficult, a polite word for bitch. Johanna's the magic word. She brings cigarettes, in trade for memorabilia and papers. C'mon. Let's go."

Trude Schellenberg sat slumped in a wheelchair. Was she awake? Or pretending to sleep? She was draped with a blanket, her gray, greasy hair barely covering her scalp. Her aide, a dark-skinned woman wearing a hijab, looked up from her phone.

"Frau Schellenberg, you have visitors," said the aide, gently rousing her.

Trude Schellenberg's head bobbed slightly. She pointed at the visitors, her outstretched arm trembling. Schellenberg's eyes were rheumy, but piercing. She focused intently on them.

"*Wer bist du? Was willst du?*" she asked, spittle flying from her mouth. Goldstein handed Frau Schellenberg a small bouquet of flowers. The old lady scowled, batted them away, and continued in German. *"Zigaretten! Jetzt!"* Cigarettes, now! Goldstein was appalled.

Angela handed her two cartons of Marlboros, wrapped in brown paper. She took over in formal German. "Thank you, Frau Schellenberg, for seeing us. I am Dr. Angela Kunisberg, a friend of Johanna, your professor from Heidelberg, who visits you. Johanna sends her best regards. This is Herr Doktor Professor Goldstein from Harvard University. He's doing research—"

"I want to smoke!" interrupted Frau Schellenberg. "This place is like a prison! They only let me smoke outside!"

"It's too cold to go out, Frau Schellenberg, you know that," said the aide.

"Shut up! Take me outside!"

The aide sighed, wrapped a blanket firmly around the old lady, and rolled her out to a small patio.

"Perhaps she'll freeze to death," the aide said hopefully to Angela. "I'll be right here. Inside." She went back into her phone.

Frau Schellenberg tore at one of the wrapped cartons, but Angela produced an already opened pack and handed Frau Schellenberg two cigarettes. Schellenberg put one behind her ear and accepted a light from Angela.

Taking a deep drag, she pointed at Goldstein.

"Herr Doktor Goldstein!" spat Frau Schellenberg, baring a few crooked teeth. *"Jude!"*

"A very important professor! Harvard! Interested in your Uncle Walter. And you, of course."

"An American and a Jew!" spit Frau Schellenberg, taking another deep drag from the cigarette. She looked like she'd claw his face if she could get out of her blankets and wheelchair.

"Ach, this is nothing new. All the Jews are interested in Walter. So, what does this Jew want from me?"

"We're not here for the Jewish question, Frau Schellenberg."

"He's only here because the Führer didn't get to finish the job!" she cackled.

"Frau, did your Uncle Walter ever talk about a special U-boat?"

"A boat? What are you talking about? My Walter was a scholar, and a lawyer, not a Navy man."

"Frau. The U-boat. After the war, did he ever mention a special U-boat—planning perhaps an escape to Argentina in a U-boat?" Angela flattered, "Taking you, too, of course, you were so important to him."

"Escaping! *Nein!* My Walter never ran away! He was not a coward! He worked relentlessly for the Reich to the final days!" She glared at them, insulted.

"But when you were talking, after the war?"

The old lady considered. "But *ja*—we talked, after the war, he regretted...so many mistakes, so many missed opportunities. But U-boats? About the U-boats...Did you know, he couldn't get Edward and Wallis Simpson to come back to Deutschland. *Ja*, now that was a tragedy. Edward and Wallis, they hated the Jews, too!"

Frau Schellenberg smoked the first cigarette down. She crushed it and turned casually to Angela. "Light my next cigarette, you *judische Liebhaberin.*"

Jew lover. Angela flinched and didn't translate that for Goldstein. Goldstein didn't need her to. The vicious old crone was almost more than he could take. He wanted to slap her. Knock her down. Shout "Six million dead!" But he said nothing.

Angela, more patient, persisted. "Frau Schellenberg, what did Walter say about the U-boat?"

"He missed Coco Chanel...do you know of their affair? I think he really loved her."

"A beautiful woman, yes. But the U-boat, Trude," Angela said, redirecting her.

"*Ja, ja.* The U-boat. Years later. He always wondered what

happened to that U-boat. They went to get the big Jew in New York! You! Goldstein! You would know! You're a big Jew!"

"I'm sorry, I don't know...a big Jew..."

Schellenberg coughed and spit into a napkin. "That Jew Roosevelt! Walter sent Skorzeny! To New York in that special U-boat!"

Could this be? "But why?"

The old lady cackled, coughed, and choked out, "To bring the old Jew Roosevelt back as a prize! For Himmler and the Führer."

"Are you saying Brigadeführer Schellenberg, your Walter, was planning to kidnap Franklin Roosevelt?" gasped Goldstein.

He was stunned. Zhao will be astonished. He couldn't wait to tell her.

"Oh *ja*," she chortled. "Capture your president! Walter was going to give him to Himmler! How do you like that, Jew man! Ach! How Walter loved the Führer!" She raised her right arm with amazing firmness and screamed "*Sieg Heil! Sieg Heil!*" almost falling out of her wheelchair.

The aide looked up from her phone, shocked, and opened the patio door. "Never a moment's peace! You've upset her. What have you two done? You have to go!"

They left quickly.

Even in the hallway, they heard the old lady shrieking and ranting about the *Juden* and *der Führer*.

Goldstein's head was spinning as they drove back along the autobahn to Hamburg.

Schellenberg had taken a special interest in U-555. Could this hideous, demented old crone be right?

Did the hulking wreck in the Hudson have any connection to FDR? He knew FDR had died peacefully, right around March, or was it April, at his retreat in Warm Springs, Georgia.

At least, that's what he'd thought he knew.

History is an argument about what happened, his professor had said. Can you trust your primary sources? Why are they

telling you this version of what happened? Contextualize. Inter-
pret. Work from only from known facts.

So what had happened? They needed more facts. More
known knowns. One more dive. Who and what was in that
submarine? Maybe Zhao could help solve the mystery. Goldstein
couldn't wait to get back to New York, share what he had
learned, and make one last dive to the submarine at the bottom
of the Hudson River.

••• ▬ ▬▬▬ •▬▬•

NEITHER KUNISBERG nor Goldstein noticed the gray Opel sedan
following them at a discreet distance. They'd have been shocked
to see the two agents of the Bundesnachrichtendienst (BND), the
German intelligence agency. These same men had made careful
notes of the romantic evening Kunisberg and Goldstein passed
in Stettin.

Even as Goldstein checked in for his flight home to New
York, messages flashed across the Atlantic and passed deep into
the U.S. security apparatus.

In the hidden corridors of power in Washington, there was an
uncomfortable stirring.

Men who dedicated their lives to protecting the status quo
came alert.

A nosy historian might stumble upon long-kept secrets with
dire consequences.

Steps had to be taken.

TWENTY-EIGHT

Franklin Delano Roosevelt lay snoring in the captain's bunk. He'd aged overnight, and his thin gray hair clung to his skull. His breathing occasionally paused for long seconds and then started with a snort. The Sodium Pentothal the Germans injected when he was brought aboard the sub was barely wearing off.

Krause reached down and pulled a blanket up over the sleeping man. "I'm so sorry, Mr. Roosevelt," said Krause softly. And to what end? he wondered. Peggy was dead. Even if they got back to Germany, could he live with himself? Krause returned to the crowded control room.

Krieger tore off his blood-stained American uniform and quickly buttoned his SS tunic. He was wild-eyed and sweating profusely. He had taken eight D-IX capsules in the last forty-eight hours. It was a massive overdose of methamphetamine. "You see, Krause! I have had my rank restored to Sturmbannführer! And you, I'm afraid you are demoted back to Hauptmann!"

Krause shook his head. He should be feeling triumphant.

Krieger was a monster. All Krause felt was regret and grief.

Krieger gestured to the captain's quarters, where Roosevelt slept. "The old man back there is the one who is really in the shit. We've stripped him of his rank! He's ours now. When he wakes up, I will have him polish my boots, maybe even scrub the floor. He's a weakling! A cripple! How does this sickly old woman rule such a powerful country? The Jewish press is full of nothing but lies!"

"You can't trust the press anywhere," retorted Krause. "Do you believe everything you read in the *Völkischer Beobachter*? I can't believe he's so deformed, but his magnetism is undeniable. His power comes from the people, Sturmbannführer. The American people believe in him."

Krause thought back to the days when his family struggled to keep their farm in Kansas and sat around the table listening to FDR on the radio. He gave them such hope. The government will help you. We'll all work together. We are doing these things in Washington, and you must help us. He had always felt better after the fireside chat.

"*Ja*, we will see how optimistic these Americans are with their dear FDR in Prinz-Albrecht-Strasse. I may even take the opportunity during the voyage back to teach him the truth about the Jews."

"Don't be a fool, Krieger. FDR is a fragile old man. And we need his cooperation to end the War in the West and turn our joint forces against the Bolsheviks."

"That's quite enough from you, Krause. True German men don't need any advice from Jew-loving Americans," said Krieger, mopping his brow.

The faint glow of hope inside Krause had flickered out. Krieger had destroyed his dream of reuniting with Peggy and starting a new life. Now had to admit to himself that Germany was ruled by madmen and that the hope of bringing America into the struggle with Bolshevism was a pipe dream. What had he done? How could he have been a part of this insanity?

"Enough politics, gentlemen. Let me tell you my plan," interrupted Korvettenkapitän Reichman.

"Excuse me, Herr Korvettenkapitän," sneered Krieger. "Did you say *your* plan? I am in charge here. This is my prisoner. We are leaving immediately for Berlin."

"This my submarine. The crew follows my orders."

Krieger's neck veins bulged. "I operate on the direct orders of Brigadeführer Walter Schellenberg! He has given me complete authority, and I give the orders. We must leave immediately for Berlin!"

"Of course, Sturmbannführer. We will leave at the first possible moment. I would like to maximize our chances of navigating down the river. And getting out of here alive," said Reichman in a steely voice. "Any minute, the Americans will realize that FDR has gone missing."

"And shit their pants. All the more reason for us to leave immediately," said Krieger.

"We can't clear the harbor by daybreak. There's not enough time. We must wait until tomorrow evening."

"There is no reason for them to suspect a submarine, Herr Korvettenkapitän. If anything, they'll be looking for a surface vessel," said Krieger.

Reichman nodded. "I hope so. Either way, we will have to remain here until sunset, 1830 hours."

"That's ridiculous!" snorted Krieger. "We are leaving immediately! I order it!"

"With all respect, Sturmbannführer, It's suicide to go now. It will be full daylight at 0600, just two hours—"

"This is a U-boat! Run submerged!"

"Impossible. We can't navigate sixty kilometers of a river submerged. The river is too narrow. Visibility through the periscope is too limited. Even if we could avoid running aground, or avoiding debris, we don't have enough battery life to make it back to the harbor at flank speed without using the snorkel."

"So we just sit here! Waiting! Like sitting ducks for them to kill us? This is your plan?"

"Yes. Wait until sundown. Make a fast run for it on the surface. With full diesel power we'll do it in about two hours. If we are spotted, we'll shoot our way out." Three U-boat crewmen stood close to Reichman and stared at Krieger with unmistakable hostility.

Krieger turned away, fuming. There was no choice but to acquiesce. He would settle scores with Reichman when they were back in Germany.

Around the U-boat, the crew prepared the ship quietly and deliberately, stowing gear, oiling bearings, and adjusting valves. In the ship's galley, the cook fried cabbages, potatoes, and sausage for dinner. The odor mingled with the sour smell of unwashed men and an over-stretched septic system.

In the forward torpedo room, the crew performed the routine maintenance. The seven-meter-long, heavily greased torpedoes were hauled out of their tubes, and the crew checked their contact pistols, battery charge, bearings and axles, rudder and hydroplane.

"Extra gentle with that one!" said the Torpedo Chief, pointing at the T7 Zaunkönig in Tube 2. The Zaunkönig was an acoustic torpedo that could home in on a target. It was a "fire-and-forget" weapon, that, when functioning properly, could track the sound-waves from a ship's propeller. This allowed the Germans to make otherwise impossible shots, including attacking a small escort vessel heading directly at them. The warhead was packed with two hundred and eighty kilos of Schiesswolle 36 explosive, a devastating blow for most ships.

The Zaunkönig was a double-edged sword. Used with skill and discipline, it could be lethal, but the slightest inattention to detail could be fatal for the U-boat firing it. The electronic components needed a minimum of four hundred meters to lock on the target. The Zaunkönig had on several occasions failed to acquire noise from the target's propeller and instead locked on the submarine's own propeller noise. The torpedo then became a "circle runner," doing a U-turn, and destroying the U-boat which fired it.

All U-boat captains knew they must dive the boat after firing, turn off their engines, and demand complete silence from the entire crew.

The torpedo men paid careful attention to the delicate hydrophones and complex steering mechanisms. When they had finished with inspection, they carefully lubricated the torpedoes and reloaded them in their tubes.

The crew was served dinner at 1600. The enlisted men ate at their stations or at their bunks. Buckets of food were passed back through the engine room to the battery compartment. Roused from his nap, Krieger ate with Krause and Reichman in the narrow passageway adjacent to the captain's bunk, where Roosevelt lay snoring. Krieger aggressively shoveled the food in his mouth. Whatever appetite Krause might have had evaporated at the sight of Krieger cramming food into his open maw and chewing loudly.

"Should we have cook reserve some food for FDR?" asked Krause

"The Jew can have some of the rotten potatoes," spat Krieger. "It will give a taste of what he'll get in Dachau."

••• ▬ ▬▬▬ •▬▬•

ON THE OTHER side of the thin door, FDR's mind began to emerge through the haze of sedation. His vision was blurred. The bright lights and loud conversation in the passageway made his head throb. He slowly became aware of his surroundings and could hear the voices speaking in German out in the hallway.

Educated at home until he was fourteen, FDR had a Bavarian governess, Fraulein Klein, and his *Hochdeutsch* was excellent. As his sensorium cleared, he began to focus on the conversation and make sense of his situation. He put together the pieces of the evening—the soldiers' appearance at Top Cottage, the story of the commando raid on Springwood, the car ride, and his transfer to the submarine. It was a nightmare and he feared the worst lay ahead of him.

The chief torpedoman entered the hallway. "Herr Kapitän, the inspection and maintenance of the torpedoes is complete. *Alles ist in Ordnung!*"

"*Der Zaunkönig*—is it functional?"

"*Jawohl*, Herr Kapitän!"

"We may have to fight our way out of this rat hole. Be sure to remind the crew of protocol. We are in shallow waters. We won't be able to dive deeply after we fire, so we will need absolute silence on the boat. If we aren't careful, the fish might pick up our noise and circle back. I think that's what happened to Kressler and U-252."

"*Jawohl*, Herr Kapitän! Absolute silence. No one wants a hot torpedo up our ass."

FDR nodded to himself and made note of the water tank near his bed.

••• ▬ ▬▬▬ •▬▬•

EIGHT KILOMETERS south of West Point, the USS Niblack DD-424, a two-thousand-ton Gleaves-class destroyer motored slowly up the Hudson, passing beneath the Bear Mountain Bridge. In April 1941, the Niblack escorted a convoy from Argentia, Newfoundland, to Reykjavik, Iceland. She'd detected U-52 on sonar, and dropped depth charges; giving her the honor of being the first U.S. Navy vessel to engage Germany in World War II. After heavy service in North Africa and the Mediterranean, the Niblack had recently returned to New York for rest and refitting.

Earlier that morning, her captain had received an urgent but somewhat vague order that morning to move upriver from New York and patrol as far north as Albany. She was instructed to be on the lookout for unusual river activity, possibly related to German infiltrators. The Niblack had pushed off almost immediately. A third of her crew, including the primary sound man who was sleeping off a hangover in a Brooklyn bordello, were left behind.

••• – ––– •––•

ABOARD U-555, FDR tried to sit up in his cot. His head pounded and his back was in spasm. He reached down and fumbled with the straps on his leg braces. These ungainly ten-pound constructions of steel and leather reached from hip to ankle and locked at the knees. Alonzo, or another aide, usually did this for him. He thought of Alonzo. Hoped he had raised the alarm. And Lucy! Had they caught her, too? He prayed she was safe at home in New Jersey. He finally unbuckled the heavy braces, and leaned them against the wall. He hated those braces, hated the limitation they stood for. For decades he had fought the paralysis, never giving up hope of a cure. The braces, like his wheelchair, were a physical manifestation of his losing struggle against polio.

He massaged his atrophied quad muscles and tried to organize his thoughts.

My God, thought FDR. I'm kidnapped. By Germans. I'm a prisoner. On a U-boat. How in God's name did this happen? That Major Krause was obviously a Nazi and that bastard Skorzeny must have organized it. Was there any way out of his predicament? He had been in tight spots before, but certainly nothing like this. Even death would be preferable to torture and humiliation.

In the adjoining control room, Krieger was drinking from a flask, and with each sip of schnapps, he became increasingly grandiose. FDR listened to Krieger and translated to himself. He remembered reading *Mein Kampf* first in English translation, then in the original German. The English translator had watered down the Nazi message of extermination; the version in the original German—Hitler's actual words, unfiltered—were a terrifying and clear description of a Master Race and World Domination.

Listening to Krieger was like reading *Mein Kampf* in the original German. It was terrifying. FDR had no illusions about what the Germans would do to him.

"When we deliver this Jew to the Führer, I will get Swords and Diamonds for my *Ritterkreuz*. I will recommend to the Führer that every crewman gets an Iron Cross! Except for the cook!" he added, throwing his meal into the garbage.

"FDR is not a Jew," said Krause.

"Jew or Jew lover, one and the same. You seem very much in love with this FDR, Krause. Maybe you are a Jew as well as an American. No matter, I will personally recommend to the Führer that you get a Knights Cross, and you, too, Reichman—if you get us out of here alive…"

The Funkmeister burst into the wardroom. "We have a contact forward, Herr Kapitän! High-speed screws!"

"Alarm! *In die Stellungen!*" barked Reichman. Battle stations!

Reichman, Krieger, and Krause jumped to their feet.

"Funkmeister—update me."

"Herr Kapitän, contact bearing zero degrees, sounds like a small escort vessel. Range five thousand meters. Closing slowly."

"Give me one-third forward! Periscope depth!" Reichman peered through Zeiss optics on the targeting periscope. He swallowed hard.

There was no mistaking the distant outline of a destroyer, heading directly at them.

"I'm picking up sonar, Herr Kapitän," said the Funkmeister, his voice trembling.

"This leaves us with no choice. We have no room for maneuver. We have to get him before he knows we are here! Load the Zaunkönig and flood Tube 2," ordered Reichman.

"This is insane!" screamed Krause. "We're trapped fifty kilometers from the harbor. Our only hope is to surface and negotiate. We have Roosevelt, we can make a deal."

"Shut up, Jew lover!" screamed Krieger, unholstering his pistol. "One more word, and I'll kill you."

"Put away the gun, Krieger! You'll get us all killed!" roared Reichman.

Krause lunged at Krieger, grabbing for the gun. The two men locked arms and grappled fiercely. Krause fought with the rage and energy of a trapped animal, but the huge SS man held the pistol in his right hand with a vise-like grip. Krause freed one hand and groped for Krieger's throat, but before he could get purchase Krieger gouged at Krause's eyes. Krause felt a searing pain in his left eye, and sensed fluid dripping down his face. He vomited and crumpled to the deck.

Krieger pounded Krause's head against the steel plates of the control room until he went still.

"Put down the gun, Krieger!" screamed Reichman

Krieger holstered his pistol and calmly put his SS dagger at Krause's throat.

"I should have taken care of you when I killed that American bitch of yours," screamed Krieger.

He slashed through Krause's jugular and carotid arteries with the razor-sharp blade. Blood spurted wildly across the room, painting the wall and dripping on the trim gauges.

Krause's vision dimmed, and through a haze, he saw his sister Hildi, his dog Schatzie, and then Peggy. She seemed to beckon him and he tried to beg forgiveness and tell her how much he had loved her.

His lips moved but no sound came.

Krause seized, then went still.

Krieger rose to his feet, wiped off his dagger, and holstered the pistol.

"I am confident, Herr Korvettenkapitän, that your report will describe this treason, and my fearless dedication to the Führer."

Reichman, splattered with blood, shook his head. These men were lunatics.

Trembling, he peered into the periscope optic. The destroyer was closing fast. "Do we have a firing solution, XO?"

"Range two thousand five hundred meters. It's a straight bow shot, Herr Kapitän. It will be difficult even with the Zaunkönig."

"A solution! I am asking! Do you have a firing solution?"

"*Ja*, Herr Korvettenkapitän."

"Then FIRE! And remember! QUIET!" The boat shuddered slightly as a blast of compressed air ejected the fourteen-foot homing torpedo. The torpedo's alcohol-fed motor spun up to 8000 rpm.

The fish streaked directly at the destroyer's bow. Perfect.

"ALL STOP!" ordered Reichman. "Silent running!"

"Fish is running straight and true," whispered the Funkmeister.

The din of the fans and blowers ceased, the lights dimmed, and the thrum of the electric motor disappeared. The crew stood stock still, some praying silently. Reichman heard his own heavy breathing. His heart was racing.

All was silent.

In the adjacent Captain's room, FDR had heard and under-stood everything, the fighting between Krieger and Reichman, the death struggle between Krause and Krieger, and now the firing of the acoustic torpedo and the call for silent running.

In a moment of absolute clarity he understood how it would all end.

For a man who had been a powerful athlete in his youth, his disability had been nightmarish. The hated wheelchair and braces were the most visible symbols of his affliction. But in the end, the paralysis he fought so bitterly to overcome, and the braces that scourged his flesh, would be his salvation.

The world slowed down around him. He let his thoughts drift to Lucy and their dreams of a quiet life at Top Cottage.

He reached for his braces.

Two hundred yards away the Torpedo knifed through the water at the oncoming destroyer.

The silence in the control room of U-555 was shattered by a loud metallic clang.

The initial concussion was followed by another and then a third.

"*Scheiss, was ist das?*" whispered Reichman. "That noise will get us killed! STOP IT!"

BANG. BANG. BANG. The metallic clanging intensified.

In the captain's cabin, FDR violently swung his ten-pound metal brace against the empty water tank. Roosevelt had lost considerable muscle mass during his recent physical decline, but his upper body was like ripcord and steel. He'd always been well coordinated, and he rhythmically struck the tank at a perfect angle.

The concussion sped through water. The sound wave traveled at 3,350 miles per hour.

Within a split second it reached the torpedo, which was only 300 meters away. The hydrophones on the Zaunkönig functioned perfectly. They detected the clanging and generated an electrical signal. A signal processor activated the servomotor, which pulled a pair of fins on the tail of the torpedo, hard to port.

The torpedo made an immediate one hundred and eighty degree turn, and headed directly at the source of the metallic banging.

Funkmeister Muller burst around the corner. "Herr Kapitän!" he gasped. "The fish is circle running!"

FDR listened and smiled.

The banging continued, louder.

Reichman yelled, "STOP THE NOISE!"

Krieger threw himself against the door to the captain's cabin. It held firm. Roosevelt had wedged a chair against the door. It was stuck fast.

At two hundred meters, the loud throbbing of the Zaunkönig's motor filled the control room.

The Funkmeister crossed himself, and wet himself.

BANG! BANG! BANG!

"Take that you Nazi bastards!" whispered Roosevelt.

Krieger threw his entire weight against the door, splintering the door and partially separating it from the frame. He recovered and prepared to launch himself again.

The nose of the torpedo slammed into the flank of the submarine.

The impact activated the firing pistol, detonating two hundred and eighty kilograms of Schiesswolle 36 high explosive. The blast tore a twenty-foot hole in the hull, obliterating everyone in the middle third of U-555. A tidal wave of cold black Hudson River water flooded the boat. It crumpled and sank slowly to the river floor.

The initial blast and flooding killed most of the crew. Six men in the aft torpedo room managed to close their watertight door. They spent their last thirty-six hours in the freezing cold and darkness beneath the Hudson until they were overcome by hypoxia.

The inattentive sound man on the Niblack had removed his earphones to get a cup of coffee, missing the torpedo explosion and death rattle of U-555.

Minutes later, the Niblack unknowingly cruised slowly over the crumbled carcass of U-555, as it settled into the silty Hudson River bottom. The destroyer crew's attention turned to the majestic cliffs and fortress of West Point, as the cadets in gray dress uniforms paraded on the Plane. Pointing to the fluttering American flags, one sailor remarked, "Pretty impressive, count on those Army guys to hold the high ground."

The Niblack cruised over the small oil slick marking FDR's watery grave... The ship continued up the Hudson River, trailing a small wake that broke silently at the South Dock of West Point.

TWENTY-NINE

It was near dusk as Zhao stood at Trophy Point, one foot on the breech block of a cannon from the Spanish American War. She waited impatiently for Goldstein. As a Firstie, she had more leeway than most cadets, but if she was late for the mandatory dinner with her company, she would have to explain her absence. She was frustrated; she was in uniform, so she couldn't even do planks and burpees, her usual way to fill ten minutes of unbooked time.

Trophy Point was the most beautiful spot on the West Point campus. Captured field guns from a half-dozen wars lay in a neat line within a grove of great oak trees. The spectacular view stretched over the high mountains on both sides of the Hudson River, over Constitution Island, and the wealthy historic town of Garrison. Zhao watched the twinkling lights of the mansions in Garrison come on, and the more industrial lights at the north, the town of Beacon.

It was a popular retreat for the cadets. The trees provided

some cover and allowed for a sense of privacy, so lacking at West Point. No sex, or even physical contact, between cadets was sanctioned at West Point, but Trophy Point was a place where cadets could meet discreetly for a stroll or a picnic dinner, or just sit on a bench and hold hands.

Standing hidden in the shadows, Zhao looked west across the Plain to Washington Hall and south to Battle Monument, a forty-six-foot polished granite column topped with a golden winged angel. The names of two thousand three hundred and sixty Regular Army soldiers who died for the North in the American Civil War are engraved on the column on bronze sheets. Cadets from southern states are prompt to point out the absence of Confederate war dead. Feeling aggrieved, they will refer to the obelisk as "The Monument to Southern Marksmanship."

Zhao saw Dr. Goldstein striding across the Plain. His bright orange L.L.Bean down coat stood out amongst the gray-uniformed sea of cadets heading to the mess hall.

As he prepared to cross the street to Trophy Point, he paused for traffic. He stood next to the statue of General John Sedgwick, USMA Class of 1837. Sedgwick was fatally shot beneath the left eye at Spotsylvania Court House, making him the most senior Union soldier killed in the Civil War. West Point lore had it that if a cadet went out at midnight and spun Sedgwick's spurs, they would pass an exam they would otherwise fail.

The street traffic came to a halt. Goldstein took advantage of the pause to cross the street, but partway everyone in uniform had come to attention. As a bugler played taps, the American flag adjacent to Battle Monument was lowered. The soldiers and cadets made crisp salutes. Goldstein stood awkwardly with his arms at his side. He looked very much a civilian. As the last notes sounded, traffic resumed and Goldstein ambled over to Zhao.

"You're late! I was worried," Zhao said.

"I'm sorry, I came straight from the airport."

"So what did you learn in Hamburg? What's the big secret? Is there an A-bomb on that sub?"

"Not exactly. I didn't want to say much on the phone. But I did hook up with an old colleague, Angela Kunisberg, and—"

Zhao interrupted, laughing. "Hooked up? Don't say that. I don't think you know what it means."

"Actually, I know exactly what it means. Angela and I have always had a connection."

Despite herself, Zhao felt jealous of whoever Angela was. "Good for you. So. Okay then. What exactly did you learn?" asked Zhao.

"Angela is an archivist for B & V, the U-boat builder. They retained some documentation related to the sub, and she found a letter that indicated Brigadeführer Walter Schellenberg, the head of Nazi foreign-intelligence services, requisitioned that sub for a special mission."

"Wow. Crazy. A mission! What sort of a mission?" added Zhao

"There is nothing else in the archives. Schellenberg died in 1952, but we managed to locate his niece—they were very close."

"And?"

"And, well, she's in a nursing home and only intermittently lucid, she's toothless and curses like a sailor, but she said that Schellenberg had told her of plans to use a submarine—to kidnap President Roosevelt! She insisted on calling him the big Jew," said Goldstein.

"Wow. Seriously? That's huge! Kidnap the president with a sub! From West Point. Or Hyde Park, it's just up the river from here. Maybe something went wrong with the sub and nobody ever heard about it!"

Goldstein nodded. "Schellenberg specialized in kidnappings."

"But this niece! How much faith can we put in a foul-mouthed, eighty-five-year-old demented Nazi?" Zhao looked dubious. "It's just her bad memory. No hard data. No smoking gun."

"You're right. We can't rely on her. We have to do another dive and find proof." Goldstein hesitated. Looking over the Hudson River view, he lowered his voice. "Zhao, I am concerned, I must tell you, before we get in deeper. The Secret Service came to my office and specifically warned me off doing any further inquiry into the sub."

"Holy shit. The Secret Service? Why didn't you tell me sooner? When? What have we stumbled into?"

"I understand if you want to back off now—"

"Where has following the rules gotten me so far? What, quit now, just when it's getting interesting?" Zhao snorted.

"The Secret Service didn't say anything about diving. They just wanted me to stop poking around in the archives. But Zhao, I'm concerned for you. I don't want to get you into trouble. We can dive one more time."

"Can we get in and out without anyone knowing?"

"It's worth the risk. One last dive. It's the only way to know. Can you get Haskins on board?"

"Don't worry about Haskins. He and I have an...understanding."

"You aren't...he's married...that's fraternization—he could get busted out of the Army!"

"Haskins will do what I ask." Zhao checked her phone. "There's no football this Saturday, but we have a physical-fitness test in the morning. Let's meet at 1200." Zhao waved and headed back to Washington Hall.

She passed close to the statue of Sedgwick. She paused, waved back to Goldstein, then reached up and spun the spurs on the general's boots.

... — ——— .—..

THE FOLLOWING SATURDAY AFTERNOON, Captain Haskins stopped Zhao before she jumped onto the Boston Whaler. "Listen, I'm sorry, Zhao, but I can't take you guys out on the boat. Not today. Not any time. And don't text or email me anything. In fact, it would be better, you should just go now. Could you just split," said Haskins, looking over his shoulder, "now?"

"What are you talking about? Dr. Goldstein will be here any minute," replied Zhao.

"Zhao. C'mon. We both know something weird is going on here. That depth anomaly is way off the charts. There has to be something down there, something bigger than the chain, some-thing you guys want to keep secret. The last dive we made, you came with sample bags and strobe lights. There must be a wreck down there. You know the Honor Code. I didn't have a choice." He looked at her sadly. "I like you. But I went and told the BTO. I had to."

"Oh, shit," said Zhao. "I'm not angry at you. Just—what did the BTO say?"

"Funny, he didn't seem very interested, just wanted me to keep my trip logs and fuel records…But Zhao, the next day I had two Secret Service agents in my office!" Haskins looked guilty. "They asked all sorts of crazy questions…Stuff about the KGB and a submarine. Maybe a U-boat? I did my best to keep you out of it. But they know you're involved—"

"Oh, man, oh man," said Zhao. She felt dizzy and sick, like she'd been punched in the stomach.

"Look, Zhao, get out of here! You're a good kid. This is trouble."

Goldstein ran down breathless to the docks. "Hey, listen, sorry I'm late! Let's get going! Why aren't we ready? Let's get out on the water. Let's go!"

"But who are these guys?"

Three black Suburbans pulled up alongside the dock, dust and gravel flying as they skidded to a halt. Haskins, Zhao, and Goldstein froze.

Six agents in dark suits jumped out of the cars. Goldstein recognized Agent Cadell. The two female agents grabbed Zhao. Two burly agents held Goldstein while they handcuffed his arms behind his back.

"You are both under arrest," announced Cadell. He read them both their Miranda rights.

"Let's go. Put them in the vans."

"Under arrest? What are you talking about? What's the charge? I need to see my lawyer, and she needs a lawyer too!"

"Hey, Officer," said Haskins. "What's this all about?"

Cadell waved his hand impatiently. "Put the boat away. Go home. And shut the fuck up about this."

The agents dragged Goldstein roughly over to the van.

"We have rights! I need to speak to my lawyer!"

Cadell looked murderous. "We warned you! Listen to me, now, you motherfucking traitor! This is an Army base not a small claims court. That one, your friend, the cadet," he pointed at Zhao. "She's a soldier, she'll be tried under the Uniform Code of Military Justice. She's off to fucking Leavenworth!"

Zhao gasped.

Goldstein felt a surge of panic and struggled to speak. "I want a lawyer. I'm a civilian!"

"We'll get you a lawyer, asshole! Right now you're going with us. Just thank God we can't send you right to Guantanamo!" yelled Cadell, pushing Goldstein into the van and slamming the door.

Cadell turned to Zhao, tears were streaming down her cheeks, and spoke to her in a low voice. "You better tell us everything you know, sister, or you really are headed to Leavenworth." He shoved her roughly into the SUV and slammed the door.

He rapped hard on the window and the SUV sped off. Cadell jumped into the third SUV and the three vehicles drove off.

••• ▬ ▬▬▬ •▬▬•

Haskins dropped the gear on the deck. He stood, stunned, mouth agape. He knew that his conversation with the BTO had set this in motion, but what choice did he have? He felt awful. Zhao was a fellow soldier and Goldstein a decent and honest guy. What the hell was going on? Should he go to the BTO? Then it hit him. His old college roommate—Peter Kim, the one who told him about the Great Chain. The last time they had spoken, Kim was elliptical, but Haskins had got the strong sense Kim worked for the CIA. Haskins knew the smart move was to lie low, but the soldier in him wasn't going to leave his buddies behind. Zhao and Goldstein needed his help. Haskins reached for his phone to call Kim.

THIRTY

Vice President Harry Truman felt at home in Sam Rayburn's cozy private office. Rayburn, the powerful and connected Speaker of the House, was an old ally from Truman's days in the Senate. The walk over had been chilly —it was a blustery spring day—and now Truman basked in the warmth and glow of logs burning in the fireplace, and the small, neat glass of bourbon in his hand.

Three months of frustration! It felt good to be back with an old, trusted friend. Despite being vice president, "a heartbeat away from the presidency," since January, Truman was marginalized at the White House. He was blocked out, not on the agenda, not included in meetings.

A naturally genial and social man, it pained Truman to be pointedly excluded from the Roosevelts' nightly cozy cocktail hour in the residential wing of the White House, where the real influence and policymaking happened. Roosevelt didn't want him in the White House. Never had. Wasn't going to include him in anything.

FDR resented Truman; he'd not wanted to jettison his progressive Vice President, Henry Wallace, and did it reluctantly, under intense pressure from party leaders. Truman wasn't even his tenth choice for replacement vice president; FDR preferred U.S. Supreme Court Justice William O. Douglas. Conservative southern legislators selected Truman in what was at the time dubbed, "The Second Missouri Compromise." FDR was stuck with Truman, but refused to work with him.

"Give us ten minutes alone, Sheila!" Rayburn shouted into the bustling main office, where four efficient secretaries and Sheila fought a losing war against ringing phones, messengers, and waiting lobbyists.

Rayburn closed the door. The two old friends were finally alone. Rayburn, a political animal, knew how important Truman could be if FDR became ill or died. He was flattered, and happy to give advice or ferret out information. He welcomed his old friend effusively, settling into the overstuffed armchair across from Truman.

Rayburn lowered his voice confidentially. "People tell me FDR's still giving you the cold shoulder, Harry. Are you sorry you took the vice presidency?"

Truman slammed his drink down, spilling the bourbon. "My God, Sam! I'm cut out of everything! The entire globe is being reconfigured! Europe reimagined! Right there at the White House! I'm completely excluded."

"Well, you're new in the job, Harry. The White House is a big step up from Capitol Hill. He probably just misses Wallace. I'm sure FDR will bring you up to speed."

"Up to speed? I can't even get a meeting with the man! He's got everyone in the whole world pleading their cases through his office—Britain, India, all of Africa! I can't even get in just to listen! I've been veep for almost three months. Sam. Look. How many meetings do you think I've had?"

Sam waited.

Truman exploded. "Two! Two, that's right! Just two goddamned face-to-face meetings with FDR! In three months! He's all smiles. He's very glib. But Sam, he won't talk to me, he doesn't respect me. He doesn't trust me."

Rayburn added more booze to their glasses. "Harry, be patient. FDR is a sick man. There's no way he survives a full term. He probably won't survive till Christmas. Try to relax, bide your time. You'll be president. This year, next. Your moment is coming."

Truman bit his lip and stared out the window at the Capitol Building across the street.

A sharp knock at the door. Rayburn looked annoyed. "I told Sheila to give us ten minutes alone."

The door swung open, Sheila protesting, and two Secret Service men barged in, ignoring her.

One spoke very quickly, handing Truman his coat and hat. "Mr. Vice President and Mr. Speaker! Orders from Admiral Leahy and Mr. Hoover. You're coming with us to the West Wing, immediately."

Rayburn stood up quickly. "What's happened?"

"Not you, Mr. Rayburn. Just the vice president. Now."

Truman had a nodding acquaintance with Leahy, who was FDR's chief of staff, but had never met the FBI chief. Hoover stayed in the shadows, but, for reasons that Truman didn't fully understand, everyone in D.C. was terrified of him.

Truman stood. "Now I'm taking orders from Admiral Leahy? What the hell is this about? Senator Rayburn and I have—"

"No, sir, I'm sorry. Now. Hurry. Admiral Leahy was very clear—it's urgent."

Truman sighed. "No doubt some goddamned funeral they want to send me off to. In Timbuktu." He slugged down the last of his bourbon and shrugged on his coat. He waved to Rayburn and headed to the door.

As he started down the hall, a second agent, carrying a

Thompson submachine gun, fell in step. Two grim-faced agents scanned the hallways, grabbed his shoulders, and almost carried him down the stairwell. Truman felt the hair stand up on the back of his neck. What the hell is this all about? Okay, then. Steady soldier, he told himself.

Rayburn put his head out the door and yelled after Truman, "I'm sure it's good news! I'm feeling it! Don't forget your friends on the hill, Harry!"

The silent Secret Service men hustled Truman into a waiting armored limousine, escorted by two other cars filled with FBI agents. They drove at high speed down Independence Avenue, and then cut across 17th Street to the White House.

Admiral Leahy, FDR's chief of staff and close personal friend, waited impatiently for him at a side entrance he'd never seen before, surrounded by four heavily armed agents.

"Follow me. Now!" commanded Leahy, adding, "Mr. Vice President, sir."

Truman stood stock-still. "That's enough ordering me around, Admiral! I'm in the dark around here. What is happening? I won't do anything more unless I understand it."

"Please, Mr. Vice President! There is a…situation."

"What are you talking about? Where is the president?"

The Secret Service men surrounded Truman in a scrum, facing outwards and back to the driveway, scanning the perimeter. Admiral Leahy put his hand on Truman's back, pushing him gently through the doorway. "Please, Mr. Vice President, let's get you safely inside. Of course, you are in charge. We'll explain it all when we get you to a secure location."

They headed down the corridor to an elevator, guarded by two soldiers with carbines. Truman felt his stride lengthen, he stood more erect, and felt a surge of adrenalin. Exiting the elevator, they walked as a group down a basement corridor to an unmarked door, guarded by two other soldiers.

"I've never come down here. Where are we?"

"It's the Map Room. You haven't had the security clearance until now."

Truman was insulted. And mystified. FDR had never invited Truman to the Map Room before. Everyone knew FDR spent many hours in the Map Room, following the war from moment to moment, planning strategy with his admirals and generals. The room was dominated by floor-to-ceiling maps of the European and Pacific Theaters. In the Pacific, an American fleet encircled Okinawa, and symbols showed the masses of Marines and Army units battling the Japanese. In Europe, the Soviet and American lines were racing toward each other, and Berlin.

Until today, Harry Truman had not been welcome. Now he was urgently summoned. Why was he asking him to the War Room now? Had we won the war? Was it over? Had the Germans unleashed some crazy explosive bombs, one of Hitler's Wonder Weapons, on American soil? No, he thought to himself, those nuclear devices were just German Army public-relations hyperbole to keep the United States in fear. There was no single bomb that could wipe out an entire city, he was sure. That's just fearmongering and science fiction.

The Map Room was busy. Young men and women in military uniform were deeply occupied updating maps and reports, typing, and on the phones. Truman noticed a particularly attractive young red-headed WAC, standing on a ladder adjusting a marker to reflect the latest update from the front. Truman did not fail to note her attractive ankles.

Admiral Leahy shouted, "All personnel out! Now." The military staff left quickly, but the Secret Service men looked askance. "You guys, too. Guard the door. Trust me, if we're not safe here, it's over."

FBI Director Hoover and General George Marshall were waiting for them. Truman noticed both men jumped to their feet, a new mark of respect. Marshall looked like the housemaster of an elite boarding school, thoughtful and intelligent. Hoover, overweight and pugnacious, looked suspiciously at everyone.

He collected secret files on everyone, including a thick file on First Lady Eleanor Roosevelt.

"Nowhere is safe," said Hoover. "Spies and traitors everywhere. Communists, too. Mr. Vice President, gentlemen, I'm sorry about the mess the Army has made. The FBI is working to straighten out this fiasco."

Marshall, a man of highly controlled temper, seethed with rage. "I am disappointed Mister Hoover! Scoring points off the Army when the president is missing!"

Truman cut him off. "FDR missing? I'm not meeting him here? Admiral Leahy, speak! What is going on?"

"FDR is missing," Leahy said.

"What do you mean, missing? How did you lose the president? If FDR is missing, I'm in charge here! I need to know everything. Now!"

Leahy cleared his throat. "The initial report is very alarming. Discovered this morning at 0600 at Top Cottage—FDR isn't there. Four people are dead, all three guards, and FDR's private valet. Two had their throats cut. Two were shot. The shell casings are 9 mm. Phone lines cut. I suspect Nazis."

Truman sat down abruptly. He thought he'd faint. FDR missing. Four dead. Nazi commandos in New York.

"And Eleanor? The rest of the family? Are they injured?"

"Oh, his family isn't anywhere near New York—"

"But what do they know—"

"Now? Nothing. They think he's up in Hyde Park, looking at his stamp collection. Only we three, and this morning's guards and staff, know."

"Keep it that way until we know more. What else do we know? Where do you think FDR is right now?"

"We conclude, well we think...FDR has been kidnapped."

"Kidnapped? By whom? Has anyone contacted us? Is there a demand for ransom? Or for peace?" asked Truman. "The Russians? The Germans?" The Republicans, he thought, but knew he couldn't say it.

Hoover added, "Let's not forget those spies the Germans dropped by U-boat on Long Island in '42." Hoover saw spies everywhere. And sometimes he was right.

"Any contact from the Germans or Japanese?" asked Truman. "Do you think they did it?"

"Nothing yet," said Leahy. "No response yet. We've made inquiries through neutral diplomatic channels. Nothing back from the Swiss, the Swedes…"

Truman looked at Hoover. "Tell me everything you know, and what you are doing."

Hoover looked at his papers. "The bodies were discovered at change of shift at 0600. Could have been anytime after 2200 when the last guard phoned in the all-clear for the night. Mr. Truman. Let me run this operation! The FBI knows how to do a manhunt. This job is our job! We've roadblocked all the roads around West Point and Hyde Park. Every car and truck fully inspected. I'm sure the kidnappers can't get far with the president's limitations."

Marshall snorted, "That's what you say, Mister Hoover. They could be miles away by now in a box truck…"

Hoover glared. "Look how well the Army protected him! Never would've happened if the FBI was watching him. FBI agents don't wander off!"

"Excuse me Mr. Hoover, they didn't wander off! They were shot!"

The thought of Roosevelt ill, hungry, bound and gagged in a trunk made Truman physically ill. He started to feel sweaty and nauseated. He had to think clearly and take command. These three men, the political guy Leahy, the Army guy Marshall, and the FBI guy Hoover, were at odds; they had to work together to find FDR, and they had to keep this completely from the American public. Remember the hysteria caused by the Lindbergh baby kidnapping. This was so much bigger. The American people would panic, feel unsafe, lose faith in the government.

Truman asked, "Marshall. What else are we doing? What other information?"

General Marshall said, "Harbor Command reported an unexplained radar contact forty-eight hours ago. Unconfirmed, though. We've closed New York Harbor to all traffic. We did get a rather garbled report from the local police in Briarcliff Manor. Apparently a ten-year-old boy reported seeing a U-boat on the river the other night."

"A ten-year-old?" Are you serious?" asked Hoover. "Is the Army depending on children for coastal security? The next thing you know an eight-year-old girl will have us looking for the Loch Ness Monster."

"Mister Hoover, your lack of collegiality is noted. I know it's not much to go on, but I've had the Navy send the destroyer Niblack up the river to investigate," said Marshall.

Truman frowned. "Closed New York Harbor? How are we explaining this to people?" The other three men looked down. "Don't you think people are going to wonder why the harbor is closed? Any other leads, anything else to find FDR?"

"The daughter of the commandant at West Point was just reported missing. She's probably the mole, the inside woman on this—"

Truman was shocked. "Is she involved?"

"Possibly," said Hoover. "She hasn't returned yet from an escapade with two Army officers two nights ago. The maid says the name was Major Krause, she thinks. An imposter, I think, in a stolen uniform. We can't find anyone in the personnel records with that name. It feels like that Nazi bastard Skorzeny is behind this. We found the commandant's car abandoned near West Point—she went for a joyride in the car—but no sign of the girl. She might just be an alcoholic on a bender. She might show up today. When she returns home, we'll arrest her and beat the information out of her."

Hoover always said the quiet part out loud. He had a file on everyone in Washington, and told them all. He liked to drop the names of married men's girlfriends or illicit trade deals, just to startle people. He had dirt on every man in the room.

Leahy cleared his throat. "So, sir, we've prepared a public statement for you to read, Mr. Truman. You must strike the right note to fully inform and reassure the American public. We need to explain the canceled shipping and the roadblocks. Are you listening to me? You need to explain that the president is missing."

"No, I don't," Truman said acidly. "I'll listen to your advice. It doesn't mean I'll take it. I will not tell the American public that FDR is missing. It will cause widespread panic, dead guards, and missing women. Marshall: people will notice the closed harbor. Have the Army take the fall for me on this. Say it's a War Department SNAFU. Loose torpedoes. Harbor net malfunction. Unexploded ordinance. That sort of thing. Call a reporter at *The Times* with a plausible explanation. You'll think of something."

Leahy asked, "And how do we explain the three dead guards?"

"Training accident," Truman responded. "Happens all the time. Especially in Albany or Syracuse or Fort Drum, where these three men tragically died. Leahy, you take care of the families, the notification letters, the articles in the newspaper about the importance of gun safety and all."

Leahy persisted. "And what will you tell them about FDR's dead valet with his throat cut?"

"The family cannot know this." Truman sighed. "He had a heart attack. Heart attack, Leahy, write that down. Cremate the body. Write a beautiful warm letter from FDR—you sign it—about his service to the country. Get someone kind and close to the family to call them—"

"But what are we going to say when he's missing appointments and meetings? People are asking to see FDR. We can't just have him vanish into thin air without an explanation," said Leahy, looking at the week's planner. "What do we tell the people where the president is?"

"He's run down. He's heading to Warm Springs to recover. Tell them...he's getting physical therapy, taking a vacation, getting his portrait painted, or some shit like that. Tell them he'll be back in a week."

"Mr. Vice President, is this a cover-up? Are you calling off this manhunt?" asked Hoover.

"Of course not. Hoover, turn up the manhunt. Turn it up high! Blame it on a serial killer loose in upstate New York. Here's an idea. Let a real convict out from Sing Sing prison. Tell him to run like hell. Put up roadblocks everywhere for him, according to official reports. Local citizens will get excited and help us look for anything unusual on the river or on the road. We have to find him." Truman sighed. "I don't know how long FDR will survive as a kidnapping victim. We have to find him soon, or..."

Leahy pushed hard one last time. Was Truman even listening to him? "Mr. Vice President, you have to make this statement. I've written it, do a press conference, you have to tell the American people what is happening."

"Tell them what is happening? How? You don't know what is happening!" He glared at Leahy, who held out the statement to be signed. "No statement. We'll tell the American people what they need to know, when they need to know it."

Leahy asked, "And for now?"

"Stay focused. Work with each other. Until we find him, I am in command. We don't have to tell the American people, but you three know it, and I know it. Use every resource to find FDR—dead or alive—as soon as possible."

Leahy gasped. "You can't believe the president of the United States is actually dead!"

Truman looked at him. "No, of course not. The president of the United States is not dead. You're talking to him." He paused. "I'm the president now. Whether I want it or not."

THIRTY-ONE

G oldstein and Zhao passed the night in manacles in the West Point brig. They were cold and hungry and desperate to pee. Finally, just as dawn was breaking, Goldstein couldn't hold it any longer and wet himself. The smell of urine filled the small room.

"God, I'm so sorry."

"It's okay, Dr. Goldstein. I've been in the field with cadets, it's pretty hard to gross me out."

"You're kind, Zhao. Kindness is in short supply here at West Point."

"No kidding. Kindness and justice both."

Zhao felt a surge of affection for Goldstein. He was quirky, but he was passionate about history and loved to teach. Unlike everyone else at West Point, he was an iconoclast. He knew right from wrong, and wasn't afraid to break rules if it meant doing the right thing. She was happy to share the discovery with him. But now what? Would she ever get a break?

"Tell me, Zhao," asked Goldstein. "Tell me how these fools here at West Point managed to make a woman like you hate them so much."

Zhao hesitated. What the hell, she thought, what do I have to be ashamed of? As the early light filtered through the barred windows, Zhao told Goldstein how it had all gone wrong. At the start of her final year at West Point, Zhao had been the odds-on favorite to be selected as First Captain, the highest honor at West Point. She was at the top of the class academically, physically, and militarily. She finished her command of summer training with excellent reviews. She was loved and respected. Zhao deserved to be First Captain, and she wanted it more than anything. As First Captain, she would command the entire Corps of Cadets. She would stand next to the superintendent and review the Corps when they marched by on parade, and be introduced to visiting dignitaries as the personification of West Point excellence. She would be the first female Asian cadet at West Point to wear seven stripes on her uniform sleeve, and seemed the perfect choice as the Army pivoted to the looming enemy in the East.

When Zhao was summoned to the superintendent's office late in August, she knew there could only be one reason. Finally, the day had come! She was bursting with pride and excitement at commanding the Corps. She would follow in the footsteps of John Pershing and Douglas MacArthur. On her way from her room in MacArthur Barracks to the superintendent's office on the fourth floor of Washington Hall, Zhao crossed the Plain and looked up at the equestrian statue of George Washington. Who knew how far her Army career would carry her? My parents will be so proud, she thought. They would meet the president when he came to speak at graduation in May!

The superintendent, Lt. General Alexander, was a broad-shouldered former Infantry Officer, with a friendly smile and relaxed manner. He liked cadets, especially high performers like Zhao. He waved her into his carpeted office and directed her to a pair of easy chairs. The walls were decorated with framed weapons and portraits of soldiers. On his desk, there was a photograph of the general with former President Trump. Zhao already felt like a colleague—after all, First Captain was part of the Academy Leadership Team.

"Cadet Zhao! Excellent job this summer running Cadet Basic Training. You seem very popular with the plebes," said the general in a broad South Carolina accent.

"Thank you, sir. I tried, well, my whole command team tried to lead by example, sir."

"Yes, that's fine cadet, just fine. A few of your PowerPoints might have been more polished, of course..."

"I know, sir, but our leadership team focused our energy on teaching the new cadets. We did every road march with them, and worked to create a strong team spirit. We even created our own motto, sir: Always the Best, Nothing Less!"

"Yes, yes, quite so. I've heard a few cadets quoting that. Morale-building with the lower ranks is important, of course. But—"

"But what, sir?" Zhao was on alert. What was he getting at? She couldn't have done a better job.

"But, Zhao, you are forgetting how crucial it is to communicate clearly with senior leadership. It's the only way to advance your career and accomplish the mission. Terrible mistake to get caught in the weeds and not see the bigger picture! Do you know Cadet Richter from the Crew team? Of course you do, you've worked with him."

Zhao remembered Richter as a brownnoser and a bully. Richter had seemed interested in her. She wanted nothing of it.

General Alexander continued. "He's quite good with PowerPoint presentations. He's very crisp and to the point. You might spend some time with him."

Zhao felt her stomach tighten.

"Let's not dwell too long on this summer, Zhao. You have

Firstie year ahead of you, and we need to make sure the Corps of Cadets has the best possible leadership."

"Yes, sir." Zhao relaxed a little. First he had to criticize. It's the Army way. But now. Now he would tell her she was appointed to be First Captain.

"Zhao, do you know what the most important element of your USMA training is?"

"Duty, Honor, and Country, sir."

"That's right, Zhao, and at this moment, my gravest concern about the Corps of Cadets is Honor. The commandant and I feel that the Honor Board isn't taking its responsibilities seriously enough. Cadets have pledged "Not to Lie, Cheat, or Steal or Tolerate Those Who Do," and sometimes I don't think the message gets through. It's absolutely my top priority this year. That's why I've decided to make you the...Brigade Honor Captain."

Zhao's mouth dried out; her tongue felt stuck to the roof of her mouth. Brigade Honor Captain! Are you kidding me? It was the worst job of all at West Point. The Brigade Honor Captain presided over the Cadet Committee that conducted trials of cadets accused of honor-code violations, mostly plagiarism. Some cheating. Egregious rule-breaking. It was a thankless job and carried no prestige or privileges.

"Honor Captain? Sir? I had thought, well, hoped for, a senior leadership role—a Regimental Command at least!—or possibly First Captain—"

Alexander interrupted her. "Yes, well, Cadet. The commandant and I have made that decision, and with a great deal of thought. David Richter will be First Captain. He's a model of efficiency. He reminds me quite a bit of his father, Wild Bill Richter. His dad's a colonel over in the 101st and was my XO back when I had the 82nd. You two will work well together." Alexander stood up. "And Zhao, take my advice..."

"Sir?"

"Get him to bring you up to speed with PowerPoint. That's all."

Alexander gestured toward the door, and picked up a file on his desk.

Zhao stumbled out of Washington Hall, flushed, angry, and mortified, and headed back to her barracks. It just didn't make sense. Too shocked to speak, unable to face friends and room-mates, she locked herself into a toilet stall in the barracks to sob, and then vomit.

Later that evening, she was alone in her room when there was a knock on the door. She opened it a crack and saw Richter, soon to be First Captain. He pushed the door open and closed it behind him.

He reeked of alcohol. This was bad. "Excuse me, Richter—the regulations—we can't be alone in the room with the door closed. It's late. What time is it?"

"Time? Who knows? We just closed down the Officers Club. Pretty late," slurred Richter. "How about a kiss, Zhao. Let's cele-brate my promotion." He leaned toward her and put his hand on her shoulder.

"It's after taps, you're drunk, and you shouldn't be in my room. I should report you to the Honor Board."

"Come on now, Zhao. I'm The First Captain and you're...you're whatever position they gave you. I told Alexander I wanted you on my team, so he threw you a bone. You owe me a kiss—or more."

Zhao was mortified. They threw her a bone? Richter leaned closer to her. He moved to kiss her and made a clumsy grab for her breasts. Zhao slapped him, hard, across the face. He stum-bled away, blood trickling down his lip.

"Touch me like that again and I'll kill you," hissed Zhao. And she meant it.

Richter moved to the doorway. Turning to leave he slurred, "Alexander asked me about you. I said you were a cold-hearted bitch. I was right."

Zhao slammed the door after him and locked it.

"I was so ashamed. I told my best friend. Everyone in First Regiment knew Richter was a predator, and a couple of girls had filed complaints, but nothing ever got done. Guys like him are Teflon-coated. Nothing sticks. Now he's First Captain."

"Did you report him?"

"I thought about it, but what's the point? It's my word against his. His dad's a colonel. People would say that I was angry that I didn't make First Captain. I gave them eight years of my life, eight years of sacrifice and dedication, and for all of that, they called me a bitch."

"So why didn't you just quit?" asked Goldstein

"It's the Army, remember—I have a five-year commitment after graduation."

"Oh right. Shit."

"That's when I decided to apply for a Rhodes Scholarship. I thought two years at Oxford would give me time to clear my head and establish some credibility. Maybe one day I could come back to the Army, and effect some change. It's a delaying action. So that's my story. And now this shitshow. I'm probably headed for Fort Polk or a dishonorable discharge."

••• ▪ ▬▬▬ •▬▬•

GOLDSTEIN WAS FURIOUS. He had always been slightly unsettled around men in uniform. This was an outrage. Was there no justice in the Army? This is all my fault, he thought. Why didn't he listen to the Secret Service and back off when they warned him? No, he wouldn't back off. This was a cover-up, pure and simple, like Watergate. This is Orange Fucking County, New York, not Chechnya, he thought. That asshole Cadell could only fuck with them so long. After all, what had they actually done? Diving in the Hudson, and found a submarine. There was no law against wreck diving. Hell, we're heroes! Sooner or later they'll let me call a lawyer.

One phone call to a judge and they would have to let him go. He'd sue the hell out of them.

Goldstein began talking to himself. "I'll call Karen Shanda. She'll rip into those bastards." Karen was a college classmate of his mother's, a long-time frenemy; both English Lit majors, his mom wound up teaching high school. Karen went to law school. Karen was belligerent. She'd never ask when she could demand. She fought with the prosecutors, the judge, her co-counsel, even her clients. Karen defended white-collar criminals, the Hamptons-Goldman Sachs crowd when they were charged with financial crimes, like fraud, and she despised the government and the police. The last time he'd seen her, at Passover, she'd been loud and drunk, and was laughing, "You should see these Wall Street guys begging me! Please take me as a client! Whatever it takes! Here's a blank check!" Oh, God. The money, Goldstein thought. Crap. That will be a problem. Karen Shanda had no family of her own and always came to the Goldstein's Passover Seder, but in the end what did that mean? Would she need to be paid upfront? he wondered. Goldstein didn't have the kind of money a big-league lawyer would want. Goldstein wondered if his parents would front him the money. They don't have much. They would have to take a mortgage on their house. Holy shit, my brother Steve will flip out, he thought. My arm is killing me. Fuck these people.

The door to the brig creaked open, and a thick-necked Military Policeman with a broken nose opened the door. Agent Cadell entered and wrinkled his nose. "Jesus Christ, it stinks like piss in this place!" he said to no one in particular. "Take off the manacles."

The MP opened the manacles.

Cadell pointed at Zhao.

"Get her out of here. You're going back to barracks. You're

confined to your room until further notice. Don't get your hopes up. We're conferring with the Judge Advocate General."

He turned to Goldstein.

"For God's sake, I can't look at him. Get him cleaned up, put him in some clothes. Then bring him next door."

Goldstein washed himself as best he could, and dressed himself in a comically large XXL set of gray sweatpants. The MP pushed him down the hall to a small conference room where Cadell sat waiting, and shoved him into a folding chair.

"Want me here?" the MP asked Cadell. "For security?"

"No, I think I can take him," Cadell laughed. "Get him some grub, will you? Here, Goldstein, have some water." Cadell threw him a water bottle. Goldstein missed the catch, got the water bottle off the floor, and slugged the entire bottle down. "That MP doesn't have the clearance for this conversation."

"I want a lawyer," said Goldstein.

"We can get you a lawyer. We can recommend one..." answered Cadell.

"Ha. Not your lawyer. I want a real lawyer," said Goldstein.

"Better get a good one. We're planning on sending you away for a long time. We warned you."

"Why? On what charge? What did I do? Dive on a wrecked submarine. Why are you here? Why is the Secret Service involved in this? *You* have explaining to do, not me!"

Goldstein knew he shouldn't talk to Cadell or anyone without a lawyer. But he was mystified.

What was happening to him? He couldn't organize his thoughts. Is this what it felt like to be disappeared? One moment you are in Heathrow Airport, and the next day some black-box CIA interrogation cell.

"We explained already. We warned you. The sub is a matter of national security. We told you to stop poking around."

"Look, so we didn't have permission to dive on that sub, but so what? It's a seventy-five-year-old German U-boat! What could it possibly have to do with national security?"

"You don't have the clearance to know. You can't hear what's so important about that sub. But now…We do need to talk to you about that little honeymoon in Germany."

Cadell opened a briefcase and tossed out photos of Goldstein and Angela, leaving her office at B & V and then checking into the inn near Stettin.

"Check these out—you and your girlfriend. The really racy ones are at the end."

"What is wrong with you people?" shouted Goldstein. He threw the photos on the ground. "You followed us! And photographed us? She's a colleague and my friend. She has nothing to do with you!"

"It looks like your personal matter has involved you with a long-time agent of the KGB!" shouted Cadell. "She's an agent, Goldstein, for twenty years."

"You bastards!"

"So we're the bastards?" shouted Cadell. "You're a fool. You're an employee of the U.S. Army and you consort with an enemy agent and share matters of national security?"

"I need a lawyer."

"You bet you need a lawyer. Thomas Goldstein, you are under arrest. We're charging you with conspiracy and espionage. You have the right to consult an attorney of your choice. If you can't afford one, we will provide you with an attorney. You have the right to remain silent, anything you say can and will be used against you. You're an arrogant prick, Goldstein. Don't say we didn't give you a chance."

Cadell stormed out.

The MP entered with a tray of greasy eggs and toast on a metal tray. He nodded at the phone on the desk. "You dial out from that, when you're ready."

Sure, he could use the phone.

If he could figure out who to call.

Goldstein got through to his parents. He'd interrupted their breakfast, doing the *New York Times* crossword puzzle together.

They were confused, then frantic. He had to repeat three times that he was under arrest, in jail. They couldn't seem to understand his words. Arrest? Jail? You, espionage? You need a lawyer? He persuaded them to send Karen Shanda to West Point.

Karen Shanda arrived late in the afternoon, wearing her usual flashy outfit: leopard-print raincoat, miniskirt, and tall leather boots. Completely inappropriate for a hefty woman in her sixties, but Karen knew it was her trademark. No one forgot the photos on the *New York Post* tabloid covers, doing the perp walk with her finance bros, or the *New York Daily News* photos of triumphant celebrations when she got them free. On technicalities. Or plea bargains. Or throwing their friends under the bus. Whatever it took to get her client out. When Wall Street traders got into trouble, they wanted the lady in the leopard-skin coat.

Goldstein jumped to his feet. "Karen! Thank you enough for coming right away. This is a total nightmare."

Karen looked very sad. She kissed his cheek. She was wearing a lot of makeup and heavy perfume.

"Thomas, you are family to me. I've known you since you were a baby. Your mom called and I dropped everything. I thought, what could that sweet guy have done? Plagiarize some research papers? Your car inspection out of date? You're such a sweet guy. What kind of trouble could you have made?"

He felt so relieved. Karen would solve this. She was wily. And she loved him.

She sat on his cot. "You were the sweetest little toddler. One time your mom caught you stealing a dollar out of her wallet. You were so ashamed. I knew you'd never make it on Wall Street."

"I remember, I remember." Goldstein rubbed his hands anxiously. "You have to get me out of here. These charges are ridiculous! It's just research, a submarine, I have photos of the sub on a memory—"

"Thomas! Stop! Don't say another word!" interrupted Karen.

"I just met with the JAG lawyer, and they have every intention of trying you for espionage. I can't help you. These Secret Service guys aren't fooling around. The last thing I want is to get involved with something like that!"

"All I did was discover the most important shipwreck since the *Titanic!*" said Goldstein.

"And share that information with a KGB agent!"

Karen and Goldstein glared at each other. Goldstein broke eye contact first.

"She's not an agent! She's my...my..." Goldstein's voice trailed off. What was she, anyway? "When we break the story about this submarine, this Nazi U-boat, directly below West Point, it will be an international sensation."

"Thomas, right now, listen to me. No one is better than me on white-collar crime. I've beaten the government on bank fraud, embezzlement, stock manipulation, insider trading, front running, you name it, but this is different. I run circles around those ADAs in financial crimes. I spoke with Agent Cadell. You've made some very powerful people scared. Scared but very angry. These guys after you are the A-team. They're not the kids right out of law school who work for the SEC. They aren't résumé building. You are up against the full power of the U.S. Intelligence Services. You cannot win."

Goldstein moaned. To hear this from Cadell was one thing; from his parents' dear friend was another.

Karen continued relentlessly. "If you weren't a citizen, they would lock you in Guantanamo forever. They have every intention of trying you in secret and throwing away the key. Thomas! What kind of a hornet's nest have you stepped into? One thing I can tell you, the only way you're telling the world about that submarine is after serving twenty years in federal prison!"

Goldstein felt his bowels loosen.

"Oh my God. What should I do?"

"I can't help you, Thomas. Maybe Judy Clarke can help you."

"Who is she?"

"She's got the kind of experience you need. She helped defend Dzhokhar Tsarnaev."

"Who?"

"The Boston Marathon bomber. She also represented Zacarias Moussaoui from 9/11."

Goldstein slumped in his chair.

"Next thing you'll be suggesting I hire the guy who defended the Unabomber."

"She did. Judy represented Ted Kaczynski, too!"

Goldstein held his head in his hands.

"I don't know what to do. I'm sorry you can't help me. Can you reach out to this Judy Clarke?"

"Yes, of course."

"My God, Karen, I feel like I'm in deep shit."

"That you are, Thomas, way over your head." Karen shook her head sadly. She kissed him on the cheek and whispered, "I'll call Judy, but Thomas, honey, I wouldn't fight this. If I were you, I would be begging to cooperate."

THIRTY-TWO

REICHSSICHERHEITSHAUPTAMT
KURFÜRSTENSTRASSE 116, BERLIN
APRIL 1945

Brigadeführer Walter Schellenberg missed the comfort of his old office. A raid over the winter had destroyed the RSHA at Prinz-Albrecht-Strasse, and the Gestapo and SD had been relocated to a cavernous, but barely furnished, building a few streets away.

The end was near. Germany had lost. Gestapo officials supervised the frantic destruction of papers documenting the Nazi police state, the sham trials, the executed political prisoners, the murdered students, dissidents, Jews, Communists, anyone who opposed the Third Reich. Aides dumped thousands of boxes of files into burning garbage cans. Many high-ranking officials had secretly arranged forged identity documents to facilitate their escape to Argentina. Soon, they would need them.

Two days earlier, the Americans had unexpectedly seized an intact railway bridge over the Rhine at Remagen, and despite every effort to dislodge them, had established a deep bridge-head. On the Eastern Front, over a million Russian soldiers almost surrounded Berlin. Newly constructed underground factories, manned by starving prisoners, continued to produce advanced aircraft and sophisticated armored vehicles, but there was no gas for them to run on. Everyone could see the Reich was finished.

One hundred hours. No report since. Schellenberg pondered what might have gone wrong with the U-555 mission and all it might have accomplished. The last communication came from the arrival at West Point. Nothing since. Had they been captured? Had they hit a mine? Had there been a technical failure with the submarine? Did Krause somehow lose his nerve? No word from the Americans. No explosion reported in the news.

At this point, he could only assume they were all dead. No reason to leave a trail for the Americans. Schellenberg doused the *Unternehmen Sturm König* files with gasoline and dropped a match. A shift in the wind blew the smoke into his face. He coughed and cursed.

He mourned his vision of the mighty United States and victorious Germany united together in the struggle with Bolshevism. He wondered when those naïve Americans would finally wake up to see the Soviets as the real threat to culture and civilization. Life was full of disappointments. He had no regrets. His plan had been genius. The failed execution of it was not his responsibility.

Now his highest priority was saving his own skin. He walked down the hall to the office of Heinrich Himmler.

Himmler's SS uniform was immaculate, and his hair was closely cropped. He seemed entirely unconcerned by the panic in the nearby offices. Despite having moved to this makeshift temporary headquarters, the Reichsführer-SS had carefully hung an autographed, gilt-framed portrait of Adolf Hitler above his desk. Earlier in the month, Himmler had concluded that the only way to save Germany, and his own skin, was to negotiate a peace treaty with the Americans and bring them into the fight against Bolshevism.

The dull thud of Russian artillery hammering the outskirts of Berlin could be heard faintly in the distance. Himmler was reptilian in his calm.

"Ah, Brigadeführer, thank you for making the time to see me. Do we have word on the guest we are bringing to Berlin from New York?"

"Regretfully not, Herr Reichsführer. We have had no reports from Operation Storm King since they arrived at West Point." Schellenberg pointed to the east. "Given the proximity of the Asiatic hordes, perhaps we need to focus our efforts elsewhere."

Himmler nodded, adjusted his pince-nez, and addressed Schellenberg in measured tones. "I reached out again to Count Folk Bernadotte in Stockholm, expressing our interest in averting unnecessary bloodshed. I suggested initiating peace talks with the Americans. As a sign of good will, I have offered to release about two thousand Jews from the Theresienstadt camp and send them to Switzerland."

"How generous of you," said Schellenberg.

"Ah, but he has been noncommittal. He might respond more favorably in a face-to-face meeting. I have a Fieseler Storch awaiting you at Templehof Airfield. It will take you directly to Stockholm. Let's hope you can convince the Swedes to talk sense into those foolish Americans."

"And the Führer?"

"I'm afraid our Führer has decided that Germany has failed, and we Germans should die with it. I disagree. We will have to pursue this initiative on our own."

"*Jawohl*, Herr Reichsführer!"

Schellenberg returned to his office and changed into a civilian suit. His career in the SS was finished. Now he was a private citizen, a lawyer, en route to neutral Stockholm. Perhaps he could still talk sense into the Americans. If not, he was sure that a man of his abilities would find his place in whatever way the world reassembled itself.

He collected a few belongings, notably the information on his bank accounts in Switzerland, and set out alone through the rubble-strewn streets of Berlin for Templehof Airfield.

Operation Storm King had come to an end.

THIRTY-THREE

T ruman, Leahy, Marshall, and Hoover met in the Map Room, cleared of all personnel. Forty-eight hours had passed since FDR had gone missing. They were no closer to solving the mystery of his disappearance. The massive manhunt found nothing. No president. No kidnappers. Nothing from the Germans.

They spoke in low tones. Their faces reflected the anxiety and uncertainty of the past two days.

Leahy paced nervously. "We can't keep a lid on this much longer, Mr. Vice President. Eleanor demands time on FDR's schedule, or a phone call. She suspects something is up. She's threatening to surprise FDR for dinner."

"I think we can handle Eleanor," Hoover replied. "I've got a file as big as a suitcase on her. But I'm worried about Stalin. That man has a nose for weakness. He's totally paranoid. If he finds out FDR has been kidnapped by the Germans, he might go after us in Europe."

"That's probably what the Germans were hoping to accomplish," answered Leahy.

"We might need to use that New Mexico experimental bomb on Stalin...Wonder if it works?" said Hoover.

"Steady there, Mister Hoover. Better to work together to rebuild Europe," said General Marshall.

"General Groves tells me it should be ready for testing in July," said Leahy.

"Well, I can hardly threaten him with a secret weapon that may or may not work," said Truman. "What are we going to tell the American people?"

Hoover answered, "If I may, Mr. Vice President, I think I have an answer. As you know, they say in Washington that I know where the bodies are buried. In this case, that's literally not true, but I think we can manage this situation to our advantage."

"Okay, Mister Hoover, exactly how is that?"

"I think it would be best for you not to know all the details. We must assume FDR is dead. How and where, we'll never know. Whoever took him is either dead or in hiding. Our best move is to tell the country that FDR is dead, and allow for a period of appropriate mourning. We need to assure them that his leadership team is firmly in control. I'll handle the details."

"Can we keep this thing from getting out?"

"I guarantee it. By the end of the week, the country will be mourning FDR and lining up behind your presidency. We won't hear any silly talk about assassinations or abductions. The nation will look forward to the future with your steady hand at the helm."

"And what is this going to cost me, Mister Hoover?"

"I need your full support for my important work at the bureau. I have serious concerns about the presence of communists and fellow travelers in our government. It's good for both of us."

"Fair enough, Mister Hoover. Deal with it. I look forward to having you close by my side, throughout my time in the White

House. You have my full support." Truman rose, indicating that the meeting was over.

Later that night, well after midnight, the armor-plated presidential limousine arrived at Union Station. The Packard V12 had bulletproof windows and run-flat tires. The Secret Service driver pulled the vehicle into a special entryway and down a ramp directly onto a poorly lit train platform. Two other vehicles with FBI agents followed.

Waiting on the track adjacent to the platform was the Ferdinand Magellan, FDR's private train. The Secret Service transferred a small man, features obscured in the darkness by a fedora, out of the car and into a wheelchair. The man in the wheelchair clenched a cigarette holder at a jaunty angle between his teeth. The wheelchair was guided by Clyde Tolson, the Assistant Director of the FBI. The Secret Service then transferred the man and his wheelchair on to U.S. Rail Car No. 1, operated under the code name POTUS. Like the presidential limousine, it was covered with half-inch nickel-steel armor on all sides.

The Secret Service maneuvered the presidential limousine and their Secret Service cars through the modified end doors of B&O Rail Car No. 748. With the presidential motorcade stowed away, the train pulled slowly out of the station. President Roosevelt disliked traveling more than thirty miles an hour. The train headed slowly south toward Georgia.

Inside the Presidential Suite, the man in the wheelchair waited until Tolson pulled the shades down over the armor-plated windows. Safely and almost hermetically sealed into the rail car, and secluded from prying eyes, J. Edgar Hoover pulled off the fedora, discarded the cigarette holder, and rose jauntily from the wheelchair.

"Oh my God, Eddie, you were so convincing! You actually startled me when you stood up! This whole thing has me jumping out of my skin."

"Relax, Clyde. I have this under control. Truman is

completely on board. The last thing he wants is for this story to break into the news. Can you imagine the headlines?"

"How much longer can we keep this thing under wraps, Eddie?" asked Tolson.

"We'll wait a couple of more days, Clyde. FDR, I mean we, will be secluded in Warm Springs. No press, no visitors," said Hoover.

"How about that Lucy Mercer girl? Isn't she usually down there with him?" asked Tolson.

"We'll send her away, tell her that FDR ordered it."

"And then what?"

"If we don't hear anything from the Germans by Monday, we will assume he's dead."

"Dead?" asked Tolson.

"That's right. Something must have gone wrong. Maybe whoever abducted him killed him and ran off. We know that at least two of them were wearing American uniforms. The maid at the commandant's told us that one guy sounded absolutely American. Maybe they've melted back into the civilian population."

"That would be smart thinking on their part," said Tolson. "We'll cut their balls off if we find them."

"Maybe they were trying to get out by plane or boat that crashed in the Atlantic. Either way, it hardly matters," said Hoover.

"The president of the United States disappears and it hardly matters? Are you mad?"

"We haven't heard a squeak from whoever did this, or from those Nazi bastards. In another week or two, Berlin is going to fall. Anyone left in Germany is worried about saving their own skin. Listen, Clyde, this is the plan. We'll tell the press that FDR is in seclusion at Warm Springs for the next few days. I've asked a doctor we can trust to come down to Warm Springs. He can make some statements about the President's health. We'll say officially that the president is overtired and resting but leak to the press that his heart failure is much worse. I've arranged to have my handpicked men assigned to this detail. They'll keep the rest of the staff at a distance. Plus, you and I can catch a little sun, and enjoy some private time," Hoover added, grinning.

"Ooh, that sounds delicious, but then what?' asked Tolson.

"When the time is right, the president will have a sudden stroke and be declared dead by our doctor. We'll load some weight in a casket and send it up north for closed-casket burial. The country will mourn for a week, and then move on."

"And us?" asked Tolson, putting one arm gently around Hoover's shoulder.

"Mr. Truman and I had a very frank discussion. I will stay as director at the FBI and you are my deputy. After this, we will be untouchable. It's the ultimate secret. We will own President Harry S. Truman."

Tolson opened a bottle of Scotch whisky, filled two crystal tumblers, and handed one to Hoover. As the train rumbled through the darkened Virginia countryside, they raised their glasses.

"To FDR's last journey to Warm Springs!" laughed Hoover.

"To President Harry S. Truman!" added Tolson, giggling.

"To us," murmured Hoover. The lifelong "friends" and confirmed bachelors looked deeply into each other's eyes, and clinked their glasses.

THIRTY-FOUR

Peter Kim, the Chief of Staff to the Deputy Director of the Defense Intelligence Agency, put down the report on new Chinese naval activity in the South China Sea, and focused on the satellite photos of looming Russian forces on the Polish border. He groaned when Karen, his administrative assistant, entered his office. The last thing he wanted was another distraction.

"Not now, Karen, for God's sake. I have to prep the Deputy Director for his meeting with the president in an hour."

"I'm sorry, Mr. Kim, it's someone named Captain Haskins. Something about the Great Chain."

Kim groaned. He really didn't have time for this now.

"It's urgent. Something about a German submarine."

Kim looked up from his papers and took the call. He made notes on a yellow legal pad. "Okay, okay. Yes, I remember, you were going to look for the chain at West Point? What? Seriously? A submarine? A U-boat? Are you sure? Secret Service. Huh. Yes,

I get it, he's been arrested and charged with espionage. Listen, I'll do my best. I'll look into it."

Kim hung up the phone and handed his assistant a request for files.

"I'll want to look at these as soon as I'm done briefing the Deputy Director."

By the time his meeting was over, the assistant delivered a file box of documents, with a Top Secret/Special Access Program seal. Kim broke the seal and worked through the yellowing pages of the Roosevelt dossier.

He was thunderstruck. It was almost too much to take in. He quickly understood the panic that was seeping through the national-security apparatus.

"Jesus Christ!" he muttered.

How had they managed to keep this under wraps all these years? he wondered. Hoover was amazing that way. But now, things were unraveling. And fast. This administration can't convince much of the country that the last election was legitimate, and now this! If word got out that the government had baldly lied to the public about FDR's death, there will be complete chaos. The QAnon people, the Area 51 lunatics, and the JFK assassination maniacs would come pouring out of the woodwork.

The nation could be paralyzed. Something had to be done, and quickly.

Kim realized that threatening to jail Goldstein wasn't the answer. As much as the Secret Service would want to throw a hood over Goldstein's head and make him disappear, that just wasn't an option. This was a very dangerous fire, but a big opportunity. If he could make this go away, he was headed to the top of the Agency.

He had a quick phone conference with the Deputy Director, who conferenced in the Director of National Security. "Yes, sir, absolute discretion, sir. I understand. I haven't spoken with Captain Haskins in years. He's the real deal: Army Ranger—he won a Silver Star in Afghanistan. We were roommates in college. Ah, no, sir, Rutgers, actually. Fraternity brothers, Sigma Nu. I'll try to work something out. Yes, thank you, sir, I appreciate your confidence."

••• ▬ ▬▬▬ •▬▬•

Kim spent the rest of the evening with the files. He would have preferred to have taken them home, but secret/SAP files had to stay at the agency. He called Haskins back and arranged a meeting for the following afternoon.

Kim and Haskins had shared a room in the Rutgers Sigma Nu fraternity. Kim had joined because it was the cheapest decent place to live near campus. The beer pong and binge drinking were idiotic. Haskins was another kid who didn't really belong in the frat. He was incredibly focused on ROTC. He didn't drink, and spent most of his time studying and working out. The two men weren't close but were good roommates, neat, studious, and quiet.

Haskins had filled him in about Zhao and Goldstein. Kim felt he had a lot in common with Zhao. They were both only children of immigrants. Kim knew what it was like to grow up under a microscope. His parents pushed him relentlessly. He had been high-school Valedictorian, and president of the Model UN. He desperately wanted to go to Harvard. The Harvard admission office did not cooperate. To them, he was just another smart Asian kid from New Jersey. Kim was crushed when he was rejected.

At Rutgers, he redoubled his efforts to excel. Kim wrote a thesis on U.S. drone policy in Afghanistan, and he worked for a summer at the Pentagon. Under pressure from his parents, Kim took a job with the management company McKinsey and worked one-hundred-hour weeks, routinely flying across the country for business. The pay was great, but he wanted more.

He kept his head down and bided his time. One day he was contacted by an old advisor, who indicated there was an opening at a certain government agency. He had jumped at the chance.

··· – ––– ·–·

The following morning, Kim was picked up by a town car at 1 p.m. Kim spent the hours on the road calling contacts at several defense contractors and Ivy League universities. Arriving at Thayer Gate, he flashed his Department of Defense ID card and was quickly waved through.

They drove along Colonels Row. American flags and Go Army banners hung from the red-brick colonial homes on their left. Across the river to their right, million-dollar mansions in Garrison were scattered on a wooded hillside, the setting sun glinting off their windows. They veered off left, passing the construction site for a massive new computer-science and engineering-science building, and pulled up at Grant turnaround.

Kim opened the door and stepped out. He found Goldstein, Zhao, and Haskins standing at the curb, guarded by Cadell. Kim presented his credentials to the agent. Goldstein and Zhao jumped into his car.

Agent Cadell grabbed Kim by the shoulder. "We've got these two. They're in deep with the KGB. We're going to send them away for a long time."

"Agent Cadell, please," said Kim, shaking free. "I'm just here to make sure we consider all the angles and protect the national interest."

Haskins stepped in, separating the two men. Kim stepped into the car.

Cadell turned to Haskins. "Watch yourself, soldier boy. You may find yourself posted to someplace dangerous."

Haskins turned and put his face close to Cadell. "Listen to me now, asshole. I can see you like playing the tough guy." He pointed at the ribbons on his chest. "This one's for the Korengal Valley and that one's for Kandahar. I've a piece of Taliban RPG in my arm. Don't you dare talk to me about dangerous places. Little men with big egos don't scare me. Fuck off." Haskins got in the car and slammed the door. He turned to the others and said, "Nothing I hate more than a cop who thinks he's a soldier."

They drove out of West Point and wound their way through Highland Falls toward the Bear Mountain Bridge. The road was lined with used-car dealerships and shuttered bagel stores. The only decent building was a Dunkin' Donuts.

"Where are you taking us?" asked Goldstein.

"We're going to dinner. Does Italian food sound good?" asked Kim.

"You bet! Holy shit, what is happening here?" asked Goldstein. "One minute we're shackled to the fucking wall, and the next minute, we're free and headed to dinner in a limo. Thank you, guys!"

"You'll have plenty of time to thank me when I explain the arrangement."

"Arrangement? What kind of arrangement?"

"Let's not talk about that right now," said Kim, pointing up at the driver. "Oh, and let's be clear. You're still very much under arrest. What happens from here is entirely up to you."

Goldstein fell silent. Haskins turned to Kim. "Hey, thanks for coming up from D.C. like this."

"Are you serious? Don't you remember the Sigma Nu pledge?"

"Actually, no," said Haskins.

"Me neither, I hated that place. I think you were the only other guy in the frat who read a newspaper. Speaking of which, I did read that piece about you in the alumni magazine when you won the Silver Star. You have a way of finding the action. This is certainly a very interesting situation we have on our hands. Tell me again how you got pulled in with these two?" He pointed at Goldstein and Zhao.

"Zhao came to me a couple of weeks ago and asked if I could help her and Dr. Goldstein with a dive project. I keep a boat up here and help out with the scuba club. Zhao's very squared away, really an ideal cadet."

Zhao smiled. "Thank you, sir. Means a lot coming from you."

"And besides, it sounded like fun." Haskins laughed. "I was wrong there."

"And Goldstein?"

"We're both in the history department. He's...not standard-issue Army material."

Goldstein snorted. "And proud of it."

"This business with the Secret Service is an outrage. It seems like something out of Abu Ghraib. Zhao and Goldstein lied to me about the wreck, and I had no choice but to report them. It was hard, but I knew I had to do the right thing. When the Secret Service blew in here like the Gestapo, throwing cuffs on them and demanding I keep silent, I knew something was very wrong."

Their car crossed the Bear Mountain Bridge and turned north through a dense hardwood forest. They drove through Garrison with its gated mansions of politicians, media stars, and financiers. There were glimpses of the Hudson and, on the opposite bank, the massive campus of West Point intermittently peeked through the trees. They crossed over a deep gorge and turned left into Cold Spring, an old working-class river town, lately morphed into a Hudson River valley tourist mecca. A well-heeled crowd of hipsters up from Brooklyn prowled the streets in yoga pants and wire-rim glasses in search of antiques, naturopathic medicines, and kayaking gear. Traffic was heavy on Main Street. They headed down a narrow side street and arrived at the Riverview restaurant.

"My admin booked us a table. She says it's the locals' favorite," said Kim. "Supposed to have great pizza. Made me think about the times we would go into town to avoid those idiotic frat parties."

"Good times," said Haskins wistfully, as they ducked inside.

It was 5:30 p.m. on a Tuesday, and they were the only customers in the restaurant. They were shown a table in the corner. Haskins and Kim caught each other up on their careers, careful not to discuss their classified activities. Zhao and Goldstein were mostly excluded from the small talk between the old friends.

They ordered pizzas, and Kim looked at the wine list.

"Can I pick the wine?" asked Goldstein. "I'm picking up the check. It's the least I can do to thank you guys."

"Don't be so quick to thank us, Dr. Goldstein. Haskins here thinks highly of you, and you seem like a decent guy, but these are strange circumstances, very delicate circumstances. Please understand that I'm not here as your friend. I'm here in my official capacity. I work for the United States Government. Specifically, the Defense Intelligence Agency."

"Didn't you come here to help us?" asked Zhao.

"I came to try to sort out this shitshow, but I am working for the DIA. Not you. Anything good that happens here, happens because it's in the government's interest."

"That's fair, at least we know what we're dealing with," said Zhao.

"Why don't you start by telling me your side of the story?"

Goldstein laid out the details of their findings. Kim made notes on a legal pad.

"We didn't start out looking for the submarine. It was all an accident. When we first found it, I was sure it was a Whiskey-class, a Soviet sub. We only figured out it was German when we went back and found the plate in the control room."

They paused when the waitress brought their pizza and opened the bottle of moderate-priced Pinot Noir. When she moved off, Goldstein continued. "Zhao wanted us to report the finding right then. I went to Germany without even telling her. I don't see why you guys arrested her."

"This is a national-security tar baby. Anyone who touches it will get dirty."

"I was afraid if we broke the news without knowing what the sub was doing here, someone would steal our thunder. This is a seventy-five-year-old submarine, what's all the concern about national security?" said Goldstein. "It's about FDR, isn't it? That's what Frau Schellenberg was screaming about!"

Kim paused and looked Goldstein in the eye. "It's a secret, we can't get into it. So you went off to Germany and met with your KGB friend."

"Don't call her that. I had no idea that she was KGB. I still don't know if that's true. Angela never asked me for anything. What secrets do I have, anyway? I don't even have a top-secret clearance."

"I can't speak to your motivation, but you did share information about the sub with her."

"Well, I told her I was investigating U-555, but I didn't tell her I found it. She found the letter in the B & V archives from Brigadeführer Schellenberg. And she took me to see his niece."

Kim put down his pizza and shifted in his seat. "What do you know about Walter Schellenberg, Dr. Goldstein?"

"Not much, just what I read on Wikipedia. He seems to have been some kind of Nazi spymaster and dirty-tricks expert."

"Yes, that's right. And Angela took you to see his daughter?"

"Not the daughter, the niece. She's crazy as a loon. I'm not sure I believe anything she told me. She ranted and raved about Roosevelt and the Jews. She suggested that her uncle was planning to kidnap FDR."

Kim took a sip of his wine. "Well, that is certainly interesting. Maybe that was the plan. We may never find out."

"I disagree. Sooner or later, the truth is going to come out. Threatening to send us to prison and covering the whole thing up isn't going to make that sub go away."

"Look, I think we can make a deal here. Nobody will be happy, but that's called compromise. You need to drop any further investigation of U-555. If you do that, I can arrange for you two to walk out of here free and clear," said Kim.

"So that's it? You want us to just forget about the most important discovery in the history of marine archeology? How about the truth? No, no, no. This thing is bigger than you and me—it's an international story. Someone has misled the American people, the entire world, in fact, for the past seventy-five years. No more lies," said Goldstein.

"If you don't listen to me, you may be headed to prison, and Zhao, too, by the way. The Army will try her under the Uniform Code of Military Justice, and that will be ugly."

"You bastards, what's so important here? This business with Goldstein and the KGB—the Secret Service probably made that up. What's the real story here? Why ruin our lives?" asked Zhao.

"Trust me, we have a lot more to worry about in D.C. than ruining your lives. There is a story here, and Goldstein, you're right, it is tied in to Schellenberg and FDR. This just isn't the time to dig into it. We have a crisis of confidence in Washington. The American people, some of them, many of them, just don't trust the government anymore. Hell, half of the electorate still thinks Trump won the 2020 election. The last thing we can afford to do is throw gasoline on that fire. West Point isn't right for you. Why don't you just walk away?"

"Forget it. If all you can offer is our silence for our freedom, you can screw yourself. This isn't Nazi Germany, brother. Try locking us up. We're U.S. citizens. We still have a free press and something called the internet. There's no way you can keep this buried for long," said Goldstein, crossing his arms and looking out the window.

Kim turned to Zhao. "I've discussed your situation with the Secretary of the Army. She can arrange the Rhodes Scholarship for you. When you're done with that, she'll release you from service, if you want. But you know, the secretary thinks you have a lot to contribute to the Army. She'd like you to stay. She's interested in meeting you to discuss nepotism and sexual assault at West Point. It's up to you. You'll be free to go to McKinsey or Goldman Sachs. By the way, I've been at McKinsey —it's awful. Either way, we need you to agree to forget about the sub."

"I think I can go along with that," said Zhao. "But it's really up to Professor Goldstein."

Kim turned back to Goldstein. "So tell me, Tom, how much money will it take?"

"It's not about the money! I'm damned if I'm going to do SAT prep for high-school kids or teach at some third-rate private college. I'm a scholar, and I want to focus on my research, and there's the matter of principle."

"Cut to the chase, Tom. How much money?"

"At an Ivy League college, my salary and benefits with housing and support for my graduate students and research would be about one million dollars a year."

Kim whistled. "Okay, okay. We have some good friends at the General Weapons Corporation. I think I could get them interested in creating an endowed professorship. You choose the place. Harvard, Princeton, Yale…"

Haskins had been listening attentively, and joined the conversation. "May I speak freely?"

"Sure."

"Listen up here, Goldstein," said Haskins. "You haven't exactly thanked me for getting involved."

"I'm sorry," said Goldstein. "My God, I am so thankful."

"Like I told Kim, the Army teaches you to do the right thing, to choose the harder right over the easier wrong. You are a decent guy. You make West Point a better place. You should stay at West Point."

"You don't want me to go? You think I should just shut up about the sub, go back to kissing Major Sanchez's ass, and turning a blind eye to the cheating by the football team?"

"No, not at all. Sanchez is a joke. The whole department knows that. People respect you, Goldstein. They're intimidated by you—you could be a better colleague, but I think you are a natural leader for the history department."

"Hah, and what will Major Sanchez and the football coach think of that?"

Kim joined in. "What Captain Haskins is saying is that I can arrange for Major Sanchez to return to a place where he can best serve the Army. If you agree to stay on as history department chair, we'll send Sanchez back to the field artillery. In South Korea."

"History department chair—that sounds amazing!" said Zhao. "Would he get one of the nice houses on Colonels Row?"

"Absolutely, and we can arrange for the General Weapons Corporation, Institute for Historical Research. That means research opportunities for the cadets, even graduate students."

Goldstein whistled thoughtfully. "And the commandant and the coach?"

"Don't worry about them. The Secretary of the Army has you covered."

Goldstein and Zhao exchanged looks.

Goldstein inhaled and then spoke. "I'm afraid that's not all. We can't just pretend none of this ever happened."

"Seriously, Dr. Goldstein, I thought we had a deal." groaned Kim.

"It's a matter of principle, Mr. Kim—Zhao's Cadet Oath. She's sworn never to lie, cheat, or steal. It's wrong to lie to the American public."

"Or tolerate others who do so. If we aid and abet you in this cover-up, I'm afraid I'm in violation of my oath," added Zhao.

Kim shook his head. "It isn't so simple. We have a crisis of faith in this country. The administration is hanging on by a thread. This is just the wrong time to break this kind of story." Goldstein and Zhao said nothing. Kim cleared this throat. "Well, let me see what I can do about that. I'll do my best. Let me make a few phone calls."

Kim stepped out of the restaurant. Goldstein, Haskins, and

Zhao sat and waited. They finally attracted the attention of the waitress and managed to get some coffee. They spoke quietly, filling him in with the details of the wreck.

Half an hour later, Kim returned. "The file will be automatically declassified on the one-hundredth anniversary of the events. That's 2045."

"That's more than twenty years from now! That's ridiculous," said Goldstein.

"I know, I know. I spoke with the White House. They've agreed to declassify earlier. The president has two years left in this term and, hopefully, four more after that. The vice president is planning on running and wanted another eight years, but I got her down to four, which will get her into her second term."

"So we'll have to wait ten years?"

"That's right, ten years, but we'll guarantee you'll have exclusive rights to explore the sub and to break the story. The American people will learn the truth and you two will get the credit, just not now. Let me be clear. We'll be keeping a close eye on you, and if you even breathe a word about the U-boat without our permission, you'll find yourselves in federal prison."

Goldstein and Zhao exchanged glances and nodded in approval.

After dinner, Goldstein and Zhao were driven down to the Foundry Dock in Cold Spring. It was a warm evening, and a light breeze blew across the river.

"Congratulations, Professor! Chairman Goldstein!" she laughed.

They looked out across at the twinkling lights of West Point, reflected in the ripples of the Hudson River.

"It's right out there, you know," said Goldstein, pointing south on the inky dark river. "All these years, it's been sitting here and we found it. They're keeping it secret. It really pisses me off."

"It can wait, Professor. Whatever is down there has waited this long. Kim is right. The country needs to heal, and people need to regain some trust in the government. What good will it do to create more chaos?"

"You're right, Zhao. Let's focus on making West Point a better place. There is so much good here. I'll finally have graduate students, and do research. I hope you stay in the Army after the Rhodes Scholarship, and improve the Army. Maybe one day they'll do an oil painting of you up next to those old white men in Grant Hall."

Zhao laughed. "You are a dreamer, Professor."

The two walked further out on the dock, gazing at the lights of West Point, still wondering what secrets were buried in U-555.

ABOUT THE AUTHOR

Dr. Elliott Sumers is a Harvard trained radiologist. His father served on the U.S. Navy Destroyer Escort Niblack during the Battle of the Atlantic of World War II. As a child Dr. Sumers was fascinated by his father's stories of hunting U-Boats. Dr. Sumers lives in the Hudson River Valley of New York with his wife Dr. Anne Sumers and their Irish Wolfhounds. For many years, the Drs. Sumers have welcomed cadets from the nearby the United States Military Academy, into their home. Operation Storm King is the natural fusion of his childhood interest in World War II submarines and tales of life at West Point, told to him by cadets.

f